TRUST
ME

BOOKS BY SHERYL BROWNE

TRUST ME

SHERYL BROWNE

bookouture

Published by Bookouture in 2020

An imprint of Storyfire Ltd.
Carmelite House
50 Victoria Embankment
London EC4Y 0DZ

www.bookouture.com

ISBN: 978-1-83888-870-1
eBook ISBN: 978-1-83888-869-5

This book is a work of fiction. Names, characters, businesses,
organizations, places and events other than those clearly in the
public domain, are either the product of the author's imagination
or are used fictitiously. Any resemblance to actual persons, living or
dead, events or locales is entirely coincidental.

For Theresa.
Stay safe in the embrace of those who love you, sweetheart.
Until we can dance together again. xx

PROLOGUE

The night of the party

'For God's sake!' He lunged for her as she grappled with the passenger door, causing the car to swerve violently across the narrow road. 'What the hell are you *doing*?'

'Let go of me!' She fought him, squirming away from him. 'Let me *go*!'

Fear constricting his throat, he tightened his grip on her arm and squinted past the windscreen wipers sloshing ineffectually against the lashing rain. Frantic, he searched for somewhere to pull over. The night was dark and moon-free, affording him little visibility. Relief flooded through him as he spotted a passing place on the single-track road. He slowed the car. And then hesitated. The entrance to Apple Tree Farm was only thirty or so yards ahead. The field beyond it would give them some privacy. There was no way he was having a full-on argument out in the open, no matter how remote an area it was.

'Stop the car! Let me out, *now*!' she cried, trying to prise his fingers from her arm.

'Christ almighty!' Cursing as the front wheels hit a pothole, he hurriedly loosened his grip on her to wrestle with the steering wheel.

Her scream was loud and piercing, jarring his already shattered nerves, as the car veered towards the woodland at the side of the road. He pushed his foot hard on the brake, realising his mistake too late as the vehicle careered into a tailspin before grinding to a nauseating stop. His heart pumping with shock, he wiped a trembling hand over his face and twisted to face her. 'What in God's name are you trying to do?'

'Get away from you!' she shrieked, lashing out at him, her balled fist pounding heavily into his shoulder.

'While the car was moving?' Disbelief and anger unfurled inside him. 'You could have bloody well killed yourself!'

'What do you care?' she retorted tearfully. 'You lying *bastard*, pretending you give a stuff about me when all you ever really wanted was to use me.'

'I do care. You know I do. I would do anything for you.' Softening his tone, he tried again to reach for her, but she recoiled.

'Of course you would. That's why you wanted to keep me as your dirty little secret. You're despicable, do you know that?' she spat. 'It's about bloody time everyone found out what you're really like. I'm going.'

'Don't,' he said, growing desperate. 'It's not safe walking around here on your own.'

'Ha!' She laughed derisively and reached again for the door. 'Save it for the next gullible fool you win over with your twinkly-eyed smile and bleeding-heart crap. It was nice knowing you. *Not*.'

'Come back!' he begged as she scrambled out of the car. 'It's pouring with rain. You'll get soaked.'

'No chance!' she yelled.

Panic knotting his stomach, he tried to start the engine as she fled, only for it to splutter and die. *Shit*. He slammed his hand against the steering wheel. What should he do now? He couldn't let her broadcast his business all over the village, ruin everything he'd worked for.

Go after her, whispered the woman whose death had changed the course of his life. *You have to stop her*.

CHAPTER ONE

Emily

Bitter wind biting into her bones, Emily stood across the street from her house, outside her life looking in. A fox cried in the distance, shrill and soul-piercing, like the cry of a terrified child. There was no other sound, no movement, apart from withered leaves scurrying across the pavement like frightened mice in the night. Loneliness seeping through her, she watched and waited. There were no lights on in the upstairs windows, suggesting the children weren't home. The only light visible was the mellow amber glow from the lamp in the large bay window, and beyond that, the flickering shadows from the television dancing across the walls of the lounge. What was her husband watching? Emily's heart constricted. Who was he watching with, if not her?

Drawn like a moth to a flame, she stepped down from the kerb and crossed the deserted road. She was on the drive, directly in front of the window, when her husband rose from the sofa. Tall and dark, wearing his almost perpetual five o'clock shadow, he was what some would call classically handsome. Attractive, undeniably. He was going to fetch refreshments, making drink signs with his hands. Doctor's hands. Steady, capable hands. She knew his every gesture. Knew every inch of him. From the scar on his knee from a fall as a child to the flecks of green and brown that made his blue eyes a myriad of ocean colours, she knew him. Didn't she? Mesmerised, she continued to watch as he smiled languidly at his companion and then crossed the room towards the kitchen. Her man: he would never hurt her in the worst possible way a husband could hurt his wife. But he had once been tempted, *the wind whispered.*

It was an embrace. A kiss, that was all, *Emily replied. He hadn't slept with her. She'd had no cause to doubt him since. Had she? Icy fingers trailed the length of her spine as the woman in her house got to her feet, coming across to the window. She waited a beat, and then, in one graceful movement, she raised a hand, placing the palm flat against the glass. Fascinated, petrified, Emily scanned her familiar features, looked deep into the eyes that were holding hers; violet eyes, peering out through a wild tangle of flaxen hair. Her own eyes. Her own hair. A mirror image of herself, looking hauntingly back.*

The fox cried jarringly.

Her heart jolting, Emily stumbled backwards, away from the woman who had once been the other half of her. She wasn't here. She couldn't be. A hard knot of fear expanding in her chest, she tried to draw breath. Kara. She attempted to enunciate the word, but her lips were like putty, her tongue glued to the roof of her mouth. 'Kara.' *It came out elongated and slurred.*

'You stole him,' *Kara whispered. An accusation.*

Emily heard it, impossible though it was, through the window between them. It was a lie. I didn't steal him. *Why couldn't she make Kara hear her? Believe that she hadn't taken away the man she'd imagined her life had had no meaning without? If anything, it had been the other way around. He hadn't loved Kara. He'd used her. Used them both.*

She hadn't meant to be so vile to her sister. She hadn't. 'Kara!' *she screamed. Why was she here? What was she trying to tell her? She watched her sister's mouth move, but the words were soundless now. Emily was glad. She didn't want to hear the dark warning she was sure Kara was trying to convey. Clamping her hands over her ears, she stepped back, but her heels sank hopelessly into the soft ground beneath her. Soon it was sucking her down, her feet, her calves, her stomach, her chest. Thick, cloying and slimy; suffocating. It was as if the earth was trying to swallow her whole and bury her along with her sister.*

'Emily!' Kara banged her hand against the glass. 'Emily ...'

'Emily ...'

She heard her name called softly again. Not Kara. A male voice, concerned, comforting. *Jake.* She snapped her eyes open to find her husband's gaze urgently searching hers.

'Jesus, you scared me.' He smiled warily. 'You were dreaming again, screaming out. Are you all right?'

Pulling herself from the pillow, Emily took a second to answer. 'Yes,' she murmured, the frenetic beating of her heart abating a little as she realised she was inside her home, safe in her bed.

'Sure?' he asked her, easing her to him and gently stroking her hair; soothing her as he would once have done their daughter. Millie would often wake crying in the night as a child. Jake had been the only one who could console her. 'You've been dreaming a lot over the last few days. You're hot, too.' He felt her forehead. 'Extremely.'

'I'm fine, honestly.' Settling into his embrace, she nodded into his shoulder. She *was* hot. Burning up. She hadn't felt well all week. She hoped she wasn't coming down with something. She was sleeping fitfully, struggling to get to sleep or waking early. And then there were the nightmares. The one she'd just had was so vivid. She wouldn't easily forget it. She thought of the text she'd received last week. *Thinking of you both on your special day*, it had said. She had dismissed it as a wrong number. Sent so close to her and Kara's birthday, though, her thoughts had been on her sister as she drifted off.

It was no wonder Kara haunted her dreams. Emily pictured her twin, identical, yet not. On the inside, they were two completely separate entities. Kara had always been their parents' favourite, the quieter, prettier, cleverer one, studious and obedient. She'd been destined for Oxford, studying Classics and English. She'd worked hard to please their parents. Emily had decided on an art degree, unleashing her creativity as an antidote to her frustration that she couldn't possibly compete with her sister. She'd been seen as the wild one, the noisy, rebellious one her parents would have to keep an eye on. It had been Emily who had started smoking and drinking first. She who'd started dating.

The local bad boy had been two years older than her, good-looking, cocky on his Yamaha motorbike. Despite his reputation – or perhaps because of it, to spite her parents for loving her less – Emily had been determined to go out with him. She was hopelessly in love with him and imagined she would be the one to tame him. She'd lived for the days when she would hang out with him, smoke weed on the canal bank, ride pillion into Birmingham, where they would go clubbing together. He'd said he loved her wild side, encouraged her to be who she was, abandoned and carefree, not constrained by conformity. The girl who would rise to the challenge when he dared her, taking what wasn't hers to fund his habit, terrified he would dump her if she didn't. How naïve she'd been. How ashamed when she'd woken up to the fact that she'd been so easily manipulated.

She'd been consumed with rage the night she'd found him in bed with Kara, unforgivably vile to her sister. Her heart twisted painfully as she pictured Kara's stricken face, the mascara she rarely wore wending black tracks down her cheeks, her lipstick smeared sideways. '*Slag!*' Emily had hissed, throwing her clothes after her as she'd screamed at her to get out of her life. 'He doesn't love you. He *laughs* at you,' she'd seethed, as Kara backed tearfully along the landing. 'We *both* do, little Miss Goody Two-Shoes with her nose always stuck in a book. He loves *me!*'

She'd been deluded. He hadn't loved either of them. Kara had loved *him*, though, she'd come to realise, as painfully as she had herself. She hadn't known how deeply until she'd read the diary her sister constantly scribbled in. He'd been the first boy she'd had sex with. And the last.

'Care to share?' Jake jarred her from her thoughts, his mouth curving into a reassuring smile as she looked up at him.

Emily nestled back into him. 'I would, but I can't remember half of it,' she said, glossing over the dream, though it had stirred up in her the disturbing memory of how Jake had been intimate with another woman, years ago now, when they'd only been going out a few months. At the time she'd withdrawn from him, pushed him away because of her emotional vulnerability. He'd felt rejected, though he swore that he hadn't slept with the woman, that it hadn't gone that far. She'd believed him and had felt safe with him since. Secure in his embrace at night, listening to the reassuring thrum of his heartbeat, as if the world and all the bad things in it couldn't touch them.

'Are you all right?' she asked, looking up at him. She'd obviously woken him.

'Fine. A bit tired.' He gave her another reassuring smile. He had a nice smile, warm and genuine; it always reached his eyes, making them more sparkling blue than ocean green. They grew darker when he was troubled, as they had been in those dreadful weeks leading up to the day she'd seen him with the woman. She hated that she hadn't been able to be honest about why she'd drawn away from him. She'd known deep down that she could trust him with her emotions. A man who'd been too shy to ask her out, visiting the café where she'd worked umpteen times on the pretext of studying before he'd plucked up the courage; who'd also had to visibly find the courage to confide in her the terrible tragedy in his own life. That tragedy had made him everything she felt he was, kind and sensitive, but she herself felt so naïve and responsible for what had happened to her. She wished to this day she had told him instead of carrying it around like a stone, living in fear that it would surface.

'*Shoot!* Also late, unfortunately,' he added, his gaze flicking past her towards her alarm clock. 'I need to be gone. I have that pharmaceutical rep coming before my first patient.' Pressing a hurried kiss to her forehead, he pulled himself off the bed.

Hell. She'd forgotten about that. Throwing back the duvet, she scrambled out after him and, feeling immediately woozy, placed a hand on the dressing table to steady herself. She clearly was coming down with something. Her mind had been like wet cotton wool lately. She must have forgotten to set her alarm. After an emergency call-out last night, Jake had obviously done the same. He would be exhausted. But now that his father had cut back to two surgeries a week, he had to go in, regardless of how tired he was. As did she. The practice wouldn't run without them.

Grabbing her dressing gown from the door, while Jake headed fast for the en suite, she listened for sounds of the kids as she pushed her arms into it. They were up, she gathered, judging by Ben's exasperated tones drifting from the hall. Millie, whom Ben dropped off at school on his way to uni, was undoubtedly keeping him waiting.

Turning to the wardrobe, Emily grabbed the first clothes that came to hand, dumped them on the bed and then headed quickly downstairs. Reaching the hall, she bypassed Millie, who was in front of the hall mirror, layering on the mascara, attempting to look half awake after a heavy night studying at her friend Anna's house. It had definitely been a heavy night, but Emily suspected it wasn't studying her daughter had been hard at. Millie's make-up had been less than immaculate when she'd eventually arrived home, her eyes slightly unfocused. Emily guessed she'd been drinking, which Millie had denied, naturally. The worrying question was where? With her own teenage rebellion in mind, Emily was treading carefully. She didn't want to set ground rules her daughter would immediately challenge, but she didn't like the idea of her sneaking off to pubs miles away, meaning she might be at risk if she had to find her way home alone.

She didn't want to preach to her daughter, but she was scared for her. Millie was young and impressionable, as she herself had once been. She could so easily be led astray. She'd tried subtly questioning her about her social life and got nothing but vagueness for answers. Telling her that she was worried for her, that she didn't want Millie making the same mistakes she'd made, only invited the roll of the eyes that accompanied her daughter proclaiming she was 'sixteen, not six'. She and Jake needed to sit down and talk to her, Emily decided. She would have a word with him later.

'Shouldn't you be leaving?' she asked Ben, who was standing in the hallway by the front door, his art portfolio in one hand, his car keys in the other and an impatient look on his face.

'I'm trying to, but she's taking forever.' He glanced despairingly at his sister.

Millie scowled at him in the mirror, and then went back to grooming her eyebrows. God forbid there was a hair out of place.

'You look fine, Millie,' Emily assured her. 'You'll need to get a move on if you're not going to be late.'

'I'm trying,' Millie huffed. 'What's your problem anyway?' she asked Ben. 'You have a free period this morning, don't you?'

'To prepare for my ceramics exhibition,' he pointed out exasperatedly. 'Can't you just get a move on, for fuck's—'

'Ben, *language*.' Jake cut him short as he hurried down the stairs, roping his tie around his neck and waggling his watch arm at Millie as he passed her.

'Sorry,' Ben mumbled. Then, emitting a world-weary sigh, he dumped his portfolio against the wall and ran a hand through his dark mane of locks – grown long since starting his fine art course, apparently to assert his individual style. Emily had refrained from pointing out that he might actually be following the herd, since the majority of the male art students were similarly hirsute. 'Mum, can you tell her, please?' he appealed to her. 'I've got loads to do and she's making me really late.'

'Come on, Mils.' Sensing her son's frustration, Emily chivvied Millie on. 'He'll leave you to walk otherwise.'

'I'm coming, I'm coming.' Millie turned grudgingly from the mirror, retrieved her shoulder bag from where she'd hung it on the stair rail and dropped her make-up bag into it. 'I have my interview after college for the Saturday job at the vet's. I can hardly go looking a complete mess, can I? This is important work experience for my future.'

'So you couldn't have got up earlier?' Ben muttered. 'Like, three hours earlier? Dunno why you're bothering anyway. They'll have loads of applicants.'

'Because I like animals – present company excepted.' Millie eyed him with disdain. 'I've decided to apply for a foundation degree in veterinary nursing. What are *your* life goals, other than to starve for your art?'

Ben glared at her. 'You have five seconds, Millie,' he warned her, a thunderous look flitting across his face. 'And then I'm gone, and you can find your own way there.'

'All right. I said I'm coming. Keep your gorgeous hair on. Agitated doesn't suit the carefully cultivated laid-back arty look.' She gave him a flat smile and patted his cheek as she sailed by him to the front door.

Ben rolled his eyes. 'Counselling,' he mumbled, picking up his portfolio and trudging out after her. 'I need advice on how to divorce my sister.'

'I'll let your father know.' Emily smiled, and cautioned herself to ignore Ben's flash of anger. It was justified, since his sister had been deliberately winding him up. 'Good luck, Millie,' she called. 'And well done on getting the interview. Don't forget you have to—'

'Concentrate on my studies as well, get good grades, don't let myself be distracted or dictated to by anyone ...' Millie picked up, with an irritated sigh. 'Yes, Mum, I know. You tell me about a thousand times a week.'

'Only because I care about you.' Emily felt a bit hurt. 'I just don't want you—'

'Making the same mistakes you did. I got that bit too.' Millie smiled flatly over her shoulder and headed out the door.

Emily tried not to mind. She probably did go on a bit. Going into to the kitchen, she found Jake swilling back an instant coffee.

'Let me know what?' he asked warily. He looked absolutely shattered. She noted the dark shadows under his eyes and wished he would slow down a little.

'Your son's decided he needs counselling in regard to his sister,' she informed him, glancing at the kitchen clock. The dishwasher needed emptying, but that would have to wait. Jake had a full list this morning and, as practice manager, Emily needed to be there. Their cleaner, Fran, who squeezed in a day at the house in between cleaning at the surgery, was due in later anyway. It wouldn't hurt her to actually do a bit of work rather than nattering.

'Again.' Jake smiled amusedly. 'Tell him I'll make a referral.'

'God forbid.' Emily walked across to him to straighten his tie. Ben did have a tendency to lose his temper, something she was naturally wary of, particularly since the episode when, escorted home by the police after drinking far too much and arguing with another youth outside the pub one night, he'd openly challenged Jake. Jake had handled it well, although he'd been shocked by Ben's sudden volatility. Emily had tried to reassure herself it was just normal teenage rebellion. Ben showed no signs of calculated malice, thank God. Underneath his moodiness, which, after all, was normal at his age, he was a sensitive soul, she was sure, artistic by nature like her. She wished he would confide in her more, but she doubted he would easily open up to anyone.

'Do you think she's serious?' Jake asked, nodding after Ben and Millie.

'About the foundation course? She seems to be.' Emily turned to grab her multivitamin tablets, washing them down with the coffee Jake had made her. He wasn't convinced they actually did any good, but the woman at the healthcare shop had persuaded her they would help reduce her levels of stress and anxiety and also improve her memory and mood. Emily wasn't entirely convinced either, but the way she was feeling at the moment, anything was worth a shot. Remembering that the bottle she kept on her desk was running low, she made a mental note to collect some more at lunchtime.

'She'll need to buckle down and apply herself at school,' Jake said, depositing his mug in the sink and then grabbing his case from where he'd left it on the kitchen island.

'As I keep reminding her.' Emily sighed, worrying afresh about the impact Millie's late nights would have on her grades. Jake had been out on a call when she'd rolled in last night. He'd been here the previous time she'd come home the worse for wear, though, and was as worried about her as Emily was. 'We probably need to have a talk to her, present a united front,' she suggested. 'Shall we have a chat about it, make sure we're singing from the same hymn sheet? Later this evening, maybe?'

'Can do. I'll make sure to get back a bit earlier,' Jake promised. 'Oh, and in case I forget, could you have a word with Ben? He left the back door unlocked again when he was out smoking last night.'

Emily noted his despairing look and sighed inside. Having met with a 'we can't all be perfect' comment from Ben the last time he'd tried to point out the health risks of smoking, Jake tried not to go on at him. Emily dearly wished Ben wouldn't smoke. Aside from the health issue, it was an addiction, and that worried her. Harsh reality had jolted her from her own addiction, but if Ben had inherited a propensity for dependency, would he be able to easily give it up?

'I'll leave him a note,' she said, as she went to the hooks on the utility room door for the spare key. At least if Ben kept one on his key ring it might remind him to lock up after himself before they were all murdered in their beds. Finding it missing, she sighed again, wearily, and added 'get key cut' to her mental to-do list.

'Are you leaving without breakfast again?' she asked, an admonishing edge to her voice as she turned back to find Jake swinging towards the hall.

'No time. I'll grab something from the village shop on the way.'

'Make sure you do,' Emily said, thinking she sounded more like his mother than his wife. But then someone had to keep an eye on him. He skipped too many breakfasts and worked far too many late nights now that his father was retiring. Jake and Tom shared partnership of the practice and Tom still worked part-time, but he'd wanted to be less involved to free up his time so he could concentrate on his role as chair of the clinical commissioning group governing body. Privately Emily couldn't help thinking his time might be better managed if he didn't spend a large proportion of it chatting up every attractive woman in the village. For Jake's sake, though, she avoided commenting.

'Yes, miss,' he called from the hall. 'Don't forget you have your blood test with Sally this morning. See you there.'

He was worried about her, thinking her recent dizziness, fatigue and general inability to concentrate might be symptoms of anaemia. She'd thought it was just due to her inability to sleep – which, Jake had pointed out, was also a symptom of anaemia, along with the bouts of nausea she'd had. She was glad that he cared, but wished he wouldn't worry with so much on his plate. It was probably just a virus she couldn't shake off.

'I'll be ten minutes behind you,' she called back. 'Don't forget you promised Edward Simpson you would oversee the duck race at the village fair on Saturday,' she reminded him. 'You'll need to ask Tom if he'll cover the emergency surgery. It won't hurt him to—' She stopped, cocking an ear as she heard Jake's mobile ring. That was probably Tom now, wondering where he was, or else their receptionist, Nicky, wondering where *she* was. It looked like she would probably be skipping breakfast again too.

'Dr Merriden,' she heard him answer. The phone pressed to his ear, his eyes flicked to hers as she stepped into the hall. 'I'll have to call you back,' he said quickly and ended the call.

'Anyone interesting?' Emily asked him curiously. He wasn't normally so brusque with callers, even unwanted ones.

'Just a sales rep,' he said, giving her a short smile as he pocketed the phone.

'Oh, right.' Emily watched him leave. He hadn't kissed her goodbye, which he always did. *Idiot.* She pulled herself up. He was tired, distracted, and she was being ridiculous. The vivid dream hadn't helped, bringing back too many memories she dearly wished she could forget. Perhaps Jake was right about the blood test, she pondered, collecting her own phone as it beeped with a text. It would be nice to get to the bottom of what was going on.

Assuming the message was from Nicky, she flicked to her texts and her heart skipped a beat. *Thoughts with you*, it said. That was all. It was a wrong number. It had to be. The message was almost one of condolence, which had to be a cruel irony. She thought of the first mysterious text, talking about her 'special day'. The sender couldn't know of the birthday she'd shared, the tragic significance of that date.

She should call them. It was a personal message. Whoever it was would want to know they were texting the wrong person. Her mind made up, her heart now beating a rapid drumbeat in her chest, she called the number, cleared her throat – and stopped breathing. 'We're sorry; you have reached a number that has been disconnected or is no longer in service,' a monotone voice informed her. 'If you feel you …'

Reaching for the hall table as the floor loomed up to meet her, Emily stopped listening.

CHAPTER TWO

After a full-on day, with their phlebotomist, Sally, going home sick in the middle of it, meaning some blood tests had to be cancelled – fortunately not hers – Emily was relieved when the last patient left. Fatigued understated how she felt. Every ounce of energy had drained from her body reading that damn text. It had obviously been sent in error, as had the previous one. She hadn't shared details of her past with anyone. Jake knew about her sister, but she hadn't told him everything. She'd wanted to. Many times she'd been tempted to, but she'd bottled out each time, knowing it could blow her world apart. Blow Jake's world apart.

She watched him come out of his office now, courteous and caring as always, as he walked Edward Simpson to the door. Edward had seemed a bit down lately, she'd noticed, which was unusual. A stalwart, backbone-of-the-village sort heavily involved in the organisation and running of charitable events, such as the upcoming summer fair, he was normally upbeat and positive. He'd been one of the first people to welcome them when they'd moved here. At the time, Jake had felt some trepidation about the move. He'd made up his mind years ago that he would never come back to the village he'd grown up in. After losing his mother so heartbreakingly, he'd felt there was nothing here for him to come back to, which Emily had thought was terribly sad. He'd been pleased to see Edward, though, and Emily had seen immediately that their neighbour had a caring, generous nature. She'd often thought it was Edward who kept the community together, giving up his time to visit people he suspected might be in need of assistance or company. Thinking about all that he did, she supposed he might be feeling a bit under the weather, particularly as he also had to care for his wife, Joyce, who suffered from polymyalgia rheumatica and unstable angina. When the polymyalgia flared up, she struggled even to get dressed in the morning. But she still generally managed to keep smiling, as did Edward.

She would pop in and see them both, Emily decided, coming around the reception desk to have a quick word with Edward. She wasn't sure he would accept any offers of help gracefully, determined as he was to do everything for himself, but she could maybe do a bit of shopping for them, help lighten his load a little. He was fit and healthy, but he wasn't exactly a spring chicken. Joyce had mentioned he would be retiring soon. At least then he would have more time on his hands to devote to the things he clearly loved doing. Walking across to where he and Jake were chatting, she reminded herself to do something about organising a party at the village hall for Edward's upcoming seventieth birthday. Joyce wanted to do something special for him, she'd confided when she'd last been in to see Jake. She would struggle with the practicalities of organising anything, though, and it might spoil the surprise a bit if Edward had to organise it for himself.

'Everything all right, Ed?' Emily asked him, giving him a cheery smile. 'How's Joyce?'

Edward smiled warmly back. 'Not bad, lovely,' he assured her. 'Joyce is jogging along. She has her off days, but still she refuses to give in and have the odd lie-in in the mornings, stubborn woman.'

'Because she has a good man to get up for,' she reminded him, giving his arm a fond squeeze.

'Her garden, you mean. It's that she gets up for. She's always out there, weeding and cutting and pruning. I can't keep up with her when she gets something into her head. I found her trying to heave the lawnmower from the shed yesterday. She'll be the death of me, I swear.' He sighed despairingly, but he had a fond twinkle in his eye, Emily noted.

'She'll have fewer off days now we've got her on the right medication.' Jake smiled encouragingly. 'She's already more like her old self. Hopefully we can start tapering the steroids down soon, which will minimise the side effects. I'm expecting you two to enjoy many happy retirement years together, Ed.'

'Fingers crossed.' Edward smiled back, but Emily noticed the worried look flitting across his ruddy features. Appearing to shake himself, he gave her a wink and nodded back to Jake. 'He's a good lad. I hope you're looking after him.'

'Too well,' Jake indulged him, patting a non-existent paunch, also reminding Emily that she'd completely forgotten to get something out of the freezer for dinner in the mad rush this morning. Ah well, Ben and Millie could have pizza and she would book a table at the pub for her and Jake so they could discuss their worries about Millie in peace, assuming he did manage to get back early, rather than working until some ridiculous time on the mountain of paperwork that came with the handover of the partnership. He'd had to work late a lot over the last few months, as his father had relinquished his responsibilities. It couldn't be healthy.

'I was so busy talking about myself just now, I forgot to thank you for your help when Joyce took ill last month, Jake,' Ed said, his voice emotional. 'If it wasn't for your quick action when she rang, she might never have seen her beloved roses bloom again.'

'All part of the job, Ed.' Jake shrugged selflessly. It hadn't been, Emily knew. The second Jake had realised Joyce might be suffering with the symptoms of a giant cell arteritis – a known development of polymyalgia rheumatica that could have rendered her suddenly and permanently blind or resulted in a stroke – he'd raced out of the surgery to drive her to the hospital himself.

'Above and beyond the call of duty, I'd say.' Ed gave him a grateful smile. 'There's not many people who would go the extra mile.'

'Time was of the essence. You only live two minutes away, so it wasn't a problem,' Jake assured him. 'We'll see you both on Saturday, yes?'

'Will do.' Ed waved as he turned for the door. 'I hope you've been keeping fit for the duck race.'

'Rigorously. Jogging, swimming, weights. The lot,' Jake lied. He jogged, but only when he could find the time, which wasn't as often as he would have liked.

'Those little buggers can be fast when the will and the tide takes them,' Ed warned.

'I'll be ready for them, Ed,' Jake promised, casting a puzzled glance in Emily's direction.

'Jolly good.' Ed chuckled as he left, with more jauntiness to his walk than when he'd come in. He certainly seemed in better spirits for talking to Jake, who always made time to listen. His appointments spilling over didn't help his schedule, of course, leaving him running perpetually behind and Emily apologising to waiting patients, but she tried not to mind. She wouldn't have him any other way.

He leaned towards her as the door closed behind Ed. 'Er, they are plastic ducks, aren't they?' he asked worriedly.

Emily laughed at the thought of Jake imagining himself wading down the river in pursuit of the flapping feathered variety. 'Yes,' she confirmed, to his relief. 'I imagine the RSPCA would have something to say if they weren't.'

'You're racing plastic ducks?' their receptionist asked, one eyebrow raised dubiously as Emily went back to the desk.

'It's called having fun, Nicky.' Emily couldn't help but smile at the unimpressed look on the girl's face. Having moved to the small village of Earlslip from London with her family a little over a year ago, Nicky often seemed bored, and just the tiniest bit contemptuous of the community's twee way of life. 'You should come along, let your hair down and enjoy yourself.'

'Er, right.' Nicky looked doubtful. 'I'm not sure wading about in wellies in freezing-cold water is my idea of fun, but thanks anyway.'

Walking back to his office, Jake exchanged amused glances with Emily as Nicky got to her feet, teetering around the desk in her preferred footwear to check the self-sign-in system. Her heels were at least five inches high and Emily couldn't help but wonder how she walked in them. She'd worn her own fair share of stilettos in her errant younger days. Still did whenever Jake and she went anywhere special. But for negotiating the treacherously uneven cobbled high street to the surgery? Sooner Nicky than her.

Jake's smile slipped as Tom emerged from his own office. He was also taking in Nicky's shoes, Emily noticed, along with every inch of leg above them. Wincing inwardly, she shot Jake an empathetic glance, to which he shook his head in a combination of despair and anger. Emily understood why he would be agitated by his father's behaviour. He'd seemed reluctant to disclose much about his family history when she'd first met him, other than that he'd lost his mother in his teens. As they grew closer and he'd felt able to let his guard down, he'd confided that his father had always been a womaniser. That his mother had turned to drink when he'd left her, renting a flat in the same village, which must have been soul-crushing for her. Jake had found himself in the role of caring for her. He felt he'd failed her, and Emily suspected he'd never been able to forgive himself for it. Her heart had stopped beating as she'd imagined the horror he'd felt walking through the front door of his house to find his mother hanging like a limp ragdoll in the hall. He'd been just sixteen years old. How did one recover from that?

He'd gone to his father's flat afterwards, he'd told her, determined to confront him. Incoherent with grief and rage when he'd found he was with another woman while his mother took her last breath, he'd accused him of driving her to suicide with his infidelity. Emily's heart had bled for him as she tried to imagine his insurmountable pain.

His father had apparently blamed his affairs on his wife's drinking, begged Jake to try to understand. Jake had turned his back, walked away before he could do something he would regret. He'd left the village almost immediately after that. He and his father had never discussed the matter since, as far as Emily knew. They avoided anything emotive, in fact, even though they worked in the same practice together and could hardly therefore ignore each other. Watching Tom now, it was obvious he still had a roving eye, confirming all that Jake had said about him. A silver-fox charmer, the man was an obvious flirt. Leopards and spots, Emily supposed.

'Quick word about the practice budget when you have a second, Jake,' he said, his mouth curving into an appreciative smile, his gaze still on Nicky.

Aware of Tom's attention, Nicky smiled back. Emily had no idea what else she was supposed to do other than blank him, but she couldn't help thinking Tom would be encouraged by the girl appearing unconcerned about his ogling. She really was going to have to have strong words with him.

'No time like the present,' Jake said tersely.

'Is it okay if I go now, Emily?' Nicky asked as Tom dragged his gaze away and turned to follow Jake to his office. 'It's just I've already worked ten minutes over and I'm meeting up with someone in Pembridge this evening.'

Emily checked the clock. 'Gosh, yes, of course. Sorry. You go. Take an extra ten minutes in the morning if you like. I can manage. Going anywhere nice?'

'The Fish and Anchor for a meal.' Smiling in anticipation, Nicky headed back around the desk to grab her bag. 'It'll take me ages to get ready.'

Emily's mind boggled at that. The girl always looked as if she'd stepped out of the pages of a fashion magazine. 'Enjoy. See you tomorrow. Not too hung-over, I hope,' she added as Nicky went to fetch her coat, a trendy black leather biker jacket similar to one Millie had. They seemed to be everywhere at the moment. Emily quite fancied one herself, but couldn't help thinking she might look like mutton dressed as lamb.

Nicky smiled sheepishly and tugged the jacket on. 'I won't be,' she promised, lifting her lustrous dark hair from the back of the jacket and allowing it to fall in loose waves over her shoulders. 'I don't generally drink during the week.'

'Glad to hear it.' Emily smiled knowingly back. Nicky had come in so hung-over once she'd barely been able to function. As she'd been out celebrating her birthday, and aware of her own propensity to judge people who leaned on mood-enhancing drugs, alcohol being one of them, Emily hadn't been too hard on her, but she had warned her not to make a habit of it.

She felt less forgiving, however, when she noticed that the girl was about to leave the surgery with her computer screen still lit and showing confidential patient data.

'Haven't we forgotten something, Nicky?' she asked, drumming her fingers pointedly against the desktop.

Knitting her brow, Nicky gave her a puzzled look.

'Your data protection training, possibly?' Emily's eyes slid towards the computer.

'Oh my God.' Nicky clamped a hand to her mouth, her huge brown eyes growing wide with alarm. 'I'm sorry,' she said, flying back towards it. 'I was distracted.'

By Tom, no doubt, Emily thought, now feeling considerably peeved.

'It won't happen again, I promise.' Leaning over the keyboard, Nicky quickly exited the patient files and closed the computer down.

'Please make sure it doesn't.' Emily softened her tone, despite her annoyance. 'We operate a clear-desk policy for a reason. Making sure there are no files left lying around and exiting all computer screens is essential. Anyone could access private medical information otherwise: a member of the public, the cleaning staff, the postman – even delivery or maintenance people, for goodness' sake.'

Nicky looked contrite. 'I know. I really am sorry. I'll put a Post-it note on my screen to remind me, and a note in my handbag.' Her eyes flicked down and back again, and Emily saw she was on the brink of tears. She felt like an old witch but couldn't let it slip. The waiting room was open to all and sundry, and protecting patient confidentiality was paramount in a doctor's surgery. As practice manager, she was entrusted to keep people's personal details safe, and she took her responsibility very seriously.

'And one on your desk to remind you to put the note on your screen?' she suggested, with a small smile. 'Try not to forget, Nicky. It's extremely important.'

Nicky nodded. 'I know. I won't.'

'Go on, off you go.' Emily sighed tolerantly. The girl had clearly got the message. 'See you in the morning,' she said, going back across the surgery to lock up behind her.

'Will do. I'll be bright-eyed and bushy-tailed and making sure to pay attention to detail, I promise.'

Emily hoped so. Watching in bemusement as the girl negotiated the steps with ease and clip-clopped off, she closed the door and walked back to do her usual check of the waiting area. Having established there were no items left behind by patients, she was walking back to reception when she heard Tom's tones drifting through Jake's open office door. 'I see all the young female patients are switching to your list,' he said amusedly.

Emily guessed from Jake's silence that he found this more annoying than amusing.

'Can't say I blame them. You're definitely a chip off the old block,' Tom went on, oblivious. 'Suave, good-looking. I hope you're not stepping too literally into my shoes, though.'

Emily sighed at the man's attempt at a joke. She very much doubted Jake would aspire to do that. Undoubtedly handsome, he'd definitely been a magnet for female patients when he'd first joined the practice. He wasn't his father, though, or anything like him. Her vivid dream popped into her mind, reminding her how easily Jake could attract the attention of a woman, and the intense heartbreak she'd felt when he had. But that was years ago. She tried hard to dismiss it, but couldn't quite manage to.

'I have no intention of stepping into your shoes,' she heard Jake reply brusquely.

'Right,' Tom said awkwardly. 'I, er, actually meant I hoped you wouldn't be taking all of my patients, since I wasn't intending to fully retire just yet.'

Jake took a minute to answer. When he did, Emily was taken aback. 'You never cease to amaze me, do you know that?' he growled. 'This bloody innuendo you come out with all the time. Don't you have any conscience?'

Tom hesitated. 'If you're referring to what I think you are, Jake,' he said, at length, 'I do have one or two regrets, yes.'

'Just one or two?' Jake's tone was caustic.

'Several,' Tom admitted. 'Look, Jake, I know what you think of me. That you're uncomfortable with some of the things I did in the past.'

'*Uncomfortable?*' Jake repeated, astonished.

Tom was silent for a second, then: 'It wasn't easy for me sometimes,' he said quietly. 'Things weren't good between your mother and me, and—'

'You sought comfort elsewhere?' Jake suggested, his voice edged with disdain.

'Your mother wasn't *well*,' Tom insisted fiercely. 'She never had been, not really. I tried, but—'

'Shall we talk about the budget?' Jake cut him short.

Oh dear. Hearing the anger in his voice, Emily felt for them both. Despite his reservations, Jake had come to work with his father five years ago because Tom had managed to persuade him that, however he felt about him, he would be an idiot to pass up the offer of a partnership, particularly with two teenagers to put through their education. Emily sensed that, beneath his sometimes glib exterior, Tom might be lonely and desperate to mend fences with his son. Jake would never be able to make himself believe his father had ever cared about his mother or him enough to want to meet him halfway, though.

'Fine.' Tom sighed heavily. 'I haven't got long myself, as it happens. I have an engagement in Pembridge this evening.'

'Ah. With anyone interesting?' Jake asked.

Emily didn't miss the sarcasm. Tom clearly didn't either. 'Some people from the local medical committee,' he answered with another weary sigh.

Quietly wishing that Jake would let his defences down a little for his own sake, and then realising that that was probably impossible, since Tom was still clearly unable to curb his flirtatious inclinations, Emily left them to it and went to clear her desk. She needed to book that pub meal and make a bit of an effort to get ready.

Heading back to her PC, she made sure she'd exited the patient app – God forbid she should leave anything on display for the cleaner when she came in; Fran Nateman revelled in a bit of juicy village gossip, and wasn't best known for her discretion – then did a final check of incoming emails. A late email had pinged into Jake's inbox, she noticed. She didn't recognise the sender's address – which began nja123 – but she ought to check it in case it was important. Good job Jake trusted her. Thanks to her job here, she had access to all his various accounts, along with his medical history. She really did know everything there was to know about him.

Smiling distractedly, she opened the email and her heart stopped dead.

Unless you want a certain person to find out about your extracurricular activities, meet me in the designated place, 3 p.m. tomorrow.

CHAPTER THREE

Her hands shaking, Emily typed the address into the email search bar. No previous emails came up. Nausea swilling inside her, she tried to make sense of it. It was some kind of joke, she tried to reassure herself. It *had* to be. Or else it was meant for Tom rather than Jake. She seized on that as a possible explanation. Might he be having an affair? Could someone be threatening to expose him? Her palms damp with sweat, she searched through Jake's previous emails, her gaze darting in the direction of the offices lest Jake or Tom suddenly come out. She went back weeks, finding nothing personal of any significance other than emails he had sent her. *Drowning in paperwork*, his last one had said. *I'm going to be at least another couple of hours. Don't worry about food. I'll get takeaway. Sorry. Will make it up. Promise. X*

She *had* worried. She worried constantly about him: his diet, the long hours he worked, his exhaustion. She swallowed hard, saw afresh the image from her dream of her sister's hand pressed against the window, as if she were trying to reach out to her. She had thought Kara was taunting her, reminding her of Jake's flirtation with another woman. She'd been angry. She'd thought her sister was jealous. In her mind, she'd been convinced that Kara was trying from the grave to take her man away, as she imagined Emily had done to her. But what if it was nothing of the sort? She recalled the frightened, plaintive look in her sister's eyes, almost as if she were mourning. What if she was mourning not the loss of years gone, but the loss to come? Emily's loss? What if she was trying to warn her?

Her heart racing, she reached for the gold locket she always wore with her sister's photo inside, trying to find some comfort from it.

Could it be true? Was this the message she was supposed to take from her dream, that Jake was having an affair? She'd thought that, in frequently working so late, he was being conscientious. She'd admired him for it. When she'd missed him in the evenings, she'd reminded herself what a good man he was, determined to do right by his patients. But an affair would explain his bone-weary exhaustion when he did finally come home, wouldn't it? His 'extracurricular activities' would be a terrible drain on his energies.

Had she been so wrong about him? Wrong to trust him? She'd loved her first boyfriend – or thought she had. She'd thought he'd loved her back. He hadn't, other than in some twisted way she would never understand. But she hadn't trusted him. Somewhere inside her, even as a gullible seventeen-year-old, her instinct had tried to warn her, gnawing away at her consistently. She'd ignored it. She was trying to ignore that same instinct now. But she couldn't.

Jake was cheating on her.

Her mind reeled. Her heart palpitated unsteadily. He *couldn't* be. She stared hard at the message that was screaming at her, telling her he could be. *God.* Looking upwards, she bit her tears back. He would know she'd been crying. What little make-up she wore would be ruined. Perhaps she should have paid more attention to her beauty regime, made more of herself. She hadn't thought it was necessary for her to look glamorous when she came into work. Jake saw her first thing in the morning and at every stage between waking and sleeping, even worse for wear occasionally after indulging too much on a night out. After childbirth, during childbirth, he'd seen her then, at her absolute worst. It hadn't seemed to faze him. She remembered how she'd felt his love like a safe blanket around her when, far from feeling powerful as she'd imagined she would be after bringing a tiny human being into the world, she'd felt vulnerable and tearful and depleted.

It had taken her a while to believe him when he'd told her he loved her; that the woman she'd seen him with all those years ago in the very same bar they drank in together meant nothing to him. As time had gone on, though, and he had been steadfast and caring, she'd felt secure in her relationship again. Finally she'd felt comfortable in her skin, something she hadn't been since Kara's death. He *had* loved her; with his eyes, with his body, he'd loved her. There had never been a day she hadn't loved him back with all of herself. But if he was being unfaithful, then his love for her had died. She felt the tears rising, her throat tightening. She didn't think she could bear it.

When she'd walked in on her boyfriend and Kara, she'd thought it was the most excruciating pain a person could possibly endure; until the acrid grief of losing her sister plunged her into a pit of despair so deep she'd thought she would never claw her way out of it. Her parents had never recovered from Kara's death. They'd split up soon after. Emily saw her father occasionally, less over time. There had been no love in his eyes when he'd looked at her, more sadness and disappointment. He'd never actually said the words, but she sensed that his disappointment was because he'd lost the better, prettier, cleverer twin, leaving him with her, the flawed one. It had all been her fault.

Was this her fault too? Despite striving to be all her family needed her to be, had she never been what Jake wanted? Was she not pretty enough? Not adventurous enough in bed? Was he bored with her? Bored with marriage and the responsibility of fatherhood?

She'd made herself trust him, but had she truly known him? Could two people ever really know each other? She'd never confided in Jake her deepest secrets, the cruel things she'd said to her sister; the fact that she'd been so naïve she'd agreed to meet the man who'd used them both and who would soon be convicted of Kara's murder. She didn't know to this day what she'd been thinking. Her mind had been so muddled, her recollection of the day Kara died hazy. Perhaps she'd hoped he would help her remember.

They shared a tragedy in common, he'd told her when he'd contacted her. He'd needed someone to talk to, someone who understood that he'd also been damaged by what had happened. He'd said he needed forgiveness in order to move on. She'd felt for him, guessed he would be hurting; believed him. She'd seen him once. Once had been enough to confirm that he was damaged, but not by Kara's death.

He'd had a far-reaching impact on her life. Emily had thought that, in a devastatingly ironical way, her experiences had stood her in good stead. They had taught her not to judge people, as she had Kara. Yet here she was judging Jake based on a single email. But was she? He'd said he hadn't slept with the woman she'd seen him with years ago, but there was definitely an intimacy between them. She was clearly flirting with him, touching his hand as they'd sat at the table, threading an arm around his shoulders as they stood, one hand resting on his hip as she'd kissed him goodbye. Emily had avoided seeing him for a while, because after what had happened to her, she hadn't known how to face him.

She had no idea how to face him now. If she asked him outright whether he was seeing someone else, he would hardly be likely to admit it. She couldn't do it. She had to wait, be vigilant. Arm herself emotionally. To look into his eyes – honest eyes, she'd always thought – and see the lies there would kill her.

Frozen with indecision, she tried desperately to compose herself. He would know she'd seen it, that she'd opened the email. Panic gripping her, she glanced again towards his office. Her finger hovered uncertainly over the keyboard as she agonised, and then she deleted the email. She needed time. She needed to think what to do.

She needed to find out who it was he was meeting.

CHAPTER FOUR

Jake's expression was wary when he finally came home, which only increased the cold foreboding that had been churning away inside Emily since she'd left the surgery.

'The rescue service came then?' she asked him, searching his face carefully. Would she know if he was lying? He'd held eye contact with her the last time he'd assured her that her suspicions were unfounded. Would he now? His car had broken down on the way back from an urgent call-out, he'd said. He'd had to wait for the recovery service. With every fibre of her being she wanted to believe him, desperate not to give in to the tears that had been sitting close to the surface since she'd seen that damn email. More so since Millie had chosen to stay out late, despite having promised she wouldn't. It was nearly eleven, an hour after her weeknight curfew, and Emily was beginning to worry. She'd promised herself she would remain the epitome of calm when Jake got back; that she wouldn't overreact, hurling accusations at him without establishing the facts first. That she wouldn't 'bang on', as she apparently did to Millie. Now, though, feeling agitated and more light-headed and nauseous than ever, her resolve was waning.

'Eventually.' Jake sighed tiredly, dropped his case on the hall floor and shrugged out of his jacket.

He wasn't looking at her. Apprehension crept the length of Emily's spine. 'What was the problem?' She tried to keep her voice casual.

'An electrical fault,' he said, hooking his jacket on the peg, collecting his case and heading up the hall. 'I'll take it into the garage tomorrow.'

Look at me, Jake, Emily willed him as she stood aside, allowing him to pass. He did –but just a brief glance. 'And the call-out?' she asked, hating the mistrust she could hear in her voice as she followed him into the kitchen.

'Rachel Brown's little boy.' Jake parked his case in its usual place on the island and went across to the kettle. 'She said she was reluctant to call, but it's a good job she did. Tea?'

'No thanks.' Emily watched him guardedly. 'I cancelled the table.'

Jake knitted his brow in confusion. 'Table?'

'At the pub,' she reminded him. Clearly he'd forgotten. Her spirits sank. 'I booked it so we could have that chat we were going to have, remember?'

'*Christ.*' Jake squeezed his eyes closed. 'Sorry. I didn't realise you'd—' He stopped, cursing quietly as his phone rang. Fumbling it from his pocket, he checked the number and then, giving Emily a weary smile, accepted the call.

'Hi,' he said, pressing the phone to his ear and turning away from her to head for the conservatory.

Watching him, Emily's heart dropped like a stone. Clearly he wanted privacy, and this, combined with the fact that he hadn't introduced himself as Dr Merriden, was a pretty good indication it was a personal call.

'No problem. I'm happy to be of service,' she heard him say in that selfless, reassuring way of his as he slid the door closed behind him.

What bloody service? Trepidation twisting her stomach, Emily checked the wall clock. It was ten past eleven. Who would be ringing him at this time of night? Not his father. Jake wouldn't have greeted him so cordially. And if it were Millie, he would hardly have shut himself in the conservatory.

Hearing the front door open behind her, Emily breathed a sigh of relief. Cautioning herself to stay calm, she tore her gaze away from the conservatory and went into the hall. Millie was home safe. That was all that mattered. Her determination not to launch into a confrontation with her flew out of the window, though, as her eyes lighted on her daughter, who was creeping unsteadily towards the stairs.

'Millie!'

She stopped in her tracks but didn't look round. It was obviously catching, Emily thought angrily.

'Do you realise what time it is?'

'Need the loo,' Millie mumbled, and took another step towards the stairs, almost reeling into the hall wall as she did.

Emily's heart skipped a beat. 'Where in God's name have you been?' she demanded, moving towards her.

Millie met her eyes at last, her own slightly unfocused, Emily noticed. 'Anna's,' she said shortly. 'Why?'

'*Why?* It's way past the time we agreed,' Emily pointed out, staring hard at her. She'd obviously been drinking, and Emily doubted very much she'd been doing that at Anna's house. 'I've been trying to ring you. I've left you umpteen messages. I also called Anna. She didn't answer either.'

'We were watching TV.' Millie shrugged indifferently. 'It's no big deal.'

Shocked that her daughter was apparently lying to her face, Emily attempted to call her bluff. 'What were you watching?'

Millie widened her eyes indignantly. '*The Sinner*, a rerun. What is this? The Inquisition?'

'It's a *school* night.' Emily's voice rose. 'We discussed this, Millie. If you've any hope of getting the five GCSE grades you need, you have to apply yourself to your school work.'

Folding her arms, Millie rolled her eyes languorously. 'Right, so I'm not supposed to chill out occasionally then?'

'You can chill out as much as you like.' Emily tried hard to hold onto her temper. 'But you do *not* stay out late without clearing it with me or your father first.'

Millie's expression was now one of belligerence, which only increased Emily's annoyance. Did she not realise how worried she'd been? Yes, she was only an hour late, but anything could happen in an hour, as Emily well knew. 'And you do *not* lie to me, *ever*,' she added. 'Understand?'

Millie boggled at that. 'That's way out of order, Mum,' she muttered, her face creasing into a scowl. 'I am *not* lying. I've been round at Anna's. Ring her now if you don't believe me.'

'I just might,' Emily threatened. 'But I think I'd much rather talk to her mother tomorrow. How much have you had to drink?'

'I haven't *been* drinking.' Millie dragged her hair from her face and eyeballed her defiantly. 'What the bloody hell is up with you anyway? It's not like I've been out the whole night.'

Enough. Emily saw red. 'That's *it*, Millie. No more going out during the week, no TV …'

'*What?*' Millie laughed, disbelieving.

'… no mobile top-ups and no computer time, unless it's for homework. Not until you learn to act like an adult.'

'You have to be joking.' Millie gawped at her, stunned.

'I've never been more serious in my life,' Emily assured her. 'You can carry on up the stairs now, assuming you can negotiate them.'

'God! You're being totally unfair. Ben's still out.' Millie splayed a hand towards the front door.

'He's older than you,' Emily argued, stopping short of pointing out that she would also always worry more about Millie simply because she was a girl. She was acutely aware that this was partly because of her own experience at the hands of the man who'd manipulated her and then taken what he wanted anyway when she'd said no. The fact was, though, that Millie was young, beautiful and vulnerable – more so for having been drinking.

'I've only been at my *friend's*,' Millie retaliated, her cheeks flushing furiously. 'I rang Dad on his mobile and told him I was going to be a bit late. He said it was fine.' Her gaze went past Emily to where Jake was making an appearance now he'd finished talking to whoever it was he was perfectly happy to take calls from this late, leaving her to deal with their daughter. 'Dad?' Millie appealed to him.

Jake glanced at Emily, as she turned to face him, and then uncomfortably back to Millie. 'I said it was fine as long as you checked with your mum, Mils,' he said, at least backing Emily up.

'Right. Thanks for your support, Dad.' Swiping a tear from her cheek, Millie threw him a mutinous scowl, and then flounced onwards to the stairs. 'I *hate* it here. I'll be glad when I can leave,' she growled, thundering up them, half tripping. 'You treat me like I'm three years old and then expect me to act like an *adult*? How does that work?'

Shaking his head, Jake gazed despairingly after her, and then looked back to Emily. 'She's been drinking again, I take it?' he asked, his face etched with concern.

It was a pity he hadn't been concerned enough to come home when he'd promised to, Emily thought, with a mixture of fear and frustration. She so wanted to believe his car had broken down, but after seeing that email, she just couldn't make herself. 'Obviously,' she said, now perilously close to tears herself. 'That was one of the things I wanted to talk to you about tonight, but of course *you* had more important things to do.'

Jake looked at her, perplexed. 'It was an emergency, Em. It's clear we do need to sit down and have a talk, preferably also with Millie, but I had no choice but to go.'

Emily nodded, trying very hard not to cry in front of him. 'I gathered,' she managed, turning back to the stairs.

'Em ...?' Jake called worriedly after her.

'I'm going up,' she said, a treacherous wobble to her voice. 'Can you check how long Ben will be, please?'

Pausing on the landing, she took a breath, and tapped on Millie's door. She wasn't sure what she was going to say to her. She couldn't apologise. She just wanted her daughter to know that she loved her.

Getting no answer, she tapped again. 'Millie?'

'I'm sleeping,' Millie mumbled moodily, which Emily supposed meant she didn't want to speak to her.

The tears fell as she went into the bathroom, bolting the door behind her. Was she wrong about all of this? Wrong to wade in so heavily with Millie, despite her gut feeling that she hadn't been at Anna's house? Wrong about Jake, despite her instinct telling her that something wasn't right? She'd been so off colour lately, stressed and anxious, her heartbeat so rapid she'd felt it like an actual pain in her chest. Millie kept accusing her of saying things she couldn't remember having said. She should talk to Jake. But he would want to examine her. Feeling as vulnerable as she did, could she bear for him to be that close to her?

'Emily?' His voice came through the bathroom door. 'Can we talk?'

She wasn't sure she wanted to, with her emotions so fraught. She could hardly avoid it, though. She would be the one acting childishly if she stayed in here. Taking a second to wipe her smeared mascara from under her eyes – make-up she'd foolishly reapplied when she'd thought they were going out – she braced herself and opened the door.

Jake was sitting on the bed, his head bowed, his hands draped between his knees, looking utterly exhausted. 'Ben's on his way,' he said, glancing up at her as she came into the bedroom. 'He should be here in five minutes. I'll go down and wait for him and then lock up.'

Emily nodded. 'Thanks.'

'He's my son too.' He frowned pensively. 'You don't need to thank me.'

Emily's heart caught in her chest, as it was prone to every time she was reminded what a good father Jake had been to Ben. 'I know. I …' She faltered. 'I'm just tired. It's been a long day.' Offering him a weak smile, she turned to the dressing table to remove her locket and earrings.

'Look, I am sorry, Emily.' Jake met her gaze finally, albeit in the mirror. 'Tonight was clearly important. I can see you're upset, and I can see why you would be, but the call-out really was an emergency.'

'I'm sure it must have been.' Emily tried to keep the weary facetiousness from her voice, but couldn't quite manage it.

Jake evidently picked up on it. 'He had appendicitis,' he said, his forehead creasing into a curious frown. 'Ethan, Rachel's little boy. I thought the appendix might be close to rupturing. I didn't want to risk peritonitis, so I got him straight into the hospital.'

Oh no. Emily closed her eyes. She'd been a millimetre away from accusing him of using his call-outs as cover for an affair. All because of a silly email. She'd leapt to conclusions, but perhaps there was some other explanation she hadn't considered. She should tell him about the email. How was he supposed to explain if she didn't? The whole thing was ridiculous. She *trusted* him. Apart from that one blip in their distant past, which she couldn't blame entirely on him, she always had. Turning from the mirror, her heart jolted.

Jake was on his feet, tugging off his shirt, his back towards her.

'What are those?' she asked, her blood running cold.

Half in and half out of the shirt, Jake paused and glanced over his shoulder. 'Scratches,' he said, looking at her cautiously as he turned to face her. 'I got caught up while I was trimming the Leylandii at the weekend. I told you, remember?'

Emily stared at him. She didn't remember. Her stomach turned over. She had no recollection at all of him coming in from the garden injured. Surely she would have? She scrambled through her memory. There was nothing. Nothing at all. She couldn't even remember him being in the garden. But the Leylandii, they had been trimmed recently. Hadn't they? Oh dear God. Fearing now for her sanity as well as his fidelity, a hard knot of panic twisted inside her.

CHAPTER FIVE

Jake

Jake had no idea how he'd let Edward talk him into this. He wasn't sure how they'd got on to the subject of swimming, let alone how that had ended up with him volunteering to wade about in wellington boots in the river. The water was low, but it was still bloody cold in there.

'We need someone competent,' Edward had told him with a hopeful smile. Jake doubted a high level of competency would be needed to make sure a raft of plastic ducks crossed the finish line without coming a cropper on the rocks or getting snarled up in flotsam. He'd agreed to do it, though, when Edward had pointed out that the majority of the spectators would be small children, who would sit up and take notice of him as he was the local GP. Jake didn't think the kids in the village were that in awe of him, but he would hate to think of a young child slipping past one of the marshals and sliding into the water. It was all for a good cause, he supposed; the money collected from sponsorship of the ducks would be put towards repairing the roof of the sports hall, which would also go some way to keeping the kids dry. And at least this way he would be on hand – numb from cold probably, but on hand if he was needed.

'All right, Jake?' someone shouted as he glanced around for Emily. Turning to the local produce stall, he spotted Dean Miller with his arm around his wife, Zoe, who was expecting their first child.

'Didn't think there was a dress code,' Dean said, looking him over with an amused grin. 'Liking the natty attire.'

Jake glanced down at the yellow waterproof dungarees someone had loaned him and decided 'natty' possibly wasn't the right description.

'Dean, stop it.' Looking highly embarrassed, Zoe gave him a nudge with her elbow. Clearly she thought Dean was being overfamiliar. She was always shy when she came to see Jake, always addressed him as Dr Merriden, as some people tended to.

'What?' Dean looked at her, now highly amused. 'Jake's all right. He has a sense of humour.' He gave her shoulders a squeeze. 'Must have to be wearing those, hey, Jake?'

'Clearly.' Jake smiled wryly and gave him a wave as the couple moved on, Dean now being severely chastised by his wife.

He'd located Emily and was about to go across to her when Edward called to him from one of the stalls. 'Ah, Dr Merriden. Glad you managed to get here in plenty of time for the off. And looking the part, I see.' He chuckled as Jake walked across to him. 'Very trendy.'

Thinking he was possibly going to be the main source of entertainment at the fair, Jake shook his head good-naturedly. Then, glancing across to where Emily was manning the bar and BBQ stall, and pointedly *not* looking in his direction, he buried a sigh. She was still annoyed with him for not coming home early when he'd promised to on Thursday. He didn't blame her. They clearly did need to sit down together and have a discussion about Millie, and think about maybe speaking to her tutors. He wished Emily would talk to him in the meantime, though. She wasn't exactly *not* talking to him, but she wasn't being very communicative. She was upset about Millie, understandably, but he couldn't escape the uneasy feeling that it was more than that. Perhaps he should suggest they go out tonight? He could book a table at the Italian restaurant in Hereford that was Emily's favourite, and ask Tom to cover any call-outs. If his father was going to insist on being hands-on, he could step in during out-of-surgery hours occasionally. It wouldn't kill him.

His mind made up, he turned his attention to Edward. 'Looks interesting,' he commented, nodding at the bottle of wine he was wrapping up in old Christmas paper, doing his bit for recycling.

'Aye, it is that,' Edward said with a wink. 'It's water.'

Perplexed, Jake knitted his brow. 'That should make sure no one's drunk while in charge of their ducks. Might be a few disappointed winners, though.'

'No, they're all getting into the *spirit* of it,' Edward quipped, adding the bottle to a row already wrapped and picking up another. 'It's a good fundraiser, this. It's called Water into Wine. The winning ticket gets a nice little …' He paused, squinting to read the label at arm's length. 'Sauvignon Blanc. And everyone else is happy in the knowledge that all proceeds are going towards maintaining the sports centre.'

'Fair enough. Count me in.' Managing to locate his jeans pockets under his dungarees, Jake fished out some cash. Handing over a ten-pound note, he marvelled at how Edward kept smiling despite his wife's recent illness and his accountancy business going under last year – something he hadn't told his wife, he'd confided. There was also his recent dementia diagnosis, which he really did need to tell Joyce about, though Jake guessed it wasn't going to be an easy thing for him to do. Joyce and Edward had been together for forty-five years. They weren't joined at the hip, both of them determined to stay independently active, but he'd noticed how close they were, always holding hands whenever they were out walking together, which was a sure sign of a strong relationship.

A stark image of his mother seared itself on his mind, reminding him how devastating the psychological consequences of feeling trapped in a bad relationship could be. He drew in a sharp breath. *Jesus.* Where had that come from? In his nightmares he couldn't avoid it, but during waking hours he tried hard not to think about the day he'd walked in from school to find his mother's body hanging limp and lifeless in the hall. Her eyes had been bulbous, bloodshot and haunted, looking right at him. He drew in another breath, tried to shake the image from his head. He'd been frozen, paralysed with fear and incomprehension. He hadn't cried. Eventually backing into the furthest corner of the hall, he'd sunk to his haunches. He'd been shaking, he remembered that, trembling incessantly, but he hadn't shed a tear. Because deep down somewhere he'd expected it. Even as a teenager, he'd seen the signs that his mother was becoming unbalanced after discovering the extent of his father's adultery. Now it seemed as if his own wife was behaving erratically, which was obviously down to him, and it scared him. He wondered how to broach the subject, try to get to the bottom of what she was thinking.

'Here you go,' Edward was saying, offering him a raffle ticket along with his change, Jake realised. 'You never know, it might be the winning ticket.'

'That's okay, Ed. You can keep the change.' Feeling hot and clammy suddenly, Jake wiped away the perspiration dotting his forehead. The dungarees were a bad idea with the temperature soaring. 'The raffle ticket too. You might as well sell it on. The more funds, the better,' he added, arranging his face into a smile. 'I'll catch up with you in a minute. I just need to have a quick word with Emily.'

'That's very generous of you.' Edward smiled delightedly. 'You're a good man, Dr Merriden.'

Yeah. Pity his wife didn't seem to think so. She'd definitely been off with him. He had to find out why. Glancing towards her again, he gave her a minute to finish serving a customer, then headed in her direction.

His progress was impeded, however, by Steve Wheeler, who ran the DIY store, and whose wife he'd recently treated. 'All right, Jake?' he asked, stopping in front of him.

'Yes, good, thanks,' Jake replied, one eye still on Emily. 'How's Jennifer?'

'Better. Much,' Steve said, a relieved look on his face as he glanced towards her.

Jake followed his gaze to see Jennifer bending to talk to one of her pupils from the primary school she taught at. She looked better, smiling and relaxed as she chatted to the little boy and his mother. Jake had been extremely concerned for her at one point. After losing her mother closely followed by the child she and Steve had both desperately wanted, he'd been sure she might be heading for a breakdown. He'd wanted to refer her for counselling, but she'd refused, worried that it would get back to her employers. The medication certainly seemed to be helping. That was good.

Seeing her notice him and give him a cheery wave, Jake waved back. 'Give her my regards,' he said. 'And tell her to come and see me any time if she needs to.'

'Will do,' Steve assured him. 'Catch you in the beer tent for a pint later?'

'I think I'll need one.' Jake indicated his attire with a despairing smile.

Steve laughed. 'I'll get them in, and remember, if you have any trouble with those ducks, give Jenny a shout. She'll keep them in line.' Giving him a wink, he headed jauntily off towards her.

'I just might,' Jake called after him, feeling pleased that he'd helped them get their lives back on track. It would be quite nice to do the same to his own, he thought, bracing himself to finally approach Emily. 'Hi,' he said, stopping in front of the barbecue, where she couldn't avoid looking at him.

'Morning,' Emily replied, and turned away to pick up a batch of burgers.

That worked well then. Jake sighed. 'Can I come in now?' he joked tentatively. 'It's getting a bit lonely out here.'

Emily's eyes flicked to his, her expression puzzled.

'In the doghouse,' Jake clarified.

'What makes you think you're in the doghouse?' she asked, glancing away.

'The fact that you seem to be avoiding me,' Jake suggested. 'We barely exchanged a word at the surgery yesterday.'

'I was busy. I spent my lunch hour looking at catering for Edward's birthday party.' Emily concentrated on the burgers she was placing on the grill. 'Plus, I'm not sleeping well. I'm a bit tired and preoccupied, that's all.'

'I gathered.' Jake studied her carefully. She looked flustered, her cheeks flushing the way they did when she was embarrassed. Or angry. 'Is there anything I can do?'

'There's something you can stop doing,' Emily mumbled, now looking definitely upset. She really was angry with him then.

'Such as?' he asked apprehensively.

To his frustration, she didn't answer.

'Em, apart from the fact that I didn't get back the other night, which was unavoidable, have I done something wrong? Because if I have, you're going to have to tell me what.'

Taking her time, Emily turned the burgers. Then, 'I'm not stupid, Jake,' she said, her eyes filling up as she looked back at him.

Extremely worried now, he stepped towards her. 'Emily, I have no idea what's going on here. You're talking in riddles. Please ...' *Leave the bloody burgers alone and talk to me*, he was about to say when someone twanged the braces of the ridiculous dungarees he was wearing from behind.

'Hiya!' a female voice said cheerily.

Sally. Jake's heart plummeted.

'Only me.' On cue, Sally draped an arm around his shoulders and leaned to press a kiss to his cheek. Jake had known her since childhood. It was the way she was, bubbly and outgoing, but he really wished she wouldn't. She'd been all over him at the 'welcome back to the village' party Edward had organised for them when they'd first arrived – five years ago now, he could hardly believe it. Emily hadn't been very impressed. Having realised she might have upset her, Sally had worked at gaining her friendship. They went out together, got on well at the surgery together – Jake nearly fell over when he'd arrived to find Sally was employed there – but the mood Emily was in, he wasn't sure Sally being so overtly tactile would go down well.

'Ooh, look at you, all dressed up for the part.' Her eyes travelled over him as she came around to his side. 'I do like a man in yellow rubber.'

Jake glanced down, trying to quash his irritation as she made a great show of patting his hind quarters.

Sally, though, seemed oblivious to the awkwardness she was causing. Walking across to Emily, who was now looking considerably upset, she hooked an arm through one of hers. 'Sorry I'm late,' she said, helping herself to a burger with her free hand. 'I know I promised to help you set up, but Dave had an emergency call-out, a sewer to unblock – ugh – and my car's still in the garage so I had to cadge a lift with one of the neighbours.'

'It's okay. We managed without you,' Emily assured her, fixing a bright smile on her face and trying for normal, where normal seemed to have been suspended – between her and Jake, anyway.

'I knew you would. I said to Dave, you two are a team,' Sally gushed in between mouthfuls of burger. 'I wish my husband would take a leaf out of Jake's book and make a bit more of an effort. His face was like a wet weekend when I told him we were coming to the fair, miserable old—' She stopped, her eyes growing wide as her gaze shot past Jake. 'I see Tash is on form,' she hissed, nodding in the direction of whoever had caught her attention.

Jake followed her gaze to see one of his patients, Natasha Jameson, waving at them.

'God, what *is* she wearing?' Looking the woman over, Sally scowled disapprovingly. 'The village fair is hardly the place for full sex-siren gear, is it?'

Intrigued, Jake glanced again at Natasha and noted the high leather boots over tight jeans. Her T-shirt was low-cut, he noticed that too, but he would hardly call it 'sex siren'.

'She's obviously on a manhunt,' Sally went on judgementally, and Jake couldn't help but feel sorry for Natasha. Relatively new to the village, she'd moved here after marrying Michael Jameson, who ran Apple Tree Farm. The tongues had started wagging the minute she'd arrived, the fact that she was fifteen years younger than Michael and didn't tend to dress in clothes suitable for hop-picking fuelling the gossip. Speculation was rife that she was only after his money. Jake guessed she would be on the receiving end of the tittle-tattle whatever she wore. A pretty woman with a good figure was a prime target for jealousy, he supposed.

'Question is, *which* man?' Sally pondered, her eyes roving derisorily over Natasha again. 'I'd gird your loins if I were you, Jake.' She looked amusedly back at him. 'She's definitely making fluttery eyes in your direction. She obviously knows a good thing when she sees it.'

Glancing away, Jake shook his head. When he looked back at Emily, her eyes were shooting venom-loaded daggers at him and Natasha both. 'Obviously,' she said, her voice strained as she scooped her bag up from under the table.

'Emily, hold on.' Bemused, Jake reached for her arm as she turned to walk past him, eye contact now nil.

'I'm busy.' Emily pulled away from him. 'I'm sure you have important things to attend to as well, don't you? Like impressing fluttery-eyed women with your rubber-duck-saving skills?'

'Oh dear. I've obviously put my foot in it,' Sally said worriedly, standing alongside Jake as he watched Emily walk away. 'You haven't, have you? Been trying to impress fluttery-eyed women?' She looked pointedly from him to Natasha and back.

'Not funny, Sally.' Jake sighed tiredly.

CHAPTER SIX

Emily

She was being absurd. Risking a full-on argument with Jake over an email that had probably been sent by some nasty individual who was quite clearly jealous of what she and Jake had together. The past was the past. Ancient history. They were a family now and they *were* a team. Sally had been right. They worked together, laughed together. Or at least they had until recently. They'd always been there for each other. She was being completely irrational. If she carried on like this, it would be a sure way of driving a wedge between them, which was obviously the aim of the email sender.

She would talk to him. She would have to. If she didn't, her suspicion would eat away at her and she would end up driving him away again. Her heart skipped a beat as she imagined it. And then another when Jake's foot slipped as he waded about in the water, causing him to stumble. He wasn't concentrating, busy watching her watching him, no doubt wondering why she was being so horrible to him.

She breathed a sigh of relief as, planting a hand behind him, he saved himself, the crowd cheering him on as he hauled himself up and reeled in a meandering duck to steer it back into line. She couldn't fail to notice Natasha, whose breasts were in danger of spilling over her top as she leaned over the bridge just ahead of Jake.

Jake glanced up at her when the woman cupped her hands to her mouth and yelled, 'Go the good doctor!', making sure to attract his attention. He looked away quickly enough, though, Emily noted, another surge of relief washing through her, concentrating instead on the slippery terrain underfoot.

He's not interested. She tried to resist finishing her thought with *you trollop.* It was plain that the woman was interested in him. It was also clear that Natasha Jameson had to be the owner of the email address beginning 'nja123'. She was one of the female patients Tom had mentioned who had transferred from his list to Jake's, clearly preferring to disclose her most intimate details along with her anatomy to someone young and good-looking. Recalling how she'd turned up for her last appointment wearing much the same look-at-me outfit she was wearing now, Emily felt her green-eyed monster unfurling dangerously inside her again.

She watched as Natasha pulled herself away from the bridge to head along the road and pick her way precariously down the slope to the riverbank in her high-heeled leather boots. And then laughed in disbelief as, acting more like one of the children she'd squeezed in between than an adult, the woman clapped her hands gleefully and shouted, 'Oh well done, Jake!', as if he were herding wild buffalo rather than inanimate plastic ducks.

Feeling miserable and dowdy by comparison, Emily moved from where she was standing on the road just before the bridge. It was possible Natasha wasn't aware she was here, watching her. Deciding to make sure she realised, she followed her, heading down the slope after her in her unsexy rubber flip-flops.

She was almost at the foot of the slope when her ankle turned over, a sharp squeal of pain escaping her as she pitched helplessly forwards. It was a squeak compared to the shriek Natasha let out as Emily lurched into her, sending her plunging into the icy-cold river.

Assaulted by a petrifying sense of déjà vu, Emily stared, horrified, down at the woman. And then it was as if the world had slowed down, the alarmed cries of those around her receding as she was sucked back to another time, another place, standing waist deep in murky water, another woman frantically thrashing before her; floundering as her muscles cramped and her efforts grew weak. There was someone there. Memories she'd pushed to the deepest recesses of her mind crept back. A figure darting through the foliage.

She heard herself shouting, 'Help! Help!' Over and over she shouted, wading further out, mud sucking at her feet, twisted metal tugging at her clothes. Minutes later, minutes lost, she saw someone on the canal bridge. A glimpsed silhouette. A man, backing away. Was he coming down? Why wasn't he coming down to help? Where was he? 'Help her! She can't swim! Please …' She heard someone screaming, a terrified, heart-jolting scream that came from the soul. Emily wasn't sure whether it was her. Had it been? Her mind hovered somewhere between then and now. She tried hard to remember, snapped her gaze back to the water.

Natasha. She wasn't moving.

Emily's chest constricted with confusion and fear. She wasn't flailing. She was floating, face down. Seeing the thin trickle of crimson bleeding into the water, a tight lump clogged her throat. She wasn't conscious. The jagged rocks …

She'd hit her head. *Oh dear God!* 'Someone help her!' she cried, her stomach knotting with panic as the man next to her scrambled into the river. *Get her out*, Emily prayed silently as another man plunged in after him. *Please get her out.*

Instinctively she limped forward, her feet teetering on the edge of the bank, and then faltered, relief crashing through her as she realised Jake was there, wading towards the woman. Efficiently he took control, crouching beside Natasha, quickly assessing the situation. Checking the alignment of her body. Emily's blood froze as she guessed he was checking for spinal damage. A beat later, he moved around to support Natasha's head.

'We have to get her out. We need to roll her,' he said, his face taut, his voice calm. 'Can one of you take hold of her torso and someone else take her legs?' He glanced at the men in the water. 'Ready?' He checked everyone was in position, then, 'On my count,' he said, his face set with grim determination.

A minute later, she was lifted onto the bank. People were milling around, trying to help, getting in the way. 'Has anyone called an ambulance?' Jake yelled.

'On its way,' Edward answered, stepping forward, and then turned to the gathering crowd. 'Come on, everybody, let's move back, shall we? Give the doctor some space,' he suggested, herding people away as Jake focused on Natasha.

'Natasha?' he called, feeling for a pulse. Turning his attention to her face, he scanned it, looking for signs of life, and then brushed her bedraggled hair aside to apply pressure to her ear. The woman didn't stir.

'Tash?' he tried again, then, 'Dammit!' He swiped at the droplets of sweat on his forehead and looked up to the heavens.

He seemed indecisive, and Emily guessed he was weighing the risk of tilting her head back, possibly causing further damage to her spine, against losing her to drowning. *Please God, no.* Her heart banging against her ribcage, she prayed hard as she watched him listen over Natasha's mouth for breaths. A turmoil of emotion twisted inside her as he moved his attention to her chest: guilt threatening to rise up and choke her; fear; jealousy. She'd felt something close to hatred as she'd witnessed the woman ogling her husband, but she hadn't wished her dead. *She hadn't.*

Had she? She swallowed hard. Her mother was right. She was evil. She heard it distinctly, her mother's hissed condemnation as she'd lain alone in her room, dark shadows flitting in and out of her dreams as the days after Kara's death drifted into nights, into days … 'She's a monster.'

That part came back to her with blinding clarity. She hadn't remembered any of it until now. She'd buried it along with her sister. Hadn't wanted to acknowledge how bitterly her parents had wished it was her they'd lost and not Kara.

'She's not breathing,' Jake said tightly, snatching her attention back to this day, this riverbank and another death she might be responsible for. Terrified, she watched as he used his fingers to gently clear Natasha's airway. He was pinching her nose, placing his mouth over hers, breathing slowly into it. Pausing. Assessing. Sucking air deep into his own lungs. Breathing. Rescue breaths. The kiss of life.

He was desperate not to lose her. Emily's fingers strayed to her own lips. She was desperate not to lose *him*, her husband, the one solid thing in her life, the one person who knew her and loved her. But he didn't know her, not all of her – he didn't know why the ghost of her sister haunted her dreams. She didn't know him fully either, each minuscule detail that had made him the man he was, or the deceit he might be capable of. She didn't *know* whether he loved her. Her heart boomed another echo of her past. He'd been looking for a distraction, possibly attempting to move on. He might have done if she hadn't called him from outside the bar that long-ago night and lied to him, telling him she'd been nervous about committing fully to another relationship after being treated badly by a man. She'd never told him how badly. How could she? The truth would surely have driven him away, and she'd needed him. She loved him – then and now. He'd taught her what love really was. She couldn't have told him the whole truth and expected him to stay.

He had stayed. When they'd talked the next day and she'd told him she was pregnant – she'd decided she would keep the baby; she'd had to – he'd walked her home, his mood quiet, contemplative. Tentatively he'd kissed her goodbye, saying he would call her in the morning. She hadn't been sure he would. An hour later, there'd been a knock on the door of her bedsit, and she'd answered it to find him standing nervously on the doorstep holding a small velvet box. 'It wasn't an expensive one,' he'd said awkwardly, seeming not to notice her old pyjamas and cried-off make-up. 'We can change it. As soon as I'm qualified, we can choose any ring you want, but for now, will you accept this one? Will you marry me?'

The box contained his mother's engagement ring. She still wore it. Had he proposed because he loved her, or had he stepped up to do the right thing? Had she forced him to?

Now, standing stock still, too scared to speak or move as she heard hushed whispers around her, sensed fingers pointing accusingly at her, she continued to watch as Jake positioned his hands over Natasha, ready to perform cardiopulmonary resuscitation. He'd done two compressions when she gasped, her eyes springing wide as she spewed out a breath.

Jake moved fast, yelling at the men who'd assisted him in the water to help roll her onto her side, keeping her spine aligned as they did. 'Try not to move. You'll be okay. The ambulance is on its way,' he said, his hand resting gently on her shoulder, his face close to hers.

Someone offered sheets hastily retrieved from tables, which Jake indicated they should drape over her while he talked reassuringly to her, keeping her calm and still. He didn't move from her side until the ambulance arrived.

He conferred with the paramedics as they checked her over, and walked with her as they transported her to the ambulance. Smiling, he squeezed her hand as they paused before loading her into it. 'You gave me one hell of a scare back there,' he said.

'Sorry,' she managed weakly.

'I'll let you off.' He gave her another warm smile. 'You're in capable hands now. I'll come and see you as soon as you're home.'

*

An hour later, they were on their way back home themselves, Jake's car loaded up with unsold goods from the stalls, the fair ruined. Despite what had happened, her guilt that she'd been the cause of it, Emily decided to broach the subject of the email. She was sure Natasha Jameson was the sender. It had to be her. 'You saved her life,' she said carefully. 'She might have died if not for you.'

'It was just basic first aid.' Jake ran a hand over his neck, looking utterly exhausted.

Emily hesitated. 'Still, it was a good job you were around.'

Jake nodded. 'I suppose.'

Natasha had been in the vicinity of wherever Jake had been that morning. Emily would have had to be blind not to notice. Might she be wrong? It was possible. But she couldn't ignore the nagging voice in her head that told her she wasn't. 'I didn't realise you knew her that well,' she ventured.

'Sorry?' Jake glanced confusedly at her.

'Natasha.' Emily took a deep breath. 'I didn't realise you two were intimate.'

'Intimate?' He laughed uncertainly.

'Tash. You called her Tash.' *And she called you Jake. Why would she do that if you weren't on first-name terms?* Her heart thundered. She was treading on dangerous ground. He would know she was accusing him. He wasn't stupid. How would he react?

He shot her another look, one of incredulity this time. 'She was unconscious. I was trying to reach her. That's what she prefers to be called, isn't it?'

Emily noticed his tight grip on the steering wheel and her heart dropped to the pit of her stomach. 'Yes … but I wasn't aware you knew her well enough to know that.' She tugged in a tremulous breath. Held it. 'Or exchange emails.'

'You what?' Jake did a double-take. 'What on earth are you talking about, Emily? We don't *exchange* emails. And I know her as Tash because that's how she introduced herself when she first came to see me. Everyone calls her that.'

Remembering that she'd deleted the email and therefore had no proof to back up what she was saying, Emily floundered. 'Why has she switched to your list?' she blurted out, and then immediately regretted it as she realised it was sure to escalate this into the worst kind of argument.

'For fu—' Stopping himself short of swearing, Jake bumped the car onto the drive and stamped on the brake. She could feel the anger emanating from him as he twisted to face her. 'Are you *serious*? The woman almost *died* because *you* fell into her. And now you're saying … *What* exactly?'

CHAPTER SEVEN

Perilously close to tears, Emily threw open the passenger door and headed fast for the house. Jake banged his door closed behind him and followed.

'So let me get this right,' he said, dragging a hand through his hair in frustration as she paused in the porch to fumble in her bag for her front door key. 'Out of the blue you're accusing me of … what? Fancying another woman? Having an affair?'

'No,' Emily replied, flustered. He was right. Natasha might have died, and it had all been her fault. She should never have brought the subject up. 'That's not what I said. I just …' Where was the damn key?

Sighing agitatedly, Jake reached around her to push his own key into the lock.

'Talk to me, Emily,' he said as she stepped quickly into the entrance hall. 'Tell me what the hell's going on.'

Her eyes flicked to the stairs. Millie and Ben had plans, so she assumed they were out, but it was possible one or the other was upstairs in their bedroom. 'I don't want to talk about it. I didn't accuse you of anything.' She hurried on through to the lounge.

'Christ give me *strength*,' Jake muttered behind her.

He was angry. Furious. Why would he be? Wouldn't he just have laughed it off if there were no truth in it? Emily walked across to the lounge window, which overlooked their pretty rear garden.

He'd been angry around his father, palpably, but she'd never known him to lose his temper. He seemed close to losing it now.

Goosebumps prickling her skin despite the perfect warmth of the summer's day, she wrapped her arms around herself and looked out past the abundance of small trees, shrubs and flowering plants to the mill stream that bordered the garden. She hadn't been sure about the property when they'd first viewed it. A barn conversion that formed part of the Black and White Trail, it was beautiful, though it had been in need of some renovation. The stream, though … She'd imagined the soft lap of the water might haunt her. In fact, she'd found it strangely therapeutic, especially on days such as this when – melancholic though her memories were – she would sit outside and allow her mind to wander to thoughts of her sister growing up, the secrets and laughter they'd shared. The stories they would tell each other – classic stories sometimes, like 'Little Red Riding Hood' and 'Goldilocks', each trying to outdo the other with surprise endings. Kara's had been tragically beautiful. She'd always been gifted. Emily remembered the games of dressing-up and make-believe they'd played: sock puppets, doctors, warriors, united in their efforts to vanquish their foe; together, always, until they'd grown up. Or imagined they had.

Her mind flew back to the first time she'd allowed her boyfriend to 'go all the way'. She'd been just sixteen. She was under the bridge with him, her back against the wall, the cloying smell of damp brickwork and aftershave in her nostrils, his body pressed hard to hers.

'I want you,' he'd mumbled, his face stuffed into her neck, his hand sliding down the front of her jeans. It had been uncomfortable, with his hurried tugging aside of her clothes, his urgent fumbling and thrusting.

He hadn't said much afterwards. Lighting up a spliff while she made herself decent, he'd slid down the wall to his haunches. Drawing smoke deep into his lungs, he'd held it for a while. Then,

'How's that sister of yours?' he'd asked her, exhaling thickly into the air. 'Do you reckon she's still a virgin?'

Emily shuddered. She would never forget the smell of his aftershave mingled with the sweat from his body; the paralysing fear she'd felt the last time she'd been alone with him. The same paralysing fear Kara must have felt.

People hadn't openly blamed her when they'd found her sister's limp body floating in the canal, but Emily had blamed herself. She'd lived with the guilt lodged like a sharp stone inside her ever since. In her heart she'd known she hadn't pushed Kara, but in her head ... She hadn't been able to remember, not everything. No matter how hard she'd tried, the details were always just out of reach, floating hauntingly on the periphery of her memory. But now ... She remembered following her, but why would she have been trying to save her if she'd pushed her?

Her mother *had* blamed her. Emily had seen the accusation in her eyes. Felt it. She'd never forgiven her for the part she'd played in Kara's death. Could Kara? Emily wished she could have had her sister's forgiveness.

Gaining no comfort from her memories today, she tightened her arms around herself and pushed thoughts of Kara to the back of her mind while she tried to think what to do about her suddenly floundering marriage. She'd opened the whole ugly can of worms now. She couldn't undo it. Should she tell him about the contents of the email? Admit that she'd followed him the next day when he'd left the surgery shortly after lunch? He was going to pick up the lawnmower he'd ordered from Leominster while he had a window, he'd said. She'd lost him at the traffic lights. He *had* picked up the lawnmower, but he'd been an extraordinarily long time, scraping back into the surgery before his first evening appointment. But she'd deleted the email. She no longer had proof to back up her story. And if she did tackle him, there would definitely be no turning back. It would be out there, real, creating a divide between them that would never close, a deep, dark chasm she would surely fall into, finding herself alone with her grief and her guilt all over again.

'Emily, what's happening here?' Jake asked, a defeated edge to his voice as he finally came in behind her. 'You're upset, and I honestly have no idea why. Please talk to me.' He ventured closer, placing an arm tentatively around her shoulders.

Involuntarily she tensed, and he immediately snatched his arm away. 'I take it we're not talking then?' he asked wearily.

Hearing his hurt and disappointment, Emily desperately wanted to turn around, rest her head on his shoulder, apologise and have him hold her. Pretending it wasn't happening wouldn't make it go away, though, would it?

Jake waited a minute. Emily didn't move. 'Right. Message understood,' he said with a sharp intake of breath. 'I think I might do better to be elsewhere for a while. I'll call you. Later.'

What did he mean, 'elsewhere'? Fear gripping her, Emily whirled around as he walked to the door. 'Where are you going?'

He stopped and turned back. 'To the surgery.'

'To catch up on paperwork?' Her voice sounded small and uncertain even to her own ears.

'There's a fair amount to do.' He shrugged disconsolately.

She nodded. 'I gathered that, from the amount of time you spend there.'

A frown crossed his face. He was clearly wondering where this was leading.

'Who were you talking to on the phone?' She finally asked him the question she'd been burning to, then braced herself.

'On the phone when?' He squinted at her, mystified.

'When you came home late on Thursday. Why did you take the call in the conservatory?'

His look was now one of astonishment. 'Because I couldn't hear over the kettle boiling.' He laughed bewilderedly.

Emily glanced down, her stomach churning. She could never hear over the kettle boiling. Several times she'd walked out of the kitchen, her phone pressed to her ear.

'It was Rachel Brown, Ethan's mother,' Jake informed her, now obviously irate. 'She called to tell me he'd had his surgery, that he was conscious, and to thank me. Are there any more questions I need to answer?'

Ethan. God, where was her mind? Jake had said the little boy had been rushed into hospital. His mother would have been beside herself with worry. As Jake had possibly saved her child's life, she would have been likely to ring him with an update. He'd probably asked her to. Why on earth hadn't she thought it through? Her cheeks heating up, she struggled for something to say. 'No. I'm sorry. I just … It doesn't matter.'

'Right,' Jake said tersely. 'I don't have a clue what this is all about, Emily, but when you feel like enlightening me, you know where I am.' Looking her over, unimpressed, he shook his head and then turned to walk away.

'I take it you two are still not on speaking terms, then?' Emily heard Millie ask as he reached the hall, and her heart dropped.

Jake's reply was agitated. 'Apparently not.'

'So where are you going?' Millie sounded apprehensive. 'I thought you were out together at the village fair all day.'

'It ended early,' Jake answered diplomatically, though his anger was still evident. 'I'm going into work for a while. I shouldn't be too long.'

Emily gathered from Millie's silence that she wasn't impressed with what was happening either.

'I'll bring a pizza back later, shall I?' Jake suggested, softening his tone. 'Assuming you're around?'

'I'm out tonight,' Millie answered after a second. 'Assuming I'm not grounded at weekends as well as during the week,' she added drolly.

'Where?' Jake asked. 'Assuming you get why we would be worried about you.'

'I get it,' Millie conceded grudgingly. 'I'm going to the Open Air Film and Chill in Hereford with Anna and a few friends. And no, we're not going anywhere near the pub, before Mum starts going on about me drinking again, as if she never did when she was my age.'

'It's only out of concern, Mils,' Jake said in Emily's defence. 'I know you think we go on, but if you're honest, I think you'd much rather that than if we couldn't care less where you are.'

'I suppose so.' Millie conceded that much too.

'You know so,' Jake chided her. 'What about Ben? Do you know whether he's home later?'

'I think so. He's gaming round at his mate's this afternoon, but he said they'd be coming back here. I'll tell him to give you a call at the surgery, shall I?'

'If you could. Thanks, Mils,' Jake said, that special fondness in his voice he had for his daughter. 'Have you heard back from the veterinary practice about the job yet?'

'No.' Millie sighed disappointedly. 'I think I messed up my application form, to be honest. And then I was so nervous I was talking rubbish.'

'That sucks,' Jake sympathised.

'Yeah.' Millie sighed again, heavily. 'I should have prepared better, I suppose,' she admitted – and Emily felt even more guilty. She should have gone through her application with her, and made time to coach her. If only she hadn't been so preoccupied with convincing herself Jake was cheating on her.

'Did you make enquiries at MacDonald and Gibbs?' Jake asked. 'They're moving premises, looking at expanding, apparently.'

'Are they?' Millie sounded hopeful.

'So I heard from Phil MacDonald. I tell you what, why don't you come in with me? We'll draft an email together, and I'll give Phil a ring and let him know to expect it. What do you think?'

Millie took a second to answer. 'That you're pretty cool,' she said, careful not to sound overly gushing.

'As dads go,' Jake added, amused.

'As dads go.' Amazingly, Millie laughed.

'Grab your stuff,' Jake said. 'I'll wait in the car.'

Hearing Millie charge up the stairs, Emily hesitated and then stepped into the hall. As Jake walked out without even calling goodbye, her heart sank without trace. There'd definitely been no kiss this time. Her marriage seemed to be crumbling and she had no idea how to repair it.

Natasha. She had to stop her. She would *make* her stop. A fresh wave of anger welled up inside her, closely followed by a now overwhelming guilt. The woman might have sustained a life-changing injury. They didn't yet know. Whatever she'd done, Emily wouldn't wish that on her.

She clutched a hand to her head, wishing she could make the incessant throbbing go away. She couldn't let her emotions get the better of her. She had to tackle this calmly, rationally. In light of the psychological damage his own father had wreaked, she couldn't believe that Jake would do anything that would rock Millie and Ben's world, but if it turned out to be true, then they would be caught up in it.

She wouldn't throw any more accusations at him; not yet. That would only make the situation worse. First she would establish how Natasha was, and then she would go and see her. It seemed to Emily that in sending the email to Jake's work address, Natasha had hoped she would see it. No doubt she'd imagined that Emily would confront Jake, raging at him about the evidence of his infidelity, thus lighting the fuse that would blow her marriage apart. She'd very nearly done just that. She still didn't know what the truth was, whether her marriage was in deep trouble. If push came to shove, though, she could fight dirty too.

CHAPTER EIGHT

They'd managed to get through Sunday relatively normally. Emily hadn't brought up the subject of Natasha again. It was Jake who eventually mentioned her, saying that he'd spoken to a colleague at the hospital and that she'd made a full recovery and had been discharged. He'd conveyed the information unemotionally, telling her pointedly that he would be checking up on her as she was a patient, leaving Emily feeling yet more guilty, if that were possible. But was she the one who should be feeling guilty?

He'd kept his phone with him constantly, she'd noticed. Or had he always done that? The nature of his work dictated that he needed to be contactable, but she hadn't noticed him keeping it quite so close before now. But then she'd never had cause to look before. She'd caught him several times guardedly watching her, perhaps because she'd been carefully watching *him*, trying to read his body language and his expression, which was largely pensive.

She'd been about to dash off to the supermarket, after realising that, once again, she'd forgotten to get something out of the freezer, but he'd suggested they all eat out. She'd proposed that he treat Millie and Ben to a pub meal instead, telling him she was nursing a nagging toothache, which had been her planned excuse to leave work early today. She hadn't actually felt like eating anyway. The constant waves of nausea, which she'd now stopped mentioning to Jake, left her with no appetite.

Seeing it was time for her to leave for her fictitious appointment, she switched off her PC and grabbed her bag. 'Don't forget to blank your screen if you walk away from the desk,' she reminded Nicky as she fetched her jacket. 'And make sure to—'

'Lock all client information away in the filing cabinet and close my computer down properly when I leave,' Nicky chipped in. 'Don't worry, you can rely on me.' Smiling proudly, she pointed to the Post-it notes adorning her screen.

Emily gave her an indulgent smile back. The girl was doing her best. Still, though, she was easily distracted. She hoped she didn't forget.

As it was lunchtime, there were no patients currently in with Jake, so she tapped on his door and went in. 'I'm off to my dental appointment,' she said, determined to remain professional despite their personal situation. 'Nicky's up to speed regarding your appointment schedule.'

'Oh, right. Thanks.' Jake got to his feet and walked around the desk towards her, then stopped. Normally he would kiss her. Sometimes, a mischievous smile curving his mouth, he would push the door to and kiss her thoroughly. Now, though, his expression was awkward as he lingered a step away from her, and he didn't appear to know what to do.

She should tell him everything. A hard lump expanding in her chest, she almost closed the door herself and stepped further in. But she couldn't bring it all out into the open here and create the very scenario she was trying to avoid: confrontation, arguments, accusations. Not until she absolutely had to. She would convince this woman to back off, praying that they could then salvage their marriage. If she could bring herself to trust him again, and feel secure that Jake thought their relationship was worth saving, then she would talk to him. She would have no choice. She couldn't bury her head in the sand and hope it would go away and just be grateful when it did – until the next time.

'Tom's popping in,' she reminded him. 'He needs to get some data together for the clinical commissioning group. Nicky's on her own so you might want to keep an eye on things,' she suggested, hoping he would get the point about his father's tendency to ogle their receptionist at every opportunity without her spelling it out.

'Right,' Jake said again. She could tell by his long intake of breath that he understood.

Her heart ached as she climbed into her car and headed for Apple Tree Farm. For herself, but mostly for Millie and Ben. She and Jake had worked to protect them from anything that might damage them growing up, particularly the harm parents could wreak. What had happened? she wondered, feeling still as bewildered and disorientated as she had when she had first glimpsed that bloody email. She wasn't sure what she was doing here, other than to try and corroborate what her head was telling her: that Jake was having an affair, despite the promises he'd made never to be like the father whose behaviour he claimed to detest.

If it did turn out to be true, she only prayed he would never utter the words he'd spoken years ago, telling her his association with the woman meant nothing, quite clearly indicating that *nothing* was worth risking his marriage for, ruining his children's lives for. She wasn't sure she would ever be able to forgive him that.

Driving into the farm, she passed the field Michael Jameson had left to fallow this year and on past the hops that were beginning to establish themselves on their strings. Michael had broken his back rescuing the farm that had been handed down to him from his parents. Emily knew that growing hops was one of the hardest crop choices in farming, the hops requiring attention all year round. Even then, farmers were at the mercy of the weather and yields varied. Michael had often joked that hop growers were resilient folk, supplementing their income with other horticultural crops such as apples. Emily wondered how resilient his heart would be if he discovered the woman he'd not long been married to, and who he'd refurbished the farmhouse for, possibly overstretching himself financially, was cheating on him.

Hoping Michael was out and about on the farm, she parked a little way down the track leading to the house. She noted Natasha's brand-new Mini Clubman parked outside and the anger that had been simmering inside her rose. She had no doubt that the purchase of that car had pushed Michael further into debt.

Bracing herself, wondering what she hoped to gain if the woman denied an affair outright, she climbed out of her car and made her way towards the house. She was severely tempted to gouge the shiny Mini with her keys as she neared it, and was shocked by this new viciousness inside her. This wasn't her. No matter what people had thought her capable of, silently accused her of, she'd never felt this out of control of her emotions. It scared her.

Attempting to steady her rapid heartbeat, she was bypassing the kitchen window when a loud crash from inside rooted her to the spot. The guttural roar that followed it – primeval, the raw cry of a wounded animal more than a man – caused her heart to jolt violently.

'*Why?*' She heard Michael cry, his voice filled with agonised bewilderment. 'I've given you everything! *Everything!*'

'I didn't! *I haven't.*' Natasha's voice, desperate. 'It's a lie! I … Michael, *don't!*'

Hearing another crash that sounded like glass smashing, Emily's heart pounded as she inched towards the window. Peering in, her eyes fell immediately on Natasha. She was scrambling away from Michael, trying to get to the door that led to the hall, but Michael was faster, grabbing her arm, dragging her back and whirling her around, and then pushing her against the kitchen wall.

Emily's stomach churned with fear as she watched arms flailing, mouths moving. Michael's face, contorted with rage, was an inch away from Natasha's, his forefinger jabbing the air close to her cheek. 'How many?' he bellowed, pushing his face closer.

'None!' Natasha cried. 'No one! It's—'

'Liar! Lying, cheap *little*—'

'I'm not!' the woman sobbed. 'They all hate me. They're doing it out of jealousy! Why else would they … Michael, *please* … Don't!'

Oh dear God! Seeing what was about to happen, Emily rapped urgently on the window. 'Michael! Stop! *Michael* …' The words died in her throat as Michael's clenched fist hit its target.

Nausea swilling inside her, Emily backed away from the window, fumbling her phone from her pocket as she flew towards the front door. Her heart almost stopped beating when Natasha emerged, fleeing for her life, blood oozing from her nose and mouth, staining her white T-shirt stark crimson.

Michael was close behind her. 'They know you're on the pill!' he yelled from the doorstep, his face puce with rage and waving a piece of paper at her, seemingly oblivious to the fact that Emily was there. 'They know what fucking brand you're on! You said you wanted children!' He scrunched the piece of paper into a ball and tossed it out after her. 'You said you wanted *my* baby!'

Emily hesitated for a second, and then moved to snatch the paper up and race after Natasha as she blundered away from him.

'It's not true!' As Natasha squirmed around to face him, Emily caught hold of her and tried desperately to lead her away. 'Why won't you believe—'

'Liar! Cheating, lying little whore!' Michael screamed. 'I *loved* you!'

Watching him sink to his knees, Emily's heart broke for them both. She'd wanted Natasha to get her just deserts, but not this. Never this. Her legs trembling, tears sliding down her own cheeks, she squeezed the woman close and steered her gently towards her car. 'It's okay,' she whispered. 'I've got you.'

'It's not okay,' Natasha cried pitifully, smearing snot and blood across her face with the back of her hand. 'It's not true. None of it. Why would someone do this?'

'Shush.' Emily tried to soothe her. 'Come on, let's get you in the car, and then I'll drive you somewhere safe.'

Helping her into the passenger seat, Emily closed the door and, one eye on Michael, dashed around to the driver's side. It was clear he was devastated, broken. He wasn't about to follow. But still, she would feel safer putting some distance between them. Feeling sick to her soul, she gulped back the rock lodged in her throat and started the engine.

Driving quickly away from the farm, she pulled into a passing space in the lane beyond it. Her heart bleeding for the woman, despite her suspicions, she reached for a tissue from her pocket, passed it to her and gave her a moment.

'I think we might need to get you to the hospital,' she suggested, once Natasha was more composed. Her face would be terribly bruised. Emily only hoped there was nothing broken.

Natasha shook her head. 'No,' she said, gulping hard. 'Thanks, but I'd rather not.'

'What happened?' Emily probed gently.

Twisting the tissue nervously into a knot, Natasha looked tentatively at her. 'You picked up the letter?'

Emily nodded. 'Would you like me to read it?'

Closing her eyes, Natasha answered with a small, defeated nod.

Emily's mouth dried as she smoothed out the crumpled piece of paper. She had no doubt the contents would be incriminating. Who would they incriminate, though?

You should keep an eye on your whore wife, she read, her stomach turning over. *Did you know she was on the pill? Microgynon 30.*

Goosebumps prickling her skin, Emily looked at the signature: *An anonymous friend.* It told her nothing.

'It was pushed through the door while I was out,' Natasha whispered. 'They wanted Michael to see it. They wanted this to happen.'

CHAPTER NINE

Sitting at Emily's kitchen island, Sally gawped at her over her wine glass. 'You're joking,' she gasped, taking a mouthful of her wine and almost choking on it.

'I wish I was.' Emily drew in a breath and reached for the bottle. 'And he actually hit her?'

Emily nodded, a shudder running through her as she recalled the incandescent rage Michael had been consumed with. 'She was absolutely terrified. I wanted to take her to the hospital, but she refused to go. She wouldn't report him either. I feel dreadful for her.'

'Well, yes, I do too, but …' Sally hesitated. 'You know, I never thought I would ever say this … I mean, I could never condone physical violence no matter how driven a person was, but I can see why he lost it. This confirms everything, doesn't it?' She looked down at the letter between them and then back to Emily. 'That she's every bit the money-grabbing trollop we thought she was.'

Emily wasn't so sure it did. Natasha had looked more like a frightened child than a sex siren when Emily had dropped her off at her mother's house in Worcester. She denied absolutely cheating on Michael, and said that she loved him. When she'd thanked Emily for being the only one in the village who would care enough to be concerned about her, Emily had felt awful. The fact was, though, that if there were any truth in the letter sent to Michael, wouldn't that confirm that there was some truth in the email?

'Possibly.' She sighed. 'But to have punched her like that …'
She felt a shudder run through her.

'I can't believe you're feeling sorry for her,' Sally huffed and
hopped off her stool to retrieve a second bottle, one she'd brought
with her, from the fridge. 'The woman quite obviously had Jake
in her sights. You only had to look at what she was wearing at the
fair, as well as the fact that she couldn't take her eyes off him, to
realise that.'

Emily's blood ran cold as she remembered the events at the
fair. Guilt weighing heavily inside her, she glanced at her friend,
who was looking indignant on her behalf, and who, ironically, was
dressed in slim-cut jeans and leather boots. She had noticed what
Natasha was wearing, of course she had. It had been abundantly
clear to her that the woman had been working to attract Jake's
attention. But hadn't Sally draped herself all over him? It was the
way Sally was, the sort of person who hugged everyone. It was
possible that Natasha was just being who she was too.

'So do you still think she was the one who sent the email to
Jake?' Sally asked as she came across with the wine, and then went
back to the work surface to refill the dishes with nibbles, which
Emily really had no appetite for. 'Not that I'm implying there
was anything in it.' She glanced over her shoulder – sympathetically, Emily noted, meaning she probably did think there was
something in it.

'I thought she was,' she said, wondering now at the wisdom of
confiding in Sally, who could be a bit of a gossip. She was always
supportive, though, and Emily had so needed someone to talk to.
She felt as if she was losing her grip on reality, as if her world was
slowly crumbling around her and she had no way to hold onto it.

'But you don't think so now?'

'I honestly don't know.' Sighing again heavily, Emily reached
to top up her glass. She would probably feel as sick as a dog in
the morning, but she did it anyway. Anything to numb the pain,

hopefully enough that she could sleep. 'She swore she wasn't cheating on Michael. She was so hurt and upset ...'

Emily really wasn't sure any more. After all, the only evidence she'd had – or thought she'd had – was the email address beginning 'nja'. The letter sent to Michael had accused Natasha of everything Emily had imagined the woman was doing, yet ... She'd been so distraught. So adamant she'd never been unfaithful.

'Hmm,' Sally pondered. 'Well, whoever sent the email and the letter, there's obviously some bitter individual in our midst determined to stir up trouble between couples.'

'But who? And why?' Emily knitted her brow. Was it just that, someone trying to stir up trouble? Other than his constantly working late, she'd had no cause to think that Jake had been cheating on her, but add to that his many call-outs and that damn email ... And he had reacted so angrily when she'd hinted she suspected something. Wouldn't he have tried to reassure her, rather than go into defensive mode, if there was nothing to hide?

'I don't know, someone thwarted in love maybe?' Sally suggested. 'Someone with a grudge, determined that no one should be happy if they're not? The contents of that letter are pretty bloody awful—' She stopped abruptly as Jake, home early, amazingly, walked from the hall into the kitchen, catching them unawares.

'What letter's this?' he asked, a curious expression on his face.

'Jake!' Sally exclaimed delightedly, distracting him as she walked back to the island, while Emily quickly scooped the letter into one of the drawers underneath. 'We weren't expecting you.'

'I gathered.' Jake smiled warily, his eyes travelling to the two wine bottles. And then over Sally, Emily noticed, with a stab of jealousy.

'So are you going to enlighten me?' he asked, his eyes back where they should be, on Sally's face. Which was meticulously made up, as it always was. Emily was suddenly acutely aware of her own lack of make-up. Since finding the email, part of her thought she should make more of an effort with her appearance. Another part of her, though, told her there was no point. She was already hurting more than she'd thought possible. How hurt would she be if she tried to attract his attention only for him not to notice?

'Sorry?' Sally blinked, perplexed.

'The awful letter,' Jake said, placing his case at the end of the island and shrugging out of his jacket.

Sally's eyes ran the length and breadth of him – Emily couldn't help but notice that too – before gliding worriedly to hers. Working to still the green-eyed monster writhing inside her, which now seemed to be suspicious of everyone, she signalled her friend not to share the information with a quick shake of her head. She intended to talk to Jake, but later, when they were alone, when she'd decided how much to disclose. She'd told herself she hadn't mentioned the email to him because she'd needed more proof. Because she didn't want the children to have to cope with the fallout. But now she wondered whether she was doing what she'd promised herself not to, burying her head and hoping it would all go away. It wouldn't. The doubt would never go if she didn't talk to him and give him the opportunity to explain. Assuming there was anything *to* explain. There might not be – she felt a kernel of hope unfurl inside her – if, as Sally said, the email and the letter had been sent by some twisted individual with a grudge. But why target Jake and Natasha? Try as she might, Emily couldn't ignore that link.

'Oh, just work gossip. You know what we girls can be like.' Getting the message, Sally deflected Jake's question and perched herself back on her stool.

'You're back early.' Changing the subject, Emily arranged her face into a bright smile. She would drive everyone away at this rate, including her best friend. Plus, she was desperate for Jake to look at her anything but guardedly. He knew she was worried; he'd always been able to sense that kind of thing. When she'd been so upset about Millie's childhood asthma diagnosis, he'd been there, strong, professional, reassuring. When she'd been devastated thinking she might be losing Ben six months into her pregnancy, he'd been there for her, so supportive, such care and kindness in his eyes, she wouldn't have got through it without him. Was he avoiding full-on eye contact now out of guilt? Because he didn't want to acknowledge how crushed she would be to find out he was cheating on her? But how unfair was she being expecting him to read her mind? She had to talk to him, however painful it might be.

'I had a call-out.' He draped his jacket over his case, ran a hand tiredly across his neck and then walked around to press a light kiss to her cheek, which was at least something. 'I came straight home rather than go back to the surgery.'

'Oh?' Emily glanced up at him, uneasiness prickling her skin as she noticed his cautious expression.

Jake took a visible breath. 'In light of … certain recent events, I thought I should tell you that the call-out was from Natasha Jameson,' he went on, causing Emily's heart to somersault in her chest. 'She sounded distraught and said she was injured. I felt obliged to go.'

Noting the hands now shoved in his pockets and his shrug, as if it were no big deal, Emily's anger unleashed suddenly inside her. 'I bet you did,' she fumed, yanking herself to her feet and striding across the kitchen with no purpose other than to open a cupboard, extract a cup she didn't need and then bang it shut again.

There was deathly silence for several long seconds, until Sally broke it, clattering her stool as she got to her feet. 'Right, well, I should probably get off,' she announced with forced jollity. 'Dave will be wondering where I am.'

Coming across to Emily, she squeezed her shoulders. 'I'll call you tomorrow, hun.'

Emily gave her a small nod, grateful for her diplomacy. Staying where she was, her back to Jake until Sally had slipped out of the door, she tried to think rationally. Natasha was one of his patients. She might have felt she needed medical attention, but … why would she call Jake from her mother's house in Worcester? And why would he go? It was over an hour's drive away. Surely, if it were urgent, he would have advised her to dial the NHS emergency helpline or go to the local accident and emergency? Emily had offered to take her there herself, for God's sake.

She couldn't ignore this. Whatever the fallout might be, there was no way she could simply say nothing. Breathing deeply, she braced herself. 'Where was she?' she asked, her voice strained. 'Natasha, where did you see her?'

Jake took a minute. Then, 'Why?' he asked.

'*Why?*' Emily whirled around, astonished. Was he serious? 'Because I know very well she isn't at home,' she pointed out, daring him to lie to her outright. 'Where did you *see* her?'

Jake narrowed his eyes. 'A hotel,' he answered eventually.

A *hotel?* Stifling a half-hysterical laugh, Emily looked up to the ceiling. What a poor, gullible idiot she was. Had she honestly believed that Natasha bloody Jameson had been telling her the truth? Confiding in her? There she'd been, confronted by her husband, fleeing from him – only to bump into Emily on the drive. She would hardly have admitted she was cheating on Michael to *her*, the woman married to the man she was cheating on him with, would she? She hadn't stayed at her mother's house, clearly – if it even was her mother's house Emily had dropped her off at. She'd gone to a hotel. Probably a pre-booked hotel. Did they think Emily was completely stupid?

'She's not safe at home,' Jake went on, oblivious to her incredulous stare, her mounting anger, 'but it appears you're already aware of that. What letter were you discussing?' he asked her. 'You and Sally, when I came in?'

Emily ignored that. Her chest heaving, she stared hard at him, hardly able to believe that he was questioning her as if she were the one in the wrong. 'Yes, and you know bloody well *why* she's not safe in her home.' She almost spat the words out. 'Because of you, you bastard!'

Jake's eyes darkened. 'What are you talking about, Emily?' he asked, his quiet tone belying his taut expression, the agitated tic playing at his cheek.

'You know very well what,' she seethed. 'I am *not* stupid, Jake. Or blind! I know all about your *extracurricular activities*. I can read, in case it had escaped your notice.'

Jake sucked in a breath. 'It hadn't,' he said tightly. 'I don't think you're stupid, Emily, or blind. I do think, however, that you might be a little ... over-tired. The symptoms you've been experiencing – lack of energy, shortness of breath, headaches and palpitations – could all be due to an iron deficiency, which you have. I got the results back this morning. But the broken sleep, this ... bizarre behaviour ... We should get you another blood test organised in case we're missing—'

'Bizarre behaviour?' Emily stopped listening. *Oh, nice move, Dr Merriden. Pop your caring professional hat on. That should ramp up the guilt a bit.* 'As in irrational?' she asked, holding his gaze, challenging him to belittle her. How long would it be before he told her it was all in her mind?

'That's not what I said.' Massaging his forehead, he dropped his gaze. 'The thing is,' he looked back at her, his expression now one of discernible agitation, 'unless you tell me, I have no idea what the bloody hell you're *talking* about!'

He'd lost his temper. Something he never did. Even when the kids tried his patience severely, even when it was obvious his father was grating on his nerves, he was restrained. Angry, but never outwardly aggressive. Why would he be now? Because she was in danger of stripping away his perfect persona, revealing him for what he was, a liar and a cheat? That would shatter his good-family-doctor image, wouldn't it, she thought, her throat tightening.

'You know that I know what you're doing, don't you?' Biting the tears back, she kept her gaze fixed firmly on his.

'For Christ's sake.' Jake raked a hand through his hair. 'What *am* I doing? Will you please just tell me what's going on, because I *don't* know, Emily. I have no clue.'

'No, nor did Michael,' Emily pointed out, her heart catching as she recalled how furious Michael had been, how violent and then utterly devastated. 'Until today, that is. It's quite sad, isn't it? That a man who worked his fingers to the bone building his business could have his life reduced to rubble by someone he'd placed his trust in. Someone everyone places their trust in, misguidedly.'

'Emily, you need to stop this.' Clearly shaken, Jake moved towards her. 'You obviously think that somehow I'm involved with Natasha. You're wrong, I promise you. We need to sit down and talk, calmly.'

Emily stiffened as he placed his hands on her shoulders. She couldn't help herself. Having him so close, smelling his scent of crisp white cotton suffused with the citrus aftershave he wore – and what else? Undertones of a woman's perfume? – was too painful.

'Somehow involved?' she repeated, an errant tear escaping her eyes despite her best efforts. 'That's the problem, Jake, I can imagine all the ways. Every position. Wouldn't you, if it were me cheating on you?'

His eyes a whirlpool of confusion, he searched her face, his own deathly pale, and then dropped his hands away. 'This is hopeless.' He breathed out heavily. 'You've got it all wrong, Emily. I have no idea why you would even think … Can we not just talk it through? Please?'

'You went to see her in a hotel, Jake. There's nothing to talk about as far as I can see, is there?' she retorted flatly, and turned away.

'She's a bloody patient!' he yelled after her as she walked towards the door. 'What did you expect me to do?'

She spun back around. 'Exactly what you did!' she yelled back. 'No, scratch that. I honestly expected more of you than this … predictable shit!'

'I am *not* cheating on you, Emily,' Jake insisted furiously. 'When in God's name do you think I would have time?'

Emily laughed scornfully. 'Um, now let me think …' she said, arranging her face into a thoughtful frown. 'When you disappear on your "call-outs" to visit your "patients", possibly? When you're sweating over the mountain of paperwork in your office? *Supposedly.*'

'For crying out *loud.*' Jake heaved in a breath. 'This is madness, Emily! Bordering on paranoia. You need to let me run some tests. If you won't let me do them, then I'll organise a referral. Please just allow me to do *something*, will you? We can't carry on like this.'

And there it was. Hardly able to believe her ears, Emily stared hard at him, stunned by his attempt to deflect his guilt, the consequences of *his* actions, by claiming she was insane. And he would be qualified to do so, wouldn't he? 'Do *not* do this to me, Jake,' she warned him. 'It won't work. I will fight you. While I have breath in my body, I swear to God I will.' Sweeping a gaze filled with contempt over him, she whirled around and flew into the hall – and then froze.

Oh God, no. This was exactly what she'd been trying to avoid: her children being caught in the crossfire. They'd clearly overheard. Ben's face said it all. Behind him, by the front door, Millie looked equally shocked. Her stomach flipping over, Emily found her voice. 'Have you just arrived?' she asked them, praying they hadn't heard all of it.

'Unfortunately.' Ben shrugged, his gaze unimpressed.

'And now I'm leaving,' Millie said bluntly, her eyes shot through with something near hatred as she dragged them mutinously over her mother.

'Millie …' Emily's heart leapt as her daughter turned to yank the front door open. 'Where are you going?'

'Anna's. I'm staying over.' She headed down the drive without looking back.

'Millie, come back!' Emily called desperately after her. 'It's late. You can't—'

'No way!' Millie shouted. 'Do you really think I want to listen to that crap?'

'Millie!' Watching her daughter flee angrily into the night, Emily felt her heart splinter. *She'd* done this. Forced her to do exactly what she'd forbidden her to do. What she herself had done when her teenage home had felt like an alien place. She'd never imagined that she and Jake would put their children through the kind of trauma they'd both suffered at their parents' hands. Jake had been blameless when his world had disintegrated. She hadn't. She'd carried her guilt all her life. And now she would be carrying the guilt of her actions all over again.

'Going up. Got some stuff to do for uni,' Ben muttered as she stepped back into the hall.

'Ben?' Emily wanted to go to him, reassure him, but he was already halfway up the stairs, her boy growing fast into a man, growing more distant from her; from Jake, too, as their personalities clashed. He and Ben were so different in nature. Ben was sensitive; he could be laid-back and easy-going sometimes, but there was also a moodiness about him, as evidenced by his challenging Jake – after being escorted home by the police, for goodness' sake. He hadn't just been moody that time, he'd bordered on aggressive. Jake had told her not to worry too much about it. He'd put it down to the large amount of alcohol Ben had obviously consumed, but Emily *did* worry about it, constantly.

Watching him disappear along the landing, she swiped the tears from her eyes and grabbed her jacket from the peg, rifling through her pockets for her car keys. They weren't there. Where *were* they? Her memory was like a sieve lately. She was searching hopelessly for her bag when Jake came out of the kitchen.

'Where are you going?' she asked him, cold apprehension slicing through her as she noticed his car keys in his hand.

'After our daughter.' He shot her a furious glance as he strode past her. 'There's no way I'm going to allow her to walk around on her own at night, upset. I'll drop her at Anna's, assuming I can't persuade her to come back.'

Bewildered, Emily simply nodded and watched him go. He didn't bang the door behind him as she'd half expected he might, but still the sound of it closing was like a death knell. A terrifying thought occurred. Might he be right? Might she really be going mad? Her paranoia, as Jake termed it, blowing things horribly out of proportion?

Her thoughts a petrified jumble in her head, she was walking shakily back to the kitchen when her phone beeped from the lounge. Hoping it might be Millie, she dashed to fetch it.

I'm watching you was all the text said. It came from an unknown number.

Emily gulped back a sharp knot of fear. She wasn't going out of her mind. Someone was trying to drive her there.

CHAPTER TEN

Jake

Jake felt desperately sorry for Zoe, who was weeping quietly in his surgery. Having seen her and Dean together at the fair, he'd been astounded by what she'd just told him. He'd bumped into Dean a few weeks back in the pub one lunchtime while waiting for Emily – before their lives had started falling apart. Dean had been over the moon about his expected baby, beaming all over his face. Zoe and Dean were both in their early twenties, only married a few months and renting a small property because they couldn't afford to buy. The pregnancy hadn't been planned, but they hadn't been daunted by the prospect of parenthood. Far from it, they'd been excited about it. And now this. Life really did have a habit of kicking you in the teeth when you least expected it.

Unable to sit there and do nothing, he went around his desk, offered Zoe the box of tissues he kept there for this sort of occasion, and then, throwing protocol out of the window, placed an arm gently around her shoulders.

'I'll try to hurry the appointment up,' he said softly, as she tried to compose herself. 'Try not to worry. There will be other opportunities.' He cursed himself then, realising how hollow that sounded. 'I can organise some counselling for you if you'd like?'

Zoe shook her head, blew her nose and dabbed at her eyes. 'No,' she said, with a shaky breath. 'I'll be okay, Dr Merriden. Thank you for being so kind.'

He didn't assure her it was just part of his job. She needed genuine kindness right now. And he really did feel for her. 'Come and speak to me if you need to. Any time.' He gave her shoulders a squeeze. 'Just let Emily or Nicky know I've okayed it and we'll fit you in.'

She managed a tremulous smile. 'I will.' She nodded and got to her feet. 'You're a lovely man, Dr Merriden,' she said, leaning to give him a hug. Hugging would definitely be deemed bad protocol, but Jake was reluctant to step away, given how upset she was. 'Emily is a lucky woman,' she added, easing away herself after a second to pick up her bag.

Jake hid a rueful smile as he followed her to the door to open it for her. He doubted Emily was thinking herself lucky right now. He had no idea *what* her thinking was, apart from the fact that she clearly thought he was the biggest bastard that walked the earth.

'Take care,' he said, making sure to offer Zoe a reassuring smile as she left.

Going back to his desk, he debated for a second, and then decided to take the bull by the horns and ask Emily to come into his office. He would never normally do that unless he needed a female present for patient examination purposes. Usually he would go out to reception, but he was desperate to talk to her on her own, out of earshot of the kids, and try to establish what evidence she had to back up her accusations. At least then he would have some idea what he was dealing with. Right now, he had no clue. Or what to do about it. Everything he said seemed to make the situation worse. His emotions were all over the place, see-sawing between bewildered and bloody petrified. What if he couldn't convince her he wasn't cheating on her? What then? It was true he'd been neglecting his family lately, but they meant the world to him and he couldn't bear the thought of losing them. Losing Emily. She'd been the one constant in his life. The only thing he'd kept going for at one point, when he'd felt that the dark cloud that dogged him was closing in on him. The nightmares had been relentless for years after his mother's death, never a night where he didn't relive the day he'd walked into the hall and his world had stopped turning. He'd never confided his fears to anyone but Emily, who'd always been there for him, always supportive. He needed to remind himself of that. He prioritised making time for his patients, to listen and try to read between the lines. He needed to do the same with his wife and attempt to put things right, if only she would let him.

His gut churning, as it had been since this whole thing started, he braced himself and picked up the phone.

Two minutes after he'd called through to reception, Emily appeared, looking cautious. She was looking good, he noticed, in leather boots with leggings. She was wearing make-up and her hair was in some sort of updo. It looked nice. He wanted to compliment her, but he really didn't know how she would take that. It was as if he didn't know her any more. She was like a different person. Whatever her thinking was, she was behaving strangely. She was clearly unwell, and he was worried.

'Was it something important?' she asked. 'It's just that with only the two of us out there and Fran coming in later to do her cleaning, we're a bit backed up.'

Noting the formal tone, Jake sighed inwardly. He guessed that Fran would be talking the hind leg off a donkey, as she always did, and he knew Emily and Nicky had their work cut out without a much-needed extra medical secretary to take on some of the load, but … 'Yes,' he said, getting to his feet again to walk around her and close the door, 'it is important. Extremely. Assuming you think our marriage is important, that is?'

Emily's eyes immediately shot to the floor. 'I'd rather not discuss our personal problems here, Jake. It's inappropriate,' she said, taking a step towards the door.

Jake had his back to it, however, and inappropriate or not, he wasn't about to move until she heard what he had to say. He took a breath. 'I love you, Emily. Whatever it is you're thinking I've done or am doing, please believe it isn't true.' He held his breath and waited.

Emily didn't answer. She wouldn't look at him either.

Jake felt his heart sink. Where was this leading? What would he do if she announced she wanted a separation? A divorce? Jesus, he couldn't handle that. He couldn't have nothing in his life but work. His father, who he actually wished had never *been* part of his life. The thought of working here without Emily alongside him caused his heart to plummet to the pit of his stomach.

'I love my kids, too, more than anything. I need you in my life, all of you,' he said gruffly. He wished she would say something, anything. 'I don't understand, Em. I really don't.' Swallowing back a jagged knot in his throat, he took a step towards her. 'Knowing what you know about me, do you honestly think I would do anything to put my family in jeopardy?'

Still she didn't answer.

'Look at me, Emily,' he implored her, his voice catching.

She seemed to prevaricate, and then lifted her head, meeting his gaze at last. Her cheeks were flushed, her wide blue eyes shiny with tears.

'Em? Please believe me,' he begged her. He was flailing. There was nothing else he could think of to say to convince her. He couldn't bear to see her like this, so down and flat. He was scared.

Her eyes flicked away. 'I know you love Millie and Ben,' she said eventually. 'I thought I knew you loved me, but …'

'I do.' Jake took another step towards her. 'I've always loved you. You must know that.'

'But how can I?' Emily took a step back. 'How can I know that you're not relying on me believing you could never be like your father in order to cover your tracks?'

'You *know* me, Emily,' he tried. 'Probably better than I do myself. I hate what he did. What he is. I would rather cut my throat than be like him.'

'But you might not be able to help yourself.' She searched his eyes, her own full of confusion.

Jake ran a hand over his neck. She didn't believe him. 'Right, so you really do think I would throw all we have away for … what? An affair with a married woman? One of my patients?' He looked at her in astonishment.

Emily dropped her gaze, indicating that she did, clearly.

'And the basis of this is that you think I'm like my father?' he asked tiredly.

'No,' she answered quickly. 'Not just that.'

He tipped his head to one side, eyeing her curiously. 'There's something else then?'

She hesitated. 'You were seeing someone before,' she said, her voice small, her eyes still cast down.

'What?' Now Jake was truly astonished. '*When?* I've never *seen* anyone else. I've never even so much as looked—'

'Before we were married,' Emily blurted. 'I saw you in the bar with her.'

He shook his head. 'You have to be joking,' he said, feeling physically winded.

'You said it was nothing …'

'It *was* nothing.' He wondered if he was hearing her right. He didn't even remember it, for Christ's—

'And I believed you. And then you proposed to me, and I thought that maybe you felt pressurised and …'

'Because I bloody well *loved* you,' Jake said vehemently as she trailed off. 'I wanted to be with you. Have you honestly been dwelling on this all these years? Imagining I was … what? A serial adulterer?'

'No.' Emily denied it, her cheeks flushing hotly. Then, 'I don't know,' she murmured, her eyes travelling down again. 'You're always working late.'

Jake pressed his thumb and forefinger hard against his forehead. 'Because I *have* to. You know how much there is to do.'

'Every single night?' she challenged him. 'You go off to call-outs without telling me—'

'Right,' he interrupted, his frustration growing. 'So you're saying that you think I've been using patient call-outs as some kind of cover-up for an affair? With Natasha Jameson, the wife of a mutual friend? A good friend? *Christ*, Emily ...'

'Don't look at me as if I'm mad,' she snapped. 'You obviously have been attracted to other women, looked at other women. Whether or not it was before we were married, you were seeing me at the time, Jake. Or supposed to be.'

'Except that you didn't appear to want to see me,' he reminded her, now utterly despairing.

'I explained all that. I'd been treated badly by a man and I was nervous.'

'Was *I* treating you badly?'

'No, I ...' Emily faltered. 'I was pregnant. I was confused. I didn't want you to be with me because you felt obliged to be.'

'I didn't feel obliged.' Jake kneaded his forehead in frustration. 'I've just told you. I—'

'But that's beside the point,' Emily cut in. 'We're talking about where we are now. Our marriage. People who are married *do* have affairs. Most marriages break up because people have affairs. If two people are sexually attracted, they tend to throw everything that's supposed to matter to them out of the window. I mean, let's face it, the thought of illicit sex is a powerful aphrodisiac, isn't it?'

'Unbelievable.' Jake eyed the ceiling. 'I am *not* sexually attracted to Natasha, for God's sake,' he grated, looking back at her. 'Why the hell do you think I would be?'

'Because she's attractive,' Emily pointed out, ridiculously. 'Slim, abundantly blessed in the breast department.'

'That's utter rubbish, Emily.' His jaw tightened. 'You can't just accuse me of having an affair out of jealousy. You're every bit as attractive—'

'She fancies you!' Emily's voice rose. 'She practically drools whenever she sees you.'

Jake studied her carefully. 'You're deadly serious, aren't you?'

Emily said nothing. Her eyes ablaze, she simply stared at him.

Cold apprehension clutched his stomach. If she'd been comparing herself to Natasha, if this notion that he was having an affair with her, this resentment, had been simmering away inside her, then might she have … 'Did you send that letter to Michael?' he asked her. 'A letter that contained private medical information that could easily have come from here. Did you send it, Emily?'

Her expression was a combination of shock and hurt. 'What?'

'The contents of that letter caused an argument that ended in physical violence,' Jake pointed out, though he knew he didn't need to, nor did he need to point out the consequences of patient information somehow being leaked. 'If it did come from here, then I need to know.'

Emily eyed him furiously. 'I can't believe you just accused me of that,' she fumed, pushing past him to yank the door open.

Me neither, Jake thought, his own temper dangerously close to spilling over. Breathing in hard, he turned to go after her.

'She obviously spoke to you about the contents of the letter then,' Emily threw over her shoulder.

'I went to see her. Obviously she told me—'

'I *know*. In a hotel,' Emily hissed, striding out.

'Emily …' Jake stopped, realising they had an audience: Nicky, who was looking warily past Emily towards him; and Fran Nateman, their cleaner, who revelled in local gossip, embroidering it or even inventing it half the time, and who looked actually excited to be getting a juicy dollop to get her teeth into. There were also patients waiting, most of whom, obviously having heard raised voices, looked uncomfortably away. Also Sally, whose sympathetic frown accompanied by a heartfelt sigh made him feel uncomfortable.

Shit. Averting his gaze, he walked back to his office, trying to recall as he went what he and Emily had just said. Closing the door, his heart jolted when he realised that he'd as good as announced they were breaking patient confidentiality.

Christ. Once the village drums started beating, that would get around like greased lightning.

CHAPTER ELEVEN

Emily

Her professional smile fixed in place, Emily exited the toilets more composed than when she'd gone in. She wasn't surprised to find Fran behind the reception desk, dusting being her excuse to natter to Tom, who'd obviously just arrived, and whom she would feel duty-bound to fill in on the gossip. All eyes swivelled in her direction and there was a sudden obvious silence as she approached.

'Okay, Emily?' Nicky asked, smiling tentatively as she went around to her desk.

'Yes thanks, Nicky.' Forcing a smile in return, Emily seated herself at her PC, behind which she hoped she might hide her embarrassment.

'Morning,' Tom said, his tone far too chipper and obviously determined to engage her in conversation. From the curious look on his face, Fran had obviously already told him about her argument with Jake and he was on a fishing expedition to find out more.

'Morning, Tom,' Emily replied, determined not to get drawn into conversation. She felt like running away, but she could hardly go home, setting an example to Nicky that relationship problems justified time off sick. In any case, the beautiful home she and Jake had built together wasn't a place she particularly wanted to be right now. It would be too painful a reminder that the foundations beneath it were crumbling.

'I was hoping to have a word with Jake sometime today about the never-ending budget problems,' Tom went on, loitering annoyingly. 'Do you know if he's free after evening surgery? About six … ish?'

'Well I assume he'll be here,' Emily said curtly. 'But then I'm not always privy to what his movements are. Why don't you ask him yourself?'

'Right. Yes. Will do.' Tom now sounded puzzled, as he would be. Emily didn't rate him, as a father, or as a man, all things considered, but she didn't usually allow her personal feelings to affect their professional relationship.

'Sorry, Tom,' she apologised, noting his perturbed expression. 'I'm feeling a bit off colour.'

'Not a problem.' Tom smiled reassuringly. 'You have a lot on your plate. I wonder how you manage to keep all the balls in the air sometimes. Let me know if I can help.'

She blinked at him, surprised. She and Tom weren't close, for obvious reasons, but was that sympathy she could see in his eyes? 'Thanks, Tom.' She managed a smile. 'There is one thing I could use a bit of help with, actually.'

'Fire away,' he said, plainly keen.

'I've decided to organise a party for Edward's seventieth birthday, and with one thing and another, I haven't been able to do much about it yet.'

'Splendid idea.' He rubbed his hands together enthusiastically. 'The man's a pillar of the community. We ought to do something special for him. How can I be of assistance?'

'You could put the word out,' Emily suggested. 'I'll be sending invitations, but as I'm a bit pushed for time, I wondered if you could mention it to your patients. I think pretty well everyone knows him.'

'No sooner said than done.' Tom nodded, looking pleased to have been asked. 'I'll drop those I have email addresses for a quick line too. I'm sure they won't mind, given the occasion.'

'Thanks, Tom.' Emily breathed a sigh of relief. Despite her own initial enthusiasm, she hadn't done anything towards making the party happen, other than check the village hall itinerary and have a quick word with Sally, who thought she might be able to get hold of a Beatles tribute band. It wouldn't be much of a party without people … and catering … and decorations. And then there was the bar to organise. Realising she might have bitten off more than she could chew now that her life seemed to be spiralling out of control, she was beginning to panic.

'Any time,' Tom assured her. 'I'd better get on. I'll have a word with Jake about the budget later.'

'I'll bring you some tea in, Tom,' Fran offered as he headed for his office.

'No need, thanks, Fran. I was just off to make one anyway. I imagine Emily could do with one. Strong and sweet, hey, Emily?'

'Please. That would be lovely.' Reaching for her vitamin pills, along with the pills Jake had prescribed for her iron deficiency, in the hope that they might boost her energy levels, Emily smiled after him. That was the third cup he'd made her in as many days. He seemed to be trying to look after her somehow, as if he truly cared about her. Was it possible he wasn't so bad after all?

'I'll do it, Tom,' Fran insisted, making to follow him. 'I'm sure you have more important things to do.'

'Nothing at present,' Tom assured her, looking awkward as he glanced back at her. Fran plainly had a soft spot for him – she couldn't do enough for him. Emily suspected she quietly fancied him and wondered how long she'd felt that way. Tom obviously didn't have any reciprocal feelings. He couldn't seem to get away from her quickly enough whenever she gazed longingly in his direction.

'Oh,' said Fran, looking deflated.

Emily glanced up at her, actually feeling quite sorry for her. It couldn't be easy bringing a child up single-handed on a low income.

Reminded of her own children, who imagined they were adults but still had so much growing up to do, she pictured their stricken faces when they'd overheard her and Jake arguing, and her heart dipped heavily in her chest. When Millie had come home from Anna's this morning to get changed, her complexion had been unhealthily pale. Concerned, Emily tried to ask how she was, but Millie's responses to her questions were monosyllabic. It was clear she didn't want to speak to her.

'You're looking nice today,' Fran observed, as Emily toyed with the idea of texting Millie now, and Ben too, suggesting they go out for a meal together this evening and have a talk. They were probably waiting for that, living in dread of the 'your father and I love you both dearly, but …' announcement. Her blood ran cold at the thought of what might be going through their minds.

'Making a bit of an effort, are we?' Fran went on.

Emily's sympathy disappeared. She couldn't believe the woman was oblivious to the fact that she was actually being insulting. Her gaze gliding in Nicky's direction, Emily noted she was also boggling in disbelief.

'*Cow*,' Nicky mouthed.

Emily frowned, but said nothing. Nicky was right. Fran pretended concern while she was nattering on about people, but Emily was aware that she wallowed in their misfortunes. Sally said it was because she was full of resentment after the father of her child had decided not to step up to the task. Emily had thought she was being a bit hard on her, but now she was beginning to think Sally was right too.

'Rum business, this Natasha Jameson thing.' Fran sighed as she flicked her duster around. 'I've no time for newcomers to the village, especially the sort that flaunt themselves, as you know,' she continued, getting into her stride. She sounded more like an old fishwife than the forty-year-old woman she was. 'But I can't help feeling sorry for her. Who would have thought that Michael

Jameson would have turned out to be a wife-beater? He's always been such a kind, sensitive man. You can't help wondering what it was she did that drove him to it, can you? Or rather who.'

Noting Fran's eyes, which were stuffed full of innuendo, gliding in her direction, Emily felt her stomach turn over. She wasn't sure how much of her argument with Jake people had overheard. She guessed they'd heard raised voices, but she'd hoped they hadn't gathered what they'd been arguing about. They evidently had.

Jake emerged from his office, his face taut. He didn't even glance in her direction as he headed towards the treatment room to confer with Sally, and she felt tears sting the back of her eyes. Their personal problems were out there for public consumption. With Fran beating the drum, the news would be all over the village in no time. Their children would be hurting because of it, and Emily had no idea what to do, how to make their world safe again. How to stop her own world from unravelling around her.

CHAPTER TWELVE

Dean

Seeing Zoe manically cleaning the kitchen worktops again as he went in, Dean shook his head in despair. The kitchen wasn't big enough to swing a cat in; it couldn't be that dirty. She'd cleaned the entire flat scrupulously over the last week. He supposed it was her way of keeping her mind occupied since losing the baby. He wished there were something he could do to make her feel better. She didn't seem to want to talk to him about it. That hurt.

He'd been absolutely gutted when she'd rung him, upset that she hadn't told him before he'd set off on his road trip that she wasn't feeling well. He got that she was concerned he might lose his job – the bastard he worked for had made it clear that if he didn't take the long haulage jobs, he'd find another driver who would – but Dean would rather have told him where to stuff his job than for Zoe to have gone through this on her own.

What he didn't get was why Jake hadn't contacted him. She'd gone to see him at the surgery only days before. Dean understood that patient confidentiality would have prevented him saying too much, but he must have known something was wrong, surely? The last time they'd had a pint together at the pub, Dean had told Jake he had to work away sometimes, that he was worried about leaving Zoe on her own. Knowing that, the bloke could have texted him, couldn't he? Alerted him to something being amiss, at least. Maybe not. It might not have been obvious there was a problem, he supposed. Still, Jake must have known when she was actually losing the baby, assuming Zoe had rung him before going to the hospital. Dean wanted to ask her about that, but didn't want her to have to go over it if she found it too painful. The doctor at the hospital had reckoned it was something to do with abnormal chromosomes. They'd also told her it was usually a one-off event and that she would most likely go on to have a normal pregnancy. Dean had been relieved to hear that. He hadn't carried the baby inside him, but he still felt, weirdly, as if he was grieving.

Noticing that she was standing on tiptoe, stretching to reach up to the top cupboards, he walked over to her. 'You shouldn't be doing that, Zoe,' he said softly. 'You need to rest up a bit. You've been through a lot.'

'I'm fine,' she assured him, carrying on regardless.

'You're not fine.' Burying a sigh, he reached to still the hand she was wielding the cloth with. 'The place is so clean we could eat our dinner off the floor. You don't need to be doing this now.'

'I'm not ill, Dean,' she said, closing her eyes, her energy seeming to deplete as she dropped back to her feet.

'I know.' He wrapped an arm gently around her waist. 'But you're going to be all over the place emotionally, aren't you? You need to look after yourself. Go out shopping and treat yourself to something nice, why don't you? I could come with you if you like.'

Zoe glanced at him. 'We wouldn't have any food to eat off the floor if I did that,' she reminded him with a wan smile.

Nodding awkwardly, Dean took a breath. 'I've been putting a bit away. You know, for when …' He trailed off, his throat tight. 'Anyway, I have a few quid. You should splash out a bit. Buy a new outfit or get your hair done or something.'

She looked at him, bewildered, for a second, and then dropped her gaze and covered her face with her hands.

Realising she was crying, Dean's heart lurched. Crap, he'd meant to cheer her up, not reduce her to tears. 'Hey,' he said, easing her towards him. 'It's okay. I'm here. I've got you.'

She pressed her face hard into his shoulder. 'I'm so sorry, Dean,' she murmured.

'For what?' He tightened his arms around her. 'Wetting my shirt?'

She laughed, a short, muffled sound. 'I don't deserve you.'

He held her closer. 'I know. Unfortunately, you're stuck with me.'

She laughed again. A laugh that turned into a sob that shook through her body. She was so petite and seemed so fragile right now that Dean felt he would die to protect her. He wished there were something he could have done to protect her from this. She'd been on her own when she needed him. He would always feel bad about that. Determined to get another job that would allow him to stay at home – he'd get some training if he had to – he held her while she cried, gently stroking her back, soothing her as best he could.

Eventually, when her sobs slowed, he eased the wild tangle of red hair he adored gently away from her ear. 'I'll run you a warm bath,' he whispered, 'with loads of bubbles, and then give you a nice shoulder massage afterwards. How does that sound?'

She looked up at him, her eyes still awash with tears and filled with heart-wrenching sadness. 'Like heaven.' She managed a tremulous smile. 'Did anyone ever tell you you're lovely?'

'Frequently.' Dean smiled, and pressed a tender kiss to her forehead. Actually, no one had ever told him he was lovely, apart from Zoe. Not even his own mum. 'Come on, let's get that bath run.' Giving her a squeeze, he steered her out of the kitchen, down the hall and towards the bedroom. 'And when you're ready, if you don't fancy a bit of retail therapy, how about we take a stroll by the river and grab a pint and a bag of crisps?'

'You spoil me.' She gave him a fond squeeze back.

'I know.' He sighed theatrically. 'It's tough knowing you're not after my body, but I can live with it.'

'Twit,' she giggled.

Leaving her to have a soak once the bath was run, Dean came out of the bathroom feeling marginally better than useless. At least he'd managed to cajole a smile out of her. He was pondering alternative jobs and what he might actually be any good at when the post plopped through the letter box. Assuming it was nothing but bills, he scooped it up and flicked idly through it as he went back to the kitchen. Noticing what looked like a greetings card addressed to both of them, he furrowed his brow, puzzled. An invitation, most likely. Hoping it wasn't to a christening, he opened it warily, the furrow in his brow deepening as he scanned the simple white card with a cracked silver heart on the front. It was a sympathy card, he realised. His own heart caught in his chest as he read the verse:

Babies who are taken too soon
Are never touched by fear.

It stopped beating altogether as he read the inscription beneath: *Was yours, Zoe? So sorry you had to have an abortion. Dean must be devastated.*

CHAPTER THIRTEEN

Jake

Jake was going through Joyce Simpson's rheumatologist's report with her, now that he'd finally persuaded her to come in for an appointment. She seemed to think she was bothering him if she requested a consultation. An intelligent, capable woman, she was coping well, but he worried that she might not understand all the technical terms in the letter she'd been sent from the hospital, and the importance of tapering the steroids down slowly. She was responding to treatment well, still having the odd temporal head-ache, meaning they had to keep an eye on the giant cell arteritis, but she'd had no recent flare-ups of her polymyalgia rheumatica, which was a good sign.

'You're doing well, Joyce.' Digesting the report, he looked up at her with a smile. 'Your ESR is slightly raised, but everything else is looking good. Your angina is under control, too. I reckon you're healthier than I am.'

Joyce chuckled at that. 'Make sure to step aside for me when you're out jogging. I'll be whizzing past you in no time. Mind you, I'll be needing one of those electric commuter-scooter things that are all the rage.'

Jake's smile widened. It sounded like she'd already looked into getting one. 'There's no stopping you, is there, Joyce? Hold your horses,' he added as she raised herself from her chair. 'I just want to check for any scalp tenderness and have a quick feel of your temporal arteries before you go.'

'Now there's an offer a girl can't refuse.' Arching her eyebrows in amusement, Joyce settled back down.

Examining her gently but efficiently, Jake assured her everything seemed fine, and then offered her a hand to assist her up. 'Such a gent.' She batted her eyelashes theatrically. 'I would say I can manage, but it's not often I get to hold a good-looking young man's … Oh dear.' She stopped, her gaze going to the door, beyond which there seemed to be a commotion in reception. 'Sounds as if there's a bit of a rumpus outside.'

'It certainly does.' He braced himself as he walked her to the door. If he wasn't mistaken, the raised voice he could hear belonged to Dean Miller, Zoe's husband, and he sounded upset.

They'd almost reached the door when it was banged open from the other side, narrowly missing them. 'I need to speak to you,' Dean said, his gaze gliding between Jake and Joyce. From the palpable fury in his eyes, it was clear he wasn't going anywhere until he had.

Jake's heart sank. He knew what it was Dean wanted to talk about. 'Okay.' He spoke evenly. 'Can you just give me a minute to—'

'*Now*.' Dean wiped the back of his hand across his mouth.

Jake's gaze drifted past him to where Nicky bobbed into view, her face pale and clearly worried. 'Emily's calling the police,' she said – for Dean's benefit, he guessed.

'No,' he said quickly, noting the flash of thunder in the man's eyes. He was close to exploding. That would do no one any good. 'Tell her there's no need.'

'They wouldn't let me see you,' Dean said, as Nicky disappeared back to the desk. 'Kept telling me I had to make an appointment. I told them I don't need a fucking appointment. I need information. And I need it—'

'*Whoa.*' Jake held up a hand. 'Calm down, Dean. Take a seat.' He indicated a chair. 'Let me make sure Mrs Simpson is safely on her way, then we'll have a word.'

Dean didn't move. Swiping a hand agitatedly over the back of his neck, he glared hard at Jake. 'You need to tell me,' he demanded. 'Was it a miscarriage?'

'Dean, wait.' Jake's heart dropped. 'This isn't a conversation you want to have here. Just give me a minute and—'

'It's a simple enough question, *Doctor* Merriden.' Dean's voice was full of contempt. 'Was it a fucking miscarriage or did she have an abortion?'

Christ. Concerned for Joyce's safety, Jake was relieved to see Emily skidding through from reception. 'Sorry,' she said, her cheeks flushed with a combination of frustration and embarrassment. 'He insisted on seeing you. I told him you were back-to-back with appointments, but …'

Jake nodded, understanding. Seeing the mood Dean was in, he guessed she couldn't have stopped him. He supposed the whole surgery had overheard what was going on, but that wasn't his major concern right now. What was worrying him was that if Zoe hadn't been honest with Dean – and judging by the state he was in, she hadn't been – then how did he know? 'I'll come out to reception shortly,' he said, scanning Emily's eyes warily. The information had come from here, as had the information in the letter sent to Michael. It had to have done. The question was, who would leak it, and in God's name, why? Lives were being destroyed here. He couldn't believe that anyone would do that.

Making sure Joyce was well out of the fray, heading back to reception with Emily, he closed the door and turned to face Dean. The man's eyes were shot through with a mixture of bewilderment and anger. He wasn't going to leave until he had answers. And Jake simply couldn't give him any.

'Well?' he demanded.

'Sit down, Dean, please.' Jake nodded again towards the chair.

Folding his arms across his chest, Dean didn't budge.

Jake wondered where the hell to start. 'I understand your frustration, Dean. I—'

'Right,' Dean sneered. 'I doubt that, Jake. I doubt that very much. Are you going to tell me what I need to know, or not?'

Jake sighed inwardly. 'I can't, Dean,' he said apologetically. 'I can see you're upset, and I sympathise, but I can't disclose private patient information.'

'Well someone can, obviously,' Dean retaliated, his look now bordering on murderous. 'Do you realise some bastard sent a bereavement card?'

Jake furrowed his brow in confusion. Had Zoe confided in a friend or her family? he wondered. If so, how had Dean learned what he obviously had, unless they'd mentioned—

'"So sorry you had to have an abortion", it said.' Dean cut his thoughts short. 'So are you going to stand there and tell me she didn't?'

Jesus. Jake drew in a tight breath. 'I'm not telling you anything, Dean. I can't. It's just not within my power to—'

'I don't give a flying fuck about your bureaucratic claptrap,' Dean spat. 'I have a right to know. We're talking about my *child*. You can't keep the information from me.'

'I have no choice but to, Dean. You need to speak to Zoe. I'm sorry, I can't tell you what you want to know.'

Tipping his head to one side, Dean eyed him narrowly. 'You just did, though, didn't you?'

Jake held his gaze for a second, and then looked away.

'So was it on medical grounds?' Dean pressed him.

Jake sighed heavily. 'Dean, I can't help you. You need to speak to Zoe.'

Dean spun around. 'I intend to. And she'd better damn well have answers.'

Christ, what was he going to do? 'Dean, *wait.*' He followed the man as he charged out of the office, but Dean wasn't about to stop. 'Dean! You need to calm down,' Jake yelled after him.

Dean kept going, striding through reception and straight out of the main door.

'*Shit!*' Jake cursed, causing patients' gazes to swivel in his direction.

He needed to call Zoe. He shouldn't, but he couldn't just leave it. The man was consumed with rage. Ignoring the heated hushed whispers around him, he turned back to his office and straight into Tom, who presumably had been tied up with a patient while all this was going on.

'I gather there's a problem?' Tom asked, his brow knitted curiously.

'You might say that, yes,' Jake answered curtly, making to move past him, desperate to alert Zoe. He also wanted to try to establish whether she'd confided in anyone. Because if she hadn't, then his fears about the information coming from the practice would be proved right, and that could have dire consequences.

'Not quite appropriate behaviour, though, is it?' Tom commented, stopping him.

'What?' Jake wondered if he was hearing him right.

His father swept a disapproving gaze over him. 'Yelling across reception. Not very seemly, might I suggest?'

Jake looked him over in disdainful disbelief. *No you may bloody not.* Anger rising inside him, he counselled himself to stay calm. 'I have a call to make,' he said.

CHAPTER FOURTEEN

Emily

Seeing Tom knock perfunctorily on Jake's door a minute later and then walk straight in, Emily couldn't help thinking he might be treading on dangerous ground. Jake had been upset when he'd come after Dean into reception, for his patient rather than himself. Judging by the tight set of his jaw, he'd been quietly fuming when his father had pulled him up in front of the medical team, including Sally, who'd stepped out of the treatment room wondering what all the noise was about. To say little of the waiting patients, who'd witnessed it all.

Passing behind two women as she came back across reception from the loo, Emily's step faltered. 'They say he's been having an affair,' said Barbara, who ran the village store, leaning conspiratorially towards the woman sitting next to her.

'Who? Dean?' The other woman looked at her wide-eyed, her expression a mixture of shock and anticipation.

'No. Lord, keep up, Wendy. Dr Merriden,' Barbara said impatiently. 'There's talk of letters being sent. All sorts of personal information being leaked. That Natasha Jameson's husband had one apparently, telling him *she* was having an affair.'

'What, with …?' Wendy's eyes flicked towards Jake's office.

'Well, this is all second-hand, of course, but …' Barbara broke off, leaving Wendy to draw her own conclusions. 'One thing's for sure, though. With all these personal details coming out, it makes you wonder who might be next, doesn't it? I hope you haven't been keeping secrets from your hubs, Wend, or you might be next.'

'Ahem.' Emily coughed loudly, drawing attention to the fact that she was there. Barbara looked abashed, she noticed. Wendy, however, had paled to the point of grey.

'I've just remembered I promised to pick my Sam up from sixth-form college,' the woman said, grabbing her bag and practically running for the door.

Clearly she *was* keeping secrets. Emily's stomach roiled with a mixture of seething anger and sick trepidation. Was there a list? Someone systematically targeting people, as Sally had said, out of some sense of spite?

'It was definitely out of order.' She realised Nicky was talking to her as she approached the desk.

'Sorry?' Thinking she was talking about one of the toilets, Emily glanced distractedly over as Nicky sat back at her PC – the screen of which she hadn't blanked when she'd left her desk, she noted with despair.

'What Tom said,' Nicky clarified, emitting a huff on Jake's behalf. 'Given the mood Dean Miller was in, I thought Jake handled things pretty well. There was no need for Tom to show him up like that. I don't know what he was thinking. He's normally so charming as well.'

Emily glanced at her askance, a prickle of agitation running through her as she noted Nicky's pensive expression and realised that Tom had clearly won the girl over. Obviously he was still a silver fox. Emily had no doubt he would have charmed the birds from the trees in his heyday. She'd accused Jake of being just like him. She hadn't thought he was, up until now. Her heart sank icily in her chest as she recalled the argument they'd had, the anger in his voice. *Was* there a side to him she didn't know? Was it possible he was the sort of man who would be cruel enough to try to convince his wife she was going out of her mind rather than confess to an extramarital relationship? It was incomprehensible. Yes, he had seen another woman, and might even have been more involved with that woman than he'd admitted, but that was years ago. He and Emily only been together a matter of months, and at the time she *had* been distancing herself from him, trying to recover psychologically and physically from the damage inflicted on her by another man. If she examined her conscience, wasn't that the reason she was so determined to doubt him? Because in her heart she couldn't trust any man?

She needed to talk to him. Calmly. For the sake of Ben and Millie, who'd both reluctantly agreed to go out for a meal this evening, she had to establish whether they still had a future together. She wasn't looking forward to the meal, nervous about what to say to the children. She was particularly worried about Ben, who was becoming moodier and more withdrawn, leaving her to imagine what might be going on in his mind. What would she say if they asked outright if she and Jake were splitting up? Cold foreboding clenched her tummy. Perhaps ignorance was bliss after all. If she'd never said anything to Jake, waited it out instead, it might just have gone away.

Suddenly perilously close to tears, she swallowed hard, arranged her face into a smile and turned to Nicky. 'Why don't you go off for lunch?' she suggested, needing some time to herself. 'I can handle everything here now things have quietened down.'

Nicky looked at her in surprise and then checked the clock. 'But it's only quarter to.'

'It's been a full-on morning, though. You might as well grab a few extra minutes. You could get some cakes from the village shop on the way back,' Emily suggested. 'My treat. We could all do with a bit of cheering up.'

'That sounds like an excellent plan.' Nicky was out of her seat and grabbing her bag and jacket in seconds flat.

'Thanks, Nicky.' Reaching for her purse, Emily handed her the money, and then, realising there was something Nicky had obviously forgotten, stopped her short of the door. 'Oh, Nicky …?'

'Hell.' The girl twirled around. 'Sorry,' she said, coming back to close her computer down. 'It went clear out of my head with all the excitement.'

Emily gave her a despairing look. She was going to have to have a firm word with her, particularly under the current circumstances.

Waiting until Nicky had gone, she blanked her own screen, picked up a file and went quietly across to Jake's office. She hated that she seemed to have turned into someone who could give Fran a run for her money, listening at doors, spying on people, but after Tom belittling him like that, she was concerned about how Jake would react. He was stressed enough without having to deal with his father winding him up. She wondered why she was worrying about him under the circumstances, but she couldn't just stop any more than she could stop loving him. And she did love him, still. So much it hurt.

Pausing guiltily outside his door, she flicked through the file she'd picked up for the benefit of anyone who might be looking in her direction as she listened. Hearing Tom from inside, she was immediately agitated.

'It was unprofessional in front of the patients, Jake,' he was saying, with a heavy sigh. 'I gather the man was being aggressive and that you were upset, understandably, but—'

'You have to be kidding.' Jake laughed scornfully. 'After the way *you* behave, you have the gall to preach to me about inappropriate behaviour. I've never heard such hypocritical bollocks in all my life.'

Tom didn't answer straight away. Emily could almost feel the tension crackling between them. 'I'm only concerned for you, Jake,' he said eventually. 'Not just from a professional point of view, but—'

'I think it might be a good idea for you to leave,' Jake cut across him angrily.

Hearing movement inside – Jake scraping his chair back to show Tom the door, she supposed – Emily stepped back.

'Look, Jake …' Tom hesitated just the other side of it. 'I know we're not as close as we should be, but I'm sensing you and Emily seem to be having a few problems. If you ever need someone to talk to …'

'Now you *really* have to be joking.' Jake's tone was one of incredulity. 'I wouldn't confide in you if you were the last man on earth.'

'I was just offering.' Tom sounded wounded. 'Sometimes it helps to talk. A problem shared and all that.'

'Right,' Jake replied flatly. 'And you would be qualified to offer relationship advice, would you?'

'Don't, Jake,' Tom said awkwardly. 'There's no need to bring all that up. It's ancient history.'

Jake was quiet for a moment, and Emily imagined him looking his father over with that mixture of bemusement and contempt she'd often seen. Then, 'Really?' he said. 'So how's the new relationship going? She's a bit young for you, I would have thought, but—'

'Okay, look, forget I said anything,' Tom interrupted irritably. 'I have work to do. I'm sure you do too.'

'Did the meeting in Pembridge not go too well then?' Jake enquired, with pointed innuendo. 'You two seemed to be getting along extremely well from where I was standing,'

Pembridge? Emily tried to think back through the constant muddle in her head. Tom had had a meeting with some people from the medical committee there, she recalled. Wasn't that the same night that Nicky had been meeting friends in Pembridge? No, surely not. She pondered Jake's implication in disbelief. Tom and Nicky? That was utterly preposterous.

'You were spying on me?' Tom's tone was now one of shock.

'No, Tom,' Jake assured him. 'Just satisfying my curiosity.'

Her mind racing, Emily headed quickly back to reception as the door opened. Jake *had* been spying on him. He must have been. Why else would he have followed him? Unless it was out of jealousy. Might she have got this all wrong? Could it be Nicky that Jake was involved with?

No. She laughed at her own absurdity. He wouldn't, not right under her nose. Her suspicion was running riot, imagining that every attractive female in the vicinity was behind that email. Nicky would never do that to her. She was woolly-headed sometimes, and Emily despaired of her continually flouting data protection rules, but she was hard-working and conscientious otherwise. A nice, genuine sort of—

As her eye snagged on the 'Meet Our Staff' board behind the reception desk, her step faltered. Oh dear God. Reading her full name, Nicky Jade Horton, Emily realised that Nicky could easily be the owner of the email address beginning 'nja', and her heart almost stopped beating.

CHAPTER FIFTEEN

Dean

Letting himself back into the flat, Dean counselled himself to keep calm. There would be an explanation. There had to be, he tried to reassure himself. No, there wouldn't. He'd been through every possible justification she could have for telling him cruel, bare-faced lies. She'd let him think it was a miscarriage, left him feeling so bloody guilty for not being here for her. Why had she done it? Why did she want to hurt him so badly? He needed to know what he'd done to deserve it, though he didn't want to actually hear it: that he was such a useless prick she'd decided she didn't want to be saddled with his kid, meaning she would be stuck with him too.

Going quietly into the bedroom, his gaze was drawn immediately to the holdall on the bed. Zoe was hurriedly stuffing clothes into it. Sensing him standing there too stupefied to speak, she paused, her gaze shooting to his. Her eyes were wide, filled with fearful apprehension. She knew, then, that he knew. Jake Merriden had obviously felt obliged to alert her to the fact that he'd been close to losing it at the surgery, and why. Pity he hadn't felt a similar obligation to keep him, the child's father, in the fucking loop.

Attempting to keep a lid on his emotions, he took a deep breath, pulled the folded card from his jacket pocket and tossed it on the bed. The cracked heart on the front of it would make the point succinctly, he thought: that she was breaking his heart into a million pieces, each piece piercing his chest like a knife.

Emitting a small gasp, Zoe glanced down at the card. She didn't look back at him.

'You need to explain,' he said over the loaded silence between them.

She didn't say anything for a second, and then, slowly, she brought her gaze back to his. 'Dean, I …' She faltered, wrapping her arms around herself. She was shaking. Was she cold? It was always cold in here. Was that why she'd done it, aborted their baby … without even *telling* him? Because she didn't want to bring a child up in a poxy two-bedroom flat with under-floor heating that was too expensive to run and black mould decorating the walls?

'I meant to tell you. I wanted to. I …' she stammered, as if reading his mind. She'd always had an uncanny knack of doing that. She'd always guessed when he was feeling down – about his job mostly, the fact that he couldn't provide for her as well as he wanted to. She'd told him not to worry, that things would get better in time. Yeah, right. He should have tried pissing off down the pub every night, spending what little money they had getting off his face with his mates, instead of putting away whatever he could for the baby. He would be a far happier bloke than he was now. Had she wanted to go back to work? it occurred to him to wonder. Was that why she'd done it? A part of him hoped it was, that in some misguided, back-to-front way, she'd been thinking of them, their future. Even then, though, to have done what she'd done … He wasn't sure he could ever forgive her.

'I should have spoken to you, I know I should have,' Zoe stumbled on, 'but—'

'*Why?*' Dean yelled over her, causing her to flinch. Anger and confusion twisting his gut, he took a step towards her.

She stepped back, her face paling, her huge blue eyes darting past him to the door. She looked like a tiny porcelain doll, so fragile. He'd always thought of her that way, as someone who needed to be looked after. She wasn't, though, was she? Appearances deceived. She was clearly as hard as nails under the surface. Emotionless. Must be.

Desperate for her to offer him something, anything that might sound remotely like a valid reason for crucifying him, Dean took another step into the room.

Zoe backed away from him, into the wall. There was nowhere to go. The room was barely big enough to accommodate the bed. She couldn't get past him. He wasn't about to let her, not until she'd offered him some kind of explanation.

'Why?' he repeated, his voice choked, his gaze fixed hard on hers.

'I *had* to,' she cried, her eyes filling up. 'The baby … It wasn't right. I didn't want to tell you because of your job. I knew you'd want to take time off and I … I should have said something, but I didn't know how to. I was—'

'Bullshit!' he grated. Jake would have told him if there was something wrong with the baby. He *would* have. That wouldn't have broken with whatever protocol crap he'd been spouting. He would have *told* him. 'Do *not* lie to me, Zoe, or I swear—'

'I'm not!' she said frantically. 'I promise you I'm not. He wasn't growing properly. He—'

'He? You knew it was a boy? You knew we were having a son and you didn't even tell me that much?' Eyeballing her with a combination of heartbreak and insurmountable fury, Dean moved towards her again.

'Dean, stop this,' Zoe pleaded shakily. 'Please. I need to get past. I want to go to my mum's. Just for a few days,' she added quickly. 'I need some time. We both do. Please let me—'

'Your mother's?' He laughed incredulously at that. 'You do nothing but argue with your bloody mother. You said you'd never go there again after she had a go at you for getting bladdered in the pub with your girlfriends last …' He trailed off, his world careering completely off-kilter as the penny began to drop. She'd stayed with one of her friends that night. On another long-distance trip, he'd been worried sick when he couldn't get her on the phone. She'd been too drunk to trust herself getting back, she'd told him. She'd stayed with that same friend a couple of times since. She'd said she'd been lonely.

His gut clenching, Dean narrowed his eyes, searching hers quizzically. Was that why she'd done it? Had she worked out her dates and realised they didn't add up? 'Where are you really going?' he asked her.

'My mum's,' Zoe mumbled. 'I said. Just for a few days. I need to get away, Dean. I …'

Lies. Dean noted the averted eye contact. 'It wasn't mine, was it? The baby …' His voice cracked. 'It wasn't mine.'

Zoe's eyes came back to his, and what Dean saw there ripped his heart from inside him. Guilt. She'd been cheating on him. While he'd been working away from home, sleeping in his cab, worrying about her being on her own, feeling guilty – always feeling so *fucking* guilty – she'd been shagging someone else behind his back. Seeing her writhing and groaning with some other *bastard* in his bed, blind fury rose white-hot inside him.

His knuckles hitting the wall a millimetre from her face jarred him from the murderous thoughts in his head. It was as if time stood still for a second. Frozen with shock, her terrified eyes were locked uncomprehendingly on his. And then, as he realised the enormity of what he'd done, she moved. Pressing both hands against his chest, she shoved him back hard, a muted cry escaping her as she ducked past him to scramble for the door.

Jesus Christ. 'Zoe!' Spinning around, he raced after her, catching up with her in the hall. 'Zoe, don't,' he begged, the flat of his hand against the front door as, tears streaming down her face, she wrestled to open it. 'Please don't go, Zoe. I'm sorry. I—'

'Get out of my *way*.' Struggling with the door, Zoe sobbed harder.

'Zoe, *please* …' Dean caught hold of her arm. 'Don't do this. Please stay. We can—'

'Let me *go*.' She wriggled away from him. 'Leave me alone!' she screamed, fleeing to the living room.

'Zoe, come back. You can go. I'm sorry. I didn't mean …' Desperation climbing inside him, Dean followed. Fear gripped his stomach like a vice as he realised she was heading out onto the balcony.

'Zoe, don't go out there.' He moved towards her.

'Leave me alone, Dean,' she warned him, stumbling over the washing rack in her haste to get away from him. 'Don't you come anywhere *near* me.'

CHAPTER SIXTEEN

Emily

Emily tried to act normally, to ignore the wild palpitations in her chest, the churning in her stomach. Attempting to calm herself, to think rationally, her eyes slid towards Nicky, who was back from lunch and talking on the phone to the medical suppliers.

Catching her looking, Nicky gave her a smile. 'They've admitted they made a mistake,' she said, placing her hand over the receiver. 'The new blood pressure monitor should be with us tomorrow.'

'Excellent.' Expelling a breath she hadn't realised she'd been holding, Emily forced a smile in return. She was wrong. She had to be. Please God she was. Nicky was acting naturally, making full eye contact with her. If she was gazing distractedly after anyone, it was Tom. But that was an even more ludicrous idea than her and Jake ... Yet Jake had *seen* her with Tom. He'd followed Tom. Why? Unless ... Had Nicky been involved with Jake and then become involved with Tom? That might explain why Jake would follow him.

Emily's heart plummeted, her stomach clenching at the thought of what might have been going on. Had Jake been meeting her here? It was perfect, after all, wasn't it? Nicky had a set of keys. No one would think anything of her coming and going. Dear God, had he ...? In his office? Absurd though they were, the thoughts came rapid-fire in her head. She simply couldn't stop them. She had to *know*.

Ask her, a little voice urged her. *She won't admit it, but you'll know if she's lying.* An averted gaze, angry denials – those would be the signs that would confirm her guilt. But on the other hand, wouldn't Emily be affronted if someone levelled that kind of accusation at *her*?

She needed to talk to someone before she did go out of her mind. The alternative would be to storm into Jake's office, which she was dangerously close to doing, and then her marriage would undoubtedly be over. Jake's reputation would suffer. Tom would imagine his own deplorable behaviour had been vindicated in some way. The children would be utterly humiliated.

She was about to ring through to Sally and ask her if she had time for a quick chat when her mobile rang. *Hell*, she thought, checking the number and realising it was Peter, the landlord at the Plough and Dog pub. He would want to know her drinks order for Edward's party. She'd been so preoccupied; she had no idea how many people might be going yet, and she was clueless about beers and ales. She'd meant to talk to Jake about it, but now it seemed they were incapable of talking without arguing. She needed to get on with organising the arrangements. She'd promised herself she would do this. She couldn't let Edward down and end up leaving Joyce in the lurch. She had to focus – not that she seemed capable of focusing on anything lately.

Was she overreacting? Might everything she thought Jake was doing be in her feverish imagination? The truth was, she *did* feel paranoid. Her emotions were out of control, her sleep patterns all over the place, which made concentrating on anything almost impossible. It was as if her body were waging a war against her. She *had* to get some perspective. Sally wasn't exactly the soul of discretion, prone to gossip with the best of them, but she was a good friend, someone who'd known Jake before he'd left the village to get away from the pain of his childhood. If anyone could help her see the wood for the trees, Sally could.

Blanking her screen, she was rising from her desk when Sally emerged from the treatment room, heading towards the kitchen. 'Won't be a tick,' Emily mouthed to Nicky, who was still on the phone, and followed her.

She was passing Jake's office when she heard voices from inside and realised that Sally had stopped short of the kitchen and gone in there. Realising she would have to catch her later, she turned to go back to reception, but stopped when she heard Jake say, 'I'm fine, Sally, honestly. I'm sure things will sort themselves out once Emily and I have a chance to sit down and talk.'

Deciding that her eavesdropping this time was justifiable, since she appeared to be the topic of the conversation, Emily frowned and stepped closer.

'Well, if you ever need a shoulder ...' was Sally's reply, leaving Emily confused. Wasn't *she* the one Sally was supposed to be offering a shoulder to?

'Thanks, but I don't,' Jake answered brusquely, which went some way to appeasing her.

'Right, well, I just thought I would offer,' Sally said, sounding hurt.

Jake blew out a discernible sigh. 'Sorry, Sally. That sounded ungrateful. It's just ... I really don't think it would be a good idea for us to ... you know, behind Emily's back.'

Behind her back? Emily's antennae stood on red alert.

'It's fine,' Sally assured him. 'I get why you would be a bit edgy. I'm not completely insensitive, Jake.'

'I know. Ignore me,' he said apologetically. 'I'm not in the best of moods lately.'

'I gathered,' Sally replied understandingly. 'You do realise that's exactly what you said all those years ago?'

'Sorry?' He sounded mystified.

'Before we went our separate ways,' Sally went on, causing the hairs to rise over Emily's skin. 'I knew you were struggling then too, but you just shrugged and said to ignore you and that you weren't in the best of moods. I got that. I mean who would be after all you'd been through, but I never did understand why you closed up on me the way you did.'

Jake hesitated before answering. 'I didn't find what happened easy to talk about,' he said awkwardly, after a second. 'It was too painful back then, I guess. Still is.'

'I know it was. What happened with your mum was unimaginably terrible.' Sally oozed sympathy. 'But … it hurt, you know, that you turned away from me. I thought we had something, and the next thing I knew you'd left the village without saying a word. I still don't know what I did wrong.'

'Nothing,' Jake said quickly. 'It wasn't you, Sally. It was me. I cared for you, a lot, but …'

Emily felt the blood freeze in her veins. They'd had a relationship? A serious relationship? *When?* Why hadn't he told her? Why hadn't Sally? Why wouldn't they have?

'You didn't love me?' Sally finished sadly.

'I was young, confused. My emotions were all over the place. I honestly wasn't sure what I felt.' Jake paused. 'I didn't mean to hurt you. I just …'

'Needed some space to sort yourself out, I know. Don't worry, I forgive you, but only because I know how badly you were affected. I'm glad you found someone you could eventually share your problems with.'

'Yeah.' He laughed ironically. 'Not any more.'

'That bad, hey?'

'That bad,' he confirmed, causing Emily's heart to fracture. 'It's the kids I'm really worried about. Millie's at that age, you know, where she's pushing boundaries. Ben's … I don't know. I'd hoped we might have a better relationship than Tom and I had, but the older he gets, the less it seems we have in common.'

'He's probably just a bit shy,' Sally suggested. 'Like his dad.'

'Probably,' Jake reflected thoughtfully.

'Not so shy lately, though,' she added, a playful edge to her voice. 'I'm liking the authoritative doctor-in-charge thing you have going on. Very hot.'

He sighed ruefully. 'Yeah, I'm not sure my wife's that impressed.'

'She'll come around. You're a catch, Dr Merriden. I doubt she'll want to throw you back.'

'I wouldn't be too sure about that.'

'I would. She won't let you go easily, Jake, trust me.' Sally paused. 'I'd better get on. I have someone due in shortly. Talk later.'

'Will do. Oh, and Sally …' Jake stopped her. 'You haven't mentioned anything to Emily, have you? About us?'

'No. Don't worry, your secret's safe,' she assured him. 'It's not the sort of thing that's easy to drop casually into conversation.'

Moving swiftly away from his office as she heard Sally nearing the door, Emily felt a surge of pure rage. *Shy?* He'd sounded anything but from where she was standing, pouring his heart out to a woman he'd had a relationship with – and hadn't *told* her about. Someone he'd 'cared for'. Now that her eyes had been opened, it was obvious, blindingly obvious to Emily, that Sally cared for him too, which explained her draping herself over him at every opportunity. Her dressing to impress him. Her anger quadrupled as she recalled the tight jeans, leather boots and abundant make-up Sally had been wearing in order to come to her house for nothing more than a girls' chat. She had thought the woman was simply flirty by nature. She'd even joked about it to Jake, to her utter humiliation. She couldn't believe that he'd been sharing details about *their* relationship with her. That he'd just told her that Emily wasn't there for him any more.

He was twisting everything, blaming her. And now she had absolutely no one to confide in. Not her best friend. Not her GP. Not her husband.

Safely ensconced in a cubicle in the toilets, Emily wondered if it was truly possible to die from a broken heart.

CHAPTER SEVENTEEN

Jake

Watching Sally leave, Jake had never felt so guilty. He'd meant to mention to Emily that he and Sally had once gone out together. It seemed like aeons ago now, but they had been fairly serious, until his mother died and his life had fallen apart. *He'd* fallen apart, wondered what the point was: of taking his exams, doing all the normal stuff that people did; having relationships. He'd begun to see people in a different light, speculating about what they were really like under the exterior they presented to the world, what secrets they kept. Or didn't. His father had certainly made no secret of his numerous affairs. Jake would never understand that, not until the day he died. It was some kind of ego trip, he supposed, a way of proving his masculinity.

Why *hadn't* he told her? He thought back to the first time he and Emily had run into Sally when they'd moved into the village. Edward and Joyce Simpson had organised a welcome-back party. Sally had been all over him. Drinking more than was healthy, she'd been openly flirting with him. Emily had been put out, understandably, and Jake had decided not to say anything then, rightly or wrongly. When Emily and Sally had struck up a friendship despite that shaky first meeting, he could see Sally working to gain Emily's trust after her 'deplorable behaviour', as she called it, and he'd again declined to say anything, so as not to destroy a potential friendship. He'd supposed Sally would mention it to Emily somewhere along the line. Apparently, she hadn't.

Given how their marriage was at the moment, he was bloody glad now that Emily didn't know. He was growing more worried about her state of mind. It hadn't helped when he'd practically accused her of sending the letter to Michael out of some sense of vengeance. Now he didn't know what to think. Who would have alerted Dean Miller to the fact that his wife had decided to terminate her pregnancy? Why would they? There was no blackmail involved, nothing to be gained as far as Jake could see, other than some twisted satisfaction from watching people's relationships fall apart. He needed to talk to the whole team, including his father, and make sure that everyone knew that patient confidentiality was crucial. He also wanted to see their reactions when he told them he suspected one of them was accessing private medical data and using it unethically – as well as illegally. If it was someone on the team, then perhaps they would betray themselves.

Deciding to ring through to reception and ask Nicky or Emily to organise a meeting before close of play, he reached for his phone and then grabbed it up when it rang.

'I have Dean Miller on the line,' Nicky said, sounding wary. 'He's insisting on speaking to you.'

Jake drew in a breath. He guessed this wasn't going to be an easy conversation. 'Thanks, Nicky. Could you put him through?

'Dean?' He braced himself as the call connected. 'What can I—'

'It's Zoe,' Dean cut in, his voice terrified. 'I didn't do it, Jake. You have to believe me.'

CHAPTER EIGHTEEN

Emily

Sitting in the waiting area along with the rest of the team, Emily glanced towards Jake as he emerged from his office. He'd asked her to let everyone know he needed to call an urgent meeting once all the patients had left. Emily hadn't been surprised he would want to talk to them all, after receiving the terrible news about Dean Miller and poor Zoe. Picturing her, a petite, pretty girl who'd looked pale and drawn the last time she'd been to the surgery to see Jake, Emily's heart broke for her. For her parents, too. What must they be going through, not knowing the extent of her injuries? If it were Millie … A cold shudder running through her, she tried to clamp her mind down on that thought, but couldn't. Where was Millie going when she disappeared in the evenings? Emily hadn't yet told her daughter that she'd rung Anna's mother; that she knew it wasn't Anna's house she was staying at. She'd hoped that Millie might confide in her, before she was forced to confront her. Why would she be so secretive unless she had something to hide? Emily could only think it was because she was afraid that she and Jake would disapprove of the person she was seeing.

Might he be controlling or aggressive in some way? Going through all the stomach-wrenching scenarios, her mind returned to Zoe. What had happened? Since he was being questioned by the police, gossip had it that Dean had been responsible for her fall from the balcony. Emily tried to imagine what could have possessed him to push her, or else terrified her so much she'd climbed up there and fallen. He'd been on the point of losing his temper at the practice today, but he was normally such a gentle, caring young man. Emily didn't consider herself the best judge of character at the moment, but she couldn't imagine him ever wanting to hurt Zoe. He'd obviously worshipped her. That much had been obvious from watching them together at their wedding. The expression on Dean's face when he'd turned to see Zoe walking down the aisle had almost reduced Emily to tears. He'd been bursting with pride, his love for his new bride shining bright in his eyes. Their first dance together had been magical. He hadn't been able to take his eyes off her as he'd led her around the dance floor to 'The Way You Look Tonight'. It truly had been the stuff of romance.

The trigger for Dean's violence had originated here. He'd become privy to information that had rocked his world to the very core, Emily had no doubt about that. She was scared. That email Jake had received had been the catalyst for all of this, and she'd said nothing about it at the time. She still hadn't told him what the email had implied. She should have. Jake was bound to think, as she now was, that they might have nipped all this in the bud. From the letters other people were receiving, it was becoming obvious that she and Jake were being targeted as part of a malicious plot of some sort. Didn't that suggest that she shouldn't be reading too much into the email? On the other hand, the information about Zoe's abortion was real. Natasha *was* on the pill, Microgynon 30, Emily had checked. Didn't that make the implication about Jake's infidelity true too? And what about the weird texts she herself had received? Might they in some way be connected?

'This all looks very official.' Tom, who'd initially been annoyed at being called away from one of his meetings, interrupted her thoughts. Looking wary, he nodded towards Jake, who looked across to them, hesitated, and then detoured towards the water cooler. He looked more in need of a strong brandy. His hands were shaking as he tipped the cup to his mouth, his complexion ashen. Emily felt a turmoil of conflicting emotion. She should hate him, yet still she loved him. Her heart felt as if it was tearing apart inside her at the thought of him cheating on her with Sally.

'Any idea what this is all about?' Sally asked. She was sitting opposite Emily, who had ignored her since hearing her intimate exchange with Jake in his office and busied herself trying desperately to catch up with the arrangements for Edward Simpson's party, firming up the booking of the village hall and returning the call regarding the bar.

'Zoe Miller.' Fran, who was standing, rather than sitting – probably so she could be first out of the door with the gossip – filled Sally in. 'Pushed over her balcony by her husband,' she said with a dramatic sigh.

'*Shit.*' Sally's shocked gaze twanged in Emily's direction. 'You're joking.'

'I wish I was.' Folding her arms, Fran shook her head dourly. 'He denies it, of course. Poor girl fell three flights, cracked her head open on the paving slabs below. Blood everywhere, awful sight it was. She looked like a little broken rag doll according to Mrs Wilkinson who works at the chemist. She was coming back from walking her dog. Said she'd never had such a shock in her life. Heard her landing, apparently. There was a dull thud and then—'

'Fran!' Noticing Nicky wiping quietly at the tears streaming down her cheeks, Emily pulled Fran up sharply. Could the woman not just exercise a little restraint, for goodness' sake?

'But couldn't she have just fallen?' Sally whispered.

'Not according to the neighbours,' Fran whispered back, her eyes flicking to Emily as she did. 'They had a violent argument, so I heard. He was in a terrible state when he was here, I gather. Bordering on violence, then, according to …'

God. Emily gritted her teeth as they whispered on. The village drums had obviously gone into overdrive. Refraining from saying anything further, for fear she might tell Fran exactly what she thought of her, and also possibly Sally, she smiled tentatively at Jake as he approached. 'Would you like a coffee or tea?' she asked him, having noticed that he'd swilled back two cups of water and had another in his hand.

'No.' Jake smiled shortly. 'Thanks.' Loosening his tie, he turned to address everyone gathered. The shadows under his eyes were darker, Emily noticed. He looked bone-weary with exhaustion.

'I gather you all know about Zoe Miller?' he asked, surveying them each individually.

'We do. Fran's furnished us with details, should any of us have been wondering,' Tom answered, a despairing edge to his voice. Fran glanced down, looking flustered and upset, which was surprising. Emily had always considered she must have a very thick skin, since she generally didn't appear to care what people thought of her gossip-mongering.

'You can hardly blame people for talking,' she muttered tetchily at length. 'Everyone's wondering what on earth's going on, where the information is coming from. Fern Jessop is worried to death about her old mum learning about her muscular sclerosis diagnosis. Says it will be enough to give her a heart attack.'

'People are cancelling appointments,' Nicky chipped in, her voice a frightened whisper as she glanced worriedly at Jake.

Jake tugged in a breath. 'Right.' He nodded tersely. 'In case any of you weren't aware, Dean Miller was here earlier. Distraught I think understates the mood he was in.'

'Fit to murder someone, he was,' Fran interjected, addressing no one in particular. 'From what I heard, his language was—'

'I'm not sure that's helpful, Fran.' Shooting her a warning glance this time, Tom cut her short. Emily noted Fran's cheeks flushing and the peeved look she gave him, at which Tom looked away uncomfortably.

'From his conversation with me,' Jake went on, clearly working to control his emotions, 'it was obvious that he'd learned certain upsetting information.'

Uneasy glances were exchanged as he paused again, allowing people to digest this.

'Personal medical information regarding his wife that was given to me in strictest confidence, as is all patient information,' he went on, with another agitated intake of breath. 'I spoke with Zoe Miller shortly before the tragedy and established that she hadn't divulged that information to anyone else. It seems clear, therefore, that it could only have come from here.' Stopping, he glanced again at everyone in turn, causing people to shift awkwardly.

'I won't say who it concerns, but it's also pretty damn clear that other patients' details have been accessed too.'

He was talking about Natasha. Emily felt her cheeks flush.

'Whether these details have been leaked inadvertently or deliberately, in what I can only assume is some kind of spiteful act of revenge, obviously has to be ascertained,' he continued. 'The police have informed me they will need to talk to me. I imagine they will want to talk to each of you individually too. It goes without saying that if anyone here is responsible for what is basically a flagrant disregard for data protection, for whatever reason, then it might be a good idea to come and see me … or Tom,' he added, almost as an afterthought, 'before that happens.'

Nicky gasped openly at that, her eyes pivoting towards Emily, her expression a combination of bewildered and horribly guilty.

'You're placing yourself above blame, then?' Fran asked in the ensuing silence. She was possibly the only person who would dare to challenge Jake on this, since she didn't have access to files or systems. Which didn't actually mean she hadn't had access to patient information. Emily had caught her peering at the computer screens on many an occasion as she fussed about, cleaning, which was one of the reasons she was so despairing of Nicky's lackadaisical attitude. God only knew what information Fran had become privy to, poking around in the various offices – especially Tom's, which she spent a disproportionate amount of time in.

'Fran …' Tom sighed, his tone now one of utter despair.

'I'm just saying,' Fran retorted. 'Just because you're both doctors doesn't mean you're beyond reproach, does it?'

Eyeing the ceiling, Tom sighed again and shook his head.

'No, Fran, it doesn't,' Jake answered for him. 'To be frank, though, as a doctors' surgery, where patient confidentiality should be our absolute priority, I think we all have a certain amount of responsibility to bear. Certainly in making sure this sort of thing *never* happens again.'

'I agree,' Sally piped up. 'It's absolutely dreadful. I can hardly believe it. And you actually spoke to her before … Poor you,' she said, locking tearful eyes on him. 'If you need me to do anything, Jake, you only need to ask, you know that.'

Like offer him a shoulder. Despite the awfulness of the situation, Emily couldn't help feeling immensely annoyed, particularly when Jake glanced awkwardly down and back. Of course, if she read anything into that, she *would* be being paranoid.

'Right, that's it for now,' he said. 'We'll clearly have to look at overhauling our systems and tightening protocol. Meanwhile, if anyone needs to speak to me, I'll be here for a few hours this evening.' He looked meaningfully at Emily. 'And I'll be in early tomorrow morning.'

'Can I have a quick word now, Jake?' Tom asked, as people made moves to leave.

'Can you give me a moment? I just need to have a quick word with Emily.' Massaging his forehead and now looking extremely stressed, Jake turned towards her.

'Right. Yes, of course.' Tom glanced warily between them.

Emily felt her heart drop. Was the breakdown of their relation-ship really that obvious? If so, it would certainly also be obvious to the woman who was intent on stealing her husband. Her eyes pivoted towards Sally.

'Do you have a minute?' Jake asked, as Tom headed off to his office, Fran heading purposefully after him. Emily tried to decipher the look in his eyes. He looked guarded, uncertain. Under the circumstances, he would be, but was his uncertainty about her?

'Yes. I just have to check on Nicky and make sure the desk is cleared and the PCs are closed down,' she said, wanting to remind him that that was what she did every single evening before she left.

Jake looked her over searchingly. 'I'll be in my office,' he said.

Nerves knotted Emily's insides as he turned away. Why was he being so formal? Of course he would be in his office. Where else would she find him?

In Sally's, said a nagging little voice in her head.

CHAPTER NINETEEN

Finding Nicky still upset, Emily sent her off home and did her usual checks. She was making Jake a coffee when Sally poked her head around the kitchen door behind her. 'I have to dash. Dave will be wondering where I am,' she said – something she said often. No doubt because Dave often had occasion to wonder where she was. 'I'll give you a ring later, hun.'

'Don't bother,' Emily replied, more shortly than she'd intended. Forcing a confrontation now after the terrible events of today would be beyond insensitive. She didn't want to do that. She was sorely tempted, though, to suggest to Dave that next time he was wondering where Sally was, he might find her tucked up with Jake, cosily reminiscing.

Stirring the coffee vigorously, and sloshing liquid over the sides of the mug in the process, she made a valiant attempt to be civil. 'I'm out with Millie and Ben tonight,' she said, and then cursed herself for announcing she was otherwise engaged, leaving the field clear for any extracurricular activities Sally might have in mind.

'Oh. Right.' Sally sounded taken aback. 'Well, I'll see you tomorrow, then.'

'First thing.' Turning around, Emily smiled brightly. 'We'll need to have a meeting before the surgery opens to discuss this vile correspondence someone has been sending.' She held Sally's gaze for a second, then headed towards the door.

Sally looked at her uneasily as she squeezed past. 'Yes, of course,' she said, her eyes skittering down and back. 'I'll make sure Dave drops me off early. It's dreadful, isn't it, what happened to poor Zoe?'

'Shocking,' Emily agreed, carrying on to Jake's office. 'Just goes to show, no matter how well you think you know someone, you never really know what they're capable of, do you?'

Glancing back as she tapped on Jake's door, she noted Sally's puzzled frown. She couldn't say what she would like to – that she was fully aware of what her *friend* was up to. She wouldn't, not with Jake and Tom – and worst of all Fran – in earshot, but at least she'd given the two-faced cow something to ponder. Hopefully Sally might glean that she should watch her back, since she seemed to have no qualms about digging the knife into other people's.

Pushing into Jake's office, she relaxed her face into a more genuine smile. 'I grabbed you a coffee,' she said. 'I thought you could use one after …' Seeing the steaming mug on his desk, she trailed off.

'Thanks,' Jake said, with a semblance of a smile in return. 'Sally's already brought me one.'

Emily drew in a breath. 'So I see. That was very thoughtful of her, wasn't it? I sometimes wonder what we'd do without Sally selflessly offering her shoulder whenever it's needed.'

Clearly picking up on her facetiousness, Jake eyed her quizzically, and then got to his feet, walking around her to close the door, while Emily parked the coffee she'd made next to Sally's.

'So,' he said, dragging a hand over his neck as he came back towards his desk, 'I think we need to talk.'

Emily looked him over carefully. Was he going to confide in her? Confess to what he'd been up to? Or was he going to maintain it was all in her mind, which, if he was cheating on her, was possibly the cruellest thing he could do, amounting to emotional abuse in her book? And she knew about abuse; she had survived physical and emotional abuse that he had no idea about. She would fight back harder this time.

'Would you like to sit?' he asked.

This made her feel as if she were in the headmaster's office, a place she'd often been as a teenager, pulled up for her waywardness, her inability to live up to being a replica of her perfect twin sister. She'd been frequently reprimanded for her failing grades and her inability to concentrate – which was due to the marijuana she'd smoked under the canal bridge with the man she'd thought she could be her true self with. Except she hadn't been. She'd been who he wanted her to be. She'd done the same thing with Jake, she realised now. She'd tried to be someone she thought he wanted her to be: supportive, the perfect mother, the perfect wife. Quite clearly she wasn't any of those things. She was imperfect.

'These letters,' Jake said, scrutinising her guardedly. 'The information they contained obviously came from here.'

'I know. I've no idea how or when anyone could have …' Emily looked away, cursing herself as tears pricked her eyes. The last thing she wanted to do was give in to her emotions and cry. She had to appear in control, competent. Show him that she was capable of doing her job.

'They've had devastating consequences,' Jake went on. 'The General Medical Council will need to be involved, obviously. I imagine the impact on the surgery will be pretty dire.'

Emily was well aware of that. Patient trust would be broken, which was all the more devastating since it was something Jake had worked hard to build up, especially after Tom's indiscretions, which Jake considered would have impacted on patient relationships. A GP should be someone the community could rely on, after all.

'I've told Nicky to make sure to be in early tomorrow. Sally, too,' she said, forcing herself to say the woman's name. 'I think we need to have a meeting and go through all the guidelines together before casting aspersions. Nicky's distraught. She—'

'Is it you, Emily?' Jake asked bluntly, stopping her mid flow.

She looked at him, astounded. 'What?'

'Is it you?' he repeated, his expression guarded. 'I have to ask. Are you doing this, leaking information, because of this ridiculous obsession you have that I'm cheating on you, which, quite frankly, utterly confounds me?'

Emily felt the blood drain from her body. 'Are you serious?' She could barely get the words out.

Jake said nothing. His blue eyes as dark as thunder, he simply stared at her.

'You are, aren't you?' Nausea rose hot in her throat. Was this what he thought of her? What he'd always thought? He hadn't suddenly imagined her a monster, had he? He'd obviously been harbouring bad thoughts about her for some time.

'Anyone could have sent them!' she yelled, biting her tears back. 'As for leaking information, do you honestly think I would do that? I'm constantly on at Nicky for flouting data protection. Do you realise how many times I've had to reprimand her for forgetting to blank her screen or shut her computer down? Not to mention the files she leaves on her desk. Tom too, come to that. It's certainly not me who's allowing all and sundry free access – delivery men, the postman, patients. Fran's always floating about the place, peering over people's shoulders. As far as gossip goes, I'm only surprised she hasn't got a loudhailer.'

Jake continued to study her. Still he didn't say anything, which spoke volumes.

He'd made up his mind. Did he really have such a low opinion of her? Or was this a way for him to justify his own despicable actions?

'Have you considered that it might be Nicky who's sending the letters?' Emily asked, careless of the tears now spilling down her cheeks. As was Jake, it seemed. He saw them, looked agonised for a second, but didn't move towards her.

Massaging his temples, he glanced down. 'That's not likely,' he said, looking confusedly back at her. 'She hasn't been here that long. Why would she do such a thing?'

'I don't know. But that's my point, we don't know *her*,' Emily said, determined now to fight her own corner since she seemed to have no one else in it. 'We don't know who she is. She could have any number of personal issues.'

Jake looked highly sceptical, which fired her temper further. He believed his wife – someone he'd lived with, someone he *loved*, or so he'd said – capable of doing something so deplorable, clearly, but not Nicky, a woman he'd known for five minutes.

'You do realise her initials are NJA, don't you?' Emily couldn't let him go on making – and possibly believing – these accusations against her. Whether he truly believed it was her, or whether he was using it as an excuse to get rid of her, she didn't know. She wouldn't creep off meekly, though, from her marriage or from her job. Being her husband's office manager hadn't been what she'd wanted to do with her life. She might not have been the clever one, as her parents had made patently obvious, but she'd had talent. Over the years she'd convinced herself that her ambitions of picking up her art training had been unrealistic, and had channelled her energies into this instead: into her marriage and her family. She'd given everything she had to give. She had loved Jake unconditionally, with her whole heart and soul. He might want to throw her love away, but she wouldn't just simply abandon the relationship. She *couldn't*.

Jake looked at her askance. 'And?'

'The emails I believed you were exchanging with Natasha.' Her heart pounding, Emily reminded him of what she'd asked him after the summer fair. 'I saw one sent to you from an address beginning "nja123". It wasn't quite as calculatedly nasty as the letters sent to Dean and Michael, but it was definitely of the same ilk, threatening to expose secrets.'

'Secrets?' Jake's expression was now a mixture of incredulity and wariness. 'What bloody secrets? You need to show me.'

'I deleted it.' Realising how implausible that sounded, Emily felt her cheeks flush. 'But I remember it, every single word,' she added quickly. '"Unless you want a certain person to find out about your extracurricular activities, meet me in the designated place, 3 p.m. tomorrow",' she recited.

Jake narrowed his eyes. 'And you're sure it was addressed to me?'

'It was addressed to you, yes.'

'And you deleted it?' He looked sceptical again.

'Because I panicked,' Emily tried to explain, though why it was her suddenly in the position of having to defend herself, she wasn't sure. 'I didn't want you to know that I'd seen it. I ... needed some time. To think.'

'I see.' Jake faltered for a second, glancing away and back. 'It was obviously some kind of prank or scam,' he said, raking his hand through his hair and dropping heavily into his chair.

'Like the letters?' Emily reminded him of those. 'Because of the address, I thought Natasha Jameson had sent it, as you no doubt gathered.'

'*Jesus.*' Shaking his head, Jake looked hard at her. 'And you really believed that I ... With Natasha?'

Emily searched his eyes, looking for the lies there. Jake seemed totally bewildered. But then it was all a bit bewildering, she supposed. 'I did, but then she was targeted herself, wasn't she? I'm thinking it must be someone closer. Sally, for instance, who is definitely close and who we do know. Intimately. Or at least *you* do.'

'Excuse me?' Jake squinted at her, disbelieving.

'Sally,' Emily repeated calmly, despite her manic heartbeat. 'She has access to files and computers, doesn't she? Information at her fingertips. It occurs to me that she might have wanted me to see that email. She also wouldn't have wanted Natasha to get her claws into you, would she?'

Paling visibly, Jake scanned her face. 'I have no idea what you're talking about, Emily,' he said shakily. 'You're really beginning to worry me.'

Emily scanned his face in turn. *Don't lie to me, Jake*, she willed him, fear piercing her heart like an icicle. *Please don't do this to me.*

'You're making no sense whatsoever,' he went on. 'First I'm supposed be involved with Natasha, and then … *what*? What are you saying? I can't keep up with you.'

She held her nerve. 'Sally's still in love with you,' she said quietly. 'Quite obviously.'

'*Christ.*' Running his hands over his face, he got to his feet and started around the desk towards her. 'You've got it wrong, Emily. She's—'

Emily stepped away from him. 'Have I, Jake?' she asked, her eyes fixed on his. 'Have I really?'

'Em, I …' He spoke her name with affection, but it was too late. Much too late. With as much dignity as she could muster, Emily tore her gaze away and headed for the door.

'Emily, wait, please. We need to talk. I need to … I—'

'*How*, Jake?' she asked, her hand poised on the door handle. 'The thing about lies is, you can't unsay them.'

'I haven't lied to you,' he insisted, so close to her she could feel his frustration. 'I—'

'Omitted to tell me the truth?' She pulled the door open. She couldn't listen to this any more. It was too painful. He must know that. The Jake she'd thought she knew would.

Grabbing her bag and coat, she was halfway out of the surgery when she heard Tom behind her. 'Everything all right, Jake? We couldn't help overhearing.'

We? Tom and Fran, Emily realised, her heart disappearing without trace.

CHAPTER TWENTY

Jennifer Wheeler

'What do you say?' Poppy Freeman's mother prompted her little girl as Jenny delivered her safely into the woman's care and handed over her Peter Rabbit school bag.

'Thank you, Mrs Wheeler,' Poppy said obediently, her eyes big and beguiling as she took hold of her mother's hand.

'My pleasure, Poppy.' Jenny smiled. 'Thank you for helping me tidy up the classroom. It will be all bright and clean for tomorrow now, won't it?'

'Uh huh.' Poppy nodded, a pleased smile lighting her face.

'Thanks for taking care of her,' her mother said, smiling gratefully. 'I hate being late for her. The thought of her standing on her own in the playground ...'

'No problem at all,' Jenny assured her, pressing a hand to her forearm. The woman was a care provider at the Haven hospice. Jenny could imagine the dilemma she'd had trying to decide whether to stay with a dying patient or leave her to pick up her little girl. She might not have children herself – something she and her husband had yearned for, tried endlessly for, eventually realising it wasn't meant to be after a third failed IVF treatment – but she loved every one of the children in her care as if they were her own.

'See you in the morning, Poppy. Don't forget your special found object,' she said. 'We're having a free imagination morning,' she explained to Mrs Freeman, who, judging by her puzzled expression, clearly hadn't seen the letter that had come home with her daughter yesterday. 'Poppy's going to choose a place and a setting and a special found object and then tell us a story, aren't you, Poppy?'

Poppy nodded keenly. 'I'm telling a story about a princess. She's beautiful and she's really strong,' she said with a determined little nod, 'but she can't swim and she's very sad because there's a tiny kitten stuck on the riverbank and she can't get to it.'

The two women swapped surprised glances. 'Looks like her imagination's already hard at it,' her mum said, impressed.

Jenny was too. 'And what's your special found object, Poppy?'

'Sticks,' Poppy said with another sage nod, 'and leaves from the princess's garden.'

'Ah.' Jenny got the gist. 'So our intrepid princess is building a life raft?'

'Yes.' Poppy looked delighted that she'd understood.

'I think we can work with that,' Mum said, clearly relieved at having the dilemma solved. 'Our garden has more sticks and leaves than it has flowers, doesn't it, Poppy?' Giving Jenny a conspiratorial roll of her eyes, she squeezed her daughter's hand and then, mouthing, 'Thanks,' turned to head for the gates.

Watching Poppy chatting to her mum as they went, Jenny felt a sense of pride. This was what had kept her going through her recent heartbreak; her interaction with the children. There was nothing more rewarding than seeing them blossom, knowing that she'd played a small part in shaping what would hopefully be a positive future. Contentment settling inside her, she went back to the school to collect her coat and bag.

Digging into the bag for her car keys, she found the envelope that had plopped through her letter box this morning. She'd stuffed it into her bag unopened, as she was running late. Climbing into her car, she dumped her bag on the passenger seat and pulled the envelope out, turning it over to look for clues as to who it was from. It was a plain white self-seal with a typed address. No stamp, she noted, and assumed it was from someone local. A parent of one of her pupils, possibly?

Thinking no more of it, she tore open the envelope, pulled out the page inside and unfolded it. As she read it, her stomach turned over. Panic constricting her chest, she took several slow breaths, then, with trembling fingers, pushed the note back into the envelope and placed it on the passenger seat. It looked so innocuous. Not the sort of correspondence that would shatter the recipient's world.

It was strange really. She'd known this day would come. She reached back into her bag, drawing out the tablets prescribed by Jake Merriden. Then, feeling calmer for knowing they were there, she pushed the key into the ignition of her little white Mini and listened fondly to its familiar cough. It was ancient. Still, she loved it. She'd been reluctant to part with it. She'd never aspired to fancy cars or foreign holidays. She preferred to holiday at home, loved the slow pace of life here in the village. The school was all she'd really needed. Seeing the smile in the eyes of a child was her reason to keep going.

Poppy's story about her strong princess making it to the river-bank on a raft made out of sticks and leaves would be beautiful. It broke Jenny's heart that she wouldn't be there to hear it.

CHAPTER TWENTY-ONE

Millie

Concerned about disturbing her boyfriend, who lay snoring quietly beside her, Millie lay still, watching the treetops sway in the soft breeze outside his second-floor flat. What was she doing here? she wondered, wiping away the slow tear that slid from the corner of her eye. She loved Louis, got that flip in her tummy whenever she thought about him, but this wasn't how it was supposed to be, she was sure. She'd imagined making love would be special. A sensual discovery of each other emotionally and physically that would bring them closer and bind them together forever.

This wasn't any of that. She'd bunked off biology, which she really couldn't afford to do – her mum would go spare if she knew – to come to his flat. This was the second time she'd been here, the third time they'd had sex, and still there'd been no mood-setting, no foreplay, no sweet endearments or whisperings of love, which she longed to hear.

Her first time hadn't been anything like she'd hoped it would be. Basic sex in the back of his car, it had been rushed and actually quite rough. Painful, too, though she hadn't told him that. *So what were you hoping for when you agreed to come, then? Rose petals scattered on the bed? Soft music and scented candles? Christ, grow up, Millie.* She was always going on at her mum not to treat her like a child, and here she was acting just like one because there hadn't been flowers and violins and exploding white lights. But wasn't that what she'd liked about Louis: the fact that he was the kind of man who knew what he wanted and went for it? He'd wanted her. He'd told her so. In fact it was the very first thing he'd said to her. Waiting for her outside the nightclub, he'd caught hold of her arm as she'd come out, leaned into her and whispered, 'You're the most beautiful thing I've ever seen. I want you.' She could hardly believe his arrogance, but she couldn't deny that the huskiness in his voice and the intense look in his eyes had sent a thrill of excitement through the entire length of her spine.

She'd noticed him watching her in the club, never taking his eyes off her as she'd danced with Anna. He was a bit old to be at Tramps, she thought at first, but he was bloody good-looking – had that dark, broody thing going on. Also, he was tall, tanned and muscular from working outdoors, definitely her type. She didn't mind that he was an odd-jobbing builder, grabbing work where he could. He'd had a tough childhood. The oldest of four children of a single mother, he'd had to leave school at sixteen with few qualifications and take whatever job he could to provide for them all, he'd told her. He'd had few opportunities in life, but he'd made the best of his situation. He still looked after his mother, who was sick, apparently, making sure she had everything she needed. That couldn't be easy for him with bills to pay on the house his ex-wife still lived in until it was sold, and debts to pay off, one of which was pressing. Millie respected him for caring enough to do that, loved him all the more because of it. She doubted her mum would approve of him, though, particularly given the age gap between them. Him being thirty was no big deal in Millie's mind. Most women went out with older men, didn't they? Sally's husband, Dave, was ten years older than her.

Her mum was bound to think it was a big deal, though. She banged on endlessly about Millie not being distracted or dictated to by anyone and doing something with her life. Wasn't *she* dictating, though, telling her she had to get her grades up, study hard, go to uni? Louis thought she was lucky having parents who were loaded and gave a stuff about her. Millie wasn't so sure sometimes. It was hard trying to live up to her mum's expectations.

Emily had warned her several times not to make the same mistakes she'd made. Millie despaired of that – her mum couldn't see that she was basically saying that she and Ben were her mistakes. That she thought being married to her dad was a mistake. Despite all that, Millie had always thought their marriage was strong, that they were okay together, but from the shit going down now, they clearly weren't. The smile seemed to have gone from her dad's eyes. He looked nothing but worried and miserable. As for her mum, she seemed to be off the bloody wall, ranting on at him constantly, which she'd never done before; accusing him of being unfaithful.

Her dad wasn't perfect, but Millie could never imagine him doing *that*. He had been working late a lot while taking over the practice, which she thought was understandable – he'd barely moved from his desk whenever she'd gone in with him on a Saturday – but he was always bringing her mum flowers, and she thought that was dead romantic. He listened to her – or he had before all this started – always looked at her with affection. He helped out around the house whenever he could. He even brought her tea in bed and massaged her shoulders when she felt tired, which seemed to be permanently recently. Was there a reason for that? Millie wondered, worrying quietly. But then she dismissed it. Her dad would know if there was. He wouldn't be looking at Mum now with nothing but bewilderment in his eyes.

Would they split up? She didn't want them to. She wasn't sure she could bear it at home if her dad wasn't around to lighten things. Goosebumps prickling her skin, she pulled up the sheet that was half covering her body and twisted her head to look at the man she'd given her virginity, her heart and her soul to. She was reassured when she felt that familiar little flip in her tummy. Things would get better, she was sure they would. She just had to be brave and explain to him what she wanted. She was a grown woman, after all. She could bring the scented candles and set the mood. It was way outdated to expect the man to do all the romancing.

He had extraordinary eyelashes, impossibly long; they almost brushed his high cheekbones as he slept. Studying him, she was tempted to reach out and touch them. A five o'clock shadow darkened his strong features, which only added to his rugged good looks. She hadn't minded that it had been scratchy while they'd made love. He'd been desperate, frustrated, counting the days since the last time, he'd said, deep longing in his cobalt eyes as he'd pulled her into his arms, which Millie supposed was quite romantic.

She hadn't been sure about going all the way with him at first. She'd wanted to take things more slowly, but she couldn't expect him to live like a monk. He was a man, not some inexperienced kid hoping to lose his virginity, like the boys she'd dated previously. *Her* man. She didn't know what the future held. She wanted to do her veterinary course. That had been her choice; her mum and dad weren't pressuring her to go in any particular direction, though there was no doubt her dad was pleased, probably more so because Ben showed no inclination towards the sciences. Her mum was more concerned about her seeing through whatever it was she chose to do.

Millie wasn't sure she wanted to study to be a veterinary nurse more than being with Louis, though. She loved him. Her hand strayed to his chest, her fingers tiptoeing downwards to trace the thin line of hair that disappeared below sheet level. She didn't care that her parents would probably go apoplectic about his age. She wanted to be with him. She could do both, couldn't she? Having a serious relationship didn't mean she couldn't apply herself to her studies. It would only make her more determined. She was doing all she could to help him pay off the man who was pressurising him for money; being dishonest, she reminded herself, a huge lump of guilt constricting her throat. Her parents would definitely freak out if they knew about that. Once she was earning money of her own, though, she could help out more, contribute to a place a bit more luxurious than the flat above the empty car workshop he was living in, which stank of oil. When the time was right, and when she'd plucked up the courage, she'd tell them that she intended to move in with him as soon as he asked her. She'd dropped subtle hints about it to him and was sure he would, now they were in a meaningful relationship.

'*Shit* …' She jumped as he moved suddenly to catch hold of her hand. 'You almost gave me a heart attack.'

His mouth curved into a slow, suggestive smile. 'That's nothing to what you're giving me, sweet cup.' Nodding down to his groin area, he looked back at her with that same deep desire he'd had in his eyes when she'd arrived. 'I want you,' he said, his voice low and husky.

Tugging the sheet aside, he leaned over her, straddling her before she could stop him.

'Not yet.' She smiled nervously and pressed her hands to his chest.

A flicker of impatience in his eyes, he scanned her face questioningly.

'I'm … a bit sore,' she said, hoping he would understand. He'd had other relationships. Many. Of course he had, at his age. With his looks, he could have his pick of any woman he fancied, which was why she was keen to move in with him where she could keep an eye on him. Meanwhile, though, she desperately didn't want to disappoint him.

'I'll be gentle,' he promised, his mouth hungrily seeking hers.

'I can't.' She used a little more force. 'I … Oh fuck!'

'What?' Louis said, taken aback as she slithered hastily from underneath him. 'You just woke me up. Why would you do that when I've been working since the crack of dawn unless you—'

'I'm late.' Millie flew around the room picking up her clothes and tugging them on. 'I'm supposed to be going out for a meal with my mum.'

'Yeah, right.' Louis reached agitatedly to grab his smokes from the bedside table. 'Give her my love.'

Millie frowned. 'What's that supposed to mean?' He was always saying things like that: 'Pass on my regards to her' or 'Give her my best', which she couldn't help thinking was sarcastic, as if he thought she was tied to her mum's apron strings or something.

'Nothing. I just have a lot on my mind, that's all.' Lighting up, he sighed and ran a hand through his tousled hair.

The pressing debt he had to pay, Millie guessed, to the man called Bear, who was as big as a bear and would rip his head off with his teeth if he didn't meet his payments regularly.

'Plus, I miss you when you're not here, don't I?' he said, lying back on the bed. 'Come over here and let me kiss those delicious lips of yours goodbye.'

Millie hesitated. She really did need to go.

'I'll sulk if you don't.' Giving her his best puppy-dog eyes, Louis stuck his bottom lip out. He looked like a petulant schoolboy. Millie laughed.

'That's better. You're beautiful when you laugh,' he said, his mouth curving into a languid smile as he patted the duvet next to him.

CHAPTER TWENTY-TWO

Emily

Having texted Millie and Ben to say she was running late, Emily attempted to compose herself as she drove home. She needed to mentally prepare herself for any questions they might have. Clearly they were both aware something was going on – Ben was shutting himself away in his room, as if he wasn't already introverted enough; Millie was storming out and staying out, which caused Emily's heart to twist with worry as she tried to imagine who she was with. She knew she had to be honest with them. To what degree, though? They'd heard her and Jake arguing. Should she say they were trying to work things out, which seemed unlikely after the heartbreaking argument they'd had? Prepare them for the possibility that their marriage might be irretrievably broken? She shouldn't be having this meeting without Jake, but she couldn't bring herself to include him when she believed he was lying to her. She couldn't just leave her children wondering either, not when it was obvious – to her, at least – that they were suffering.

She still couldn't believe that Jake seemed to think she was the one sending the letters, let alone that he had voiced his accusation – in earshot of Tom and Fran, of all people. Even Millie called the woman 'Megamouth'. It would be the topic of conversation in no time, everyone imagining that she was responsible for what had happened to poor Zoe. To Natasha.

Her own husband believed she was. Emily felt a cold hollowness inside her, as if he'd already left her. He'd decided she'd sent the notes before he knew the contents of the email. In telling him, she realised that she'd only given him more reason to think that she had. Did he imagine now that she'd deleted the email to cover her tracks, assuming he believed it ever existed? He probably thought she'd sent the letter to Dean to deflect suspicion from the fact that she'd sent the first one, to Michael.

Why was she bothering trying to fathom out what he thought? she wondered, dangerously close to tears all over again as she pulled onto the drive outside their beautiful house. The painful reality was, he did think it was her. His anger had been palpable, the accusation and disappointment in his eyes unbearable. It seemed to Emily that there was no coming back from this. He clearly considered her capable of such a horrendous thing, as other people had in the dark days after Kara's death. She'd wondered for a very long time herself whether she was. Whether that was why she'd blanked out the details of what had happened on the canal bank on that fateful day – because she didn't want to imagine herself capable of such horrific actions.

Her heart heavy, she let herself in through the front door. 'Just me,' she called. Getting no reply, she glanced into the kitchen and the lounge, and then, realising that Millie and Ben were upstairs, went up herself to freshen up.

Hearing Millie's voice coming from Ben's room, she paused on the landing, surprised. Then, wrestling with her conscience, she took a step closer. She couldn't quite believe she was now eavesdropping on her children as well as her husband, but if it meant she might find out more about how they were feeling, then she felt she had no choice.

They appeared to be having a conversation, rather than bickering, which was miraculous. 'Do you think Dad has had an affair?' she heard Millie say, causing her heart to expand excruciatingly in her chest.

'Strikes me it's one of the perks of the job,' Ben answered moodily. Emily supposed he was referring to Tom, whose reputation both the children were aware of. 'Makes you wonder why you'd bother having a meaningful relationship, doesn't it?'

'Like you wouldn't want a meaningful relationship with Nicky,' Millie teased.

Now Emily was definitely surprised. Ben had feelings for Nicky? Nicky at the surgery? She'd had no idea. He had been in a few times, but he'd barely uttered a word to her. He had looked at her, but now that Emily came to think of it, she did remember being slightly wary of the *way* he had looked at her. She supposed it was natural for a teenage boy to give a young woman an appraising look, but it had caused her a moment's consternation. She didn't know what was going on in her children's lives, she realised, the knot of guilt in her stomach twisting itself tighter. Ben wasn't one to share unless she prised it out of him, and Millie closed up like a book every time she tried to talk to her, especially about the subject of sexual relationships.

'You do know that Nicky's into older men?' Millie went on.

Emily held her breath, her mind immediately swinging to Jake.

'Sorry to shatter your illusions,' Millie sighed expansively, 'but she's lusting after the silver fox, according to Anna. I mean, I get the older man thing – they're so much more mature than younger men.'

'Shrewd conclusion, Einstein,' Ben mumbled facetiously.

'God knows what she sees in him, though. He's so ancient, he's practically decrepit. I'm surprised he can get it up. Viagra, I suppose.'

'Pack it in, Mils. That's gross,' he muttered.

'Poor Ben.' Taking no notice, Millie emitted another theatrical sigh. 'Spurned in love at the tender age of eighteen.'

'Fuck off,' Ben growled. 'I'm not in love with anyone. It sucks.'

'Right,' Millie replied amusedly. '"'Tis better to have loved and lost than never to have loved at all."' She quoted Tennyson tauntingly at him as she headed for the door.

Stepping away, Emily ducked quickly into her own room. Closing the door, she leaned against it, a whirlpool of emotion churning inside her. Was it her imagination, or had Ben's tone been bordering on aggressive? As for Millie's Viagra comment, Emily didn't know whether to be relieved or appalled. It couldn't be true, of course. However much of a womaniser he was, surely Tom would never allow himself to become involved with someone as young as Nicky. But hadn't Jake seen them together? More worryingly, on the subject of age and relationships, what was this 'I get the older man thing' Millie had come out with? Emily had guessed she was seeing someone. She was assuming now it was someone older. But how much older? She had to talk to her, and carefully. She needed to get her daughter on side, not alienate her. She needed to confide in her in the hope that Millie might feel safe to do the same. She had her whole future ahead of her. Emily didn't want her involved in a damaging relationship, which she knew all too well she easily could be.

'Mum?' Millie rapped on the door, causing her to start. 'Are we going soon? I'm starving.'

'Yes. Won't be long. I'm just touching up my make-up,' Emily called, and headed for the en suite to wipe the telltale smudges of mascara from under her eyes. Finding there wasn't a great deal else she could do to improve things, other than scrubbing her face and starting over, she went to the dressing table to reapply her lipstick. Surveying herself critically, she reached to untie her hair, which she'd worn up in the hope of looking less of a bedraggled mess. Fran had complimented her, saying she looked nice, but Emily doubted she did. Jake certainly hadn't noticed that she'd made an effort. She felt like a fool for trying. Sighing, she raked her fingers through it, heaved out another despairing sigh, and then tied it haphazardly up again. Millie's hair was just like hers, but she always managed to arrange it artistically. She'd ask her for some tips, Emily decided. They had been close once, sharing girly things. They'd lost their way somewhere along the line. Was that her fault too? In pushing Millie to be all that she could be, had she driven her away?

Emerging from her room and gathering from the sound of the TV downstairs that Millie was in the lounge, she headed for Ben's room to hurry him up. Realising he was on the phone, she hesitated short of the door. 'We'll be downstairs when you're ready, Ben,' she called.

'Right. One sec,' he answered.

Emily sighed as she reached the hall only to realise she'd left her handbag upstairs. Turning around, she went back up again, and stopped dead on the landing.

'Yeah, right, she's gone back to her husband, hasn't she, despite the fact that he's an aggressive git?' she heard Ben say. 'Probably because he's loaded. She's not likely to look at me, is she?'

Natasha? It had to be. Rumour had it that Natasha had married Michael for his money. She'd gone back to him despite what had happened between them. Emily had wondered why. But then, though Michael might have to work for every penny he had, his assets in terms of the land and the farmhouse weren't to be sneered at, were they? She'd imagined her husband would be attracted to Natasha – other men in the village certainly were – but her eighteen-year-old son? She felt the floor shift beneath her.

CHAPTER TWENTY-THREE

'So, what's the occasion?' Millie asked, once they'd ordered.

'No occasion,' Emily answered, smiling her thanks to the waitress had who delivered their drinks. 'There doesn't have to be a reason for us all to have a nice meal out together, does there?'

'Right.' Millie pulled her Coke towards her, a pensive frown on her face as she twirled the glass around. 'So we're having this nice meal together, without Dad, because …?'

Emily felt the heat rush to her cheeks. She felt wrong-footed, defensive already. She was sure that if her marriage really was irreparable, Millie and Ben would blame her. She would rather that, though, than for their relationship with their father to be irretrievably damaged. Whatever he'd done, was doing, or might not even be doing – she didn't know any more – she wouldn't run him down in their eyes. She couldn't. He'd been the best father a man could be to both of them.

'We know that you and Dad have been having problems,' Millie went on, looking guardedly at her. 'We're not stupid.'

'Or deaf,' Ben muttered pointedly.

'You might as well level with us, Mum,' Millie said. 'Just …' she faltered, her eyes flicking down and back, 'spare us the *we love you, but* … chat, yes?'

Emily's heart grew impossibly heavy. She'd been about to say something exactly along those lines, and had no idea where to start now they'd made it obvious they weren't going to accept anything less than honesty. Bracing herself, she took a breath. 'We have been having problems, yes. I know you overheard some of it, and I'm sorry you had to. I was upset. I—'

'Are you splitting up?' Ben asked bluntly. The look in his cool blue eyes was so dark and intense that Emily's heart faltered, her instinct to shield him rushing to the fore, as it had so many years ago. She would die to protect him, protect them both. But she couldn't protect them from this.

'I'm not sure,' she answered quietly. She wished now that she'd had this conversation at home. Had she really expected that she could deliver the news to her children that their parents' marriage was falling apart and they would just say 'okay' and then tuck into their meals? She should have been focusing on them through all of this, their feelings. She should never have tackled Jake with Ben and Millie in danger of overhearing. She was already worried about Millie, who so often lately needed treating with kid gloves. She was no less worried about Ben, though, who seemed to be a riot of conflicted emotion. She was sure she sensed an anger under the surface that truly frightened her.

'Has he cheated on you?' Millie got succinctly to the point.

Emily had no idea how to answer. 'I don't know,' she replied hesitantly. 'I thought he had. There was an email sent to him. I—'

'Like the letters being sent out?' Millie interrupted, her eyes growing wide.

Emily looked at her, surprised.

'I called into the newsagent's on the way home,' Millie explained. 'Fran was in there.'

Emily sighed inwardly. So the drums had started beating. 'Yes,' she admitted, 'but not as destructive as those.'

'Sounds pretty fucking destructive to me,' Ben growled, shocking her. 'So has he cheated on you or hasn't he?' he asked, levelling his gaze unnervingly on hers.

'I honestly don't know, Ben.' Emily reached for his hand. 'It's more complicated than that.'

'I can't see what's so complicated.' He drew his hand away. 'You asked him, right?'

'You know she did.' Millie sighed. 'We heard.'

'And he denied it?' Ben pushed.

'Of course he did.' There was a bitter edge to Millie's voice. 'Wouldn't you?'

She was judging her father, Emily realised, angry with him because of accusations *she'd* made, which might be groundless. Oh, how she wished now that she had buried her head in the sand. But could she really have sat back and done nothing but wait for the day her husband might come home to announce he was leaving?

'Have you ever cheated on him?' Ben asked, catching her completely unawares.

It was an innocent question – he wanted to know whether his father might have had just cause – but still Emily's stomach lurched. 'No,' she managed, past the parched lump in her throat. It wasn't a lie. To cheat on someone was to make a conscious decision, wasn't it? Hoping to God Ben couldn't see the guilt she still felt in her eyes, she held onto that. She had to.

They fell quiet as their food arrived, each lost in their own thoughts, Ben and Millie looking as if they had as little appetite as she did for the dishes they'd ordered after barely glancing at the menu. Ben was furious; Emily could feel it. Millie seemed contemplative. They both sat with their gazes glued to the table.

Millie waited for the waitress to leave. Then: 'Can you forgive him?' she asked, looking at Emily hopefully. 'Assuming he did cheat and that he admits it, could you?'

Emily was stumped for a reply. She couldn't see how she could answer truthfully without going into the awful details. She didn't want to talk to them about the devastating argument they'd had, the things Jake had accused her of – or about his relationship with

Sally, which for reasons she could only imagine he'd neglected to tell her about. 'I'm not sure,' she replied slowly. 'Things were said that can't be unsaid.'

'So you are going to split up, then?' Ben practically glared at her.

'Nothing's been decided yet, Ben.' Emily tried to reassure him, though she knew it didn't sound very reassuring. 'Your dad and I have to talk. We—' Before she could say anything more, Ben scraped his chair back and yanked himself to his feet.

'Ben …' Emily jumped up too as he stormed away from the table. 'Your food.'

He headed fast for the exit without looking back.

Emily was about to go after him, but Millie stopped her. 'Leave him,' she said, reaching to catch hold of her hand. 'He probably needs some time alone.'

Emily scanned her eyes, and her heart jolted as she realised what Millie was trying to convey. Ben considered himself a man. He didn't want his mother fussing over him while he was upset. How would the disintegration of his parents' marriage affect him in the long-term, though, his relationships with women? Having heard his 'love sucks' retort earlier, that was Emily's overwhelming worry: that he would become bitter or cynical and lose his capacity for love.

'If it helps, I understand,' Millie offered, as Emily dropped heavily back into her seat. 'If my boyfriend cheated on me, I don't think I could forgive him,' she went on hesitantly, her expression a mixture of sympathetic and nervous.

Emily felt a smidgen of hope unfurl inside her. Millie was opening the door, inviting her in. Her daughter needed to talk to her. No; *wanted* to talk to her. Emily had worried for a while that she was losing her. But now she realised how deep that fear had become; a cold foreboding in the pit of her stomach, warning her that one day her daughter might disappear from her life, never to return. She knew she couldn't bear that. She knew because she'd already lost someone.

Losing Kara had been like losing a limb. Losing Millie would be like losing a vital organ. And now her daughter was reaching out to her, albeit tentatively. Squeezing back her tears, Emily found herself clinging to that, a tiny life raft in the sea of turmoil her life had become.

CHAPTER TWENTY-FOUR

Noting Ben's coat slung over the newel post as she and Millie came through the front door, Emily felt a surge of relief.

'I'll go and put the kettle on,' Millie said behind her as she looked warily up the stairs, clearly understanding that she was worried about him. 'I'll do some cheese and crackers as well, since we didn't eat very much.'

'Thanks, Millie.' Emily smiled gratefully.

'No probs.' Millie gave her a rare smile back and headed for the kitchen.

Emily closed her eyes and silently thanked God. The foundations of her life were rocking, but she seemed to be getting her daughter back. *Hope from the ashes*, she thought sadly. Millie had obviously sensed she needed support and was trying her best to offer it. She was grateful, but also felt guilty. She desperately didn't want Millie taking her side against Jake, for the special father and daughter bond between them to be broken.

Deciding she would have to gently broach that subject with her, she took a breath and climbed the stairs to check on her son first. Ben was struggling, that was clear. She had to talk to him and let him know he could confide in her. As concerned as she was about his tendency to fly off the handle, she also had to tell him it was okay to be angry. If he learned to suppress his emotions because of signals she sent out, it might ultimately be so much worse.

Tapping on his door, she waited a second, and then tentatively pushed it open and poked her head around it. Ben was in his chair, headphones on. Gaming, she saw. Stepping into the room, she waited until she had his attention, and then mouthed, 'All right?' She knew it was a ridiculous question. How could he be all right, having just learned his parents were falling apart?

He jabbed his controller a couple of times and then parked it on his PC table and pulled his headphones off – a reliable indication that he was far from all right. Normally it would take an earthquake, or the ring of the doorbell promising pizza, to tear him away from his gaming.

'Yeah.' He shrugged and wiped a hand under his nose. 'Shit happens, doesn't it?'

'Nothing's decided yet, Ben.' Emily stepped closer. 'We're going through a bad patch right now, but we really do need to sit down and talk. We might be able to work things out.'

'Right.' He laughed scornfully. 'Like he's going to admit he's screwing around.'

Emily's heart wrenched with unbearable guilt. She should never have lost her temper, and shouted those awful things in earshot of her children. 'I don't know that he is yet, Ben,' she said softly. 'I know you overheard some things, but try not to judge him. I haven't really given him a chance to defend himself, have I?'

Ben shrugged again and then nodded reluctantly.

Emily supposed it would have to suffice. 'Millie's doing cheese and crackers if you fancy some.' She tried to tempt him downstairs.

Ben drew in a breath. 'I'll come down in a bit,' he said, and reached for his controller again.

'I'll ask Millie to put some out for you.' Reading his body language, Emily gathered he wanted to be on his own, and turned for the door.

'Mum.' He stopped her. 'Just so you know, you can talk to me.'

Stunned, Emily turned back. In that short sentence, he'd shown he cared, and it meant so much to her. She'd been judging him, she realised, looking for signs, trying to interpret his moods … and misinterpreting them. He was confused and angry. Temperamental. He would be all of those things without everything that was happening, because, though he was technically an adult, he was still of an age when he was full of raging testosterone. She had to stop. After all, his natural reaction to being constantly judged would be to withdraw further into himself.

'If you need to,' he added, shrugging awkwardly again.

Emily swallowed back a lump of emotion. 'Thank you,' she said, going back to give his shoulders a squeeze. 'That goes both ways. Just so you know.'

He nodded, smiled faintly and fixed his attention back on his game. Evidently he considered that was enough outpouring of sentiment for the moment.

He was undoubtedly trying to process things. Hopefully he would open up to her, but she knew she would need to tread carefully. 'We'll be downstairs when you're ready,' she said, giving him another quick squeeze and leaving him to it.

Finding Millie in the kitchen making coffee, she counted her blessings. She'd expected tears and tantrums from her daughter. Instead she'd got maturity and understanding. It was enough to make sure she got out of bed in the morning, whatever awfulness the day might bring.

'I put some out for Ben,' Millie said, nodding towards a cling-filmed plate on the worktop. 'I'm assuming he's got his face glued to some juvenile game?'

Emily hid a smile. It wouldn't be Millie without the smart quip. She really was beautiful, radiating the freshness of youth. Her make-up was meticulously applied, her glossy, sun-kissed locks arranged into a bun, making her look tall and sophisticated.

Grown-up. Emily's heart caught in her chest. But she still had so much growing up to do emotionally, which only ever came with experience. Emily desperately didn't want her experiences to be the wrong kind – the sort that might damage her and shape who she was.

'You'll have to give me some tips,' she said, walking across to her.

'What, on making cheese and crackers?' Millie arched an eyebrow as she turned around to carry the coffee over to the island.

'On what to do with my hair.' Emily glanced mournfully upwards. 'How to make it less straw-like.'

'Ah. You need to use a moisture repair shampoo and conditioner.' Millie nodded knowledgeably. 'A bit of Moroccan oil wouldn't go amiss either. And a heat protector. That's essential if you're going to keep blasting it with the hairdryer and using straighteners. You can use my products if you like. See how you get on with them.'

'Really?' Emily was growing more surprised by her daughter's thoughtfulness by the second. 'That would be brilliant,' she said, tears pricking the backs of her eyes. 'It's driving me mad at the moment. I can't seem to do anything with it. I just give up and tie it up in the end.'

'I noticed.' Millie didn't look overly impressed as she eyed her updo.

Emily sighed in despair. 'It's a mess, isn't it?'

'No.' Millie widened her eyes in admonishment. 'It looks nice. It shows off your high cheekbones, but … well, it's not very creative, is it?'

'I don't have much time to be creative in the mornings,' Emily said, her shoulders sagging. She'd have plenty of time if she and Jake separated, she thought sadly. She would hardly be able to work at the surgery then. With Sally there, it would definitely be a case of three in a relationship being one too many. The thought of Jake becoming openly involved with her was more than she could bear.

'Here, let me have a go,' Millie suggested, going around behind her and tugging off her hair tie before Emily had time to object. 'Tip your head forward,' she instructed.

Emily did as she was told, and waited patiently while Millie gathered up her hair.

'Right …' Millie paused thoughtfully. A second later, she'd lowered her own head to peer up at her. 'You can braid your hair, I take it?'

'Just about,' Emily said uncertainly.

'Good. So, you divide it into three at the nape of your neck and then plait it.' Millie demonstrated, talking her through it as she did. 'If you do it with your head forwards, it will encourage it in the right direction, do you see?'

Emily gave her an upside-down nod, not that she could actually see much.

'You're braiding about halfway up, just as far as the crown, then … Head up.'

Emily obliged, and Millie gathered her hair up on top of her head and secured it with a tie. 'What you do then is twist the loose hair into a bun and tuck the ends under the tie to secure it.' She set to work again, the tip of her tongue protruding as she concentrated.

'All done. One fabulous topknot with braid detailing at the back,' she said, stepping back and then steering Emily to the hall. 'You might need the odd hair grip for any stray bits, and some hairspray, but … What do you think?'

'Wow,' Emily said, admiring her more stylish look in the mirror. It was a massive improvement on her own attempts.

'Wow indeed.' Millie smiled as she led the way back to the kitchen. 'The lady looks hot.'

Emily felt a heavy sadness spread through her. She doubted Jake would think so. 'It's gorgeous, thanks, Millie,' she said, smiling gratefully.

'Any time,' Millie assured her. 'You should wear it like that more often. It suits you. Makes you look younger.'

Emily smiled, accepting the compliment. Her daughter, she knew, was trying to boost her confidence; bless her heart for realising it would be flagging. She didn't yearn to be younger, though. She yearned to be who she was. But she didn't know who that was. She wasn't sure she had done for a long time. She'd put away her paints after Kara's death, giving up her art, which had been her way of expressing her individuality, and trying to conform. Wild was dangerous, she'd learned. If you lived life craving the unexpected, it happened. She hadn't wanted to be different any more. She'd wanted safety in normality. She'd thought she'd found that in Jake. Once they'd married and settled into what she'd thought was a happy routine, she hadn't expected the unexpected, yet still it had suddenly happened.

'So are you going to tell me a little more about this boyfriend of yours?' she asked, shaking off the ghosts of her past and collecting up their food to carry it across to the island.

'Nothing much to tell.' Millie shrugged from where she sat on her stool.

Emily noticed her stiffen a little. 'Have you been going out long?' she fished, sitting opposite her.

'A few months,' Millie replied vaguely.

Emily sipped her coffee and waited for her to offer more. 'Is he someone from your school?' she asked, when it became apparent she wasn't going to.

'No.' Millie played with the cheese on her plate. 'He's working.'

'Ah.' Emily nodded. 'Older than you then?' she asked, trying to sound interested rather than as if she were judging.

Millie looked uncomfortable. 'A bit.'

Emily waited, thinking she might tell her how old and what kind of work he did. Millie, though, kept her eyes fixed on her plate. *Careful*, Emily warned herself. She didn't want to undo the progress they'd made this evening. 'Does he live with his parents?' She pushed it a little, needing to know at least that much to be able to form some kind of a picture in her mind.

'No.' Millie shook her head. 'He has his own flat and his own car, and he's okay.' There was a challenge in her eyes as her gaze flicked to hers. 'Caring, you know?'

Someone a good few years older than her, then. Emily felt a ripple of apprehension as she noted two bright spots blooming on her daughter's cheeks. She was hiding something. What, and why?

'Well that's a relief,' she said, manufacturing a bright smile and tucking into her cheese and crackers, though she was sure they would stick in her throat. 'As long as he respects you and what you want to do with your—'

'He does,' Millie cut in, her tone agitated and her forehead creasing into a scowl.

Emily swallowed her food slowly. 'Good,' she said, and searched for something else to say. She was about to ask where they'd met, thinking that might be a safer avenue, but stopped herself. Millie had opened up to her a little, and instead of allowing her to go at her own pace, offer more if she wanted to, she was cross-examining her, effectively pushing her away again. She didn't want to do that. She just wanted her daughter to be safe and happy, to not have regrets she might carry for the rest of her life. She dearly wished Millie could see her as a friend, someone she could feel safe confiding in, rather than the enemy.

Clearly, though, she didn't. It pained her to think it, but Millie was more inclined to confide in Jake than her lately. She should have asked him to talk to her – talked more to him herself, admitted why she was so scared for their daughter, who was beautiful and wilful and vulnerable, and could so easily fall into the same traps she herself had, because she'd imagined the most important thing in her life was the man she'd thought she was in love with.

'Look, Millie …' Taking a breath, she reached across the worktop for her daughter's hand. 'I'm sorry if I seem to be grilling you. I don't mean to. I'm just worried for you, that's all. I don't want you to make the same mistakes I did and then—'

'Oh *here* we go.' Snatching her hand away, Millie scrambled off her stool.

Now what had she done? Emily looked at her, astonished.

'You just don't get it, do you?' Millie glared at her, her eyes ablaze with bewildering anger.

Shaken, Emily got to her feet. 'Get what?' she asked. She *didn't* get it. She really didn't. She hadn't said or done anything, as far as she could see, except be concerned.

'What you're *saying*,' Millie yelled. 'The "I don't want you to make the same mistakes I did" crap you keep spouting with that dour bloody look on your face. You really don't understand, do you?'

Emily was speechless for a second. 'No, I don't,' she managed, her mouth parched, her heart palpitating wildly, as it seemed to do permanently lately. 'Millie, what's going on? What is it I—'

'You're saying *we're* your mistakes!' Millie swiped a hand across her face. 'Ben and me. You've said it several times. How do you think hearing that makes *us* feel? How do you think it makes *Dad* feel?'

Emily felt the blood drain from her body. 'Don't be ridiculous.' Stunned that Millie would even imagine such a thing, she took a step towards her. 'I don't mean you. Why on earth would you …'

Millie backed away. 'Right, so now I'm ridiculous, am I, as well as a burden and a disappointment?'

'No!' Emily shook her head, astounded. Nothing could be further from the truth. She was proud of her children. She loved them. Sometimes she felt her heart physically ache with a combination of love and fear for them. 'Millie, please don't think that. That's not what I meant. I never dreamt you thought—'

'I'm not *you*!' Tears sprang to Millie's eyes. 'I'm *me*. I can't be bloody perfect just because you want me to be. I will make mistakes, loads of mistakes probably, but they'll be *my* mistakes. I can't breathe around you sometimes, trying to be everything you want me to be, to study hard, get good grades, not be distracted. I have a life, Mum. I *want* a life.'

Emily felt her head swim. Suddenly the overhead lights were too bright, yet everything around her seemed ill-defined and blurred. She felt as if she was swimming underwater. As if she couldn't breathe. A slow, cold awareness was seeping into her that no matter how many times she reached out a hand to her daughter, she only moved further away.

'I can't be like you,' Millie continued, as Emily tried grimly to hang on, sure that this time she might not surface. She wasn't well. Something was dreadfully wrong with her. She needed to talk to Jake, tell him about her symptoms, which were getting worse. But how could she when they were barely speaking unless to argue? Unbidden, her mind flew back to her mother, who'd instilled in her as a teenager the same angry frustration she could now sense in her daughter. She could feel her mother's seething fury when she'd smelled marijuana in her hair. *Why can't you be more like your sister?* she'd growled, eyeballing her with equal measures of despair and disdain. Kara had modelled herself on their mother, working so hard to please her. Terrifyingly, Emily saw her sister now, not an ethereal image, floating on the periphery of her consciousness as she tried to wrench herself from her nightmares, but real. Solid. Here, standing right behind Millie. Her heart skittering like a terrified bird in her chest, Emily drew her eyes back to her daughter.

'I don't want to feel guilty all the time,' Millie was shouting tearfully. 'I don't want to feel like a disappointment. I—'

'Millie, stop.' Willing herself to focus, to banish the apparition conjured up by her own guilt, Emily moved towards her daughter, desperate to make her listen. 'Please, calm down and listen to me. You weren't a *mistake*. From the second I realised I was pregnant, I wanted you. I wanted Ben, with every fibre of my being.' She *had*. She *would* kill to protect her children. Surely Millie must know how much she loved her.

She took another step towards her. Millie took another step away.

'Please sit down,' Emily begged her. 'Please let's just talk calmly.'

Tears streaming down her face, Millie shook her head. 'You need to sort out your own fucked-up relationship,' she said pointedly, hurtfully, 'not meddle in mine.'

Emily's heart banged. 'I wasn't meaning to. I …' Moving again towards her daughter, she faltered, her legs trembling beneath her. 'Millie, where are you going?' Cold fear constricted her stomach as Millie spun around and headed for the door.

'Out,' she retorted, over her shoulder.

No. She couldn't, not like this. 'Don't you dare walk out, Millie,' Emily warned her.

Millie hesitated. Breathing in deeply, she looked back at her. 'I thought you told me not to let anyone dictate what I did?' she spat, and walked on.

'Millie!' Emily went after her. 'Millie, come back here. Now!' she shouted, her own tears exploding with anger and frustration as Millie flew to the front door and yanked it open.

'Where are you *going*?' Clutching the door frame for support, Emily called frantically after her as Millie raced from the house.

'To see Louis!' Millie shouted back. 'At least *he* bloody well wants me.'

Shaken to the core of her bones, Emily froze.

'Mum?' Ben called behind her. 'What's happening?'

Trying to assimilate, failing, Emily turned to look up to where he stood at the top of the stairs, his earphones in his hand, his expression wary.

'Nothing. It's fine. Millie … she was a bit upset,' she stammered. 'She's gone to her boyfriend's. You wouldn't know where he lives, Ben, would you?'

Ben shook his head. 'Not a clue. She doesn't talk to me much about that sort of stuff.'

No, Emily didn't suppose she would, particularly if it was someone she was nervous about people meeting. Or possibly nervous *of*. Recalling Millie's defensiveness, her reluctance to divulge information about him, Emily felt as if her world had stopped on its axis. As if it were slowly grinding backwards.

CHAPTER TWENTY-FIVE

Jake

Reading the results of the blood test that had been languishing in his in tray throughout the chaotic day, Jake struggled to digest the information. Reeling, he read them again. She was taking *amphetamines.* How the hell had this happened without his knowing about it? There was no way he would have prescribed Emily Ritalin. Why the bloody hell would she be taking a drug used in the treatment of attention deficit hyperactivity disorder, for Christ's sake?

Grabbing up his mobile, he logged back into his computer, pulling up her record and scrolling through it with one hand while doing something he rarely did – calling his father – with the other. 'It's me,' he said, attempting to contain his emotion when Tom picked up.

'I gathered. To what do I owe the pleasure?' Tom asked drolly.

'Has Emily consulted you recently?' Jake asked, an edge to his voice despite his efforts. 'Have you written her a prescription for anything?'

'Such as?' Tom sounded perplexed. Jake suspected he might have sounded rather more wary had he been treating Emily without his knowledge.

He took a breath. 'Ritalin.'

Tom hesitated before answering, which Jake immediately read something into. His heart dropped as he realised how little he trusted his own father. 'No, Jake, I haven't,' he answered eventually, categorically. 'Patient confidentiality aside on this occasion, Emily hasn't talked to me on a medical basis. I doubt she would discuss anything personal with me anyway, don't you? I'm not sure she rates me that highly, understandably.'

Jake ignored that. If Tom was waiting for reassurance that Emily had a good opinion of him, he would have a long wait. 'I need some information,' he said, having found nothing relating to the drug in Emily's medical history. 'I realise you're not in front of your PC, but I was hoping you might recall anyone else you might have prescribed it to.'

He wasn't sure where he was going with this, but he didn't need the sick feeling in his gut to tell him something was frighteningly amiss.

Tom thought about it. 'Off the top of my head, only once recently, for Alison Wright's young boy.'

It wouldn't be her. Jake recalled Alison, someone he'd been at school with years back and who was now one of Tom's patients. She was a bubbly, cheerful woman. Married with two kids, she worked at the bank and still smiled readily whenever she saw him. He wasn't aware that Emily knew her, other than to say hello to when she came in to the surgery. 'What about in the past? Any adults you might have treated for ADHD?'

'Not that I can recall. Feel free to check my records if it helps,' Tom offered. 'Oh, and it might be worth checking with the pharmacy vis-à-vis prescriptions issued from here. It might shed some light on it if you're worried, which I'm assuming you are.'

'I might. I'm thinking there's been some sort of mix-up, though. I'll have a word with Emily when I get home. I'd better get back there now. It's late. Thanks,' he added awkwardly.

'Any time,' Tom assured him. 'And the offer stands. If you need to talk … well, you know where I am.'

'I'll bear it in mind,' Jake said, forgoing the facetiousness. His father really was the last man he would want to confide in. He was already regretting revealing as much as he had.

Taking a few minutes to check the dosage prescribed for Alison Wright's son and finding no anomalies, he closed down the computer and grabbed his jacket, his mind whirling as he tried to think where else Emily might have obtained the tablets. Had she been self-prescribing, imagining they would help her insomnia and resulting tiredness? They wouldn't. If anything, taken incorrectly, they would make her disturbed sleep patterns worse. The side effects could cause all sorts of problems: nausea, loss of appetite, hallucinations, irritability, panic, paranoia … psychosis. His heart sank further, a knot of panic taking root inside him as he realised that she had been displaying several of those symptoms, all of which he'd initially put down to anaemia.

He'd accused her of being paranoid, lashed out at her in his anger and frustration because of what was happening in their marriage and here at the surgery. That a young girl had been seriously injured because of information that had come from the practice was incomprehensible. Jake was struggling to get his head around how anyone could deliberately send such poison out, knowing the devastation it would wreak, let alone *why* they would do so. He hadn't considered the impact his wild speculation would have on Emily, who he knew was dedicated to the welfare of their patients. Her behaviour had been erratic, there was no doubt about that, but once his mind had stopped racing and he'd been able to think rationally, he'd realised she couldn't have had anything to do with what was going on. Now, though, he wasn't so sure.

How long had she been taking the tablets? Was it possible that, unable to concentrate, she was inadvertently leaking information? That she might be doing things and not remembering? She'd been so distracted, so unlike herself. Why hadn't she come to him? Because she didn't trust him. *Christ.* He needed to talk to her properly. Whatever was going on between them, he needed to get to the root of this. The long-term effects of taking amphetamines could be catastrophic, possibly causing damage to major organs, and that was without the danger of psychological dependence.

She was registered at the surgery, so she wouldn't have got the tablets from another doctor, and there was no way he could imagine her obtaining them illegally. There was one other possibility, which was that she didn't know she was taking them – and the implications of that were truly terrifying. Someone right here in their community was actively trying to drive a wedge between couples. In doing so, they were driving people to desperation. Whoever it was obviously got some perverted kick out of the power they were wielding. How far might they go to satisfy that perversion?

He was heading across the car park when his mobile rang. Cursing when he couldn't locate it, he finally scrambled it from his inside pocket. 'Dr Merriden?' he answered shortly, his focus on getting home and on how he was going to broach the subject of Emily inappropriately medicating, assuming she would even talk to him.

'Jake, it's Steve Wheeler. Sorry to bother you so late …'

Hearing the shakiness in the man's voice, Jake's stride faltered. 'Hi, Steve. Can I help with something?'

'It's Jen …' Steve hesitated. From the sharp intake of breath, Jake guessed he was trying to compose himself. 'She's taken something.'

Jake stopped in his tracks. 'I'm here, Steve. Take your time,' he said, apprehension knotting his stomach. Jennifer Wheeler was on antidepressants. There was no way he could tell the man to call back during surgery hours.

'Pills,' Steve went on, his voice choked, 'I don't know how many. She's conscious, but … I don't know what to *do*, Jake. I …'

Shit! 'Have you called an ambulance?'

'Yes. I wasn't sure whether to, but—'

'Right. Good.' Jake raced to his car. Working on the assumption that she'd overdosed on her antidepressants, she might need urgent intervention. Depending on how long they'd been ingested, her airways might need to be kept open. She would need an electrocardiogram as soon as possible. 'It's Hawthorn Lane, isn't it?' Pressing his key fob, he threw himself behind the wheel.

'Thirty-three,' Steve confirmed. 'Left-hand side, just past the church.'

'I'm on my way,' Jake assured him. Calculating how long the ambulance would take to reach them, he knew he would be quicker.

'What do I do?' Steve asked. 'I'm scared, Jake. I …' A sob catching in his throat, he broke off.

'Sit with her and try to keep her calm,' Jake advised, pulling fast out of the car park. 'Don't give her anything to eat or drink. If she loses consciousness, put her in the recovery position: on her side, a cushion behind her back, upper leg pulled forward. Don't try to make her vomit. I'll be with you in a few minutes.'

'*Shit. Shit.*' He drove at breakneck speed, calling Emily on his hands-free as he went. Getting no reply, he cursed liberally again, and then called Ben.

'She's in the bath,' Ben told him. His tone was abrupt, distant. Jake didn't need to wonder why. He knew Ben had heard the arguments. As had Millie. They were probably assuming there was no smoke without fire. Christ, where would this all end?

'Could you tell her I have an emergency?' he said. 'I'll be back as soon as I can.'

'Yeah, right,' Ben said, definite sarcasm in his voice.

Realising he'd ended the call without saying goodbye, Jake's heart plummeted to the pit of his stomach. Emily had spoken to them, he guessed. What had she told them? If his kids thought he was anything like his own father, Jake knew from bitter experience that they would despise him. He didn't think he could bear that.

Seeing the front door open as he pulled up, he parked the car askew on the pavement and raced to the house. 'Steve?' he called, going straight in.

'In the lounge,' Steve shouted.

Jake went through, his gut twisting as the man turned his anguished gaze towards him. He was on the sofa, his arms around his wife. She was slumped against his shoulder, close to unconsciousness. 'Jennifer,' he said, dropping his bag and crouching down in front of her. 'It's Jake. Jake Merriden.'

She lifted her head, looked drowsily towards him as he took hold of her hand, moving his fingers to her wrist to feel her pulse. It was rapid, her cardiac rhythm escalated to dangerous levels. Her pupils were dilated. Even the temperature of her skin told him she was running a fever.

'Jake,' she murmured, attempting to focus. 'I'm sorry. So …'

'We need to get her on her side. *Now*,' Jake instructed, as her hand went limp in his.

Jake had never been so glad in his life to see an ambulance arrive. He prayed fervently as he followed it that Jennifer didn't have a seizure before it reached the hospital. Why hadn't he *seen* this? She'd been doing well, sounding so positive when she'd last come in, as if she'd thought life was worth living again. Clearly she hadn't. He thought back to her most recent appointment. She'd been in a rush, she'd said, due to take the kids she taught on a nature trail through the park. He thought now that maybe she'd been putting on a front, feeling down and ashamed and reluctant to talk about it. Why the hell hadn't he picked up the signs?

He found Steve outside the resuscitation unit while his wife was being attended to inside. Jake should be at home with his own wife, but there was no way he could simply just leave him. There wasn't anybody else to support him – Steve's family wasn't local and Jennifer had lost her mother at around the same time they'd lost the baby she'd finally conceived through IVF treatment. As far as Jake knew, she had no other family.

'Do you want to tell me what happened?' he asked gently, thinking the man might need someone to talk to.

Steve swiped a hand over his eyes, sucked in a tight breath and reached inside his jacket pocket. 'This happened,' he seethed, handing Jake a letter. 'There's some sick fucker in this village in serious need of medication, or locking up.'

Jake swallowed back the constriction in his throat. He knew what it was before he read it. When he did, his blood froze.

Do the parents know their children's teacher is a suicidal criminal reliant on antidepressants?

'Her job is her life,' Steve said, choking back his emotion. 'She's been terrified she'll lose it since she was arrested for shoplifting.'

Jake knew all about it. Jennifer had been so lost in her grief, she'd walked out of the baby shop with a pram. That was when she'd reached her lowest ebb, unable to see a future where life seemed worth living.

CHAPTER TWENTY-SIX

Finding Emily curled up on the sofa in her pyjamas, her eyes fixed on her tablet, Jake walked across to her. She didn't look up. He hesitated to sit down next to her. He doubted she would want him anywhere near her considering how they'd parted, thanks to his damn idiocy. 'Browsing anything interesting?' he asked, and held his breath.

'Sixties tribute bands,' she answered with a shrug. 'I wanted to hire one for Edward Simpson's birthday party.'

He furrowed his brow. 'I hadn't realised you were still organising that,' he said, surprised. He recalled her mentioning it, but it seemed like aeons ago now. She'd discussed bands with Sally, he remembered. He'd forgotten all about it since. He'd imagined Emily might have too, with all that had happened.

'I thought I would, despite everything.' She looked up at last. Her eyes, skimming his, were filled with soul-crushing disillusionment, which pierced his heart like a knife. Was he losing her? The woman who'd been there for him, supported him even when he'd questioned his own ability? The person he wouldn't know how to be without?

'I don't appear to be able to do anything to stop my family falling apart,' she went on, 'but I thought, with all that's going on, this might be a way to try to keep the community together.'

Jake felt the guilt he'd been carrying since he'd accused her of sending the letters weigh heavily in his chest. This was who Emily was: thoughtful, caring. Now that he knew she was taking Ritalin, he couldn't be sure she hadn't been distracted and inadvertently leaked information that someone else had used, but she wasn't capable of causing the unbearable suffering that whoever was sending these letters was clearly intent on. That was born of pure evil.

Unfurling herself, Emily rose from the sofa. Barefoot, she was a head shorter than he was, and looked so small and vulnerable right now, he just wanted to hold her. He didn't think she'd allow him to. Why in God's name had he said the things he had? He hadn't meant to. Why hadn't she shown him the email she claimed to have seen? She'd said she'd deleted it. Had she? Jake wondered if it had even existed, but it would certainly explain her paranoia, her unshakeable belief that he was having sex with every woman in the vicinity.

'Emily …' He moved towards her, searching for a way to begin to talk to her, to apologise. 'We need to—'

'You managed to make it home then?' she asked.

Hearing the facetiousness in her voice, he prayed they weren't heading for another argument. 'I had a call-out,' he said guardedly.

'Gosh, now there's a surprise.' Glancing at him with a mixture of disdain and hurt, Emily turned away, heading for the kitchen.

Jake followed, a chill of trepidation running through him as he noticed the open wine bottle and a half-filled glass on the island. The effects of Ritalin were similar to those of speed when taken by people who didn't need it. Mixed with alcohol, those effects were intensified, masking the impact of alcohol on the system, which made it a dangerous combination. He needed to talk to her, but first he had to convince her she could talk to *him*.

Bracing himself, he tugged in a breath. 'It was Steve Wheeler. His wife took an overdose.' He said it bluntly, disclosing information he shouldn't, particularly under the circumstances, because he needed her to know why he'd had no choice but to go. He hated himself for it, but he also needed to see her reaction.

'Jenny?' About to fill up her glass, Emily stopped. 'But …
why?' She shook her head, as if not quite comprehending. 'She
was doing so well.'

'She received a letter threatening to reveal her medical history,'
Jake answered, watching her carefully.

'Oh my God, no.' Pressing a hand to her mouth, she stared
at him, horrified. He felt his heart clunk shakily back into its
moorings as he saw the tears in her eyes, which confirmed how
wrong he'd been. Emily was aware of all that Jennifer Wheeler had
gone through. She'd looked after her when the woman had come
broken and bereft to the surgery. She would never be involved in
something as despicable as this. He *knew* her. She was the only
person he'd ever felt safe confiding in. What the hell had he been
thinking?

'Is she …?' Faltering, she locked her eyes on his, her fear
palpable.

'She's out of the woods,' he answered, gathering what she
meant. 'They'll monitor her for twenty-four hours. Run ECGs.
Hopefully there'll be no lasting physical damage. The emotional
damage, though …'

Tears sliding down her cheeks, Emily wrapped her arms around
herself. 'Why would someone do such a terrible thing? If they're
aware of her medical history, they would know that she might try
to take her life again, wouldn't they?' She blinked bewilderedly at
him. 'It's as if they were driving her to it, pushing her.'

Jake stepped forward as a shiver ran through her. Wrapping his
arms tentatively around her, he eased her to him. He felt his heart
breaking as she cried hard into his shoulder. How he wished they
could stay like this, safe in each other's embrace, lie together without
this cold ocean between them and find some comfort in each other.

'I'm all right,' she said, pulling away from him as her sobs slowed
to a stop. 'I'm sorry,' she said, apologising, as if she shouldn't have
given in to her emotion.

'Tears are allowed, Emily,' he assured her softly. 'They're thera-peutic.' She didn't know it, but he'd cried a few of his own once he'd left the hospital and got back to his car. Tears of frustration and anger. For Jenny and Steve. Zoe and Dean. Natasha and Michael. For himself. He'd only ever felt this lonely once before, years ago, when his life had been blown apart. He wasn't sure he would survive if he lost everything that mattered to him all over again.

Emily nodded and reached for some kitchen towel. 'I was feeling upset anyway,' she said, dabbing her eyes. 'Millie stormed out again.'

Jake's heart jolted. He'd heard Ben on his phone upstairs when he'd come in, but he hadn't even asked where Millie was. He'd assumed she was in her bedroom; that both kids were less than happy with him and therefore avoiding him. 'What happened?' he asked warily.

'We argued,' she said with a rueful sigh. 'I knew Millie would be emotional, thinking we were breaking up. She was really trying to be there for me, but I managed to put my foot in it again.'

Jake felt the foundations of his world shift another inch. 'Are we?' he asked throatily.

She took an agonising minute to reply. 'I don't know,' she said eventually, going back to the island to pick up her wine glass. She didn't take a drink, contemplating the contents distractedly instead. 'I can't see how we can work things out when you clearly hate me.'

She couldn't think that that was how he felt, surely? 'I don't hate you, Emily.' Guilt wrenching his stomach, he walked across to her.

'No?' She emitted a hollow laugh. 'It feels that way, Jake.'

'Christ, Emily, I could never feel that way about you. I love you. I've always loved you. I fell in love with you approximately ten seconds after I saw you.'

He was exaggerating, but not by much. She'd made him smile, something he hadn't done for a while. It had felt good. A switch had flicked inside him that day. He'd felt something other than a need to work, to keep studying to stop himself from thinking. He'd felt hope. She'd saved him. She must know that.

'Please believe I'm sorry,' he begged her. 'I should never have said the things I did. I have no idea what was going on in my head. I thought, after what you accused me of with Natasha, that ...' Struggling to explain, he trailed off hopelessly.

'That I'd sent that vile letter to her? And then another to Zoe to shift suspicion from myself?' Emily searched his face long and hard.

'I was wrong. I'm sorry,' Jake reiterated.

She nodded. 'And Sally? Are you sorry about her?'

Jake glanced awkwardly down. 'I should have mentioned it,' he admitted. 'It just ...' He was about to add that it hadn't occurred to him it wasn't common knowledge by now when Emily spoke over him.

'It's her, isn't it? Sally? It's her you're seeing?'

His gaze snapped back to her. '*What?*' He looked at her, stunned.

'She obviously hates me. She must, to be doing what she's doing,' Emily continued, confounding him.

She actually believed that ... *Jesus.* 'She's not doing anything, Emily,' Jake said, his heart plummeting all over again.

'Oh, I see.' She drew in a breath. 'So you think I'm quite capable of the evil you accused me of, but not her? I think that sums up how you really feel about me, don't you?'

'You mean you think it's Sally who's sending the letters out?' Jake searched her eyes, saw the conviction in them, and felt trepidation run the length of his spine.

'She knows I check your email,' Emily pointed out. 'It was the perfect way to cause trouble between us. And she would definitely have wanted to warn Natasha off if there were some basis in it, wouldn't she?'

'And the letters to Zoe and Jennifer?' He tried very hard to keep his voice calm.

'To deflect suspicion from herself. Isn't that what you thought *I* was doing?'

He felt hopelessness wash through him. 'I don't believe that, Emily,' he said quietly. 'I've known her for some years and—'

'Evidently.' Sweeping a disappointed gaze over him, she planted her glass back on the island and turned away. 'I rest my case.'

'Emily …' Jake caught hold of her arm. 'I was confused back at the surgery. Devastated for Zoe. I said some cruel things and I'm truly sorry. I can't say I think Sally's involved, though. I can't imagine her doing something like this.'

Emily pulled away from him. 'You need to talk to Millie,' she said, changing the subject. 'Assuming you have time in your busy schedule.'

Jake sighed in utter despair. 'I will,' he said, guessing that Millie must have been considerably upset when she'd left. 'Is she at Anna's?' he asked, glancing at the wall clock, wondering whether he should call her.

'No. I've spoken to Anna's mother,' Emily said, her tone flat. 'Millie's seeing someone. Someone unsuitable. Someone older than her. She refused to tell me anything more about him.'

Jake buried another sigh. She'd obviously got Millie's back up. He knew she was concerned about her. He was too. But she needed to back off a little, allow her some space. 'We have to let her make her own mistakes, Emily,' he said carefully. 'We can't dictate who she can and can't see. That's a sure-fire way to make sure she—'

'I don't want her making mistakes!' Emily snapped. 'The kind of mistakes she'll regret for the rest of her life.'

'Right.' Jake plunged his hands in his pockets. 'Like you, you mean?' He'd heard her warning Millie. He'd dismissed it, telling himself she was referring to things she might have regretted doing before they were a couple. Now he wasn't so sure. Did she regret marrying him? The life they'd had since?

Her cheeks flushing furiously, Emily's gaze shot to the floor. Then, as if summoning her courage, she looked back at him. 'I do have regrets, yes,' she said. 'But not about you, in case you're wondering. I've never regretted a day I've been with you, Jake. Until now.' The last was added with a heartbreaking smile. 'The point here is that Millie could possibly be involved in a damaging relationship. Why else the evasiveness? She knows we're in trouble. She's emotional and vulnerable. So if you have time in between your own various relationships, could you please try to talk to her?'

'For God's sake!' Jake couldn't help himself. 'When are you going to stop this, Emily? The only *relationship* I'm having is with you! Will you not just listen to me?'

'I'm going to bed,' Emily replied flatly. 'It's late.'

'Are you taking medication?' he demanded as she walked away. He hadn't meant to blurt it out. He'd planned to broach the subject more carefully, proposing that they run another test to see if there had been a mistake somehow. But now … Her moods were all over the place, as was her reasoning. And he'd had enough.

She turned around. 'What?' she laughed.

'Medication,' he repeated, holding her gaze. 'Are you taking anything? I need to know.'

Her gaze darkened. 'So now you're accusing me of stealing drugs from the surgery?'

'You're acting irrationally, Emily. You're fixated, defensive, irritable, exhausted. I don't know how to talk to you half the time.'

'Well go and talk to bloody Sally then!' she snapped. 'I'm sure you two have plenty to discuss. Driving me out of my mind, for one!'

Jake felt his heart free-falling into the vast space between them as she spun around again, storming into the hall.

'*Christ.*' Inhaling hard, he went back to the island, raked his hand through his hair in frustration, then snatched up the wine bottle, filled Emily's glass and knocked it back.

'Have you two finished?' Ben said behind him.

Shit! Jake swung around. 'Ben, I'm sorry. I—'

'Full of fucking apologies, aren't you?' Ben drawled. 'You know what, I don't think we want to hear any more.' He stopped as Emily reappeared, her face ashen.

'You've had a text,' she said, holding Jake's phone out to him. 'Apparently she's pregnant.'

CHAPTER TWENTY-SEVEN

Emily

Emily had never imagined there would come a time when she and Jake would sleep separately. He hadn't come up to bed again. She'd lain awake most of the night worrying about where Millie was, what sort of man she was with; praying to God that her instincts were wrong and that he wasn't treating her badly. She'd listened for sounds of Jake below her, wondering whether to go down to him, to try somehow to fix things, but how could she if he was lying to her?

He'd followed her upstairs when she'd raced from the kitchen, hammering on the bedroom door until she'd had no choice but to let him in. He'd been so angry, furious, his eyes thunderous. 'Whatever this crap is,' he'd seethed, practically thrusting the phone at her, 'it has *nothing* to do with me. *Or* Sally, as far as I can see. It's sent from a blocked number, for fuck's sake. Check it.'

Emily hadn't believed him. She was struggling to believe anything he told her, yet there was a part of her that did, that saw the desperation in his eyes begging her not to condemn him without real proof. But wasn't the email, the fact that he and Sally had been in a relationship – *were* in a relationship – proof enough? She didn't know what was happening any more. Why would he accuse her of the cruel things he had? Of taking *drugs*? She hadn't been able to believe her ears. The only pills she took were the iron pills *he'd* prescribed her, along with her vitamins, and paracetamol for the headaches that followed the endless sleepless nights. She couldn't understand why he would think she'd taken anything else. As in, stolen from the surgery. She didn't doubt he'd meant that.

She'd screamed at him in the end to just stop, her hands clamped over her ears, until he'd eventually backed from the room. She couldn't take any more. She'd felt like running into the night, like going to the surgery and stuffing whatever damn drugs she could lay her hands on down her throat, anything to shut it all out. Until she'd remembered poor Jenny and how desperate she must have been to do what she had.

She'd finally been lulled to sleep by the sound of the dawn chorus, only to wake with a choking jerk, images of her sister's lifeless body floating through her mind. Kara's eyes had snapped open. She'd seen it too: the face of the man on the bridge. The man who'd watched Emily struggling to save her. The man who'd pushed her. The recollection when it finally surfaced was stark in its clarity, where up to now it had been jagged and incomplete. It wasn't her. She'd been there, she *had* followed Kara, but she hadn't pushed her. Relief mixed with acrid grief crashed through her as her mind had flown back there. She'd been on the canal bank, paralysed with fear for an instant. And then she'd run, her heart hammering, choking screams rising inside her. She'd waded into the water, tried to reach her, tried desperately to pull her out. She herself had eventually been dragged from the water hysterical but still breathing. Kara had never drawn breath again.

Perhaps her mind racing so feverishly that she felt she was going insane had its advantages. She was seeing things clearly now. Wasn't she? Reminded that she was also seeing things during the day that belonged in her nightmares, cold fear settled like an icicle in her chest. *Was* she going mad?

When she went downstairs, she'd realised Jake had slipped off early. He hadn't woken her, but he'd left her a note. Her heart had stopped beating when she'd found it propped against the kettle. And then squeezed painfully when she'd dared to read it: *I'm sorry. I love you*, was all it said.

Even having read those last three poignant words, she wondered now as she walked to work, late and not really caring, what it was that he was sorry for. How much would it suit him if he could claim that he couldn't cope with any more? That it was her, his mad wife, who'd driven *him* away? He'd get to keep his reputation intact then, wouldn't he? If there was one thing she knew about Jake, it was that he couldn't bear the thought of being likened to his father.

Approaching the village shop, she wondered again how Millie was. She'd sent a short text – *Back later* – which was at least something, but Emily knew that, in seeming to be interrogating her daughter, she'd destroyed any chance she might have had of getting her to open up. She was jolted from her thoughts as she heard two women chatting outside the shop.

'I mean, all marriages have secrets, don't they?' Ally Jones, the owner of Evolution hairdresser's, was saying.

'Definitely.' Leah Connolly, whom Emily knew to be in a bad marriage, sounded worried.

'I've heard tales from my customers that would make your hair stand on end,' Ally went on. 'More than one or two of them are living in fear of the letter box flapping, I can tell you. They need to catch whoever is doing this before someone is seriously—' She stopped, her gaze snapping to Emily as she approached.

Emily noted the nervous apprehension on Leah's face as she too glanced in her direction. They were frightened, and had every reason to be. But … was it *her* they were frightened of? Her stomach tightening, she mustered a smile and pushed on towards them, but both women hurriedly averted their gazes. Realising she would have to speak to them in order to access the shop, Emily lost her nerve, walking on instead to call into the grocery store for milk for the surgery.

Paying for the milk, she tried to engage Fred Jackson – who ran the store, and who was also looking at her warily – in conversation. 'Will you be coming to Edward's party?' she asked him with forced jollity.

'I'll be there,' he assured her, searching her eyes curiously as he plonked her change in her hand. 'I reckon we all need to present a united front. Show this bugger who's trying to split the community up they won't succeed.'

'My thoughts entirely.' Emily smiled tightly. 'See you there.'

'Aye.' Fred nodded, his expression still cautious as he looked her up and down.

Hardly able to breathe, Emily whirled around. She was about to step out of the store, but faltered and moved back. Sally was just a yard away outside. She was the absolute last person Emily wanted to run into. She would have to talk to her at some point – she couldn't avoid her at work – but she needed to prepare herself. She didn't particularly want to see Michael Jameson either. She didn't think she could look him in the eye after what she'd witnessed him doing to Natasha. So what were the two of them deep in conversation about? 'Jake Merriden needs to get to the bottom of this,' she heard Michael say. 'He needs to get the police involved, and fast.'

'He will now,' Sally replied, clearly privy to information Emily wasn't. 'Did you hear what happened to Jenny Wheeler?'

'No.' Michael's face creased into a curious frown. 'What's that, then?'

Sally moved closer to him. 'Overdose.' She said it quietly, but Emily still thought it spiteful of her to gossip about it. Did she not realise how devastating it would be for Jenny to realise that her personal life had become everyone else's business?

'I'll bet my bottom dollar that it has something to do with all these appalling letters being sent out,' Sally went on. 'Jake was distraught enough when he found out about poor Zoe. I've never seen him so furious. This will be the last straw.' She paused, emitting an elongated sigh. 'It's Emily I'm concerned about. I'm sure Jake thinks it's her, but she's such a stickler about client confidentiality, I honestly can't understand why he would.'

No, Emily couldn't understand either – nor why Sally would provide Michael with fodder for gossip. No matter what Jake thought, Sally wasn't above suspicion in Emily's mind. She wouldn't have thought it possible a short while ago, but now, aware of her secret relationship with her husband, her deceit, Emily thought she was capable of anything.

Waiting a minute to compose herself, she watched as Sally walked off, giving Michael, the man she'd condemned for being violent to his wife, a cheery wave as she went.

She hadn't realised Edward was in the store until he slid an arm around her shoulders. 'Take no notice, my lovely,' he said, giving her a reassuring squeeze. 'You know what they say: gossip is just a tool to distract people who have nothing better to do from feeling jealous.'

Reminded why she was organising his party and why she loved him so much, Emily managed a genuine smile, albeit a small one. Edward was the sort who lived by the idiom that if you hadn't got anything good to say about a person, it was better to say nothing at all. She'd never heard him or Joyce utter a bad word about anyone. The man was a breath of fresh air. 'I'm not sure they have anything to be jealous about, Edward.' She leaned into him, needing his comforting arm around her for just a second longer.

'Nonsense.' Edward gave her another fatherly squeeze. 'You're an intelligent, competent woman, and extremely easy on the old eyes, if I may say so. I'm not sure you've looked in the mirror lately, but you should.'

This time she managed a whole smile. 'You most certainly may,' she said, turning to press a kiss to his weathered cheek. 'You're not so bad-looking yourself, if *I* may say so.'

Edward chuckled. 'I'll tell Joyce you think so. She'll be mad with jealousy. Go on,' he said, nodding her towards the surgery. 'That husband of yours will be lost without you.'

Emily glanced down. *Would he?*

'He won't know whether he's coming or going.' As if reading her mind, Edward chivvied her on. 'He's a good man, Emily,' he added more seriously, causing Emily's heart to catch. 'It seems there's someone intent on splitting couples up. Don't let them do that to you and Jake, hey? You're stronger than that.'

Tears filling her eyes, Emily blinked them back hard. She didn't feel very strong right now. She wanted to fight, but didn't know how when she wasn't sure who the enemy was. 'I won't,' she promised him anyway, giving him a tight hug. 'Thanks, Ed. Give Joyce my love. Tell her I'll pop in and see her soon.'

'I'll make sure to. She'll look forward to talking to someone with half a brain.'

'Only half?' Emily laughed, and headed onwards to the surgery, feeling buoyed up and more determined. To do what, she wasn't sure, but she couldn't just give up on her marriage, on Jake. He'd once jokingly accused her of being a glutton for punishment, sticking with him when she hardly saw anything of him. Maybe she was, but wasn't that what she'd vowed to do, stick with him for better or worse? This was about as bad as it could get, admittedly, but she couldn't just roll over. As tired and confused as she was, she had to fight. She hated Jake for the things he'd said and the things she imagined he was doing, so graphically that sometimes she could feel her heart breaking. Yet she loved him – she loved the caring Jake she knew him to be.

Going into reception, she stowed her bag under her desk, mouthed an apology to Nicky, who was on the phone, then headed to the kitchen with the milk. Her mood deflated in an instant as she heard Fran's unmistakable tones drifting out.

'Well, I'm not one to stir things,' she said, 'but I can't say I blame Jake for losing his temper. The information in those letters can only be coming from here, after all. Whichever way you look at it, it means *someone's* not doing their job properly, doesn't it? A job they're getting paid well to do, I might add.'

'Well, yes, but ...' Sally had the grace to sound uncomfortable. 'Even so, I can't believe Emily had anything to do with sending the dreadful things out. I mean, why would anyone want to do such a thing?'

Fran drew in a long breath, meaning she was gearing herself up to impart her invaluable opinion. Emily froze. 'Out of jealousy, obviously. Think about it. Michael was the first person to get one, wasn't he? Now, I'm just speculating, but if it had been *my* husband Natasha had been fawning all over and fluttering her eyelashes at during the duck race... Well, let's just say I would have been tempted to drown her too.'

Emily's stomach roiled, nausea rising hotly inside her. She'd wondered how long it would take her to say that in front of her face. She was bound to have been spreading vicious rumours. Everyone in the village would think she'd pushed her on purpose. That it was her sending the letters, now that Fran had got her teeth into this too.

Her legs felt as if they might slide from underneath her, and she stretched a hand to the wall for support. Taking several deep breaths, she was desperately trying to slow her frantic heartbeat when Nicky said behind her, 'Emily? Are you all right?'

Hearing the concern in her voice but not sure if it was genuine, whether there was anyone she could trust any more apart from lovely, dear Edward, Emily nodded quickly. 'Fine,' she assured her, her voice sounding strained even to her own ears. 'I felt a little faint, that's all. I didn't get chance to eat anything this morning.'

Willing herself not to pass out, which would give Fran – and Sally now, it seemed – yet more juicy gossip to bury her under, she turned to Nicky, a forced smile on her face. 'Did you need something?'

Nicky looked her over, unconvinced. 'Jake rang through,' she said. 'He wondered whether you could step into his office.' She hesitated, her gaze flicking worriedly down and back. 'The police are here. They'd like to have a word with you.'

CHAPTER TWENTY-EIGHT

As she approached Jake's office, Emily's urge to run was almost overwhelming. He'd apologised for the things he'd accused her of, and admitted he'd been wrong, but what might he be telling the police? He couldn't state categorically that it wasn't her leaking confidential information, if not posting these vile letters through people's doors, any more than she could state categorically it wasn't him. The reality was, in Jake's eyes she was ultimately responsible, as Fran had just unkindly pointed out to Sally. No matter how many times he apologised, he couldn't take back the fact that he'd thought she was.

The worst part of it all was that he was right. Emily couldn't escape the fact that, as practice manager, the blame for what was happening rested squarely on her shoulders.

Might he have mentioned to the police his ludicrous notion that she was taking some kind of medication, as he called it? A fresh bout of nausea swilled inside her. If asked about the competency of his staff, he might have felt obliged to. There was only one way to find out. Her stomach knotted with nerves, she drew in a breath, knocked on his door and pushed it open.

'Hi.' Jake smiled uncertainly as she went in. 'This is my wife, Emily. She's our practice manager.' The two officers glanced in her direction. Getting to his feet, he walked around his desk towards her, his forehead creasing into a troubled frown as he looked her over.

'Sorry I'm late. I felt a bit off colour this morning,' Emily said, trying to keep things businesslike despite what was going on between them and the fact that they'd spent the night in separate rooms. Sally was right here in this building, no doubt desperate to see her fall apart. To see her marriage fall apart. Fran was probably in Tom's office right now with her ear glued to the adjoining wall, poised to share her malicious gossip the second she left the room. Emily wouldn't give them the satisfaction of seeing her crumble. She had to stay strong for her children.

'But you're okay now?' Jake asked, his hand brushing her arm, deep concern clouding his eyes, sending a turmoil of conflicting emotion right through her.

'Fine,' she assured him. 'I think it's just a touch of that bug Millie and Ben both had,' she added, pointedly reminding him that they had children. Children who were already troubled and whose futures were in danger of being marred by all of this.

'There's a lot of that going about. My little one's just had it.' The female officer smiled as she got to her feet to offer Emily her hand. 'Liz Regan, Detective Sergeant,' she said.

Shaking her hand, Emily made herself smile back. Regan seemed nice. She had an open, amiable face, short brown hair peppered with highlights, and sharp hazel eyes, which seemed to be weighing her up but not judging her badly. She was grateful for that much. 'Emily Merriden,' she said.

Regan dipped her head. 'I gathered. This is Detective Constable Morse.' She nodded at her colleague.

'Dave,' the man said, shaking Emily's hand. 'And no, no relation.'

Emily had to smile at that. He seemed friendly too. She felt a surge of relief wash through her. Shorter than DS Regan, he had a ready smile and a warm handshake. She relaxed a little.

'Your husband's filled us in,' Regan picked up. 'I imagine you're all pretty shaken by events.'

'Very,' Emily said, swallowing as her mind conjured up an image of poor little Zoe lying in a medically induced coma with no certainty yet as to her prognosis. She thought of Natasha and the violence she'd suffered at her husband's hands. Of Jenny and the emotional devastation that would impact on the rest of her life.

'We know all our patients on a personal level,' she confided, and then almost wished she hadn't. 'It's a small community. Tight-knit,' she added, feeling her cheeks heat up under Jake's scrutiny.

DS Regan nodded sympathetically. 'We'll be taking statements, trying to establish who knew what about whom, and talking to everyone here individually. Is there an office we can use temporarily?' She looked between Emily and Jake.

'Sally's?' Jake suggested, his gaze flicking awkwardly down and back, Emily noticed. 'She's our phlebotomist. It's actually the treatment room. She has some patients in this afternoon, but she can use Tom's – my father's – office. He's a partner, but he's only here part-time. I'm sure we can reschedule any existing appointments.'

'Great, thanks. It will make things easier.' DS Regan turned to Emily. 'Your husband tells me you've updated all your PC logins and access codes.'

Had they? She looked at Jake, confused.

'That's right,' he said, his eyes wary as they skimmed hers before going back to DS Regan. 'Nicky did it first thing this morning, on Emily's instruction.'

Emily's guilt intensified. She'd organised a meeting, she recalled, but she hadn't been here because of their personal problems … and because she'd had very little sleep again. Jake had gone ahead and asked Nicky to do it; of course he would have done. It clearly indicated that he trusted Nicky, though, where he hadn't trusted his own wife.

'And access to paper files?' DS Regan asked.

'We have lockable filing cabinets.' Emily collected herself. 'I'm tightening up the signing-out system for anyone who needs to access them.'

'Excellent.' Regan nodded approvingly.

'We'll be checking who logged in to the computers and when,' Morse added. 'We'll check out any printers as well. Hopefully, if the letters came from here, we'll be able to establish which printer was used.'

'Can you do that?' Jake asked, surprised.

'It's possible,' the DC confirmed. 'Printers can leave two kinds of identifying marks: one sort that comes from imperfections resulting from unique wear in the mechanism, plus a digital fingerprint that points to a specific printer, model and unit.'

'I'm impressed,' Jake said, looking actually concerned. Also looking at her, Emily noticed.

'Meanwhile,' Regan continued, 'we were just about to ask your husband if anyone else has access to the surgery, apart from staff and patients and the usual people who come and go obviously – delivery people, sales reps and so on. Family, possibly?' she asked. 'Do any of the staff bring their children in?'

Emily felt her nerves tighten all over again.

'Just us,' Jake provided, now looking as wary as Emily felt. 'My daughter, Millie, sometimes comes in with me on a Saturday. She's aiming to do a veterinary course. She finds the environment more conducive to study,' he explained. 'My son, Ben, has been in on the odd occasion, but only to meet up with one of us.'

'And do they have boyfriends or girlfriends who might have come in with them?' the woman asked.

Emily glanced at Jake. She could see his apprehension as his eyes as swivelled to hers. No doubt his mind was on Millie and the concerns Emily had raised about her boyfriend before their conversation degenerated into another argument.

'No,' he said adamantly. 'Never. Ben's not seeing anyone. And Millie is only recently in a relationship.'

'That's fine,' Regan said. 'If you could let us have the boyfriend's address, though …'

'Yes, right.' Jake's eyes flicked uncertainly again towards Emily. 'I'll, er, have a word with Millie.'

Regan studied him thoughtfully for a second. 'You understand that due to the serious consequences resulting from the circulation of these letters we do have to talk to anyone who might have had access to the building?' she asked.

'Of course.' Jake ran a hand over his neck. 'Not a problem.'

Emily could see from his tense body language that his thinking was on a par with hers, about this at least. They knew nothing about Millie's boyfriend, other than that he was older than her and that Millie was reluctant to divulge more about him. From the very nature of that fact, their daughter was bound to be questioned in detail about him.

'Right, well, I think that's it for now.' DS Regan checked her watch. 'We're off to have another word with Dean Miller. We'll—'

'How is he?' Emily asked. His life had been ripped apart. Whatever happened to him now, he would never recover from any of that.

'As well as can be expected,' DS Regan answered. 'We're still making enquiries.'

'He claimed he wasn't involved – when he spoke to me on the phone,' Jake said. 'I know you can't give out information, but …' Pausing, he drew in a breath. He was obviously as concerned as Emily was. Probably more so. Knowing how much he cared about his patients, she didn't doubt that. 'I don't suppose it counts for much, but I believed him.'

Nodding, DS Regan looked between them, then seemed to make a judgement call. 'There's a neighbour who claims to have seen Zoe on the balcony after Dean left. She also thinks someone else might have called on her. As I say, we're still investigating. It would help him if Zoe were able to tell us, of course.' She glanced questioningly back to Jake.

'They're hopeful,' he said, his expression one of obvious relief, on Dean's behalf, Emily guessed. 'They've managed to minimise the swelling.'

'Excellent. Fingers crossed.' DS Regan smiled. 'We'll be back in an hour or so to set up in the office you mentioned, if that's okay?'

'I'll let the team know.' Jake offered her a small smile as he walked them out.

Emily turned to go too. She desperately wanted to talk to Jake. The problem was, she wasn't sure they knew how to talk any more.

'Emily, can I have a word?' He stopped her as she approached the door. Glancing into the corridor, he closed it behind him, and turned back to her. 'Have you spoken to Millie? Is she back?'

Emily could see the worry in his eyes. He had so many things coming at him, he wouldn't know which way to turn. He would have turned to *her*, not so long ago. And she to him. She was tempted to say, *You remember you have a daughter then?*, but refrained. The pain he was causing her was excruciating – she felt as if her heart was tearing apart inside her – but she didn't want to hurt him back. 'She texted me,' she said. 'She said she'd be back later.'

Closing his eyes, Jake nodded. His relief this time was palpable. He loved his daughter. Ben, too. She could never do anything to damage his relationship with them. She couldn't lie for him, though, either. He must know that.

'But she still hasn't given you any information about the boyfriend?' he asked hopefully.

Emily shook her head. 'She'll have to if the police need to know, though, won't she?' She desperately didn't want Millie dragged into any of this, but she was beginning to think it might be a blessing in disguise if she was forced to disclose more information about the man, such as who he was and where he lived. Emily needed to know. She needed to protect her daughter. The cold foreboding in the pit of her stomach told her she did.

Jake nodded. 'She won't have much choice,' he said, searching her eyes, a kaleidoscope of emotion in his own: confusion, despair, frustration.

'I'd better get on and make sure Tom's office is available for Sally to use.' Emily moved towards the door. She couldn't stand here, so close to the man she loved, with this vast space between them. The man who once would have soothed away her worries with soft kisses, whose comforting embrace around her would have made her feel safe. She'd thought he was her rock, that he would catch her if ever she fell. And now … Did he realise she was clinging on by her fingernails? Would he be there if she let go?

'Emily, wait.' He stepped towards her. 'There's something else,' he said, a flicker of hesitation in his eyes.

She looked at him cautiously.

'I tried to talk to you about it last night. Clumsily, stupidly. I wasn't thinking straight. I was tired, overwrought after what happened with Jennifer Wheeler. And then when we argued, I …' He faltered, kneaded his forehead and looked back at her. 'I need you to take another blood test,' he announced.

She stared at him, stunned. 'You're not serious?' She struggled to get the words past the constriction in her throat.

Jake locked his gaze on hers. 'Deadly.'

'A drugs test?' She felt every sinew in her body tighten. 'You actually think that I'm self-medicating? Writing out my own prescriptions? Or am I stealing drugs from the safe, Jake, is that it?'

'Emily …' He glanced over his shoulder. 'Please just hear me out.'

Clearly he was worried the police might overhear. Let them. He was insane. Or else he really was trying to drive *her* insane. Emily had heard enough.

'Let me past, Jake,' she said, sure that the contempt in her eyes must be obvious. She didn't care. What was it he wanted? For *her* to attempt suicide? Tears welling up so fast they almost choked her, she tried to step round him.

'Emily, *don't.*' He caught hold of her arms. 'Just listen to me, will you?'

He was keeping his voice low. So she would be seen as the volatile, drugged-up, aggressive one? 'Let me *go.*' She tried to pull away. Whatever she'd done, she wouldn't stay here to be tortured by him.

'Jesus! *Listen* to me.' Jake only held her tighter. 'If you're not self-medicating, someone is feeding you these drugs, do you understand?'

Emily stopped struggling, blinked uncomprehendingly at him.

'Amphetamines.' His face was pale, his eyes fearful. 'You're being poisoned, Emily. You *have* to take another blood test.'

CHAPTER TWENTY-NINE

'There's no way I'm letting Sally take my blood,' Emily said, looking shakily at Jake over the glass of water he'd fetched her. She half expected him to say *Why?* or *It's not Sally*, such was his propensity to jump to the woman's defence.

But he didn't. Nodding instead, he reached to relieve her of the glass, placed it on the table and went to collect the appropriate equipment to take the specimen himself.

'Who would do such a thing?' she asked him as he helped bare her arm and attached the tourniquet, all of which he did calmly and efficiently.

You? she wondered, icy fingers tugging at her heart as she noticed the taut set of his jaw, the small tic playing agitatedly at his cheek. Might he be capable of it? The notion was absurd – she must truly be going mad. He would hardly have told her about it if it was him. Then who? She couldn't believe anyone would do something so terrifyingly wicked.

Jake met her gaze as she studied him, her mind ticking frantically in tandem with her heartbeat. He would be desperate to hold onto all that he'd worked so hard for here. Was it possible that there really was a whole other side to him she'd been too blind to see before? Some part of him that had been so badly damaged by the trauma of his mother's death and the role his father had played in it that he couldn't bear the thought that in the end he had turned out to be a chip off the old block?

'You're wrong about me, Emily,' he said quietly after a second, his look intense, his ocean-coloured eyes growing a shade darker.

It was as if he was reading her mind. Emily looked away while he searched for a suitable vein. She *was* going mad. Her thoughts were firing scattergun through her mind – because of the drugs? Someone was trying to poison her. He was trying to help her, not kill her. He'd never been anything but caring and gentle and kind. This was the man who'd cried openly, tears of wonderment, when he'd first cradled his newborn baby daughter in his arms. What was the *matter* with her?

She squeezed her eyes closed as he inserted the needle. He wasn't going to hurt her. She knew he wasn't. But still she couldn't look.

'All done,' he said, pressing a gauze gently to her arm.

Emily looked up at him, a tight lump rising in her throat that she couldn't seem to swallow.

Jake gave her a small, reassuring smile and turned to fill an empty vial with the sample he'd taken. 'In answer to your question, I have no idea who would do such a thing,' he said. 'Excluding anyone at home,' he glanced pointedly back at her, as if he really had heard the ridiculous ramblings of her mind, 'my thinking is that it has to be someone here.'

Sally?

'It would have to be someone you see on a regular basis,' he continued.

Sally. Emily's blood ran cold. She didn't see anyone else on a regular basis. Certainly not anyone she regularly drank or ate with.

'In answer to your other question ...' He turned back to her.

Emily looked at him, confused. Had she asked another question?

'The one that's eating away at you,' Jake clarified. 'I'm not cheating on you, Emily. I love you. Sadly, I can't seem to make you believe it, but I do.'

He held her gaze, such palpable sadness now in his eyes, it tore another hole in her heart. She had no idea what to say. She wanted to believe him, to bring a stop to all of this and just hold him, be held by him; she longed for that, but … *the email.* The intimacy between him and Sally. She hadn't imagined it. *Wasn't* imagining it, however addled her mind was. It was a fact that he hadn't told her about his relationship with Sally. As much as she wanted to, she couldn't believe it had just slipped his mind. She hadn't imagined his involvement with someone else years ago either. No matter how innocent he'd claimed it was, the fact was, he had been seeing another woman.

'Can we talk?' he asked her, his expression hopeful. 'Calmly, rather than arguing?'

They had to. They couldn't go on like this. For the sake of Millie and Ben – for their own sakes – they needed to try to communicate amicably, whatever the future might hold. That thought causing her heart to wrench afresh, Emily closed her eyes and answered him with a small nod. She was about to ask him if he could come home early when there was a knock on the door and Nicky peered in.

'Sorry to bother you,' she said, her eyes gliding curiously between them. 'It's just that I need the keys to Tom's filing cabinet. I have some notes to type up for him and I need to cross-check an address.'

'Yes, of course. Sorry.' Realising the keys were still in her bag, which actually they shouldn't be, Emily got to her feet.

Jake smiled ruefully as she passed him. 'I have to pop out to take a sample to the hospital,' he said, nodding towards the vial of blood he'd just taken from Emily. 'We still have that patient treatment plan we need to discuss, though. We'll talk later, yes?'

'Okay.' Reading between the lines, Emily nodded. He was taking the sample personally. He'd clearly guessed that she might be concerned if he didn't. Managing a small smile back, she followed Nicky out.

Once in reception, she found her bag and the keys therein, handed them to Nicky and, reminding her to sign the file out, braced herself to face Sally. There were two patients due in for blood tests immediately after lunch, she recalled, thankful that her brain seemed to be functioning on some level. With the police due back and a full evening surgery ahead, they needed to get organised. People were scared. They would need reassuring. Emily was determined to offer that reassurance, whatever rumours might be flying around. Also to be the epitome of efficiency. The person responsible for all this wanted her to fall apart, for her life to fall apart, just as the lives of the recipients of the letters had. They wanted things at the practice to fall apart, for which Jake would then blame her. Emily had decided she would die before she allowed that to happen – although, she pondered, given how seriously the other victims were suffering, perhaps that was the intended outcome.

Was it her? Seeing Sally appear from the treatment room, looking as attractive and immaculate as ever, she gave her a guarded look. Was she the one who was drugging her? Sending out those disgusting letters? It had to be the same person.

'Ah, at last.' Sally beamed and hurried towards her. 'I was wondering where you'd got to. Do you fancy a quick cuppa?'

'No,' Emily said, panic hitting her as the reality of being slowly poisoned sank in. 'I've not long had one, thanks,' she added quickly, not wanting to alert Sally to the fact that she knew she was being fed drugs. She wasn't likely to catch her in the act if she did that.

'Oh, right.' Sally eyed her curiously. 'Not to worry, I didn't really want one anyway. I've been peeing all morning as it is.'

Emily eyed her curiously in turn as Sally came around to hook an arm through hers. 'I wanted to let you know I've confirmed the sixties band for Ed's birthday bash. I hope that's okay?'

'Yes, fine,' Emily said, feeling slightly derailed by her friendliness. Also relieved, she conceded, that Sally appeared to be acting perfectly normally, chatty and bubbly as always.

'Brilliant.' Sally nodded, pleased. 'I thought with it only being a week away it might be better to grab them rather than relying on Dave to DJ. Don't get me wrong, he's good – until he's on his third pint, at least – but I thought it would be nice to make things a bit special for Ed and Joyce. He does so much for the village, after all.'

Listening to her friend, who, for all her tittle-tattling, was still the caring person she'd thought she was, Emily swallowed back the lump of guilt lodged in her throat. She'd been wrong about Sally. Wrong about Jake. She'd played right into the hands of the psychopath who'd sent the email and those vile letters. It seemed almost as if they'd known she would. As if they really knew *her* and the insecurity she felt; her deep-rooted belief that no matter how many times Jake told her he loved her, he couldn't possibly. She'd lived in fear that one day he would find out her secret and realise that whatever feelings he had for her were misplaced. She still felt that fear.

Her mind went to Kara and the plaintive look in her eyes when she'd reached out to her in her dream; she was sure her sister had been trying to convey a warning. She thought of the man she'd loved in her youth, who had reciprocated with the worst kind of twisted love that became control. Even now, she could remember clearly and with a cold dread his parting words to her. 'I know you, Emily! I fucking *love* you!' he'd shouted, right there in the courtroom, his face contorted with rage as they'd tried to lead him away. 'I'll find you, I'm warning you. You belong to me!'

'So, how are you?' Sally asked, snapping her back to the present. 'I called you last night, but your phone went to voicemail.'

'Yes, sorry.' Emily drew in a breath, attempting to banish her demons from her head. 'I felt a bit off colour, so I grabbed an early night.'

'Oh no.' Turning to face her, Sally blinked at her sympathetically. 'But you're all right now?'

'Fine.' She mustered a smile. 'It's just a virus I can't seem to shake off, I think. How's things with you?'

'Well …' Blushing, Sally glanced down and back. 'I wasn't going to say anything yet, but … we're expecting a happy event.'

Emily stared at her, cold foreboding clutching her stomach.

'I'm pregnant,' Sally announced, and waited.

Emily reeled with a mixture of fear and confusion. Jake had categorically denied that the text had anything to do with him or Sally. He'd been seething with anger that she would think it did. Yet here Sally was announcing that she *was* pregnant. 'Congratulations,' she managed. 'I bet you're thrilled to bits.'

'I am.' Sally smiled excitedly. 'It wasn't planned, but now that I'm getting used to the idea, I'm over the moon. Dave is, too. Mind you, he's a big kid himself. He's probably out shopping now for Lego or footballs or something.'

'Really?' Emily's heart thrashed wildly against her chest. 'That's very decent of him … under the circumstances,' she said, and watched her friend's face slowly blanch.

'What circumstances?' Sally murmured, eyeing her warily.

Emily said nothing. Nausea swilling inside her again as she wondered whether she was horribly wrong, whether she was truly going insane or whether the lies she was being told were designed to make her think that she was, she turned and walked away.

CHAPTER THIRTY

Millie

'Just one more time,' Louis said, wearing his best winning smile as he leaned across from the driving seat to peer up at her. 'I'll have this guy off my back after that, and then no more, promise.'

Millie felt her heart drop. 'But can't you just ask him for a bit more time? You've paid him regularly, so he knows you're making an effort. And it's not like he doesn't know where you live.'

'Yeah, that's the problem, though, isn't it?' Sighing heavily, Louis leaned back and pulled one of his smokes from his shirt pocket. 'He's already given me a week's grace. He wants me to settle my debt, which I don't have a snowball in hell's chance of doing. He won't hesitate to pay me a visit if I don't give him something.'

Watching him light up, Millie wished he wouldn't smoke that stuff in the car. Opening her window, she tried not to mind. He was obviously stressed. 'Can't you just pay him a bit more each week? I could help,' she offered. She wished she could do more to help him pay it off. But she didn't have anything worth selling apart from her PC, which she needed, and the fifty pounds she had in the bank wouldn't make much of a dent in the three hundred pounds he said he still owed the man.

Louis drew smoke deep into his lungs, held it a second and then blew it out slowly. 'It's drugs money, sweetheart. I don't think he's going to be very impressed if I offer him a cut of your pocket money,' he said, a droll edge to his tone that made Millie feel about twelve years old, like some silly kid who didn't get it. She did. She wasn't naïve. She knew it was dangerous to owe people drugs money, and this was before Louis had pointed out the man he owed it to in the pub when they'd gone into Worcester one night. He'd said he was called Bear because he was built like one. He was right. A great bloody bruiser of a bloke with an ugly scorpion tattoo on his neck, he definitely looked dangerous. Louis said the scorpion represented intimidation and fear, and then told her that the last person who'd owed him money had gone missing, eventually turning up in bin bags floating in the canal. Several of them. 'They never did find his head,' he'd said, a nervous swallow sliding down his throat as he'd eyed the man with deep trepidation.

'Can't you go to the police?' she asked now, immediately realising that she actually did sound naïve, as Louis almost choked on his joint.

'Yeah, right.' He rolled unimpressed eyes in her direction. 'They'll be falling over themselves to offer me protection, won't they, when I tell them this bloke I owe a shitload of money to for drugs is threatening to part me from my balls.'

Millie's heart sank. Of course he couldn't go the police. What a dumb thing to have said. 'But you don't do hard drugs any more. They might take that into account,' she suggested, her heart dropping another inch when Louis shook his head, laughing scornfully. 'You don't, do you?' She glanced worriedly at him, wondering whether he was telling her the whole truth. 'It's just … you seem to have been paying him off for ages.'

It was the reason they hardly ever went out. She didn't mind, not really. She supposed she couldn't be seen out locally with him anyway, at least not until she'd had the dreaded conversation with her parents about their age difference. She had wondered, though, on the odd occasion, whether he might still be seeing his wife. Whatever spare cash he had left he said went to her – supposedly to help with the bills on the house until they got a buyer. She'd thought that was nice of him at first, generous and caring, but she couldn't help being a bit suspicious when she'd seen the woman leaving his flat once. Louis had said she'd popped by to drop some of his stuff off. She'd no reason to disbelieve him – he and his wife weren't living together, after all – but she couldn't help wondering. She'd smelled perfume on him, too, not hers. He'd explained it away, telling her it was some stuff he'd bought for his mother, and she'd liked it so much she'd sprayed it all over the place. Seeing how pleased he'd looked as he'd told her, she'd tried to believe him, but now a seed of doubt was niggling away at her.

'I don't, apart from the odd joint,' Louis said. 'I told you, I went on a treatment programme. I knew I had to when my old mum got sick. I have to look after her, don't I? I'm not shoving her in some old people's home, no way. She deserves better than that. It doesn't earn you brownie points where bastards like Bear are concerned, though. He'd laugh in my face if he knew, before chopping my fucking head off, that is.'

Millie felt an avalanche of conflicting emotions. He was trying so hard to stay clean, caring for his mother. She was proud of him for doing that. She was also scared for him. And terrified for herself. If someone discovered what she was doing, she would be in deep trouble.

'I just need a bit more stuff, Mils,' he said, reaching for her hand and giving it a squeeze. 'Enough to keep him happy. My ex reckons there's a buyer for the house who's a dead cert. I'll be out of the woods then and we can start to make plans. Proper plans for you and me.'

'I don't know, Louis.' Nerves clenching her tummy, Millie dropped her gaze to her lap. She wanted to make those plans more than anything, wanted desperately to move out to somewhere of her own, especially now, with the arguments at home and the prospect of her parents splitting. She wouldn't have to sneak around any more then, and they could hardly tell her she couldn't see Louis if she lived with him, but … 'What if my dad finds out?' she asked, her heart twisting at the thought of how much hurt she would cause him. 'They're bound to notice that pills are going missing soon. And they're going to realise it's someone with a set of keys. My mum will be apoplectic. And my dad … I don't think I could bear to see the disappointment in his eyes.'

'He's not going to think it's you.' Louis repeated what he'd told her the first time they'd done this. 'He'll think it's an inside job. That nurse, Sally, helping herself to medication to fund her Botox, or the receptionist – she likes her fancy clothes, doesn't she? He's never going to suspect his own daughter of stealing from him. Let's face it, sweet cup, you look like butter wouldn't melt. He probably thinks you're an angel.' He gave her a reassuring smile and chucked her under the chin. He meant it affectionately. He was always doing it, but now Millie felt about three years old.

'But he might. They only keep so much stuff in the safe. If he realises drugs are going missing, he'll have to call the police. There might be evidence, and then …' She stopped, the hard knot of panic in her stomach twisting itself tighter.

'He's not going to find out,' Louis said, his tone sharp. 'Not unless someone tells him.'

Millie's gaze swivelled back to his. His eyes were narrowed, flint-edged and hard. What did he mean? How would anyone tell him when only they knew?

Louis looked away. 'Look, just forget it,' he said, taking another agitated suck on his joint. 'I'll work it out. I'll just have to make myself scarce, leave the area or something. There's this bloke I know in Manchester who owns property to rent. He might have somewhere he can let me doss. It would have to be somewhere cheap until I can find work, but—'

'No!' Millie's heart leapt. 'Don't do that.'

'What's up?' He looked back at her, surprised. 'You can come with me. I thought that was what you wanted: me and you to get a place of our own.'

'I do, but …' Millie faltered. *Manchester?* What would she do there? She could apply for courses, she supposed, but it seemed like a million miles away. She wouldn't see her parents. For the first time, it occurred to her that she would want to. That she would miss them, even her mum, for all her banging-on.

'You don't want to give up your home comforts and move into a bedsit. I get it. Can't say I blame you.' Louis sighed dejectedly. 'I suppose you wish I was more like your perfect old man, a fully trained doctor who's so loaded he can keep your mum in any style her heart desires. She fell on her feet when she met him, didn't she?'

'No,' Millie refuted hotly. 'I love you. I don't care what you do.'

'I suppose I could always move back in with the missus,' he pondered, as she struggled with her guilt and her conscience. 'She's keen. Me, not so much, but …' He trailed off with a shrug.

Closing her eyes, Millie swallowed back her nausea. 'We'll have to be quick,' she said, fetching her bag from the footwell and delving in it for the keys she'd had copied. 'And you have to be careful not to take too much.'

'In and out.' Louis reached for his door. 'And don't worry, I only want quantities I can shift easily.'

Avoiding the CCTV camera on the high street, they were making their way down a side street to the back of the practice – Millie thanking God for the cover of dark – when it occurred to her to wonder: how did he know about Nicky? She might have mentioned Sally, but as far as she could recall, she'd never talked to him about Nicky and how fashion-conscious she was.

She couldn't help wondering about him further when, once he'd taken what he wanted from the safe, he began to mooch around behind reception, despite her imminent heart attack.

'Louis, we need to go,' she urged him, close to tears as she kept watch at the front. She was monumentally pissed off with her parents, considering how they'd gone on at her about screwing her life up and then thought nothing of screwing it up for her. If her dad ever found out about this, though, it would kill him.

'One second,' Louis said. Then, '*Shit!*' he cursed, knocking something from one of the desks. Her mum's vitamin pills, along with her pen holder, Millie realised, scurrying around to retrieve the bottle as it rolled.

'Well, well. Not that bright, is she, that little receptionist?' Louis commented from where he was now crouched down peering up at the underside of Nicky's desk, on which she'd taped her passwords.

CHAPTER THIRTY-ONE

Jake

Jake sat on the drive for a while before going in. He'd thought that he and Emily might be making the tiniest bit of headway towards getting back to some sort of normality, despite the atrocities happening around them. Now he had no idea what to think. What to say to her. He was desperate for them to talk to each other calmly, but after what he'd just found out, he was struggling to see a way forward. Drugs were going missing from the surgery. He hadn't been sure the first time he'd noticed stocks were low. He was sure now. It could only be her. It was Emily who did the stock check and the ordering of medication to be kept on the premises. Emily who kept the keys to the safe they were locked in. Emily who was taking unprescribed drugs. How the hell was he supposed to talk to her about that?

Running a hand over his neck, he glanced towards the house. He had no choice but to ask her about it. He couldn't ignore it. It wasn't just amphetamines being taken. There were painkillers and antipsychotic drugs missing too. Whatever the consequences, he was duty-bound to report it. Even stripped from their packaging, batch numbers meant the drugs could be traced back to the surgery. Aside from which, his own conscience wouldn't allow him to stay silent in the hope of establishing for certain who was stealing drugs, and why. The consequences for anyone taking non-prescription drugs might be fatal.

He tugged in a breath and pushed his car door open. He'd never imagined he could feel like this. He didn't want to go inside his own home. Worse, he felt his family would rather he didn't. Millie was clearly angry and troubled, retaliating to her world unravelling around her by challenging boundaries and possibly jeopardising her future. Ben was furious with him, as indicated by the cutting sarcasm in his voice when Jake had tried to apologise to him. Despite his best efforts, everything was spiralling out of control and he had no power to stop it. He only hoped his relationship with his children was mendable. Being caught in the middle of warring parents was soul-destroying. Jake knew all about that. As for Emily, he was scared for her. For himself. The whole village community. People's lives were being maliciously and systematically destroyed through information gathered from his surgery, the place that should be saving lives, and he had no power to stop that either.

Pushing his key into the lock, he wondered at the irony of his situation. He'd thought his father was a total fuck-up, been determined not to be seen as anything like him. It seemed now he was worse, by far. Certainly in Emily's eyes.

Meeting Ben in the hall, he tried a smile. 'Hi, how's it going?'

'Pretty shittily, as it happens.' Ben smiled flatly back.

'Right.' Jake had no idea what to say to that. 'Ben, I—'

He was about to ask him if they could go for a drink together in the hope of trying to have a proper conversation, but Ben cut him short. 'Mum's in the kitchen,' he said, nodding over his shoulder and then more or less pushing past Jake towards the stairs.

'Right.' Jake glanced warily in that direction.

'Just so you know, no earphones,' Ben added acerbically, pointing to his ears.

Understanding that his son was warning him that he would be listening for any hint of an argument, Jake buried a sigh. 'Where's Millie?' he asked.

'Out,' Ben said, sliding a derisory glance in his direction as he mounted the stairs. 'Not that she knew you were coming home early or anything.'

It hurt that his kids suddenly seemed to hate him. Jake gulped back a tight knot in his throat.

Dropping his phone and keys on the table, he steeled himself and went through to the kitchen. Emily was stuffing things into the dishwasher. She didn't acknowledge him, or even appear to notice him as he dumped his case in its usual spot.

He felt his heart go into free fall. What had happened? he wondered, feeling disorientated. Just a short time ago he would have walked over to her, massaged her shoulders when she straightened up and then kissed his way down the tempting soft curve of her neck. She would have chastised him for interrupting whatever she was doing, but she would always turn and lean into him. Now, like Ben, she seemed not to want to even make eye contact.

'Is there anything I can do to help?' he asked, though glancing around, he could see the kitchen was pristine. In her frustration, Emily had obviously been cleaning everything to within an inch of its life. Memories of his mother compulsively cleaning, of her manic behaviour in the dark days before her death assaulting him out of nowhere, Jake reeled inwardly. Standing in his own kitchen, his wife just feet away from him, his son upstairs, he felt suddenly and hopelessly alone. It was his own fault. She was paranoid, and behaving erratically because of the drugs, but he knew in his heart that it was his behaviour that had helped fuel it.

'It's all done,' she said, clanging the dishwasher door closed, sending out a signal that, regardless of the small step they'd made towards each other earlier, they were poles apart again. 'You managed to get back early then? I'm surprised,' she added, before he could answer. 'I thought after the news you received you might have cause to be out celebrating.'

Out celebrating? There was precious little to celebrate as far as Jake could see. He looked at her askance. 'What news?'

'You know, the text you received,' Emily answered, glancing at him with a short smile. 'Sally told me herself earlier. I imagine you're both ecstatic, though I can't imagine Dave will be. I take it you'll be moving out?'

What the …? Jake almost dropped through the floor. She was talking about Sally's news that she was pregnant? Imagining the baby was his because of some text that had quite obviously been sent by someone aiming to cause trouble?

'Jesus Christ, Emily, can you hear yourself?' He'd spent the time after the police had gone looking at discreet treatment programmes for her. He *cared* about her. How the hell was he supposed to convince her of it?

'I was reasonably civil to Sally, you'll be pleased to know. I even congratulated her, although I did feel like killing her, obviously,' Emily went on, busying herself wiping work surfaces that were perfectly clean and completely oblivious to the implication of what she'd just said.

'For Christ's sake! It's nothing to do with me!' he yelled, making her start. 'That text was sent as part of the cruel, manipulative communications that are destroying so many people's lives, can you not see that?'

'All of which are based on information that's true,' Emily pointed out.

Jake nodded, watching her carefully.

'Like the email,' she added, looking him over scornfully.

Jake felt his temper dangerously close to the surface. 'What fucking email?' he challenged her. 'The one you deleted? The one sent by … who? Sally? Natasha?'

'Don't make me say it, Jake.' Emily dropped her gaze. 'This is humiliating enough without you—'

'Did you get it into your head I was having an affair with Zoe
Miller and Jennifer Wheeler as well?' His jaw tight with anger,
he ignored her. 'Is that why Zoe ended up plummeting from her
balcony and Jennifer had her stomach pumped?' He'd told himself
it couldn't be her sending the letters; that he knew her. But now,
with the discovery that drugs were being taken from the surgery,
he was beginning to think he didn't know her at all.

Emily paled visibly. 'That's a wicked thing to say, Jake,' she
said shakily. 'I don't know what you're trying to do to me, but it
won't work.'

Jake studied her. There was no point even trying to answer
that. 'There are drugs missing from the safe,' he said bluntly. He
couldn't do this, skirt around it. He didn't know what the hell
was going on, but he clearly couldn't contemplate doing nothing.
'Did you take them?'

Emily baulked. 'You really are serious, aren't you?' Searching
his face, she laughed bewilderedly. 'Is this part of the plan too?
This evil game you're playing to … what? Drive me away? Drive
me mad, so that everyone says, *Oh dear, poor Jake, having to put
up with his deranged wife. It's no wonder he had an affair?*'

Jake pressed a hand to his forehead. He felt like weeping. 'This
is ridiculous, Emily,' he said throatily. 'You're wrong about Sally.
She's—'

'I think you should go,' Emily stopped him angrily.

She was looking at him now with something close to hatred,
he noticed, feeling sick to his soul. 'I'm not going anywhere,
Emily,' he said quietly. 'Do you honestly think I would leave my
children to this?'

CHAPTER THIRTY-TWO

Emily

Hearing no sound from Millie's room, Emily pressed the handle down and inched the door open, then breathed out a sigh of relief when, clearly disgruntled at being disturbed, Millie burrowed further under her duvet.

'You'll be late,' Emily warned her.

'I have a free period,' Millie mumbled and dug herself further in.

Emily didn't think she did have a free period, but she decided not to push it. On top of the devastating argument she'd had with Jake, she couldn't face another one with her daughter. She would have to try to have another talk with her. Apologise for seeming to not trust her. Jake was right: she would have to allow her to make her own mistakes. She couldn't wrap her up in cotton wool. Millie was feisty, strong-headed – a teenager with her own views and her own life to lead. All Emily could do was pray she would stay safe and be happy. That was all she wanted for her.

Closing the door quietly, she went downstairs in search of Ben, worrying about him as she always did. He'd clearly overheard the row she and Jake had had, judging by his sullen expression when she'd passed him on the landing last night, and his reluctance to say very much other than that he was tired and going to bed.

Seeing him heading for the front door as she reached the hall, she hurried down the last few steps. 'Ben?'

He stopped and turned back.

'Are you all right?' she asked, knowing he wasn't.

Ben nodded. 'Is it true?' His eyes flicked angrily to hers. 'Is Dad having an affair with Sally?'

Emily hesitated. 'I don't know, Ben, not for sure,' she answered cautiously, and then decided it was better he knew. At least some of it. He would find out eventually, just as she had. And then he might possibly be angry with her for not being honest with him. 'They're obviously close. They did have a relationship, a while back apparently, before we were married.'

Ben considered. 'Right,' he said at length, 'so they just had a shag for old times' sake then?' His tone was one of loathing, his eyes furious as he spun around to yank the front door open.

Emily went after him as he stalked out. 'Ben, wait. Don't go off upset.'

'I'm not,' he retorted without looking back. 'Just do me a favour and tell him I don't want anything to do with him, yeah?'

Emily stopped, her heart sinking as she watched him stride away, and then dropping like a stone to the pit of her stomach when Fran rounded the gates. She'd forgotten it was her day to come in and clean.

'He's got one on him, hasn't he?' Fran observed, a disapproving look on her face as she nodded after Ben.

'He's fine,' Emily lied, her voiced strained. 'He's just deep in thought about his next project.'

'Still, he could have said hello,' Fran couldn't resist adding.

Gritting her teeth, Emily tried to ignore her.

'You're late going in again, aren't you?' Fran observed as she followed her towards the house.

She'd obviously noticed that Emily was still in her pyjamas. Her red-rimmed eyes, too; the eagle-eyed cow couldn't have failed to notice those. Cautioning herself not to lose it and tell her where to stuff her observations, Emily turned back to her. 'Actually, Fran,

I went a bit mad cleaning yesterday. I don't really think there's that much to do.'

'Oh.' Fran furrowed her brow. 'You're not dissatisfied with my services, I hope,' she said, looking put out.

'No, Fran.' Emily gave her a short smile. 'It's just that it seems a bit pointless, so you might as well take some time off. I'll still pay you, of course.'

Fran nodded, placated somewhat, but she had a cagey look in her eye. 'As long as you don't have any complaints,' she said. 'You have made one or two comments at the surgery in the past – in front of other people, I might add – which I found quite hurtful.'

Yes, because you were doing more gossiping than working. Emily felt bad, nevertheless. 'I'm sorry, Fran,' she said. 'It was wrong of me to reprimand you in public. It won't happen again.'

Fran nodded once more, a pious look now on her face as she accepted the apology. 'I do take pride in my work, you know,' she said. 'I consider it crucial to the running of the surgery, even if other people do look down their noses at it. Germs breed germs, after all.'

'It is,' Emily agreed. The woman might as well be quoting her. She'd always told Fran she was part of the team, that her job was as important to patient safety as theirs was. If only she would spend more time actually doing it, Emily would never have cause to have words with her.

'It's not been easy, you know, doing two jobs while bringing a child up on my own,' Fran went on. Emily really wished she wouldn't. She was feeling extremely nauseous, despite not letting a morsel past her lips she hadn't prepared for herself.

'Some of us don't have … well, let's just say the *privileges* in life others have.'

Emily's jaw dropped. Fran was judging her when she couldn't possibly know anything about her life. It was quite unbelievable. She was having a conversation on the drive in her pyjamas about her cleaner's injured pride while her world was crumbling beneath her.

'I'm not looking down my nose, Fran. I appreciate what you do,' she assured her with forced patience. 'I just don't need you this morning. I'll pay you, obviously, as I said. Now, I'd better get on. As you pointed out, I'm running a bit late.'

Drawing in a deep breath, she waited, wondering whether it might occur to Fran that she might have her own problems to deal with.

'Well, as long as you're sure. I don't want rumours going around that I don't do my job properly.'

'No,' Emily said weakly. She wasn't sure whether to laugh or cry.

'As it happens, I could do with going into the surgery at lunchtime rather than this evening.' Fran checked her watch, and then looked Emily over pointedly. 'I was hoping to catch Tom and have a quick word with him about something.'

Yes, and if Tom's worried looks and tendency to walk in the other direction every time he noticed Fran heading in his were anything to go by, he wouldn't want to be caught.

'Righto. See you later.' Emily twirled back towards the house before she was tempted to remind Fran that her contract actually stipulated times and hours to be worked. She'd contemplated not going in today. Since Jake had levelled such serious accusations at her, she didn't think there was any point. But then, in meekly bowing out of his life, she would be smoothing the way for Sally, wouldn't she? She had no intention of doing that. Sally had never seen her as anything but amenable. It was time she knew there was another side to her. A side that, if pushed, could be just as viciously calculating as Sally was herself.

Fran was already in, flicking her mop around reception, when Emily finally arrived, having tried to make herself presentable. She hadn't bothered trying to emulate Sally's perfectly made-up, flirtily sexy look, ditching the leggings and boots in favour of a smart slip dress that was reasonably figure-hugging. Her make-up was minimal in keeping with her desire to appear professional. Jake probably thought she would be too embarrassed to show her face. But he was wrong. She'd worked side by side with him for years, helping him build up this practice. This was her job. If he wanted her to leave, he would have to sack her.

Sailing through the reception area to her desk, she gave Fran a nod and then smiled brightly at Nicky. 'Afternoon,' she said.

'Afternoon.' Nicky looked at her uncertainly. 'Are you feeling better?'

'Much,' Emily assured her, parking her bag under her desk, and turning to slide out of her jacket.

'Ooh, I like the dress,' Nicky said, sounding like her usual self, to Emily's relief. She'd imagined that the gossip would be rife. 'Very smart. Love the colour.'

'Thanks, Nicky.' Emily appreciated it. She knew powder blue suited her, enhancing her eyes, which were probably her best feature. She felt a deep pang of sadness as she recalled how Jake had once said how much he loved them. There'd been nothing but seething anger in his own eyes the last time he'd looked at her.

'Definitely an improvement on the pyjamas,' Fran commented, her ears pricking up. 'I don't know how you managed to get dressed and get here so quickly.'

'With practice,' Emily said, very aware that Fran was desperate to advertise that she'd been in a state of undress on her drive not so long ago. She thanked God it was lunchtime and there were no patients waiting in reception. The colour of her pyjamas would be common knowledge by teatime.

'Have you heard the latest?' Nicky lowered her voice as Emily sat down at her PC, about to pull up the drug orders.

Emily braced herself. 'No,' she said, her eyes on her screen.

Nicky waited a second, watching Fran as she disappeared towards Tom's office. Then: 'They didn't find anything,' she whispered. 'The police. They haven't checked Tom's printer yet, but they haven't been able to match up any of the other printers.'

Emily felt a huge surge of relief run through her. She'd thought Nicky was about to say something about the medication Jake claimed had gone missing. He clearly hadn't mentioned it to anyone else. But why wouldn't he have? Her relief was short-lived as she considered that it was probably because he had made up his mind that she was responsible and wasn't sure what to do about it.

'They haven't been able to get any forensics either,' Nicky went on with a sigh. 'No fingerprints on the letters or envelopes, no handy CCTV footage of anyone posting letters though doors. I heard them talking to Jake. He's obviously worried sick, isn't he? He's been walking around with a permanent frown …' She trailed off as Jake himself appeared, frowning pensively, as Nicky had said, his complexion pale and looking so exhausted that, even with what was happening between them and the awful things he'd said to her, Emily felt for him.

Coming around the desk, he smiled at her. A short smile that didn't reach his eyes. He looked distracted, uncomfortable. Emily willed back the tears that stung her eyes. She couldn't function if she was permanently crying. She wasn't sure she would ever function properly again. 'Okay?' he asked her, his expression a combination of sadness and regret.

He could never feel as awful as she did. She felt as if he were slowly ripping her heart from inside her. 'Yes, thanks,' she said, arranging her face into a smile.

He nodded and plunged his hands in his pockets. 'I had a call from Sally,' he said awkwardly. 'She's going to be off for a while.'

'Oh no.' Nicky looked up at him worriedly. 'Is she poorly?'

Emily glanced down. Knowing why Sally was off, and learning that she'd communicated directly with Jake rather than just ringing in sick, she felt almost bereft. 'I'm just off to make tea,' she said, swallowing back her tears as she heaved herself to her feet. 'Anyone want one?'

'No,' she heard Nicky say behind her. 'Thanks, I've just had one.'

Tom's door was open as she passed it, Fran's tones drifting from inside his office. Emily didn't need to guess what the topic of conversation was. '… She's usually so efficient, as well, always here on the dot up until recently.' She heard the tail end of Fran's remark and guessed she was filling Tom in on the terrible pyjama crime. 'Are they going through a bit of a rough patch?'

Tom had obviously picked up on the prying edge to her tone. 'I've no idea, Fran. It's really none of our business, is it?' he replied curtly, to his credit.

Fran was silent for a minute, astoundingly. Then: 'There's no need to be quite so sharp, Tom,' she said, evidently put out. 'I was only enquiring.'

'Yes, so I gathered.' Tom sighed knowingly. 'I don't have the inclination or the time to chat about other people's problems, though. I have patients due.'

'I see,' Fran answered, after another pause. 'You never do have time to chat, do you, Tom? Considering how close we once were, I find that quite hurtful.'

Close? Fran and Tom had had a relationship? Emily's eyes widened with surprise. It seemed they might well have done. Was that what her comment about privileges had been about? Edward was obviously right. The woman was jealous. Of *her*. She had everything, after all, didn't she? A well-paid job. A marriage to a handsome doctor who in everyone else's eyes was a good man, caring, faithful. She was living the luxurious life Fran had imagined for herself. Emily was almost tempted to put her right.

CHAPTER THIRTY-THREE

Jake

Reading over the text he'd typed, Jake hesitated before sending it. Telling Emily he was spending the night at the surgery would only make the situation between them worse. Could it get any worse, though? he wondered despairingly. Doubtless she wouldn't believe he was here anyway, probably imagining he was off with another woman. However, he'd found out today that the CCTV at the back of the office had been tampered with, indicating that someone was possibly entering the premises at night, so he didn't have any other choice but to watch and wait and hope he would catch them in the act. There was no sign of a forced entry, so whoever it was had a set of keys. It clearly wasn't Emily taking medication from the safe, he now realised, once again bitterly regretting having accused her. If she'd wanted to do that, she had many opportunities when she was here on her own. She would have no reason to sneak in out of hours. She'd been forgetful, unable to concentrate even before the trouble between them – Jake's gut twisted as he reminded himself that that might have something to do with the drugs she'd been ingesting. It was feasible therefore that someone had taken her keys and copied them without her knowing.

Sighing, he hit send, guessing she wouldn't reply. He'd texted her earlier asking how she was. She hadn't responded. He wished she would talk to him, if only in a professional capacity. Now that they'd eliminated all conceivable sources of the drug, disposing of any vitamins she'd been taking at home and at the surgery, writing out a new prescription for her iron tablets, and making sure she only swallowed food and drink she'd prepared for herself, she would be going through withdrawal symptoms: aches and pains, mood swings, poor sleep, feeling that people were out to get her – him, mainly – even hallucinations. She would be terrified dealing with that on her own, which was all thanks to him.

Taking her aside after delivering her blood sample, he'd asked her if she wanted any medication to help ease the symptoms of coming off amphetamines. She'd refused – she couldn't trust her GP, after all, could she? Christ, he wished he'd handled things better, taken a step back and looked at things less emotively. He'd said she was being paranoid. She was. It was obvious why now, but his reaction hadn't helped. He'd immediately been defensive, which could only have fuelled her fears, and he'd made some brutal accusations. He was losing her. Because of his own inexcusable behaviour, his world was disintegrating. He would lose his kids too, the only family he'd felt he'd ever had. His gut wrenched as he felt it again, the loneliness that had been his constant companion until he'd met Emily, the woman he'd felt safe opening up to, the woman he loved. He always had. There didn't seem any way to convince her of that now. She was deeply suspicious of him. He couldn't escape the fact that she was right to be.

Checking his phone in the hope of a reply and finding none, he sighed in despair and toyed with the idea of ringing Ben and asking him to check on her; then decided against it. His son wasn't busting a gut to speak to him either. He'd rejected his two previous calls, making his point succinctly. Jake didn't blame him. He was very aware of the bewilderment and anger Ben would be feeling, the impotency of watching his parents' marriage disintegrate and knowing there was nothing he could do to stop it.

Not sure whether Millie would be keen to talk to him either, he debated for a second, then braced himself and called her. He was surprised when she answered. 'Hey,' he said uncertainly. 'How's things?'

'Not great,' Millie replied bluntly. 'Not likely to be, really, are they?'

Jake's heart dropped. What else had he expected her to say? 'Not out with the boyfriend tonight then?' he asked, careful to keep any hint of disapproval from his voice. He had no idea who it was she was seeing, and despite telling Emily she was overreacting, that she should allow Millie to make her own mistakes, he'd been quietly worrying. Emily had said he was older. Jake had begun to wonder how much older. And how long Millie had been seeing him. If it was serious, it had occurred to him also to wonder why they knew nothing about him. DS Regan obviously hadn't contacted her yet. Jake was pretty sure Millie would have shared that information if she had.

'No. Did you want to speak to Mum?' She cut the subject dead, sending a ripple of apprehension down his spine. 'She's lying down so her phone's probably off. I could go and get her if you like.'

'No, don't disturb her. She's still struggling with this viral infection,' Jake lied, for Emily's sake. He doubted she would want the kids to know about the amphetamines. 'Could you give her a message for me? I texted her but she might not have seen it.'

'Shoot,' Millie said.

'Could you tell her that in light of the possible break-ins here, I'm spending the night at the surgery?'

Millie went quiet. 'Break-ins?' she repeated curiously after a second.

'Looks like it.' Jake sighed tiredly. 'The CCTV out back was smashed. The security firm have supplied an urgent replacement, but—'

'When?' Millie cut in. 'I mean, when were you broken into?'

'A couple of nights back. Other occasions before then. I'm not sure—'

'What did they take?' Again Millie interrupted him.

'Drugs.' Jake guessed it wouldn't hurt to tell her. 'Why else break into a doctor's surgery?'

'Shit,' Millie responded after a second, sounding shocked. 'Are you going to the police?'

'Not yet,' Jake said. He couldn't tell her why he wasn't; that he wanted to be sure he wasn't implicating her mother. There was no way Emily would be up to answering questions from the police right now, and there were bound to be some. 'I'll have to eventually, but I'm hoping the new camera will pick something up.'

'Is there no chance of retrieving anything from the old one?' Millie asked.

'I'm not sure. The security firm's taking a look. They're getting back to me, but I'm not holding my breath. I thought maybe I'd get lucky if I stayed on the premises.'

'Right.' Millie now sounded uncertain. 'You'll be careful, though?'

'I will,' he assured her. 'Don't worry. I'll get straight on to the police if anything happens.'

'Okay,' Millie replied hesitantly. 'Sorry, Dad, I have to go. I have another call.'

The boyfriend, Jake guessed. 'Talk soon,' he said softly. 'Watch what you're doing, Mils. You know I …' He realised she'd already gone. More pressing things to attend to, obviously. He only hoped she knew how much he cared about her. That he would give anything to undo all of this, if only he knew how to.

Deliberating for a second, he took a breath and then called Sally. She'd been worried about Emily's reaction to her news. Upset that she'd walked away, apparently refusing to say another word. He wasn't sure what reception he would get, given the situation, but he wanted to at least check on her.

'Hi,' he said, relieved when she picked up. 'I just wondered how you were doing?'

'Okay, considering …' Sally answered. Jake gathered from her evasive tone that she was reluctant to discuss things further. 'How's Emily?'

'I'm not sure,' he told her honestly. 'I'm still at the surgery.'

Sally didn't reply for a second, then, 'We should have told her about us, Jake,' she said.

CHAPTER THIRTY-FOUR

The night of the party

Leaving him to ponder the consequences of what he'd done, she strode away from his car with as much dignity as she could manage, which wasn't a lot. She heard him trying to start it behind her, futilely. No doubt he would be pissed off about that. Good. He'd treated her like some cheap tart, stringing her along. Choking back a sob, she trudged through the sludge, the monsoon-like rain plastering her hair to her head and soaking through her biker jacket right down to her bones. She'd given him everything, risked everything for him. She'd thought he felt the same – he'd said sex with her was the most mind-blowing he'd ever had in his life. He'd obviously been lying about that as well. She should have thought to tell him it hadn't been that great for her. That might have hit him where it hurt. God, she'd been such an *idiot*.

He'd said he loved her. Gulping back her hurt and humiliation, she pushed on, tears stinging her eyes and careless of her expensive leather boots, which would undoubtedly be ruined. Sensing his interest might be waning, she'd worn them with her new faux-leather skirt to get his attention. He hadn't complimented her as he usually would, his eyes on her thighs and sex on his mind. He'd hardly even glanced at her.

He'd said he was riddled with guilt, feeling bad about using her when he couldn't be fully committed. Such a liar. He didn't care about anyone. *Bastard.* And now, no doubt, he would be looking for some other naïve young thing to reel in with his flattery, his easy smile and twinkly blue eyes. Lying eyes. She'd thought she'd seen his love for her there; warmth and affection, which she'd badly needed. She'd been wrong. They were as cold as ice.

A chill running through her, she wrapped her arms about herself, tucked her hands under her armpits and hurried on. After a moment, she stopped, sure she could hear footsteps behind her. His, obviously. He was clearly struggling with his conscience. Well, he knew what he could do, didn't he? Huffing out a steamy breath, she quickened her pace, then faltered, again, certain she'd heard branches snapping in the woodland beside her. Animals, probably, she tried to reassure herself. Foraging nightlife. *Shit.* What kind of nightlife?

Her bladder full to bursting suddenly, she tightened her arms around herself and took another few steps. Then she stopped again, swallowing back her racing heart as something screamed in the woods, loud and shrill, like a banshee. Standing stock still, she listened. Hearing nothing now but the sound of the rain plopping through the leaves, she laughed in despair at herself. It was obviously a fox. What *had* she been thinking, climbing out of his car in an area she knew to be one of the remotest places possible? The alternative, though, would have been to stay in the car with him. She would rather drown. Steeling her resolve, she forged determinedly onwards.

A short while later, she hesitated again, positive now that she could hear footfalls echoing her own. There *was* someone there, she was sure of it. Her antennae on red alert, she dared a glance over her shoulder. Seeing nothing but the dark shadows of overhanging branches, she took another few tentative steps. Her stomach lurched violently as another sound reached her – not the roar of an animal this time, but the rev of an engine, growling full throttle.

Shit. Her heart thrashing, she surged forward, the soles of her boots slipping and sliding beneath her. She heard the impact, dull, sickening. Felt white-hot pain jarring every bone in her body as she was tossed in the air to land heavily on the unforgiving tarmac. Seconds later, her heartbeat slowed, a slow pulse at the base of her neck, as a warm breath brushed her cheek. 'Sorry, but I couldn't let you tell,' whispered a voice tinged with regret.

Swallowing back the salty, metallic taste in her mouth, she was vaguely aware of who it was. Strangely, she didn't feel pain any more, didn't feel anything other than that the lifeblood that flowered slowly beneath her was pleasantly warm. Blinking away the droplets of rain that ran like saltless tears down her cheeks, she stared up at the tiny pinpricks of light that held a promise of another life.

He'd never loved her, she realised as the ink blue of the sky faded to a blanket of black. He'd never intended to be with her.

CHAPTER THIRTY-FIVE

Emily

As Emily came away from the makeshift bar in the village hall, Joyce hurried across to her and caught hold of her hands. 'Thank you,' she said, nodding across to Edward, who was doing his thing on the dance floor, along with several of their neighbours, to the Liverpool Lads' version of 'Twist and Shout'. 'You've done him proud. The band is tip-top. You'd almost swear it was the Fab Four themselves.'

Emily smiled, pleased that Joyce and Edward were happy, though she herself was struggling to relax. She was aware that part of this might be due to withdrawal symptoms. She'd gone from feeling flat this morning, lacking in energy, to feeling jumpy and anxious. Not least because Jake was here. She hadn't been sure he would come, having spent several nights in the surgery, bar one, when he'd slept in the spare room, at her suggestion. She'd said it was because her sleep patterns were worse than ever. She hadn't told him the other reason: that if he received a call-out in the middle of the night, her suspicion would have gone into overdrive, inciting more arguments between them. She didn't think she could bear that.

She looked across now to where he stood with one of his patients, who was no doubt trying to pick his brains about some illness or other. Jake was listening attentively, nodding politely, still as handsome as ever in a simple white polo shirt and jeans. Still the man she'd fallen in love with – on the outside, anyway. Her heart, which had been sinking steadily since discovering the email, settled like a cold stone in her chest as she acknowledged that she'd obviously never really known him as well as she'd thought she had. Was it poetic justice, she wondered; her just deserts for keeping secrets from him?

Joyce was still talking, she realised; she hoped the woman hadn't noticed that her mind had drifted off. 'They even look like them,' she was saying, her gaze on the band.

Emily resisted pointing out that the mop-top wigs and collarless grey suits possibly helped. 'Sally organised them,' she said, leaning close to Joyce's ear. She couldn't take credit where it wasn't due. They wouldn't have had a band if not for Sally. Tears welling up out of nowhere, Emily bit them back. She missed her. She'd lost her two best friends overnight, it seemed.

'Oh, well I must go and thank her too,' Joyce said, glancing around. 'Is she not here yet?'

Emily shook her head. 'She's been a bit poorly.' She actually had no idea how Sally was. She hadn't heard a word from her. And she could hardly ring her or ask Jake.

'I'd better go and rein in my husband before he does himself an injury.' Joyce rolled her eyes tolerantly. 'You might want to rescue yours too, before he dies of boredom.' She indicated Jake, who was doing his best to look interested as his patient pointed out various parts of his anatomy, obviously listing his aches and pains.

Nodding weakly, Emily watched Joyce head for the dance floor, a little twist of her hips in evidence as she did. Emily smiled. At least she'd managed something successfully, even if she had failed at everything else in her life. She was feeling sorry for herself but couldn't help it. She also felt like a spare part at a wedding, standing on her own. She glanced around, wondering who she could talk to; someone who wouldn't look at her with suspicion, trying to work out if she was vicious enough to send out the poison pen letters that had been circulating. Apart from Sally and the couples whose lives had been torn apart by the letters, most of the villagers were here. Some were searching for a sense of solidarity, which had been Emily's aim once it was growing obvious the village community was becoming fractured. Some of them possibly wanted to catch up on the latest gossip. Fran was here, her eyes seeming to be attached to Tom on strings as they followed his every move. She was drinking a lot. Emily noted her going to the bar for the third time since she'd arrived. The woman's expression was peeved as she all but glared at Tom, who was deep in conversation with the barmaid from the pub. Emily now knew why Fran might be disenchanted with him, and almost felt sorry for her. Unrequited love was painful. She couldn't imagine a time when the love she still had for Jake despite everything wouldn't cause her to hurt unbearably.

Could she risk a small glass of wine herself? she wondered, glancing after Fran and meeting Jake's gaze as she did. He nodded and smiled uncertainly. Emily managed a small smile back, watching as he attempted to extricate himself from his patient, who was now rolling up his trouser leg, clearly about to show Jake his painful bits. Jake's expression was one of bemusement as he glanced down at the pale limb the man offered him. Emily might have laughed but for the constriction in her throat.

Minutes later, as the band went off for their break, he walked towards her. 'Hi,' he said apprehensively.

'Evening,' Emily replied, saddened by the obvious awkwardness between them.

'Okay?' he asked her softly, his expression concerned as he searched her face. She looked into his blue eyes, the brown and green flecks making them a myriad of ocean colours: light and sparkling when he was happy, darker when he was troubled, as Emily could see he was now. Hidden depths, she thought distractedly.

Nodding, she glanced down. 'Coping,' she said. 'You?'

'Reasonable,' he answered, kneading his neck, a sure sign he was stressed. She would have helped him free the knot in it once, just a short time ago. How had they suddenly become strangers, standing here in front of each other on opposite sides of some invisible fence?

'Is Millie not with you?' he asked.

Emily shook her head. 'She's at Anna's. I don't think this is her thing.'

'As in actually at Anna's?' Jake's eyes were definitely a shade darker. He was finally admitting she wasn't wrong about that at least then; that they might have cause to be worried about their daughter.

'I dropped her off there earlier. I've given her money for a taxi home,' Emily assured him. This wasn't the place to go into family business.

Jake nodded, clearly relieved.

'Did Ben get off all right?' she asked, knowing that their son had been reluctant to ask his father for the use of his car. His was off the road, but as she'd had to use her car today to pick up Edward and Joyce and bring them to the village hall, he had realised he didn't have much choice. He'd had to visibly to steel himself to talk to Jake on the phone. Emily had been immensely relieved that he had, and that Jake had agreed he could take his car. Ben was going to a party. He had a date, he'd told her. Emily's relief had been immense. She prayed it would lead to something; that Ben might have found himself a girl his own age and would forget all about his crush on Natasha.

'He did.' Jake's mouth curved into a small smile. 'I'm glad he asked. At least I was able to do one small thing other than mess up his life. Yours too.'

Emily widened her eyes in surprise. Was he finally going to admit that what was happening between them wasn't all in her mind?

'DS Regan called this morning,' Jake went on, his expression wary. 'They found the email. On the company server.'

She stared at him in disbelief for a second, then closed her eyes. 'Not a product of my fevered imagination then?'

'No.' He drew in a breath. 'I owe you an apology, Emily. I doubted you. I shouldn't have. I'm sorry.'

Swallowing, she nodded slowly. It was something. It couldn't take back all he'd said, but at least he wasn't looking at her as if he didn't know who she was. 'Did they manage to trace the email address?'

He shook his head. 'They're working on it.'

Nodding, Emily paused, checking that they weren't being overheard, then lowered her voice. 'The letters … did they mention whether they'd made any headway?' Nicky had told her they hadn't been able to find any forensic evidence, but she'd hoped …

'Nothing,' Jake said, sighing heavily. 'Whoever sent them was obviously wearing gloves, making sure to—' He stopped, emitting a weary sigh as his father joined them.

'Well done, Emily. You've done an amazing job with the hall,' Tom said, indicating the bunting and birthday balloons Emily had roped the landlord of the pub into helping her string up. 'Ed and Joyce are tickled pink. It was a lovely thing to …' He trailed off as Nicky hurried towards them – with a young man in tow, Emily noted.

'I took your advice, Tom.' She stretched to plant a kiss on Tom's cheek, to Emily and Jake's surprise. 'Meet Drew, my new boyfriend.'

Tom turned to the young man. 'Nice to meet you, Drew,' he said, looking him over critically as he shook his hand. 'I hope he knows you have high standards, Nicky?'

'I do.' Drew smiled, as Tom arched an enquiring eyebrow at him. 'I think I'm actually on trial at the moment.'

'Good.' Tom nodded approvingly. 'Make sure you treat her with respect.'

'He will,' Nicky assured him. 'I've told him he'll have you to answer to if he doesn't. Back in a second, Emily. We're just off to get a drink.' Beaming them all a smile, and looking very pleased with herself, she dragged Drew towards the bar, while Emily and Jake exchanged glances.

Tom clearly noticed. 'She'd been stood up – at the pub in Pembridge where I happened to be with some of the members of the medical committee,' he explained. 'I couldn't help but notice her sitting on her own looking upset. Obviously I made my excuses to my colleagues and went over to her. We had a long chat.' He paused, now looking pointedly at Jake. 'The man in question texted her as we were talking, gave her some lame excuse about having to give a mate a lift somewhere. I told her to dump him. It seems she—'

He was cut short by Nicky, who reappeared to grab hold of his hand. 'They're playing "Love Me Do",' she said enthusiastically, as the band, back from their break, struck up again. 'Drew has a rugby injury, so I'm in need of a man.'

'Another one?' Tom chuckled, allowing himself to be tugged towards the dance floor while Emily and Jake looked on, bemused.

'Jesus.' Jake did a double-take as Tom got into his stride with a slow jive. 'Looks like I might owe him an apology too,' he said, looking awkwardly back at Emily.

'It certainly seems so,' Emily agreed, her gaze travelling from the dancing couple to Fran, who was coming back from the loo. She looked unsteady on her feet and was now glaring daggers at Tom, Emily noticed, with some trepidation. She hoped she wasn't going to cause a scene and spoil the party for Ed.

Oh no. Her heart sank as Fran stumbled towards the dance floor, reached out a hand to steady herself and knocked a drink from a table. All credit to them, the band didn't miss a beat as the glass smashed noisily, sending slivers of glass shooting across the wooden floor.

Emily watched nervously as Phil, who ran the farm shop, stood up to try and help. Fran shrugged him off, her eyes narrowed to slits and plainly fuming as she took another precarious step.

'You bastard!' she shouted suddenly, causing Emily's heart to flip in her chest. 'You just can't resist, can you?' she snarled, as the band twanged to a discordant stop. 'Chatting up every little slut in a skirt, making a bloody fool of yourself.'

Jake stepped towards her, taking hold of her arm. 'Come on, Fran,' he said, sympathetically but firmly. 'You're obviously upset. You've had too much to—'

Fran yanked her arm away. 'Don't you tell *me* what to do,' she seethed, turning on him. 'You might employ me, but what I do in my own time is *my* business. You're no better than *her*,' she flailed a hand in Emily's direction, 'looking down your nose, thinking you're better than me.'

'Fran, you need to stop this.' His face visibly paling, Jake moved back towards her, trying to reason with her. Edward and Joyce joined him after a second, and all three of them attempted to steer her gently towards a chair.

'Don't you touch me!' Again Fran pulled away, dragging derisory eyes over Jake. 'You're no better than him either. Peas in a pod, the pair of you.' Her lip curling in contempt, she looked from him to Tom. 'Impressing deluded, gullible women with your good looks and your charming smile. Imagining everyone's blind to what you're up to, including your own wife!'

'Jesus.' Massaging his forehead agitatedly, Jake backed away.

'Did you know he's having an affair with someone young enough to be his *daughter*?' Fran went on bitterly, her eyes swivelling again from Jake to Tom, causing Emily's heart to jolt. Who was she talking about?

'Ask him,' Fran growled over the stunned silence. 'Go on, *ask* him. I'm only surprised he hasn't tried to chat up his own—'

'Come on, lovely.' Edward wrapped an arm around her shoulders. 'I think you might have had a drop too much of the old sauce. Come and have a little sit down,' he suggested kindly. 'Less said, soonest mended, hey?'

'Don't you bloody well start with your do-gooding, pillar-of-the-community bullshit,' Fran seethed, pulling away from him too.

'Oh dear.' Eyeing Jake in quiet despair, Edward shook his head.

'You're nothing of the sort, are you, Ed?' Fran went on. 'You're just the same as them, pulling the wool over people's eyes, hiding who you really are behind that amiable smile of yours.'

'That's enough, Fran.' Finding his voice, Tom stepped angrily towards her.

'He's a thief!' Fran exploded. 'A thief and a liar!' she went on, spitting venom as Tom caught hold of her arms. 'Collecting the football club fees, taking people's money at events he's organised *supposedly* to plough back into the community. Lies, all of it! Half of it goes into your pocket, doesn't it, *Ed?*'

Edward said nothing, as she eyeballed him accusingly. The colour draining from his ruddy cheeks, he simply looked at her for a second, and then dropped his gaze and turned away. The silence was so profound you could hear a pin drop as, avoiding the astonished gaze of his neighbours, he walked silently towards the door.

Trembling, Emily looked disbelievingly towards Fran. It was her. *She'd* been doing this. Destroying people. Driving them to the edge of despair, with no thought or feeling for the devastating consequences. Her heart banging as the whispers began to ripple around her, she looked towards where Edward had disappeared through the exit door, and then went after him.

CHAPTER THIRTY-SIX

Frantically Emily scoured the road back into the centre of the village. She breathed out a huge sigh of relief when she spotted Edward sitting on the bench overlooking the river. His hands resting on his knees, his shoulders slumped, he was gazing out over the water; seeing nothing but his world crashing around him, she imagined, supposing any of what Fran had said was true. Judging by his reaction, she had an awful feeling it might be.

Careful not to startle him, she made her way down the path and sat down beside him.

'First you take a drink, then the drink takes you,' he said quietly after a moment. 'It obviously loosened her tongue. She would never have said the things she did otherwise.'

Emily wasn't so sure about that. Fran might have spat out her accusations in a drunken rage – she'd clearly had much more to drink than the three glasses of wine she'd had at the party – but the woman's tongue worked perfectly well with or without alcohol.

Thinking it better not to voice her opinion, she watched Edward carefully as he fell silent again. She wanted to reach for his hand, to reassure him in some way, but guessing from his long intake of breath that he was trying to hold himself together, she waited instead, allowing him the space he might need.

'She was talking about Tom, by the way, not Jake, you do realise that?' He glanced at her briefly. 'I can't abide gossip, as I think you

know, but since Fran has opened that particular can of worms …
Her daughter, Leah. If you look, you can see the likeness. I don't
think Tom ever has.'

Leah? Emily stared at him in a combination of bewilderment
and disbelief. Fran's daughter was Tom's? And she'd never told
him? *Why?*

'She was married at the time,' Edward explained intuitively.
'Definitely a case of throwing stones in glass houses, I'd say. It's not
common knowledge, incidentally. She confided in me once – had
a drop too much to drink then, too, I suspect – so …'

He was asking her not to say anything. But didn't Tom have a
right to know? Didn't Jake?

'I expect you're wondering if what she said about me has any
truth in it?' Edward asked, taking another long breath. 'It shames
me to say it, but I'm afraid it does.'

Oh God, no. Emily's stomach dropped.

'I believe Fran overheard me on the phone to my mortgage
provider. She cleans the building I worked in, as bad luck would
have it,' he continued. 'I wasn't sure how much she'd heard.
Enough, obviously. I think she's had eyes on me ever since. Been
doing a bit of sleuthing. You can't blame her.'

Obviously she'd been gathering information to fuel her nasty
gossip. Had Edward been about to become the next recipient of
a letter? Emily wondered. None of this information would be on
his file, though, which might have cast doubt on the assumption
that someone from the surgery was sending them out.

'I'm basically bankrupt.' Edward cut through her thoughts,
stunning her.

Bankrupt? But how? When? 'Edward, you don't have to tell me
any of this,' she said quickly. She dearly wanted him to know he
could talk to her – he'd offered his shoulder to so many people –
yet if she was honest, she didn't want to hear it, didn't want any
of it to be true.

He reached for her hand, squeezing it gently. 'I think I probably do,' he said gruffly. 'There are no excuses, but I'd like to try to explain, if I may?'

Emily nodded, glancing down at her hand as he tucked it back in her lap, patting it gently as if she were a child. She felt like one. Felt like sobbing like a child, for Edward, for Joyce. For Fran, ludicrously.

'I hit a few problems at work,' he admitted. 'My accountancy business went under, a while back now. That new firm, Affordable Accountancy, opening up next to the bank did for me, I suspect. I couldn't compete. I was obviously getting a bit slow in my old age.'

'Oh Edward ...' Emily's heart broke for him.

'I tried to keep going for a while, relying on my savings and investments. I ran out of funds eventually. The thing is ... the investments were supposed to fund our retirement. I haven't made any other pension provision. Damn bloody foolish thing to have done.'

He had no income? Nothing coming in at all? Bewildered, Emily searched his face. It was riddled with shame and regret.

'I tried not to worry about it at the time, thinking I would cross that bridge when I came to it. They have a habit of coming up on you faster than you expect them to, though, don't they?' He smiled ruefully.

Emily had no idea what to say. 'Couldn't you have sold up?' she asked hesitantly.

'Downsized?' He met her eyes sadly, and then looked away. 'That was the plan,' he said. 'I hadn't told Joyce, unfortunately. I knew she'd stand by me, but ... Pride, I suppose, stopped me initially. Then I thought I would choose my time, break the news gently. Time waits for no man, though.' He sighed heavily. 'Joyce got ill, as you know, and when she told me she would be happy with whatever time she had left as long as she could potter about in her garden and smell her roses ...'

Emily wiped away a tear that spilled down her cheek. 'So she doesn't know any of this?' she probed gently.

Edward shook his head. 'I couldn't bring myself to tell her,' he said, his voice catching. 'I haven't told anyone apart from Jake, and even then I only hinted at how bad things were, for obvious reasons.'

Jake knew? Why hadn't he mentioned it to her? Because they'd hardly been speaking unless to argue, she reminded herself, her heart twisting. *Why?* Why did people tear each other apart when life was so short?

'He was sympathetic, of course. He's a good listener, that husband of yours,' Edward said, with another sad smile. 'He suggested I look at equity release. He was going to research options for me, but I couldn't take that route either without Joyce finding out. I was trying to buy time, imagining I could replace the funds at some point. I'm not sure how. I'm not sure what I was thinking, to be honest. I've never done a dishonest thing in my life until now. This will kill her.' He stopped, holding his breath, desperately trying to rein in the emotion.

'God, Edward, I'm so sorry.' Emily turned to him, wrapped an arm around him. 'It will be all right. Joyce is stronger than you think. She *will* stand by you. She loves …'

Seeing someone approaching from the path, she trailed off. 'Jake …' she breathed, never so glad to see him. He would help. He would know what to say.

Wiping a hand across his eyes, Edward blinked in his direction. 'Talk of the devil,' he said with a strained laugh. 'Looks like I managed to spoil the party, hey, Jake?'

'It doesn't matter,' Emily told him firmly. 'None of that matters.' She glanced up at her husband. His eyes were anguished, filled with obvious concern.

'How are you doing, Ed?' he asked, crouching down in front of him.

'I think I've done better,' Edward said, his voice hoarse. 'Where's Joyce?' He looked anxiously back along the path.

'She's okay. Tom and Nicky have taken her home,' Jake reassured him, exchanging glances with Emily. 'Come on, let's get you back too. She'll be worrying about you.'

'She will.' Alarm crossing his face, Edward attempted to lever himself up. 'She does insist on fussing about me. I told her she would worry herself into an early …' He faltered, swallowing hard. 'I'll be all right, Jake. You go on and see to your own family. I can walk from here.'

'I'm taking you home.' Jake reached to support him as Edward wobbled on his feet. 'Can I take your car, Emily?'

'There's no need for all that,' Edward insisted. 'I can manage.'

'That's what friends are for,' Emily said firmly, coming around to his other side to thread an arm through his. 'To offer you support when you need it.'

Edward nodded appreciatively. 'Just mind you support each other. It's easier to dam a river than it is to stop gossip,' he said, nodding towards the flowing water. Emily tried not to see the ghosts that floated there. 'There's a saying: divide and conquer. Whoever is sending these evil letters out is aiming to drive a wedge between you two, for whatever reason. Don't let them. Stand together. You're a team. You always have been. Don't let them win.'

CHAPTER THIRTY-SEVEN

Listening to Jake moving about downstairs, Emily rolled onto her side, her heart constricting as she reached out to trace the empty space in the bed where he should be. It was almost dawn. She hadn't had a wink of sleep. She'd heard Jake going to the kitchen a couple of times in the early hours and guessed he hadn't had much sleep either. They'd had broken nights over the years, many, but they'd rarely slept apart until recently. Edward had been right: they needed to stand together for the children, for the people they'd come to know and love around them. And for themselves, if there was still any hope for them, if the person who was doing all this hadn't already won. Did she want to be with him, still not knowing for certain whether he had cheated on her, nothing but the email and his relationship with Sally, which he'd insisted was over years ago, to go on? Did he want to stay in this marriage? The endless questions rattled around in her head. She wondered whether he'd stayed here tonight rather than at the surgery, where she had to trust he'd been sleeping, because Millie hadn't come home. They'd called her, only to reach her voicemail. Emily had checked with Anna, every terrifying scenario possible crashing through her mind when she'd found Millie wasn't there.

'She's probably out with the boyfriend.' Jake had tried to reassure her, but she'd seen the flicker of doubt in his eyes, the worry that was now obviously eating away at him too. She was torn between frustration and fear. Millie had done this too often lately, and she had no idea what to do. Attempting to ground her would only drive her further away. Jake had said he would try to talk to her. Emily had agreed, suspecting he might be able to reach her where she couldn't.

Turning onto her back, she stared at the ceiling in the semi-light, her mind instantly conjuring up her sister's face, her violet eyes staring at her through the window of her dreams, the accusation in her gaze, the warning Emily had sensed there. But might it be that in interpreting the dream as some kind of prophecy, she herself was making it happen? Because she felt she *deserved* to lose Jake, to lose everything, just as her sister had? She recalled again the awful things she'd said to her, as she had countless times since the day that came back incessantly to haunt her. 'He doesn't love you. He *laughs* at you,' she heard herself screaming. 'We *both* do, Little Miss Goody Two-Shoes with her nose always stuck in a book. He loves *me*!'

'Why?' she remembered Kara screaming back through her tears. 'Because you're different? Unique? You think you're the only one who can give in to her wild side, don't you? You're wrong, Emily! We can all do what we want on a whim without giving a shit about anyone. The difference between you and me is I *care* about the people around me too much to hurt them!'

'Right, as you've just fucking demonstrated,' Emily had sneered.

'You just don't get it, do you?' Kara had stared murderously up at her from the hall. 'The more you rebel, because you think you have some God-given right to do what you like, the more *I* have to be perfect. And I'm *sick* of it.'

Emily's heart wrenched as it all came flooding painfully back. They'd been so busy fighting each other, they hadn't realised that the man they'd thought they loved was using them, pitting them against each other, getting his perverted kicks from it.

Emily had wanted to take her words back. She'd never had the chance. She'd apologised over and over, for years in her dreams, every time Kara slipped into her mind, but she couldn't undo what had happened. She needed to stop. Punishing herself wouldn't bring her sister back. She would probably never stop feeling guilty, but she had to stop dwelling on the past and concentrate on the here and now. Someone had tried to take away her ability to function by drugging her, but she *would* function. If it took every ounce of strength in her body, she would fight. The only other option, as Edward had pointed out, was to let the malevolent person who was trying to harm her and her family win, and that actually wasn't an option.

She had to talk to Jake, swallow her pride and try to find a way to move forward with him, together on some level, for the sake of their children.

Thinking she would ask him to go for a walk where they could talk out of earshot of Ben, she tugged on her tracksuit bottoms and a T-shirt, pushed her feet into her pumps and made her way quietly along the landing. She didn't want to wake Ben. He'd come home early, while they'd still been out, taking Edward home and making sure the village hall was secure. He hadn't said very much, going up to bed looking sullen instead. His date hadn't gone well, Emily had assumed, and promised herself to make time to talk to him properly. She wanted him to believe he could open up to her, however angry he might be feeling.

Reaching the lounge, she stopped, heart sinking, as she heard Jake's phone ring. A patient? she wondered, and then clamped down hard on her next thought.

'Jake Merriden?' she heard him say, having clearly snatched the phone straight up.

A chill of apprehension running through her, Emily listened for a second and then tentatively pushed the door open, her stomach lurching as Jake's alarmed gaze shot to hers. Her stomach turned over as he said, 'Joyce, you need to slow down, I can't hear you.'

Getting to his feet, the phone pressed to his ear, he appeared to be searching for his trainers. 'What? When?' His eyes slid in gratitude to Emily as, seeing them where he'd obviously kicked them off by the coffee table, she went to grab them and pass them to him.

'What's happened?' Ben appeared by the door, looking as if he hadn't had much sleep either.

Emily moved quickly across to him. 'I'm not sure,' she whispered, though she guessed from the urgent tone of Jake's voice that something had. Something bad.

'And he didn't say where?' Jake dropped to the sofa to shove his feet into his trainers. Standing again, he raked a hand through his hair. 'What time did he go out, Joyce?' he asked after an interminably long minute, his voice tight with obvious emotion. 'Right.' Checking his watch, he breathed in hard. 'And your neighbour's called the police?'

Emily's heart froze as he waited again, his face drained of all colour.

'Is she with you now? Okay.' He nodded, heading towards the hall. 'Try to stay calm, Joyce. Tell the police everything you've told me. We'll find him, I promise.' He ended the call.

'What's happened?' Cold foreboding clutching her insides, Emily spun around after him. 'Jake, what it is?'

'Ed went out, walking, he told Joyce,' Jake said, searching the hall table, his jeans pockets and then his jacket pockets. 'When she realised what the time was and came down, she found a note. She thinks … *Dammit*, where …?' He looked past Emily to where Ben was hovering. 'Ben, car keys?'

'*Shit.*' Clearly understanding the urgency, Ben parked any issue he had with Jake and hurried to grab them from his jacket hanging on the peg.

'What did it say?' Nausea churning her stomach, Emily followed Jake to the door.

Jake paused, his eyes flicking worriedly to Ben. 'She thinks it's a suicide note,' he said, his voice tight.

'Oh God, no.' Emily reeled on her feet. 'Not Ed.' Panic clenching her stomach, she followed as Jake raced to his car, climbing beside him as he threw himself into the driver's side. 'I'm coming with you.' Edward's last words to her rang loudly in her head: *Stand together. You're a team. You always have been.*

Jake didn't argue. His faced etched with fearful trepidation, he glanced at her with a small nod and started the engine.

'Wait!' Ben called, stepping onto the drive.

Jake hit the brake. 'You need to stay here, Ben,' he shouted, opening his window. 'I don't want Millie coming back to an empty house.'

'Queens Lake Woods,' Ben said urgently. 'Me and my mates have seen him up there a couple of times when we've been biking. He goes there birdwatching. He's usually in the same place, looking for wood warblers or something. There's a bench dedicated to the founder. It's up by the Tall Trees Trail. That's where we saw him.'

'*Jesus.*' Jake sucked in a breath. Exchanging glances with Emily, his eyes were shot through with palpable terror. Guessing that his mind had flown back to the darkest day of his life, that he was imagining Edward might have chosen this spot to end his life in the same devastating way his mother had, Emily's heart constricted.

'Thanks, Ben,' he managed, his throat hoarse, nodded appreciatively in Ben's direction, and reversed sharply.

CHAPTER THIRTY-EIGHT

'Why did I leave him?' Jake gripped the steering wheel hard as they drove through the arboretum towards the Tall Trees Trail, scouring the woodland left and right as they went. 'I should *never* have left him.' Lifting a hand from the wheel, he slammed it back down hard, causing Emily to jump.

'Jake, don't,' she said, tears springing to her eyes, fear for both him and Edward clutching her chest. 'You couldn't have done any more. He said he was tired. He said he was going to bed. He looked bone-weary. What else could you have done, other than what you did? You told him to come in and see you first thing.'

He shrugged hopelessly. 'I could have stayed. Made sure he did.'

She reached across to him, squeezing his forearm. 'You can't do that for all your patients,' she reminded him gently.

He drew in a breath, nodded and exhaled slowly.

'Do you think he couldn't bear the humiliation?' she asked, her heart aching excruciatingly as she thought of Edward's pain, the agony he must have gone through coming to such a horrendous decision.

Jake shook his head. 'He didn't do this for selfish reasons. I don't think he has a selfish bone in his body. My gut tells me he's doing it for Joyce. It was her he was worried about when he came to see me a while back. I'm guessing he thinks this way he will save her from the ignominy of his being charged with theft, a court case. She said he reminded her in his letter where his life insurance was.'

'Because he wanted her to be able to stay in her beloved house.' Emily understood immediately that that would have been exactly what Edward was thinking. He would have imagined she would need the money more than she needed a man who was about to bring shame to her door.

Swallowing back a jagged lump in her throat, she turned to the window. It was time to stop arguing, stop hurting each other. If all she'd thought about Jake were true, if he didn't want to be with her, then she would have to try somehow to forgive him and let him go.

A few seconds later, Jake pulled the car to an abrupt stop. Behind Edward's, Emily realised, her heart leaping into her mouth. 'Please don't let me be too late,' he prayed out loud, shoving his door open and scrambling out.

Quickly Emily reached for her own door and climbed out.

'Wait,' Jake said as she headed into the woods, and raced around to the back of the car to grab the emergency medical bag he carried in the boot. His face deathly white, he heaved the rucksack onto his back and then, meeting her eyes briefly, nodded her on.

Passing a bench bearing no memorial plaque, they'd gone several yards down the trail when they reached the one Ben had described. Emily watched Jake looking up at the tall trees. She knew what he was thinking. Her heart bleeding for him, she tried to imagine what he was feeling, the unbearable heartbreak he would have suffered walking through his front door to find his mother's limp form hanging in the hall.

Calling Edward's name, they ducked into the trees, passing redwoods, maples and oaks, the smell of damp earth mingled with moss permeating the air, birds chirruping in the top branches, frantically or so it seemed to Emily. Keeping within earshot of each other, they separated but kept calling. Where was he? She prayed he had come to his senses and realised that Joyce would be lost without him; that all the money in the world couldn't replace

him. She'd almost convinced herself they would find him safe …
until Jake said his name once again, his throat thick with disbelief.

'Jake!' she shouted, running urgently towards him, branches
and brambles whipping her face and tearing at her clothes. It took
a second for comprehension to dawn as she reached the small
clearing he stood frozen in, and then her heart stopped. *Oh dear
God, no. Please, God …*

'*No!*' Jake emitted a cry that came from his soul; raw, primal,
that of a wounded animal. And then he moved, dragging his
rucksack from his back, running, half stumbling, towards the
body that appeared lifeless as it swung from the trees.

Terror crackling like icicles through her veins, Emily flew after
him, grinding to a petrified halt as Jake wrapped his arms around
Edward's torso, attempting to take his weight. 'Don't you die on
me, Edward Simpson,' he growled, his voice ragged. 'Don't you
dare fucking die on me!'

'Jake …' Acrid grief and shock crashing through her, Emily
stepped closer.

'We have to cut him down,' Jake gasped, clearly struggling to
support him.

It was too late. Surely there were no signs of life. 'Jake …' She
took another tentative step.

'We have to cut him down!' Jake screamed.

CHAPTER THIRTY-NINE

Clearly worried, Ben came tentatively down the stairs as they finally walked through the front door. His gaze went from Emily to Jake, who came in behind her. 'Did you find him?'

His face ashen, Jake looked warily at him, and then answered with a small nod.

'And?' Ben's tone was impatient.

'He's alive, but we don't know for sure yet what the outcome will be,' Emily provided hesitantly.

'Which means what?' Ben asked.

'Your dad intubated him, but he couldn't resuscitate him at the scene. The paramedics tried. He'll need assisted ventilation, intensive care treatment.'

'Why, for fuck's sake?' Ben seemed furious. 'What did he do?'

Emily moved quickly towards him. 'Don't, Ben,' she said, her eyes flicking towards Jake, who appeared not to know what to say or do.

After a second, he looked at Ben, his expression haunted. 'He attempted to hang himself,' he said, his voice a hoarse whisper.

Ben stared at him, thunderstruck. Emily could almost feel the turmoil of emotions he was struggling with, and then his tangible fury gave way to obvious sympathy – and she quietly thanked God. She'd known this side of her son existed, despite the traits she'd seen in him and worried herself sick about.

'Sorry, Ben, I ...' Kneading his forehead hard, Jake looked away. He too was struggling emotionally. His voice had quavered several times as he'd spoken to the paramedics, and then to the police. They'd almost had to force him away from Edward. He wouldn't leave him. After intubating him as best he could with rudimentary equipment in the clearing in the woods, he'd stayed where he was, kneeling beside him, until the emergency services had taken him away.

I've failed him was all he'd said, over and over, tears running unashamedly down his face, as Emily had driven him home. She'd tried to reassure him that he hadn't. That he might well have saved him, in fact. Lost in his anguish, he wasn't hearing her.

Her mind went to poor Joyce, the devastation in her eyes when they'd called around to tell her. Her heart had been broken. Even then, she'd been so grateful to Jake. Emily truly believed that she and Edward loved him like their own son. It broke her heart that he believed Edward attempting to take his own life was his failure. He'd spent his entire life trying to oust the ghosts of his past, just as she had, tormented by the thought that he'd failed his mother in some way. At just sixteen, for God's sake, he'd blamed himself, carried his guilt with him every day since. And now it had come back to haunt him. Emily wasn't sure he would ever recover fully from it. Whatever he might or might not have done, she *had* to try to forgive him. He might have lied, but wasn't hers the biggest lie between them?

'I think your father might need some time,' she said to Ben, as Jake hesitated, appearing disorientated, before slowly climbing the stairs.

Ben gazed after him, then looked back to her, his eyes full of apprehension. 'Do you think he'll make it?' he asked, his voice choked.

Emily hesitated. Her first instinct was to protect her son, but there was no way to lie to him. When they'd first come to the village, Edward had been like an uncle to Ben and Millie, taking them under his wing and making sure they were involved in village activities, convincing Ben to join the local football team.

'I'm honestly not sure, Ben. They've promised to ring your dad as soon as they see any signs of a clinical recovery.'

Ben nodded and dropped his gaze to the floor. 'Fuck,' he muttered, swallowing hard. 'Why did he do it?'

Emily saw the tears squeeze from his eyes, and went to him, instinctively pulling him into a firm embrace. He didn't fight her, allowing her to hold him. 'He wasn't in his right mind,' she whispered, stroking his back, holding him closer as a shudder shook through him. 'Your dad's broken-hearted, blaming himself. He might need your support, Ben. Joyce, too. Do you think you could be strong enough to help them?'

He sucked in another breath and nodded into her shoulder, then eased away. 'I'll go and see her. See if there are any jobs she needs doing,' he said gruffly, wiping a hand across his eyes and glancing towards the stairs. 'Do you think he ... Dad ... could use a cup of tea?'

'Definitely.' Emily smiled and swallowed back emotion of a different kind. She was more grateful than he could ever know for this sensitivity she hadn't been sure he was capable of. 'Is Millie back?' she asked, suspecting she wasn't. Ben would have told her what had happened. Knowing why they were searching for Edward, she would have come downstairs, not stayed ensconced in her room.

'No. I left her a message, but she obviously couldn't be arsed to ring back.' Ben shrugged agitatedly. 'She really is acting like a brat.'

'Ben ...' Emily admonished him.

'Well, she is, let's face it. I know she's dealing with shit, but we all are, aren't we? If she wants to be treated with respect, then she needs to stop thinking about herself and grow ...' He stopped, an alarmed look on his face as his gaze travelled past Emily to the front door.

Emily turned around, her heart catching as she recognised the unmistakable silhouette of a uniformed police officer through the opaque glass, along with another person. DS Regan, she realised.

'They're probably here about what happened,' she reassured Ben, trepidation prickling her spine nevertheless as she went to the door, wavering briefly before pulling it open.

'Mrs Merriden.' DS Regan gave her a short smile. 'Do you mind if we …' Her expression unreadable, she nodded past her to the hall.

'Yes, of course.' Stepping back to allow them access, she glanced at Jake, who was descending the stairs.

'Is this to do with Edward Simpson?' he asked, his face taut. Emily hoped it wasn't. They'd given the police all the information they could.

DS Regan looked cautiously between them. 'No,' she said, her gaze flicking to Ben. 'We heard the news. Here's hoping he pulls through. I gather he's well liked.'

'He is.' Emily searched her face, her apprehension growing as she wondered what it was they had come for.

'We're actually here about a separate incident,' DS Regan said, taking a breath. 'One we believe occurred somewhere between eight and ten o'clock last night.'

Incident? Emily's stomach turned over.

'I'm afraid a young woman has been found,' the detective went on, causing Emily's heart to stop beating, 'on Orchard Lane, not far from Apple Tree Farm. She's critically injured.'

CHAPTER FORTY

Millie

Watching Louis' flat, Millie saw him finally return from God knew where. She gave herself a moment, staying where she was a short way down the lane.

He'd refused to answer her calls and texts warning him that her dad was probably on to them. From his lack of contact, it was obvious that he didn't give a shit about the consequences for her; that he probably never had. Where had he been, the bastard, going off without so much as a word? Anger bubbling inside her, she took several slow breaths, cautioning herself to calm down. She needed to act naturally. She needed evidence to confront him with. He'd been using her. She'd suspected it, but was still struggling to believe it. He'd been lying to her, stringing her along to get access to drugs – and what else? Why had he been so bloody interested in the passwords under Nicky's desk, even writing them down? And why, she wondered again, had he familiarised himself with the staff at the surgery? Precisely how much bullshit he'd fed her Millie wasn't sure, but he had, she had no doubt about that, and she intended to find out.

More composed after a minute, she checked her make-up, wanting to appear as normal as possible, though inside she was crushed, petrified and confused, then headed up the lane and across the forecourt of the derelict car workshop, avoiding the patches of oil and petrol in her new chunky leather boots as she went. She normally didn't go to his flat unless by prior arrangement, at designated times to suit him. She knew now why. He hadn't bought the perfume she'd smelled on him for his poor ailing mother. He'd been shagging his ex, she would be willing to bet, or else some cheap trollop. He'd probably brought her back here.

Trying to still the nausea swilling inside her as she recalled the times he'd made love to her here – had sex with her, she corrected; there had been no love there, she now realised, no tenderness or affection – she swallowed back her hurt and made her way up the concrete steps to his flat. Forcing herself to smile, she knocked and waited.

She could hear him moving around inside, but he didn't answer. Wondering if he would if he knew it was her, she braced herself and knocked again, harder this time, calling out his name as she did.

A minute later, Louis swung the door open with an audible sigh. 'Hi, sweet cup,' he said, a tight smile on his face. 'I wasn't expecting to see you.'

She'd bet he wasn't. He hadn't clicked his fingers, had he? 'No, but I was worried about you,' she said. 'You didn't return my calls and I thought something might have happened. That that Bear guy might have come after you or something.'

Her eyes trailed over his bare torso as he backed away from the door, allowing her in. A ripple of revulsion ran through her as once again she caught the scent of perfume. *God,* she'd been so naïve, acting just like a love-struck teenager. Her mum had been right to go on at her. She couldn't bear to imagine the heartbreak she might be about to cause her. And her dad … She would shatter his illusions about her forever.

'Yeah, sorry about that, babe. My mum's been ill,' he said, furrowing his brow in that concerned way he did whenever he talked about her. 'I would have rung, but in between doctors and hospitals …' Shrugging sadly, he trailed off, leaving her to surmise what a selfless soul he'd been. *Liar.*

'Oh no.' Millie frowned sympathetically. 'Is she all right now?' she asked, working to keep the contempt from her voice.

Louis nodded, emitting another heavy sigh. 'She's doing okay. She's getting on a bit, though, so … you know. Look, I'm just about to take a shower. Grab yourself a can from the fridge, why don't you?' he said, and turned away to head for the bathroom. 'I won't be long, and then we'll have a chat about what to do about your old man, yeah?'

'Okay.' Millie swallowed and went through to the tiny kitchenette. What did he mean, 'what to do about your old man'?

Pausing as the bathroom door closed, she listened for sounds of running water and then slipped into the bedroom and looked hastily around, relief crashing through her when she spotted what she wanted lying on the bed.

Quickly she grabbed his phone and, her eyes flicking to the door, selected his texts. She didn't have to scroll down too far to find what she was looking for: a whole ream of messages between him and some woman calling herself Sweet Cup, the term of endearment he used for Millie herself. Probably because he couldn't remember her fucking name. She suppressed something between a laugh and a sob.

Can't wait to fuck you again, his last message read. *Your old man doesn't know what he's missing.* If she was looking for evidence of what he'd been up to, it couldn't get more damning than this, could it? Bastard! Nausea roiling inside her, she dropped heavily onto the bed and read the reply. *Just remember it's worth waiting for*, the slut had sent back with a silly winking face.

She checked the dates. The texts had been sent a couple of weeks ago, but he was obviously still seeing the woman, or some other cheap tart, as evidenced by the reek of perfume.

She really had been naïve, hadn't she? How much had it turned him on, using her the way he had? He probably hadn't even wanted to have sex with her. Her heart plummeted at the thought that she might have repulsed him. He was using this woman too, though, she would bet her life on it. She was tempted to text her and tell her just how much of a bastard he was, but that would only alert him to the fact that she knew.

What had she got herself involved in? *Why* had she? Humiliation rising hot inside her, she swallowed back the bile in her throat and got to her feet. She wasn't going to face him with it. She'd thought she was, but he wasn't worth wasting the emotion on.

Disgusted with herself more than anything, she tossed the phone onto the bed, then hurried to retrieve it as it slid off the edge of the duvet onto the floor. Cushioned by the carpet, it hadn't made any noise – thank God.

As she bent to pick it up, her eyes snagged on something under the bed. His Banksy Ratapult T-shirt. She'd bought it for him online from the Banksy Shop. It had a stain on it, deep crimson, stark against the white cotton. Her eyes sliding once again to the door, she reached tentatively for it and shook it out. And her heart somersaulted in her chest.

Dropping it as if it might bite her, she tried to imagine where the blood had come from, but couldn't. He'd had no visible injuries recently. Had he? Nerves knotted her stomach as, taking another breath, she peered back under the bed, sure she would find something terrifying there. There was nothing apart from an old laptop gathering dust, and a box. A shoebox-size box. The sort in which he kept the medication she'd helped him to steal.

Hesitating, she went over to the door to listen, then, hearing him shaving, eased the door to and went back to the box. She couldn't just take it. He'd know it was her. But she could maybe take a photo of what was in there, one of the shirt too. She might need to. He'd worn gloves at the surgery. She hadn't. She was sure she hadn't touched anything near the safe, and her fingerprints would be around the place anyway since she'd been there many times with her dad. But what if she'd left some piece of DNA that would alert the police to her involvement? He would deny everything, probably that he even knew her, and where would that leave her?

Dropping to her knees, she held her breath and prised the lid off the box, a deep furrow forming in her brow as she studied the contents. It was full of old photographs. She recognised him in some of them, unmistakable with his twinkly eyes and sex-loaded smile, cultivated to reel women in. He was wearing a biker jacket and motorbike helmet in some, his hair, dark and long, like Ben's, escaping from beneath it. Looking like a poser astride his bike in others. But it was the girl straddling the bike in another photo that really caught her attention.

She squinted at it, her heart almost stopping inside her. It wasn't. *Was* it? It couldn't be. Her heartbeat a sluggish thud in her chest, she picked up another photo, of the same girl. Wearing jeans and a strappy vest, she was sitting cross-legged against a graffiti-covered brick wall, sticking her tongue out, cheeky, confident. Confused, Millie picked up another photo. The girl looked nervous in this one. She was standing, her shoulders slightly slumped, her hands tucked behind her back. She was the same, but not. Wearing the same strappy top, but not. It was a different colour.

Hands shaking, Millie compared the two photos side by side. The girl was wearing a locket, a distinctive gold-embossed locket. They both were. Her mum still had hers, a tiny photograph of a blonde-haired girl in it. She'd told Millie her twin sister had been buried in hers.

Her mouth dry, she pushed the photographs into her jacket pocket and delved further into the box, extracting an envelope; a white self-seal envelope, the sort she'd heard had been stuffed through people's doors. With trembling fingers, she extracted the letter from inside it.

Does your husband know about your son? she read. *You belong to me, Emily. You can run. You can hide. I will find you. YOU'RE MINE.*

Her head snapped up as she heard the door creak open.

'Find anything interesting?' Louis said behind her.

CHAPTER FORTY-ONE

Jake

'Natasha Jameson?' Jake shook his head, his heart still pumping with shock. 'But who …?' He brought his gaze cautiously back to DS Regan's. 'How?'

'We're treating it as a hit-and-run,' she said, 'for the moment.'

Jake noted her dubious expression. 'I take it you're not convinced that it was.'

'We're keeping an open mind. It was dark. She was wearing black, not easy to see on a secluded country lane. From the location, we're surmising she may have climbed out of a car. It may have been an unfortunate accident, the driver running scared, thinking he or she had hit an animal, possibly, but …'

'You think she may have argued with someone.' Jake read between the lines.

Regan shrugged non-committally. 'It's possible.'

'Michael?' Jake eyed her warily.

'It seems her husband has an alibi, which can be corroborated,' Regan answered. 'We'll know more when Natasha regains consciousness, which we're hoping she soon will. We've been doing some digging around meanwhile, and it appears the general consensus is that she might have been cheating on him.'

Jake's eyes slid to Emily. She looked deathly pale, clearly as shocked as he was. Before Regan had told them who the young woman was, it would have been Millie she'd seen lying in that lane. Jake had felt the fear emanating from her in palpable waves. This wouldn't help her state of mind.

'So rumour would have it,' he said, his gaze gliding after Ben, who, also visibly shocked, was heading for the kitchen.

'They split up for a while after her husband received one of the letters that have been circulating,' Regan pressed, 'which suggests that there might be some truth in it.'

Jake could sense Emily watching him steadily and prayed this wasn't going to cause more friction between them. 'I really couldn't say,' he said. 'They got back together. I hoped, for her sake, she'd made the right decision.'

'I gather from your frown that you don't approve?' Regan commented.

Jake hadn't realised he was frowning. 'It's not my place to approve or disapprove,' he said, with a short smile. 'I have to remain impartial. Michael Jameson is one of my patients too.'

DS Regan arched an eyebrow curiously.

'I can't say more,' Jake said, holding her gaze. 'Not unless I'm obliged to. I'm sure you understand.'

Regan conceded the point with a small nod. 'We'll be making further enquiries locally, obviously, trying to trace anyone she might have been involved with. A man driven by jealousy can just as easily be a lover as a husband, after all.'

'Assuming it was a man,' Jake suggested. 'Also assuming it wasn't an accident.'

'Assuming both of those things.' Regan smiled enigmatically. 'I'm sorry, but I do have to ask … Rumour being what it is, I'm sure there's no truth in it, but one or two people have speculated about whether you might have been involved with her.'

Jake glanced down and then back to her with a wry smile. 'There's no truth in it,' he stated categorically. 'I've never been involved with Natasha.'

Regan scanned his eyes quizzically for a second. Then: 'There was also a suggestion that your father might have been,' she said, watching him carefully.

Running a hand over his neck, Jake laughed cynically. 'I really don't know,' he replied. 'Maybe you should ask him.'

'We've spoken to him. He says not,' Regan informed him. 'Just out of interest, can you confirm where you were last night, Dr Merriden?'

Her tone was devoid of any particular inflection, Jake noted. He was about to ask why she wanted to know, but guessing that would make him sound defensive, thought better of it. 'I was here,' he provided. 'We'd been at Edward Simpson's party. There was an incident there, as you've no doubt realised. Edward left upset, and we – Emily and I – went in search of him and took him home.'

Regan had the good grace to look sympathetic. 'You do understand we have to ascertain people's movements around the time of the incident?' she asked.

'Of course.' Making a conscious move to show her to the door, he wished to God she'd chosen to do her ascertaining when Emily wasn't present.

'So you were here all night?' Regan continued, to his dismay. He'd hoped she would just leave it there and go. He needed to check on Ben and talk to Emily, whose expression, he noted, glancing in her direction, was one of bewilderment. 'You didn't have any reason to go out in your car. No call-outs?'

Recalling that Ben had been using his car, Jake answered cautiously. 'No, not until Joyce called,' he said, willing his eyes not to stray towards the kitchen as he heard the back door open and close.

'Right. Thank you.' Regan turned to go at last, to Jake's immense relief.

He opened the front door for her. 'Do you have information regarding vehicles in the vicinity?' he asked, trying to sound casual.

Her eyes flicked curiously to his.

'From what you've just said, I'm presuming you do,' he added.

'Could be,' she answered evasively. 'I'd better get on. A police officer's work is never done.' She glanced back at Emily with a small smile, and then at Jake. 'No doubt we'll have a few more things we might need to clarify with you.'

Jake nodded. 'Anything I can do to help,' he offered, 'providing it doesn't breach client confidentiality.'

'We'll make sure we have the requisite paperwork should we need it,' she said, stepping out – and almost into Tom, who was coming up the drive.

'We meet again.' Tom offered her a guarded smile. 'Any further news?'

'Nothing yet. We'll keep everyone informed as deemed necessary,' she replied, giving both Tom and Jake a long, searching look.

Tom shook his head. 'Nasty business,' he said with a despairing sigh.

'Very.' Regan drew her gaze away and headed onwards to her car.

Tom watched her go, then turned to Jake with a worried smile.

Jake eyed him quizzically. Tom might do the odd house call, but this wasn't a house he was generally welcome in.

'I came to apologise,' Tom said, confounding him completely.

'For?' He furrowed his brow.

'Pranging the front of your car,' Tom said, running a hand sheepishly through his hair and nodding towards where it was parked on the drive. 'Damn silly thing to have done. I was in a bit of a rush coming out of the car park the other day. Pushed my foot a bit too enthusiastically on the accelerator and went straight into yours, I'm afraid.'

It took a second for Jake to digest what he'd said. When he did, his heart skipped a beat. The police were showing an interest in his car, which was newly dented around the same time as a hit-and-run – and around the time Ben had been driving it. Christ, how was that going to look to them?

CHAPTER FORTY-TWO

Millie

Her heart banging, Millie stuffed the letter hastily into her pocket and got shakily to her feet. 'I was looking for paracetamol,' she improvised, walking towards him. 'I wondered whether you might have some in your bedside cabinet.'

A frown crossing his face, Louis looked her over thoughtfully. 'In the bathroom,' he said, nodding in that direction, and then looking past her to the bed.

'Thanks.' She cursed the tremor she could hear in her voice. 'I'll just go and grab some.'

His eyes narrowed, he nodded again and she took her chance. Her instinct was to run, but he was much taller than her, his stride longer. He would be on her in an instant.

Her nerves jangling, she willed herself to stay calm as she walked to the hall. She'd made it past the bathroom door, the front door almost in reach, when he said quietly behind her, 'Where are you going?'

She froze. 'Just outside for some fresh air,' she said, trying hard to sound casual. 'I have a really bad headache. I—'

'You've been going through my things,' he stated flatly.

Her heart lurched. 'No I haven't,' she denied quickly. Too quickly. 'I was just looking for the paracetamol. I wasn't—'

'You're scared, aren't you?' he said, an intrigued edge to his voice.

Sensing him walking towards her, every hair on Millie's body rose.

'Wondering about the blood?' he said, right behind her.

Fear constricting her throat, Millie launched herself forwards.

'It's *mine*,' Louis growled as she grappled with the ancient Yale lock on the front door. 'It's *my* blood, you silly cow.' He slammed his hand against the door. 'What? Did you think I'd *murdered* someone?'

'I need to go.' Millie caught a sob in her throat. 'I don't feel very well.'

'It's *my* blood,' he repeated, pressing his other hand to the door, one now either side of her head. 'I cut my leg on some scaffolding. I wrapped the T-shirt around it, forgot where I'd left it. I'll show you the scar if you like.'

He wasn't going to let her out. Millie's heart thrashed wildly. Even if she pretended to believe him, he probably wouldn't. Her mind racing, groping for a way to make him move away, she stopped struggling with the door and turned slowly. His face was inches from her own, his breath sweet with mouthwash, his eyes … They were frightened. Her blood pumped. He was as scared as she was.

'And the photographs?' she asked, taking a gamble and praying hard.

He pulled his hands away from the door as if he'd been electrocuted. 'What photographs?'

'My mother.' She held his gaze, shaking inside as she watched his eyes grow thunderously dark, seething suddenly with contempt. For her. He didn't want her. She'd been a means to an end, that was all. He'd been in a relationship with her *mother*. Was he still? Her mind reeled as she tried to make sense of it. *No.* He'd been stalking her. He was *threatening* her. He wanted to destroy her family. She wouldn't let him. 'I saw your phone too,' she said, her fear giving way to the hatred bubbling up inside her. 'You should know I dialled 999 on it and left the call open.'

He squinted at her, sneering disbelievingly for a second. 'Fuck!' he spat, and spun on his heel, slamming his fist into the wall as he stormed back to the bedroom. Almost choking on the fear lodged in her throat, she whirled around, her survival instinct lending her the strength she needed to wrench the door open.

She'd reached the steps when she felt his arm slide around her. 'Let me *go*.' Terror gripping her, she struggled against the hold he had around her neck.

'Not until you give me my fucking stuff back,' he hissed close to her ear.

Millie squirmed. He only squeezed tighter, hauling her backwards. 'I've done time in prison thanks to your mother,' he snarled. 'Suffered perverts and bullies, counted the days until we could be together. And what did she do?' He paused, as if he expected her to answer. 'She moved on. Made a nice cosy life for herself with your fucking perfect father and tried to forget me, that's what she did. But she *knows*.' He jerked his arm a fraction tighter. 'She *knows* she belongs to me. I was her first. I'll be her fucking last. Do you honestly think I would let some pathetic little schoolgirl rob me of that? Give me my stuff! Now!'

He was deranged. Out of his mind. Millie's stomach twisted. 'All right,' she rasped. 'All right. Stop, *please*,' she begged, gagging against the constriction in her windpipe. 'You're going to kill me.'

He jerked her chin upwards, sending her a warning, then relaxed his grip enough for her to draw breath. 'Piss me about and you *will* be dead, do you hear me?'

She nodded hard.

'Good,' he spat, heaving her around by the scruff of her neck. 'My things.'

She fumbled in her pockets, tugging the photos out first, her heart jolting as one fluttered to the ground.

'Careless bitch,' he muttered, bending to retrieve it – and Millie brought her knee up hard, a combination of satisfaction and nausea sweeping through her as she heard bone crack against bone.

'Bastard,' she seethed, thundering down the steps as, groaning and spitting blood, he dropped to his knees. Did he honestly think she was so pathetic she wouldn't rather die fighting than allow him to do this?

CHAPTER FORTY-THREE

Jake

His mind racing, Jake walked with his father to his car. His heart stalled, undiluted fear ripping through him as he looked the front of it over, noting the dent in the bumper.

'I take it you hadn't noticed it?' Tom said.

'No.' Jake glanced at him cautiously. His father was studying the damage, a perturbed look on his face.

Jake drew his gaze back to the car. Had he really not noticed the dent? He possibly wouldn't have done this morning. He'd been in a rush, his thoughts on Edward. Had it really been there before, though? When Ben had taken the car? Surely he would have noticed if it had? Swallowing back the nausea climbing his throat, he looked again at his father, his eyes narrowed. 'You know Ben had the car last night?' he asked.

Tom widened his eyes in surprise. 'Did he?'

'He was at a party in Malvern.'

'In which case, I'm glad I came by. I wouldn't want you thinking he'd been drink driving.' Tom held Jake's gaze for a second, then looked away. 'I wasn't drinking and driving when I bumped into your car either, incidentally, before you add that to my list of sins. I was on my way to a meeting, running late.'

Jake nodded, his stomach twisting as he tried to work out what was going on here.

'Anyway, I thought I would let you know I'm the culprit,' Tom went on, 'should the police wonder how you came by the dent.'

'Right.' Jake took a breath and massaged his temples, trying to release the band of tension that was tightening between them. He glanced again at Tom, who searched his eyes for a second and then gave him a small smile, one tinged with regret, which only added to Jake's confusion.

'I'd better get off,' Tom said. 'I thought I might drop by the hospital and check on Edward, if that's okay with you? I realise he's your patient, but you look as if you could use a shower and a couple of hours' sleep.'

He could. But he doubted he would manage the latter.

'Thanks. I appreciate it,' he said.

As he watched Tom head off, Jake wrestled with a riot of conflicting emotions. *Had* he driven into his car in the car park? If so, why hadn't he just come back into the office to let him know? Why hadn't he rung or texted him? Was it possible he'd just noticed the dent and was covering for him or for Ben? Why would he do that? And where the bloody hell was Ben? More worryingly, if it was Ben who was responsible for the damage, where had he been last night?

Disorientated from lack of sleep and too many things coming at him, Jake went back to the house. He needed to shower, try to get his head together. Going up the stairs, he met Emily coming out of Millie's room. 'Okay?' He scanned her face worriedly, hoping she hadn't read anything into DS Regan's questions. They were basically routine, after all, the same questions she was probably asking generally around the village. Or so Jake hoped.

'Millie's still not back,' Emily answered, evading the question. 'I was just checking if there was anything in her room that might give us a clue to where she might be.'

'*Shit.*' Jake's gut twisted. The last thing they needed in the midst of all this was no contact from their daughter. 'She'll be okay,' he said softly, quietly praying that this was true.

Emily didn't look convinced. 'Could you call her? I tried earlier, but …'

Millie wasn't answering Emily's calls, Jake guessed, still imagining she knew best. When would she grow up enough to realise that you never knew what was best, no matter how old you were? That being human meant you made mistakes, and that Emily had only been trying to look out for her, albeit she might have waded in too heavily? Did Millie not think they would be worried now, wondering whether something might have happened to her? A woman had been critically injured, and then there was what had happened to Zoe. Hadn't DS Regan said there'd been someone else other than Dean at their flat before she fell? That sent a chill right through him. Millie might not be aware of any of this, but why the hell couldn't she just try to understand how worried they both were and keep in touch? 'I'll do it now,' he said, pulling his phone from his pocket.

Dropping her gaze, Emily nodded. 'You know Ben had a crush on her?' she said, looking cautiously back at him. 'Natasha. He thought he was in love with her.'

His mind swinging immediately to the car, Jake felt as if the air had been sucked from his lungs. 'No,' he said, his voice tight. 'No, I didn't.'

CHAPTER FORTY-FOUR

Jake was just out of the shower when his phone rang. *Millie.*

'Dad, can you come and fetch me?'

Hearing the obvious distress in her voice, he tossed the towel on the bed and grabbed his clothes. 'Where are you?' he asked, his throat tight.

'I'm in the village, not far from the surgery,' she said, now sounding tearful. 'I need to talk to you. There are some things I need to tell you.'

'Wait outside the front entrance,' Jake instructed, his gut twisting afresh. Something was wrong. He needed to get to her. 'I'm on my way.'

'Okay. Dad …' She stopped him before he ended the call. 'Can you come on your own?'

Jake felt the hairs rise over his skin. There was something she didn't want Emily involved in. What, for Christ's sake? His gut turning over as he wondered whether Millie might be in danger, he dressed in record time and raced downstairs, stopping only to grab his keys and yell something to Emily about an emergency – a lie, which never sat well with him, but he didn't want to take any risks. The fact that Millie had asked him to come on his own meant she might well be in danger. He needed to be focused on her.

His heart banging as he drove, exhaustion catching up with him, he tried to reassure himself it was probably just an argument with her boyfriend, nothing more. Why then the fear in her voice, though? He'd definitely heard that. Hoping to God he didn't get stopped by the police, he drove fast, very aware of the dent in his bumper. His heart almost stopped beating as he realised Millie wasn't outside the surgery where he'd asked her to wait.

Panic rising sharply inside him, he headed for the back of the building, pulling haphazardly into the car park rather than leave the car on show outside. If this man she was seeing had dared hurt his daughter in any way …

Pushing his door open, he climbed hurriedly out to search for her on foot – and stopped. She was sitting in the doorway at the back of the surgery, her knees pulled to her chest, her head resting on them. She looked small and vulnerable, more like a child than an adult. Jake's gut clenched. Why hadn't he been there more for her?

'Millie …' He walked tentatively towards her, hesitating as her head snapped up. Her face was tear-stained, her make-up all over the place. She was more than scared, he realised. She was terrified.

She got to her feet as he approached, her eyes wide. She had beautiful eyes, just like her mother's, full now of the same uncertain agony he'd seen in Emily's lately. His guilt weighed heavier by the second.

'Let's go inside,' he said, his gut wrenching further as she took a step away from him. A small step, but a significant one nevertheless. He wanted to hold her but she'd moved away from him.

Swallowing, growing more scared himself than he dared let show, he reached to search his pockets for his keys, but Millie stopped him.

He looked down at the keys that rested in her outstretched palm, confused at first, before comprehension kicked in hard. His gaze shot to her face. What he saw in her eyes confirmed what he desperately didn't want to believe.

'I'm sorry,' she whispered. 'Please don't hate me.'

His stomach turned over. What had she done?

'Please don't hate me,' she repeated, a ragged sob escaping her.

He felt his heart crack. 'I don't hate you, Millie,' he said, his voice thick with emotion. 'I could never hate you.'

'You should.' Her red-rimmed eyes were frantic as they searched his. 'I would. Mum will. How can she not when she realises it's me who's been taking the drugs?'

Jake swallowed back his spiralling emotions. He needed to concentrate on Millie, on her feelings. 'She won't.' He tried a step towards her. Millie only took another step away, her eyes flicking to the side, as if she might run. His chest constricted painfully at the thought.

'I didn't mean to,' she said, swiping at the tears rolling down her cheeks. 'I thought I could help him. I loved him and …' She choked out another sob.

'You thought if you did this, he would love you back?' Jake asked softly.

She nodded and pressed her hands to her face. 'He doesn't. He never did. He … I wish I was *dead*.'

'*Don't*. Don't *ever* say that, Millie.' Anger doing battle with the bewilderment inside him, Jake moved fast towards her, wrapping his arms around her and yanking her to him. 'It would kill me to lose you. Please …' Squeezing his eyes closed, he pressed her head gently to his shoulder, his face to her hair. His child. His baby. He would kill for her. 'Don't ever say that again.'

Holding her close, he wiped a salty tear from his own cheek and waited. 'We should go inside,' he suggested quietly when her sobs stilled to a shudder. It was the weekend, and they were unlikely to be disturbed. Shoppers sometimes used the car park, though. He didn't want anyone seeing her like this.

Minutes later, with Millie safely in his office and less tearful, he fetched her a cup of tea – as if that could cure any of their monumental problems, which he felt were largely down to him.

His life seemed to be slipping away from him, like sand through a timer – his children, his wife – and he could do nothing to stop it.

'So what made you see the light?' he asked carefully, sitting in the chair next to her, rather than opposite her like an inquisitor. He didn't want to bombard her with questions, which might only make her close up. Nor did he want to add to the guilt she was obviously feeling. That was as evident in her eyes as the fear he'd seen there.

She wiped a hand under her nose, dropped her gaze further. 'He was seeing someone else,' she murmured, her heart clearly breaking. 'Someone older. Married, I think.'

Jake felt his jaw tense. 'And he's how old?' He was having to work now at sounding non-judgemental.

Millie hesitated, studying her thumbnail intently. 'About your age,' she admitted eventually, her voice small. 'He lied about that too. He told me he was thirty. I thought he might be a bit older, but …'

He nodded slowly. Indescribable rage burned inside him, an inclination to murder possessing him. The urge to find the bastard and remove his testicles without the benefit of anaesthetic was almost overwhelming. 'You're obviously well out of it,' he said, his voice choked.

Millie looked up at last, her eyes troubled, uncertain. 'There's something else,' she began uncomfortably, then stopped as a police siren sounded right outside the window. 'Why are there so many police in the village?' she asked, worry flitting across her face.

Studying her carefully, he debated whether to tell her. It would only upset her more than she was already. But then she would find out anyway. 'There's been an incident,' he said cautiously. 'A woman has been run over. Natasha Jameson. The police are treating it as a hit-and-run, but I think they're suspicious about the circumstances surrounding it.'

'Oh my God.' Millie's complexion drained of all colour. 'His shirt … it was covered in blood.'

Jake heart rate ratcheted up. 'Whose shirt?' he asked, his mind shooting to Ben.

'Louis'.' She stared at him, shocked. 'It was soaked in blood, hidden under his bed. There was other stuff too.' Her eyes filled with tangible panic.

Icy trepidation trailed the length of Jake's spine 'What stuff, Millie?' he asked warily.

'A letter. Photos.' She looked away and nervously back again, then reached into her jacket pocket. 'It wasn't just the drugs he wanted,' she said, her hand visibly shaking as she handed the contents to him.

Jake's heart stalled as he looked from her to the photographs. Reading the letter, it splintered inside him.

CHAPTER FORTY-FIVE

Emily

Hearing the front door open, Emily stopped uselessly pacing and flew to the hall, almost wilting with relief when Jake and Millie came in. Her relief was short-lived. Seeing her daughter's face, her make-up cried off, her complexion chalk-white, her heart folded up inside her. 'Millie, what's happened?' she asked, moving towards her daughter.

Her eyes furtive, her expression fearful, Millie didn't answer, taking a step away from her and looking back at Jake, as if for guidance.

'Give us a minute, Mils, will you?' Jake smiled reassuringly at her, but Emily could see that his eyes were deeply troubled. 'I think your mother and I might need to have a chat.'

Millie nodded, looked uncertainly back at Emily, and did as he asked.

Jake glanced after her as she climbed the stairs, then turned to place his keys on the hall table. He didn't look at Emily. Staring down at the keys, his brow furrowed pensively, he turned them around as if not quite satisfied with their arrangement, then removed his jacket, hanging it on one of the pegs, his movements precise, restrained almost. 'Did Ben come back?' he asked eventually, still not looking in Emily's direction.

'Yes,' she said, nerves knotting her stomach. Something had happened. He and Millie had obviously talked; there was an unspoken communication between them. Why wasn't he talking to *her*?

'Is he okay?' Jake checked, concerned as she'd known he would be.

'Not brilliant,' Emily answered. 'He's devastated about Natasha, naturally. I managed to get him to open up a little. He was reluctant, but he obviously knew we would be concerned about why he came home early and clearly upset last night.'

'And he told you?' Jake looked at her at last, his expression fraught with apprehension.

'His girlfriend stood him up, apparently. He was too embarrassed to say anything.' Emily had prayed that was the truth. She'd thought it was. After hearing about Edward, Ben had taken a step back towards her; been more like the child she'd thought she'd had no cause to worry about – until he'd reached his teens.

Jake nodded thoughtfully. 'Where is he now?'

Emily noted his guarded expression. 'At his friend's, gaming, I expect,' she said, watching him carefully.

'Right.' Jake took a breath. 'We need to talk,' he said, indicating the kitchen.

Confused, Emily followed him as he walked past her. She had no choice if she wanted to find out what on earth was going on.

Once in the kitchen, Jake turned to close the door, and stayed there, his hand resting on the handle, his shoulders tensing, as if he were bracing himself. Finally he turned to walk to where she stood at the kitchen island, feeling adrift and bewildered.

Stopping in front of her, he looked at her full-on at long last, studying her intently. His ocean-blue eyes were a swirl of emotion: confusion, accusation, hurt; he seemed to be looking right down into her soul.

She felt a chill of trepidation sweep through her as he pulled something from his pocket and placed it on the worktop. 'Meet Millie's boyfriend,' he said, his voice tight with palpable fury. 'But you've already met him. *Haven't* you?'

'Paul Lewis,' she whispered, icy fingers tugging at her heart, her mind, dragging her back there in an instant as she looked at the photographs Jake was now splaying out on the island. Nausea swilled inside her as she pictured him, the amused look she'd mistaken for affection in his cold cobalt eyes. She could smell him, the scent of aftershave mingled with sweat, cannabis and damp brickwork assaulting her senses. She could feel him as if he were here now, his tongue pushing into her mouth, his fingers exploring intimate parts of her body. *Paul Lewis.* She swallowed back the sour taste in her mouth. He'd found her. He'd hurt her *daughter*.

'What does he mean?' Jake asked, snatching her thoughts back to him.

Blinking back the tears clouding her vision, Emily looked at the letter he was pushing along the work surface towards her. *Does your husband know about your son?* she read, and her mouth dried.

'Are you still not going to tell me?' Jake asked quietly. 'Not even now, when this bastard has come after our daughter?'

Her heart beating so fast she could barely breathe, Emily looked at the girl in the photograph, who stared accusingly back. *You think you're the only one who can give in to her wild side, don't you? You're wrong, Emily!* She heard her as if she were standing here in the room with her.

'Talk to me, Emily,' Jake demanded. 'Or I swear to God—'

'It's not *me*,' she blurted.

'What?' He laughed, incredulous.

'They wanted me to be like Kara.' She looked back at him, saw the disbelief and confusion in his eyes and looked away again. She was making no sense, she knew, but she had to try to explain. She *had* to. 'They wanted me to be like her ... like Kara,' she stammered.

Jake sucked in a breath. 'I have no idea where any of this is leading, but—'

'Kara wanted to be me!' she cried, realising, finally, that the blame hadn't been solely hers to carry. 'She stole my boyfriend, and I hated her.' Tears streaming from her eyes, she relived the emotions as painfully as she had on that dark day. 'I *hated* her!'

Fear crossing his features as her voice rose, Jake stepped towards her.

Emily backed away. 'I said terrible things to her, wicked things, but it wasn't her I should have hated, it was *him*.'

'Emily …' Jake's eyes flicked to the door, warning her that Millie might hear. Her poor, innocent, feisty girl. He'd *hurt* her.

'He killed her!' Stuffed too long inside, the words came tumbling out. 'He *pushed* her. They argued on the canal bank and he pushed her. And I knew he had. I *knew* it. In here I knew it.' Choking back her sobs, she banged a hand against her chest. 'But in my head … I couldn't *remember*. I tried, but … I believed him. I went to him. Before he was convicted, I went to him. He was distraught, and I …' She stopped, reliving that night, desperately not wanting to.

'After we were together?' Jake surmised correctly.

Closing her eyes, Emily answered with a feeble nod.

'Were you still in love with him?' His voice was hollow.

Pressing her hands to her face, she shook her head.

'Yet you carried his child.' His voice now full of insurmountable hurt, Jake spoke the words that would send the rest of her world crashing down.

Emily looked back at him, her heart so swollen with sorrow and regret she felt it might burst right out of her chest. 'You knew Ben wasn't yours?' She could barely get the words out.

He smiled heart-wrenchingly. 'I'm a doctor, Emily, remember?'

He'd done a test, she guessed. He must have suspected. Of course he had. He wasn't stupid. She was the stupid one.

'I got that you wanted to keep the child. I understood. What I didn't understand was why you didn't tell me,' he went on, his voice strained. 'I could have forgiven you cheating on me. It wasn't as if we were already planning our wedding. I would have forgiven you anything, but ... All these *years*? Why didn't you just *tell* me?'

Emily didn't answer. She couldn't.

'You should have told me.' Shaking his head, Jake looked her over disappointedly and turned away.

'I didn't!' Emily called after him as he walked towards the door. 'I *didn't* cheat on you,' she repeated wretchedly. 'I didn't want to. I didn't plan to have sex with him. I didn't *want* to. He ...'

Jake stopped.

'Jake?' Emily moved towards him.

'Are you telling me this bastard raped you?' he asked gutturally.

Recalling again the cloying smell of him, his hands all over her body, the words he'd whispered close to her ear – *I want you* – her stomach roiled violently. 'Yes.' She voiced it finally. 'I should have gone to the police,' she added quickly. 'I know I should have, but after the court case ... They didn't believe that I couldn't remember. No one did. They convicted him anyway, but ... I couldn't go there again, giving statements, being questioned. Not being believed.'

'*Bastard!*' Jake exploded.

'Jake! Where are you *going*?' Undiluted fear gripped her as he yanked the kitchen door open.

'Where the fuck do you think?' he seethed, grabbing his car keys as he strode to the front door.

'Dad ...?' Millie said shakily, part way down the stairs.

Jake's step faltered. 'Stay with your mother, Millie,' he said throatily, then he pulled the front door open and slammed it hard behind him.

CHAPTER FORTY-SIX

'Where's he going?' Millie asked, her voice a hoarse whisper.

'I'm not sure.' Coming back from the kitchen, Emily grabbed her bag from the peg and snatched up her own car keys.

'*Mum* …' Hearing the sob in her daughter's voice as she reached for the front door, she stopped and spun around.

Millie's eyes were wide, her face, free of make-up, that of a petrified child.

Her heart catching, Emily moved quickly towards her as she stepped falteringly down the stairs, yanking her into a firm embrace. 'I have to go after him, Millie. Stay here,' she said, breathing in the smell of her, the scent of her child, her flesh and blood. Her baby girl; she would always be that no matter how grown-up she was. She had to make her world safe.

Gulping back a knot of raw emotion, she pressed a kiss to the top of her head. 'Call Ben. Tell him we need him to come home. And stay here until I ring you.'

Millie eased away to look tearfully at her.

'I won't be long, I promise,' Emily assured her, giving her another firm squeeze then turning back to the door before her courage failed her.

She wasn't sure where Jake had gone, but the cold fear in the pit of her stomach told her he might do something terrible, something completely out of character. Though perhaps *in* character when it came to protecting his children. Both of his children. He had never considered Ben to be anything but his son. Even when Ben had treated him abysmally, whether because of who he was or the age he was – Emily only wished she knew – Jake had been there for him. She couldn't let this happen. She had to stop it. She had to protect her family, Millie, Ben, Jake – the people she would die for. She knew that she was the only one who could.

Deep down, she'd always known this day would come. *I know you, Emily! I fucking* love *you! I'll find you, I'm warning you. You belong to me!* She heard his voice when they'd handed the sentence down. Saw his face contorted with rage, the intent in his unfocused eyes as he'd pinned her down, the night she'd foolishly gone to him. She'd fought him … until she'd been too frightened of what he might do. She'd fought the ghost of him ever since, just as she'd fought to rid herself of the ghost of her sister. He wasn't going to go away – not unless she made him.

She stopped a short way from the house to grapple her phone from her bag and search for the text she'd tried so hard to convince herself wasn't what she'd thought it was, the warning she'd tried steadfastly to ignore. How she wished now that she hadn't. She could have put a stop to this earlier, prevented so much pain and heartache. Knowing what she now knew, that Paul Lewis had been using her daughter, hurting her to hurt *her*, to gain access to her, she had no doubt it was him who'd been drugging her. He who'd been responsible for what had happened to poor Zoe, to Natasha.

I'm watching you. She read the text over again, each word piercing her heart like an icicle, and then, nausea clenching her stomach, she switched to hands-free, called the number it had been sent from and drove on.

'What do you want?' she asked when he picked up.

He didn't answer for a minute. Then, 'You,' he said simply.

CHAPTER FORTY-SEVEN

Jake

Blind anger burning inside him, Jake struggled to concentrate on the road. He should call the police. The fact that this Paul Lewis had been stealing drugs from the surgery was enough to make sure he was investigated. But he couldn't do that without implicating his daughter, something that piece of *scum* had undoubtedly factored in.

He slowed for a second, his breathing ragged, sweat beading his forehead. If he did inform the police, potentially risking Millie's whole future, would it even be enough to put this animal back where he should be, behind bars? Lewis was obviously responsible for everything. Jake's gut twisted as he pictured Natasha lying bleeding in the road. She could have died. Had it been *him* in Zoe's flat? He obviously thought it was his right to abuse any woman he fancied. Would Edward have been a target too, a man who would have given his life to help other people, only to almost have it snatched away because he'd made a mistake? One single mistake. Jake felt sick to his soul imagining the pain he must have been in as he'd tortured himself with what he believed was his failure. And Jennifer Wheeler: the bastard had taken away everything she'd thought had made her life worth living.

This vermin, Paul Lewis, Louis – bile rose in his throat even thinking his name – had hurt his daughter. He'd hurt his wife, more than Jake could ever have contemplated. And he *had* contemplated it, many times over the years; he'd tried to understand why she'd seen another man after he and she were together. Why hadn't she trusted him enough to tell him? How could she have thought that one day he wouldn't find out about Ben? Ben didn't look like him, and wasn't anything like him in character. He'd watched Emily worry about it, been close so many times to asking her to be honest with him.

A simple blood test when Ben had had suspected appendicitis as a child had told him what he'd needed to know. And he'd waited, and he'd hinted, and he'd prayed that she would tell him. He'd waited in vain. Finally she'd broken his trust in her. What did he do with it? he'd asked himself. What did a man do with that information when he still loved his wife despite it? His family. His daughter. His son. He'd loved Ben from birth. He *was* his father. No one could ever take that away from him. Even with Ben pulling away from him lately, he'd made up his mind he wouldn't let that happen. And now this. His world was disintegrating all over again because of this *bastard*. Millie would have to live the rest of her life with the psychological damage he would undoubtedly have caused her. Emily had lived with it for years, for some inexplicable reason feeling unable to confide in him.

Jake doubted that an individual who clearly revelled in people's suffering would experience any kind of remorse. He didn't deserve to live.

Hatred settling like ice in the pit of his stomach, he pushed his foot down, heading to the surgery. The man wanted drugs; he would have them. The worst fucking trip of his life.

Half an hour later, he reached the address Millie had given him, a run-down car repair shop on the road out of the village towards Worcester. Lewis apparently lived in the flat above it. Jake slowed, his heart hammering like a freight train. Was he really going to do this? Seeing again his daughter's terrified face when he'd found her cowering in the doorway of the surgery, knowing this monster had used her, coerced her, that he'd abused his wife in the worst possible way, he knew he couldn't walk away. He'd made mistakes. Several. He'd failed to put his trust in the people around him he claimed to love. He'd imagined his father possibly capable of this evil, he'd accused Emily, he'd even doubted Ben, to his shame. He'd sat in judgement on Emily all these years for not telling him the truth, and then, when he'd finally given up hope that she would, he'd made an irrevocable mistake, one he'd lived to regret. On top of all that, busy with his own life, shut away in his office feeling sorry for himself, he'd let his daughter down. He should have been there for her, for his family. He hadn't been. He needed to put right some of those mistakes.

His mind made up, he checked his jacket pocket, making sure the syringe he'd collected was easily accessible, as well as some extra ampoules of morphine should he need them.

CHAPTER FORTY-EIGHT

Emily

Icy fear gripping her stomach, Emily climbed the concrete steps leading up to the flat, a forties-style brick-built property with metal windows, one of them boarded up. The paintwork on the front door was peeling.

He'd left it open.

The bastard was so sure she would come, that he would get what he wanted, he'd left the door open for her to walk straight back into his life. He'd been right to be sure. He'd said he knew her, that day in the courtroom when she'd prayed she would never see him again. Perhaps he did, after all, enough to be certain she would never let him hurt another member of her family. This time she would make damn sure that he paid properly.

Pushing the door open, she stepped into the hall, a fresh bout of nausea swilling through her as the unmistakable smell of cannabis reached her nostrils. Noting the damp wallpaper speckled with black mildew, her stomach turned over. This was where Millie had been going all those nights she was away. Where he'd taken her innocence and broken her life to satisfy his own urges, to … what? Throw her away? Murder her? Wasn't that his ultimate turn-on?

Fury unfurling steadily inside her, her heart leapt when he stepped into the hallway. And then it hardened. It was him. His hair was shorter. He was still good-looking and as tall and muscular as she remembered. Still wearing the cocksure smile that had permanently adorned his face, still with that glint in his eyes she'd mistaken for admiration or love.

'Hi, sweet cup,' he said, his smile widening languidly. 'Long time no see. I've missed you. Bet you've missed me too, haven't you? Did you think about me?'

'You've cut your face,' she said, her eyes going to the angry gash across the bridge of his nose.

'A parting memento from your daughter.' His smile slipped, just for an instant, a flash of humiliation now in his eyes. 'She's as feisty as you are. She obviously inherited your genes. Come in.' He nodded behind him.

To the bedroom, Emily gathered, having noted the living room to her side, the kitchenette beyond it.

'I'm just packing a few things,' he said, turning.

To make good his escape, presumably. With her? Or was it her fate to go the way of her sister? Her hand curling around the sharp boning knife in her pocket, she followed him, her heart squeezing painfully as her eyes fell on Millie's pretty crystal hairclip on top of the chest of drawers, the only furniture in the room apart from the bed. Her heart turned to stone.

'So, what now?' he asked, collecting a handful of T-shirts from one of the open drawers and stuffing them into a holdall on top of the duvet. Stopping, he glanced at her. 'You know we're destined to be together?'

Emily said nothing, and tried very hard not to communicate her feelings through her facial expressions.

'We share a secret, Emily,' he went on casually. 'One we'll both take to the grave. We both know who really pushed Kara that day, don't we?'

Liar! Emily seethed inwardly. He'd told her all those years ago that she'd killed her sister out of jealousy. Deeply shocked, grieving, not trusting her own memory, she'd believed him. Unbidden, scenes from that terrible day crashed into her mind. She wasn't even supposed to be there. It was Kara that Lewis had agreed to meet on the canal bank that day, not her. But Kara had been angry. Emily saw her, her flaxen hair wild, her violet eyes full of fire, spitting fury, telling him what a vile bastard he was, that she would rather die than let him anywhere near her again. Emily hadn't pushed her. *He* had.

'Leave them alone,' she said. 'My family. Leave them alone and I'll come with you.'

He studied her narrowly, for a long, bone-chilling moment. 'Ben's my son,' he stated flatly, and went back to his packing.

He was insane. Surely he couldn't hope to have anything to do with Ben after all that he'd done?

'We can start afresh.' She kept her voice even.

'Right.' He smiled cynically. 'So you'll give your family up to be with me? Your perfect husband with his big fat salary? You're lying, Emily.' His eyes flicked back to hers. 'You're blushing. Didn't I tell you I know you?'

She didn't flinch. 'I'm not lying. I'm nervous. I'm bound to be after everything.' She glanced down and back. He didn't know her that well. Couldn't see that it was white-hot rage burning her cheeks. 'I've only ever wanted to be with you. I thought you didn't want me.'

'And that's why you tried to push me away the last time we were together?' He eyed her sceptically.

'I was angry.' Emily told him the lies he wanted to hear to salve his ego. 'Because of Kara.'

He thought about it. 'So you don't love him then, the upstanding Dr Merriden, with his flashy car and his big house? You don't love your nice lifestyle, your fine clothes,' he looked her over, a hint of contempt in his eyes, 'your fancy holidays. You love me.'

He was *jealous*. Emily couldn't quite believe it. Of Jake. Of what she had with Jake. Was that what had driven him to do what he'd done, to destroy so many people's lives? Pathetic creature. She would have given anything to tell him just how disgustingly contemptible she found him, but she kept her counsel and held his gaze instead. 'I've never loved him,' she said, the words almost choking her. 'He's looked after me, looked after Ben. I care about him, but I don't love him.'

He swept his gaze over her. Her flesh crawled as she watched the incredulity in his eyes give way to lust. 'Prove it,' he said, nodding to the bed. Removing the holdall, he dropped it on the floor and then looked back at her, a challenge now in his eyes.

Emily's insides lurched. Bile rising in her throat, it took her a second to find her courage, to make her legs move.

Walking across to him, she noted the stunned disbelief on his face as she snaked an arm around his neck, heard a groan deep in his throat as she pressed her mouth over his, her tongue seeking his, the taste of second-hand cigarette and cannabis smoke in her mouth, the familiar scent of him, sickly-sweet lemon mingled with body odour, assailing her senses.

He pulled back after a second, reached to free himself of his T-shirt, yanking it over his head too fast for her to be ready. Greedy lust in his eyes, he scanned her face briefly, then leaned back into her, his mouth covering hers, his body hard against her, his hands all over her as he steered her around, urging her backwards towards the bed.

Emily's heart thundered. Her fingers found cold steel. Now she was ready.

The point of the blade was a millimetre from the vertebrae in his back when her blood froze, her shocked gaze pivoting to the man with a syringe in his hand and cold murder in his eyes.

Paul Lewis looked ludicrously surprised as the needle slid smoothly into the side of his neck. Then his eyes darkened, his face contorting with rage as he whirled around.

Jake stepped back as he advanced towards him.

One hand pressed to his neck, the other a white-knuckled fist at his side, Paul Lewis took another step. 'What have you given me?' he snarled.

'Just ketamine,' Jake said, his mouth curving into the reassuring smile Emily had seen so many times. There was no reassurance in his eyes, though. What she saw there, a mixture of hatred and burning anger she would never have believed him capable of, shook her to the core. 'A large dose. Nothing a big man like you can't handle, though, hey, *Louis*?'

'You *bastard*,' Paul spat, taking another step towards him.

Jake took another step back. He didn't look fazed, though Emily's heart was banging so fast she thought it might explode.

'I'll fucking *kill* …' Paul started. Then he stopped, his legs buckling, the drug Jake had injected into him bringing him heavily to his knees.

'Probably best not to fight it,' Jake advised, moving back towards him. One shove with his foot was all it took, and Paul Lewis keeled over.

Moving fast, Jake reached past him to grab Emily's arm. 'Out,' he instructed.

'But … what do we do?' Emily asked, terrified, as she watched the man's eyes roll. 'They'll know; the police, they'll know it was—'

'It's not enough to kill him,' Jake said sharply. 'I doubt he'll be going anywhere near the police. We need to go, Emily. *Now*.'

'Were you going to …? Once he was drugged, did you intend to kill him?' Emily struggled to speak the words as, his hand firmly under her arm, he guided her out of the flat, almost dragging her down the concrete steps.

'Yes,' he snapped. 'I'm still fighting the urge not to. Keys?' he asked, as they approached her car.

She fumbled in her pockets.

'Are you okay to drive?'

She nodded and pressed her key fob.

'Go,' he instructed, pulling her door open. 'Straight home. I'll be right behind you.'

She'd started the engine and was reversing when she heard him shout. 'Ben! For God's sake, don't!'

Emily slammed on the brakes. Shoving her door open, she looked towards Ben, who was facing away from them, taking a draw on his cigarette before tossing it towards the workshop. Her mind didn't register what was happening until Jake threw himself towards him, pushing him to the ground just as a whoosh of flames spewed out.

CHAPTER FORTY-NINE

Jake

'Ready?' Jake asked Millie as she came downstairs. She still looked pale, but she was holding things together. She and Emily had talked, tentatively at first. Jake had guessed that they'd made some headway towards healing their wounds when he walked into the kitchen to find them hugging each other fiercely and crying together.

Giving him a plucky smile, Millie nodded. Jake smiled reassuringly back. Holding eye contact with her for a second, he saw that she understood he was trusting her to use her initiative regarding how much she disclosed to her friend. Three days had passed, and they'd had no contact from the police. Thinking they would have done by now had they been under suspicion, Jake breathed a little more easily.

'We're off,' he called to Emily upstairs.

'Okay. Ring me if you need a lift later, Millie,' Emily called back.

Once Millie would have rolled her eyes and told her she was sixteen, not six and perfectly capable of walking home on her own, but now she looked relieved – that her mother cared enough to be worried about her, Jake surmised, which was definitely progress.

Leaving Emily with Ben to have a more in-depth conversation with him – about the incident that had turned his life upside down and Lewis's flat into an inferno, as well as historical events that were painful for both of them – he picked up his car keys. Opening the front door to let Millie out before him, he gave her shoulders a squeeze as they walked towards his car.

Millie was quiet for a while on the journey. Eventually she turned to him. 'I'm sorry I told Ben about Lewis being his father,' she said, almost blurting it out, as if she'd had to summon her courage.

Jake reached for her hand. 'It's okay, Millie,' he said, squeezing it. 'He had to know.'

'Yes, but it should have come from Mum, not me. I should have thought about it, been more mature.'

'You were distraught, Mils. We all were.' Pulling up outside Anna's house, Jake took a breath. 'We can't undo things, Millie, but we can learn from them. I think that's the lesson to take from this, don't you? The mature thing to do?'

Millie nodded, but Jake guessed from her expression that she would still beat herself up for some time to come. 'Are you sure you'll be okay?' he asked.

She took a second, and then nodded firmly. 'I'm fine,' she lied – for his sake, he guessed. 'I need some space, to try and get my life back, you know?'

Jake nodded in turn. He understood, but knew she had a long journey ahead – it wouldn't be easy for her to get over what had happened. He was reluctant to let her out of his sight, but smothering her wouldn't help her rebuild her confidence. They were just going to have to trust her to tread carefully in future. 'Remember, if you need to talk about anything, anything at all, I'm listening.'

She glanced at him. 'I know,' she said, and then surprised him by leaning over to give him a neck-breaking hug. 'Remember, if *you* need to talk, whatever shit's happening between you and Mum, I'm there for you too.'

Hearing her sounding more like the spirited Millie he knew, Jake felt some of his apprehension abate a little.

'Love you,' she said, turning to open her door.

'Love you right back,' he said throatily as she climbed out. 'Remember to call your mum when you need a lift home.'

'I will.' Closing the door, Millie gave him a wave and then turned towards Anna, who was standing on the doorstep waiting for her.

Guessing that she wasn't going anywhere else – that she had learned from her experience and hopefully wouldn't easily make the same mistake again – Jake breathed a sigh of relief and drove on to the hospital. He wanted to visit Edward, who was making a good clinical recovery, thank God. He also wanted to check on Natasha, who hadn't yet regained consciousness, and bring himself up to speed with her expected prognosis. He'd been hugely relieved to hear that Zoe had been brought out of her medically induced coma. She was still under ICU observation, but the swelling had been considerably reduced, thereby reducing pressure on her brain and preventing secondary injury. Dean had sounded nothing but relieved when he'd called him. Jake very much doubted he'd had anything to do with her fall. All he could hope was that Zoe would remember enough to exonerate him.

Parking in the hospital car park, he texted Emily, telling her how long he expected to be, and then walked to the main entrance.

'Dr Merriden,' someone called as he approached it.

Looking up, his stomach knotted nervously as he saw DS Regan.

'I just wondered whether you were aware of any other letters sent out that we might not know of?' she asked when she reached him.

Thinking she might have been about to mention the explosion, possibly asking him his whereabouts, Jake felt relief flood through him. 'None that I've heard about,' he said, guessing she would be thinking that someone might have confided in him. 'I take it you're not making much headway?'

'Not much, no.' She sighed disappointedly. 'We'll keep on it, but I'm afraid we're coming up with nothing forensically yet. I'll let you know if we do.'

'Thanks.' Jake smiled his appreciation, though with Millie and Emily in mind, he was praying it might all just fade away. 'Any idea what might have caused the car workshop fire?' he asked, holding her gaze and hoping to Christ she couldn't read anything in his eyes.

Regan shook her head. 'Looks like it was an unfortunate accident,' she said. 'There were cigarette and spliff ends littering the forecourt. It seems Lewis was fond of tossing them out of the window. Not a smart move when you live above a tinderbox.'

'No. Not a nice way to go.' Jake looked suitably concerned. He'd been hoping that Ben had tossed the cigarette without thinking. Learning that Millie had filled him in on much of what had happened, including that Lewis was his biological father, he couldn't help feeling that Ben's justifiable anger might have got the better of him. He and Emily could live with what had happened, just. The psychological impact on Ben, however … He guessed they would have to go slowly and cross one bridge at a time.

'The worst. He was a nasty piece of work, but even so …' DS Regan grimaced. Jake assumed she would have seen what was left of Lewis, and sympathised with her. A blackened and burnt-to-the-bone corpse wasn't a pleasant sight. At least the man had been unconscious. He tried to salve his conscience with that knowledge.

'I've spoken to Zoe,' Regan confided. 'Only briefly, as she's still very weak. She's told us it was Lewis she was seeing. I had to cut the interview short before we were able to establish whether he was the person who called on her before she fell. We have the eyewitness statement. It's not one hundred per cent reliable, so we'll need her to confirm it, but it looks as if Dean Miller might be off the hook.'

'That's excellent news.' Jake felt another surge of relief, though his gut twisted as he thought about the decision Emily had also had to make all those years ago. Had she chosen not to go through with her pregnancy, Ben would never have been part of his life. The boy had been hard work since hitting puberty, but Jake couldn't imagine an existence without him. He loved him. He was going to have to work hard at convincing him how fiercely, that he would do anything to protect him – even lie for him, which he had, and would keep doing if he had to. In his mind, Ben's life had been blighted enough, learning about his parentage. The kid was struggling with his conscience; that was obvious. He'd realised, though, that in going to the police, he would be allowing Lewis to achieve what he'd set out to do: destroy their family.

'And Natasha?' he asked, wondering if they'd made any progress with their investigations into the hit-and-run. Aware now that Lewis had wanted to destroy his and Emily's relationship, destroy whatever confidence she'd found by ruining the lives of their patients, the life she'd made for herself, Jake had wondered whether he might have been involved with Natasha too.

'We're still working in the dark there,' Regan admitted, with a disconsolate shrug.

'Do you have any physical evidence?' Trying to sound casually interested, Jake dug a little.

'We have some tyre impressions,' she offered, and his mind shot immediately to the damage to his car. 'I'm not sure they'll be much use, though. They're not clear enough to identify the manufacturer. There's no chance of picking out any individual identifying characteristics. I'm thinking we'll have to wait until we can talk to Natasha herself.'

'Hopefully that will be soon,' Jake said. 'I'll check how she's doing and let you have any information I can glean.'

'Thanks. The consultant thinks she'll make a good recovery, but he's not overly forthcoming.'

'Protective of his patients.' Jake understood that.

'Definitely.' Regan rolled her eyes. 'I'd better get going. A detective's work is never done,' she added. Jake managed a smile. It was obviously her catchphrase. 'I'll keep you informed if we do come up with anything regarding the letters.'

'Cheers.' He allowed himself to breathe out.

*

Speaking to one of the nurses, Jake was surprised to learn that his father was here. Checking again on Edward, perhaps. He'd been a couple of times to Jake's knowledge. Walking towards the side room Natasha was in, he pondered his relationship with Tom. He supposed he should try and make more of an effort to get on with him. It was good of him to look out for Edward, and he'd obviously been trying to cover for him or Ben, thinking they might be dragged into the enquiry. He was Ben and Millie's grandfather at the end of the day, and a more amicable personal relationship might make for a better working one.

About to go into Natasha's room, he paused. His father was in there with her. Frowning, Jake watched through the viewing pane in the door. Why would Tom be turning off the alarms on the life support machine?

A second later, he understood. His heart slammed against his chest as he watched him reach towards her breathing tube. *Jesus Christ.* He hadn't been covering for them. He'd fabricated the whole story. He was covering for himself.

Jake shoved the door open. 'Don't you fucking *dare*,' he warned him.

CHAPTER FIFTY

'I couldn't have her broadcasting things all over the village.' Tom looked beseechingly at Jake as he was led away by the police. 'We were making progress. After all these years, you'd finally started looking at me with something other than contempt. I couldn't have her spoil what we were building together, don't you see?'

Strangely, Jake didn't feel contempt any more. Other than pity, he wasn't sure he felt anything.

'I never meant to hurt your mother, Jake. I never stopped thinking about her. There hasn't been a day when what happened to her hasn't haunted me.' Tom searched his eyes hopefully. Jake turned away.

'*Jake*,' Tom called desperately. '*Please …*'

Jake kept walking. He had no idea what his so-called father thought they'd been building together, but it wasn't fucking fences, that was for sure.

Banging out of the entrance doors, he strode across the car park, cursing the tears that slid from his eyes. *Don't.* He swiped them away. The man wasn't worth wasting the emotion on. He never had been.

'Jake, wait.' DS Regan caught up with him as he reached his car. 'Are you all right?' she asked, placing a hand on his arm.

Jake laughed sardonically. 'Never felt better,' he said.

Regan gave him a smile of commiseration. 'They have a lot to answer for sometimes, don't they, parents?'

Too choked now to speak, he nodded and dropped his gaze.

'Your father's sins are not yours, Jake,' she said, and hesitated. 'Mine was a teacher, a headmaster actually.'

Sensing from her silence that there was more, he looked quizzically back at her.

'He liked children. Not me. Fortunately,' she added, smiling tightly.

He saw the flash of humiliation in her eyes and understood. 'Sorry,' he managed.

She shrugged, her gaze flicking down and back. 'It's okay,' she assured him. 'I've moved on. You need to do the same. You're not responsible for your father's actions. Let go of the guilt and get on with your life. Be there for your family.'

Jake couldn't help thinking he *was* responsible in some way for all that had happened. In coming back here, attempting to build a life from the ashes, digging up old ghosts that were better left buried, he'd lost sight of what mattered. His children. Emily. He *should* have been there for her. He hadn't been.

In his car, he leaned his head against the headrest and tried unsuccessfully to get his breathing under control. As for letting go of the guilt, he didn't think he would ever be able to do that.

Pressing the heels of his hands against his eyes, he swallowed hard and reached for his phone to tell Emily he was coming home.

Could they get through this? he wondered. Come out the other side of it intact? Would Emily want to stay with him once he'd told her all he had to? He thought again of Liz Regan's comment about him not being responsible for his father's actions. He couldn't help wondering whether, if he hadn't despised him so passionately, Tom might not have been driven to do the unforgivable thing he'd done. But he'd tried, hadn't he? To let go of the hatred. He'd been wrong, as it turned out. His father was fundamentally who he was. Jake wasn't responsible, though growing up he'd felt he was. In the same way, Ben wasn't responsible for *his* father's actions. Whatever happened between him and Emily, he had to make sure the boy knew that.

Jake was responsible for his own mistakes, though. He couldn't escape that fact.

CHAPTER FIFTY-ONE

Emily

Emily had no idea what to do. She was *so* tired. She sat in the kitchen for a while, too stunned to even contemplate making a cup of tea – as if that would help, as if anything could. Wine might possibly. A vat of it. But she wouldn't go down that route. Wouldn't drinking herself into a stupor make her exactly what Paul Lewis had wanted her to be: a woman out of control? Dependent on drugs? Emotionally volatile?

Pulling herself to her feet, she headed for the lounge. Bypassing her vitamin pills on the worktop next to the kettle, she smiled ironically. She kept a bottle here and one at the surgery. He'd obviously accessed the house through the back door Ben constantly left open. A shudder ran through her at the thought that he'd been here, in the very spot she was standing, with his son just a floor above him. Obviously he'd rooted through her things at the surgery. He really had known her, hadn't he? Her rituals at least, her dependencies. Fury surging through her that she'd allowed such a despicable human being access to her and her family, she scooped the tablets up, thrusting them in the bin. She wouldn't need those any more. Vitamins *or* amphetamines. She would make time for herself. She would be there for her children, but she would look after herself first. Eat sensibly, exercise. She was no good to anyone unless she was in possession of her faculties and fully functioning.

Finding Jake in the lounge, his hands thrust in his pockets, staring through the window, she took a breath. 'We need to talk,' she said.

He turned to face her, and her heart twisted. He looked utterly exhausted, jaded to his very bones. She wanted to go to him, hold him, have him hold her and make this all go away. But she couldn't. It just wasn't possible to close her eyes. She wasn't sure it ever would be.

Jake's gaze flicked up towards the bedrooms.

He was thinking about Ben overhearing, she guessed. 'Outside?' she suggested. The garden was big enough to allow them some privacy. It was her thinking place. She would be able to get her thoughts in better order there.

The evening was mild, the piquant smell of newly mown grass fresh on the air. It was a beautiful garden, a tranquil place. Emily had been so glad her demons had allowed her to overcome her fears and live here. Would she be able to in future? Her heart wrenched painfully again at the thought that she might have to leave her home, leaving her only good memories behind. She'd had no plans to.

Waiting until they were well out of earshot of the house, she broached the most urgent subject first. 'Ben's wondering whether he should go to the police,' she said.

She felt Jake's gaze snap to hers. 'Did he say he'd caused the fire on purpose?'

She shook her head. 'He says he went there because Millie told him she thought you were there, that I'd followed you. He said he saw us come out. That he wasn't thinking about anything other than confronting him. What he planned to do then ...'

Jake nodded.

Glancing at him, Emily could see his uncertainty; that his thinking was on a par with hers: that Ben might have gone to the garage intending to do what he did, despite his denial.

'Do you want him to?' he asked.

'No,' Emily answered honestly. 'But if he can't live with his conscience … I misjudged him,' she admitted. 'I imagined his genes might make him the cold, unfeeling person his father was. I was wrong. His volatility is more to do with rampant teenage hormones and his world falling apart around him. That's my fault, not Ben's.'

'You can't blame yourself, Emily,' Jake said forcefully. 'I wasn't here. I should have been.'

She didn't pursue it, though she might have done, because he was right: he hadn't been. Raking over old coals wouldn't achieve anything, though. She needed to let go of all the guilt and the negativity and move forward. 'Will you support him? If he chooses to go to the police, will you be there for him?'

Jake didn't hesitate. 'He's my son,' he said adamantly. 'As long as he wants me to be, I'll always be there for him.'

Emily closed her eyes, breathing in the clean air, listening to the soft lap of the mill stream as they walked towards it. 'I tried to save her,' she said, stopping on the bank. 'My sister, I tried to save her. I couldn't.'

I'm sorry, sweetheart. We'll be together again one day, and we'll have such magical stories to tell. Seeing her sister's face as she glanced down into the water, she prayed silently. There was no plaintive look in Kara's eyes any more, no fear. It was possible she might even be smiling.

'I have to let her go now.'

Jake nodded. He didn't speak for a while. Then, 'Can we save each other, Em?' he asked, his voice choked.

'I'm not sure,' she answered. If they separated, they would be making sure that the monster who'd haunted her achieved his aim. He'd wanted them to fall apart. He'd ruined people's lives to that end. He'd even tried to ruin Millie's. He hadn't had a caring bone in his body, no compassion for anyone. Jake was completely different. He cared for her, she knew that without a single shred of doubt. He cared for Millie and for Ben. He hadn't realised that she was watching from the bedroom window, but she'd seen him come out here after the dreadful events on the day of the fire. He'd stood for a while looking up at the stars, then he'd buried his head in his hands and sat down and wept.

He cared for his patients, every single one of them. He cared for his bastard father too, hence his anger whenever he was around him, the agony in his eyes every time he spoke about him. Those weren't the emotions of an unconcerned man.

Could she forgive him?

Could he forgive *her*? They hadn't had a moment alone together since Paul Lewis had met his just deserts – the animal deserved to burn in hell as far as Emily was concerned. She knew Jake cared, but was that enough? Did he love her? After all she'd felt over the years, imagined or otherwise, she couldn't contemplate a life where she might be second best.

She braced herself to ask what she had to. She would know immediately whether there was any hope for them. Any way to move forward together. Marriage was a two-way street. Respect and trust were too. Without honesty, they had nothing. 'Is it yours, Jake?' she asked quietly. 'Sally's baby, is it yours?'

She heard his sharp intake of breath, felt his apprehension. 'No,' he said emphatically, after another agonising pause.

She waited. His next statement would seal their fate. Jake would know it. Lies in a relationship, after all, were the worst hurt of all. She'd hurt him immeasurably. His response now would tell her whether they were strong enough to move on, whether he wanted to.

She kept her gaze on the water, sure she could hear the frantic beating of her heart above the gentle swell of it.

'How did you know?' he asked eventually, his voice hoarse.

And there it was, honesty. And it hurt, so very much. 'I'm a woman, Jake, remember?' Wiping a tear from her face, she paraphrased something he'd said.

Nodding, Jake plunged his hands in his pockets, stared out at the water.

'How many times?' she asked.

'Once,' he answered, glancing down, his expression ashamed.

'Recently?' She didn't want to know, yet she had to.

Jake nodded barely perceptibly. 'I have no excuses, Emily, other than that I felt so bloody lonely. The way that you were looking at me when things started to decline so rapidly, as if you truly hated me... I suppose I thought that maybe you'd never really loved me. I started thinking more about Ben, why you could never bring yourself to trust me enough to tell me and ... It was a mistake, the worst I've made in my life, and I'm sorry.' He ran a hand over his neck. He didn't say any more.

'Do you love her?' She asked the most important question of all. She couldn't stay in a marriage where the love had died.

'No,' he replied instantly. 'I care about her, I can't say I don't, but I'm not in love with her. Sally ... she doesn't want her marriage to break up. It shouldn't have happened.'

Emily hesitated. 'Do you love *me*? As you *should* love me, I mean?'

'I've never stopped,' Jake said hoarsely. 'I don't want to go, but if you ask me to, I will. I need you to know that I do love you, though. I always will, no matter what happens.'

It was enough. Emily breathed out. Now she could start rebuilding her world. With her bare hands, brick by brick if she had to. But she would get there – with Jake by her side, God give them strength, because they *were* a team. They always had been.

EPILOGUE

'I still think we should have had a puppy,' Ben said, gazing down at his new baby sister.

'Says the man with the soppy grin on his face,' Millie quipped. 'I hope you're going to treat Aurora with more respect than you do her big sister.'

Ben looked up from the tiny bundle in his arms. 'I put up with your nuisance, don't I? He gave her a flat smile. 'And she's not Aurora, she's Ophelia, aren't you, little pickle?'

'Pickle?' Jake mouthed, exchanging bemused glances with Emily, who was watching her two oldest offspring with wry amusement. She supposed it was too much to hope that they would stop arguing for a whole hospital visit. Still, at least they were arguing good-naturedly.

'Ophelia?' Millie eyed the ceiling. 'No way. What are they going to call her at school? Ophe?'

'Lia, obviously,' Ben retorted, 'which has to be better than Rory or Rora. That's a dumb nickname for a … Uh, oh.' He looked at Jake, alarmed. 'You'd better take her, Dad. She's moving.'

'Yeah, they do that, Ben.' Millie rolled her eyes sky high.

Jake laughed, and then shot off the bed as Ben held their precious new bundle awkwardly towards him. 'Careful.' Taking her from Ben, he eased her gently into the crook of his arm. 'I'm not sure she's an Aurora or an Ophelia. What do you think, little one, hey?' he asked, gazing wondrously down at her as he walked back to the bed.

'Why don't you two go and grab a coffee while your mum and I try to think of an alternative to Pickle,' he suggested, settling carefully down beside Emily and bringing their much wanted – if somewhat surprising – new addition to the family to her.

'Er, right, good idea,' Millie said, and waited.

Sighing indulgently, Jake nodded towards his jacket hanging on the visitor's chair, inside which was his wallet. 'Grab one for us while you're there,' he said. 'And don't forget the cake,' he added, as Millie helped herself to his cash and headed for the door, Ben close behind her.

'Willow might be quite cool,' Ben pondered, disappearing into the corridor.

'Uh, uh.' Millie's decisive tones floated back. 'We want her to have a strong name. Something short and punchy, like … Aria, maybe?'

'Shall we think of a name before they christen her?' Jake suggested amusedly.

'I've already thought of one.' Emily glanced tentatively up at him.

Jake tore his gaze away from the baby to look at her curiously. 'Which is?'

'Rosie,' she said quietly.

Jake sucked in a breath.

'I know you might have mixed feelings about naming her after your mother, Jake, but …' She reached to press a hand softly to his cheek. 'I'd like to acknowledge her in some small way. Without her, I would never have had you … or this latest little miracle.'

A LETTER FROM SHERYL

Thank you so much for choosing to read *Trust Me*. I really hope you enjoyed it. If you did enjoy it, and would like to keep up to date with my new releases, sign up at the link below:

www.bookouture.com/sheryl-browne

Someone tagged me in a tweet and asked me to sum up the story in three words. I chose 'twins', 'jealousy' and 'obsession'. I think the word 'guilt' should have been in there though. Guilt can come in many forms. It can eat away at us over something as small as not answering the phone, possess us when we might be feeling jaded or angry and snap at someone. It can consume us when a choice we made in the past fundamentally affected our lives, or the life of someone else, forever. This book therefore looks at the need to stop saying 'If only I'd made this choice differently …' We can't undo the past but in order to move forwards we need to forgive ourselves, perhaps reshaping the expectations we have of ourselves, and see all the good that we do, the good that we are, and the goodness we have in our lives.

For my main character, Emily, it's about letting go of the guilt she carries – some of which was never her burden to carry – rather than being weighed down by it. Exorcising ghosts, if you like, and being there fully for herself and her family. The past is the past.

She can't change it, but she can grasp each new day as it comes and be active in shaping her future. Is she strong enough to forgive those she loves for the decisions they made, though? I hope so.

As I pen this last little section of the book, I would again like to thank those people around me, who are always there to offer support, those people who believed in me, even when I didn't quite believe in myself. To all of you, thank you for helping me make my dream come true.

If you have enjoyed the book, I would love it if you could share your thoughts and write a brief review. Reviews mean the world to an author and will help a book find its wings. I would also love to hear from you via Facebook or Twitter or my website.

Stay safe everyone and happy reading.
Sheryl x

 SherylBrowne.Author

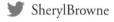 SherylBrowne

 sherylbrowne.com

ACKNOWLEDGEMENTS

Once again, massive thanks to the fabulous team at Bookouture, whose support of their authors, particularly throughout these extraordinary times, has been amazing. Special thanks to Helen Jenner and our wonderful editorial team, who not only make my stories make sense, but make them shine. Huge thanks also to our fantastic publicity team, Kim Nash, Noelle Holten and Sarah Hardy. Thanks guys, you've really had my back this time. To all the other super-supportive authors at Bookouture, I love you. Thank you for cheering me on.

I owe a huge debt of gratitude to all the fantastically hard-working bloggers and reviewers who have taken time to read and review my books and shout them out to the world. It's truly appreciated.

Final thanks to every single reader out there for buying and reading my books. Knowing you have enjoyed our stories and care enough about our characters to want to share them with other readers is the best incentive ever for us to keep writing.

CPSIA information can be obtained
at www.ICGtesting.com
Printed in the USA
LVHW092127130621
690142LV00016B/372